BLUE
RISE

BLUE RISE

A NOVEL BY

Rebecca Hill

WILLIAM MORROW AND COMPANY, INC.

NEW YORK   1983

Library of Congress Cataloging in Publication Data

Hill, Rebecca.
  Blue Rise.

  I. Title.
PS3558.1442B5   1983   813'.54   82-14329
ISBN 0-688-01875-0

Printed in the United States of America

    2   3   4   5   6   7   8   9   10

BOOK DESIGN BY ELLEN LOGIUDICE

For FRED; and for
MEADOR AND MEREDIETH,
JENNIFER AND KATE

The writer who works with a narrator styled "I" runs the risk of being questioned to death about autobiography. Let me say it here: This is a work of fiction, set with people and places as real as I could create them. But they are created, and therefore always more than and less than autobiography. I have borrowed freely from what I know of South and North, from stories, from experiences of others, from as many real and imagined characters as I could usefully lay hands on. None of the characters in this novel represents a real God-given person, living or dead.

BLUE
RISE

"It's not true that life is one damn thing after another. Life is the same damn thing over and over."

—EDNA ST. VINCENT MILLAY

1

Family gatherings in rural Mississippi are sober to a fault in the absence of anyone who will come forward and risk changing iced tea into wine. When the Groves family gathers together, no exceptions arise. It is a certainty that iced tea will be drunk, just as it is a certainty that the men of the family will gather before the TV while the women cook and set the table and feed the children and call the men to come on and are themselves the last to sit down.

My mother and I are descended from a long line of such Groves women who take as their motto and creed *I suffer, therefore I am.* Well: The heart of Christianity is sacrifice, and these be Christian women. These be, in point of fact, Southern Baptist Christian women.

Groves women see to the men and the children and then proceed to take what is left of the fried chicken, fish the brown field peas from beneath the net of ham fat already beginning to congeal on the pot liquor, dig into the eroded mass of ambrosia salad and marvel in advance over Eola's pimento-cheese sandwiches and Bethany's baked beans and onions, and since the men have already taken their burdened plates back to the TV, they pull chairs up to the table with its company-best tablecloths of hand-crocheted lace over store-bought damask and eat, their plates wedged between the serving bowls. And then they clean the table, leaving half-empty bowls of food where they are in case some of the men or the children get hungry or want something else, and they wash the dishes and scrub the pots and exchange atrocity stories and trade vows of things they wouldn't do for love of children and Lord Jesus and family. They would never part with their children for more than a few days at most, they just couldn't, they love them so much. My cousin Felicia rinses soap-suds from her plump hands over the sink and wipes them on Aunt Lottie's embroidered dish towels.

She is saying, "Y'all remember when I tried taking that job at the post office. It just broke my heart to go off and leave Kimmy and that little ole Jason—left all day in some woman's house cryin' Momma—"

She stops here, and shakes her head.

A chorus rises from the women standing in the small fra-grant kitchen.

"Pore-little-thangs, bless-their-hearts."

They just didn't know how anybody could do without their children. They just didn't know *how* I'd been able to come off down here for over a week without Laura. Wasn't she just five in April? How could I stand it?

Now. A word about those men in the other room. It has al-ways been clear that the women in my mother's family go to some trouble to pick out deficient men to marry. I thought it probably was unconscious, the same way hostility escapes from them, but here I appear to be wrong. Consider the lineup: Aunt Lottie, married to a man thirty years her senior, thus guaranteed the long-term widowhood she is now living out. Aunt Bethany, married to a man who professes socialism and unemployment right here in the rural South. My own mother, married to a man who dealt in violence and who eventually won big. Aunt Lola, married to a man whose family ritually succumbs to heart disease before age forty, he himself picked up dead off the streets at forty-five, still in his jogging outfit. All these women are the daughters of a mother who was called in Jasper County "Widow Groves"—though her perfectly sound husband was off in the next county sawing logs. People saw her plowing the fields behind a horse alone, and when she went into town to buy feed, she drove her own team and hoisted her own sacks. She passed along her talent for choosing unsatisfactory husbands, and the trait sur-vives all else, is virulent. Aunt Bethany's daughter Eola married a faithless charmer who deserted her and "her" three girls fifteen years ago. But Eola would be scandalized at the notion of divorce; after all, Delbert Charles is her Husband. That comes with a capital H in these parts. My cousins Berniece, Pauline and Felicia are the three daughters of that brief but consecrated union. They are nearly all into their twenties now and are married (respectively) to a pyromaniac, a drunkard and a cripple.

Mind you, I'm only citing the Groves women who were in attendance that day. As for myself, the fact that I am having trouble with my marriage would not make me fit in here. This is a shame of which one does not speak. Not speaking is itself a virtue. And I sense that my mother holds out some hope for me as we get into the car to go home. She still expects that I will become a mature woman, that I will yet grasp how it is that fulfillment is attained through selflessness.

So she says to me aloud what all the rest know by heart.

"That little Felicia," she says, speaking of my cousin who weighs some 240 pounds.

Obesity is another virulent family trait, and to my mind these traits are not unconnected.

"That little Felicia," she says again, securing my attention as she throws her gold Malibu into reverse on the soft sand of Aunt Lottie's driveway. "Isn't she just the sweetest thing you ever saw? She could have married anybody, but just think, who would have married James with his poor withered leg, if she hadn't?"

Momma takes the back roads past Gethsemane Baptist Church. The back roads are shaded and beautiful in the late June sun, but they command attention any time. Basically they are a one-lane track of packed red clay. When there has been a lot of rain, you avoid them, go the long way up to the Rise by the highway. When there hasn't been rain, you have a chance of telling when another car is on the road by the cloud of red dust that rises through the trees. Though the many curves and corners are absolutely blind, it is a matter of custom—faith in God, perhaps— that everybody drives fast and uses no horns. I understand that.

At sixteen I attempted these roads on one of our annual visits "back Home." After I'd sounded the horn twenty times in the space of three miles, for no apparent reason other than cowardice, I, too, gave it up.

We get to the Blue Rise that way in silence. Blue Rise is the highest section of the clay ridge that stands above Gethsemane Valley. It gets the name from the way everything that can be seen from up here seems to turn blue with distance. More than that: At times a hazy bluish shimmer seems to hang in the very air.

Once we round Uncle Odell Hinton's place on the broad northern slope of the Rise, the house appears. Gray brick with white wood trim, tapered pillars bearing up a graceful portico. The effect is as trumped-up as all the other brick-with-white-trim Colonials that now litter the South. But this one does have in its favor excellent proportions. It looked good even when its only façade was tar paper, as it was for many years after my father built the house. For we moved North before the finish work was done. Sixteen years later when he and my mother returned here for his retirement, as they called it then, the place had been nearly ruined between rats and renters. That's when the renovation was done, capped by all these pillars and porticoes. When southerners return, they come all the way back.

But the result is handsome, as my father was in the habit of remarking at this point on the road. The house comes into view with its setting: bluish valley hues in the background, and in the foreground tree-fringed pastures, woods behind the house and barn, and my mother's front-yard profusions of flowers. And, these recent years, Uncle Odell's two mammoth chickenhouses beyond the garden. Not far enough beyond, as any breeze from the north testifies.

Today there is such a breeze awaiting us, and Momma grimaces, showing her molars and tightening the rigging of her neck in fresh disgust. "I hate that dirty chicken smell."

"The wind is wrong today."

"It isn't the wind. It's farming. Wait'll you get a noseful of that manure in my barn. In the middle of the day it will knock you speechless. That scent! It don't come out of your clothes, it don't come out of your hair—" She glances over at me. I am so innocent of familiar odors, so still. Though I am not a practicing Christian martyr, it is possible that I may have become that other thing: a lady. A thing she desires for me, fears in me. "Aren't you proud to have a farmer for a mother?"

"As a matter of fact, I am."

"Hunh. You must be worse off than I thought."

She turns the Malibu into the far end of the semicircular drive past the house. The near end has been closed off, piled with the sawn trunk and limbs of the old pecan tree. The tree died the same winter my father did, two years ago. It stood at the corner of the yard, and as children my brothers and I played there, fished in doodlebug holes between its roots and hid from each other in its branches. Its trunk and limbs are piled at one end of the driveway because Momma put them there. The spring after my father died, she herself sawed the old tree into the sections she needed. She herself pushed, pulled, lifted and dragged them into place. Teenagers in cars, she said. A widow alone, and all.

At sixty-five my mother is an extraordinary-looking woman. A pretty woman, the eyes arresting in that collapsed face, the teeth certainly passable. But it is not her face but the fierce vitality that plays through the face, through the still flexible, still mannishly strong body. The vitality is at times gentle, her beam turned low for radiance, for light rather than heat. But that is not to be depended upon. Better count on this woman for strength; count on the gentleness as you do the intervention of saints.

Her body has always been ten years younger than her face, and as she ages, the lag increases. Only a body like that could bear the dictates of her will, which has no relation to face, flesh or anything else mortal.

She brings the car to a stop at the center of the semicircle, in front of the white columns of the porch. While the dogs are still jumping at the car doors, I say, as though the idea is fresh, "Momma, think I'll go over and see Carrie Dean for a while."

Wordlessly Momma tosses me the keys and gets out.

She does speak to the dogs who, however foolishly and adoringly, are in her way. "Get on out of here," she says, and strides onto the porch and into the house.

The front door slams. The same momentum will carry her right through the place, through the dusty rose velvet and satin brocade in the parlor, through the magnanimously cluttered family room and kitchen, and out the back door to check on her animals, her garden. She will change her shoes on the back steps. My mother is never one to waste motion, words or much of anything else. Yesterday, after we drove in from the airport, we toured the flower beds in the front yard. Day lilies and infant crape myrtle were in vivid bloom around the birdbath, but something drew my eye to the petunias. The glazed white pot they were banked in.

"Mother, that isn't the old . . . ?"

The lifted chin gives hauteur to the reply. What you might call finality. "It's porcelain."

I slide into the driver's seat and start the car. My father had liked cars to have automatic transmissions; there had not been a stick shift in the family since the 1949 Hudson. Automatic transmissions spoke to my father of his executive days; they also covered his inveterate clumsiness with machinery of any kind. But after he died, Momma couldn't bear to drive his Pontiac Grand Prix; the purring automatic windows that were his pride, and also the pine tar matting up the carpet underneath the driver's feet, reminded her too much of him.

So she bought this gold Malibu, with four on the floor.

It wasn't that she was a racy driver, waiting to show her true colors. Lord knows she has nearly ground the gears into flywheels. This fancy car was a windfall of the sort that comes to those who only buy on sale. Occasionally they strike a deal for something enviable. If not exactly appropriate. But this car was gold, not red, so how was she to know? I can still hear her stricken tones over the telephone, the recent widow appealing to Larry and me in useless, far-off Iowa, "You don't mean to tell me I have bought *a sports car*?"

* * *

I turn the Malibu off Highway 24 onto the gravel of Carrie Dean's road, pausing an amateurish three seconds to find the gear low enough to get me up the hill. I can see Cal in this car on his stopovers Home, slipping from gear to gear with masculine accomplishment. My brother learned to drive on these roads at age ten, not unusual for a farm boy. I learned in the side streets of suburban Detroit at seventeen, sharing the controls with my high school's driver-training instructor.

But many things changed for us in that move North. Certainly religion, for even Baptists are northern in Detroit. We found ourselves exiled in a foreign culture, no longer interwoven among family like one lateral of a spider's web. In Detroit's Houghton Park we were rednecks; in Mississippi on those annual trips back Home, we talked funny. We belonged nowhere. My father, who was fond of the applications of molecular theory, told me we had become isotopes. An isotope is an element with the same character as another element in the periodic table. They occupy the same place, he explained, but the isotope can be distinguished in various ways. By differences in mass, for example, or radioactivity.

This notion seemed to satisfy him, and by junior high I could grasp most of what it meant. But it was not the kind of wisdom that counted on the playground.

At some point Sumrall Hinton found that neither exile nor executive privilege nor the elegance of molecular theory satisfied as well as drinking. One result was his dismissal—fifteen years in a sensitive research job earned him that many minutes to clear his desk and leave the factory complex. Northern industrial concerns are a different sort of spider's web. And so it was back Home to Mississippi for him and my mother. With the children grown, a retreat from the North at last, back home to the clay ridge, home to the house he had built and abandoned on Blue Rise, home to his daddy's land, home to the farm life he'd hated as a child and loved as a sentimental adult from a distance. Blood ties are slow to give up their knots.

This gravel road is the one I have traveled to Carrie Dean's house since childhood, although back then it wasn't really her house, any more than that chartreuse-trimmed ornament that now sits overlooking the highway is the same house that used to wait at the end of this drive. When we were growing up, the usual thing was for those big old wood-frame houses—they were big but often not as big as the families they held—to grow shabby and gray from lack of paint or improvements. Or maybe it was lack of conviction that things should be any different. For sooner or later a family would tear one house down and build another, often on the same spot. If the building had to go, the home place was permanent. By succession. Whatever was left of the old structure would be hauled several hundred yards away, and put to use as a barn or shed.

Both my grandmothers had got new houses in this way. As children my brothers and I spent hours playing in the old ones, diving into the mounds of soybean meal or sacks of cottonseed that occupied what had been Grandma Groves' living room, or Grandma Hinton's kitchen. Walking in the weeds between the new house and the old one, we had periodic finds of buttons, pencil stubs, a nickel or, less spectacularly, an embossed lid from one of Grandpa Hinton's tins of snuff.

When my father built our house on Blue Rise Road, Grandma Hinton's new place was one road over, around the next curve. As it is now. Renters live there. But Aunt Opal and Uncle Vinnie's house used to be there, too, right across the road between two pecan trees. Uncle Vinnie was my father's brother and when we moved to the house on the Rise I had my cousin Serene to play with. I was seven years old, and I thought life was not only perfect but permanent. Uncle Vinnie had a brain tumor, which meant only that we were to play quietly when we played at Serene's. Then we buried Uncle Vinnie; and, to my complete amazement, Aunt Opal moved their house. The very house! Men came and jacked it up, set it on blocks and then on log rollers, and shifted it onto a flatbed truck. Away down Blue Rise Road went the frame house, leaning perilously.

No new house was ever built in its stead, and the family was considered unfairly cut off, out of place. It was a kind of shame, just as it was for my father to take his college education off to Detroit all those years.

Serene grew up in the next county beside her other grandmother's place. After she left, I used to go up the road and play alone between the two pecan trees. Once I found a tiny square gold locket where the back steps had been. It must have belonged to Serene, but for some reason I got to keep it. It has since been lost again, out in the larger world of other people's houses and apartment buildings.

Carrie Dean Wentworth now lives in what was her mother's new house some twenty years ago. The Wentworths' old one had indeed been gray and weathered, but it was taken before its time by fire. Flames had run their tongues over the roof beams and licked out the eaves before Mr. Elmer Wentworth woke in his bed to a vision of fire and brimstone raining down like a judgment. He got his family to safety and was reaffirmed a Christian before the ashes cooled.

Mr. Elmer died later that year, and when her mother parceled up the Wentworth land among the children, Carrie Dean, as the only girl, was given title to the new house. The brothers by that time had built houses on their land for themselves and their families. The mailboxes along Highway 24 read in succession: R. W. Wentworth, Buford Wentworth, Tillis Wentworth, Harley Wentworth, Vernon Wentworth. Farther down the road are five or six more Wentworths who are Carrie Dean's uncles and cousins: Matthew Wentworth, Beulah Wentworth, Nelson Wentworth, and the rest. It's the same all over the community of Gethsemane, all over the whole rural South as far as I know. Roads of Wentworths give way to roads of Maxeys, roads of Groveses to roads of Drennans. Along Blue Rise Road mailboxes with Hinton printed on them in various uneven hands are strewn two miles in three directions.

Of course, Carrie Dean's name is not Wentworth anymore. The mailbox at the foot of the road where gravel spills out over the blacktop says Parrish. And it is something unreasonably difficult for me to remember. Carrie Dean Parrish.

She sits waiting for me on the porch of the house with the

chartreuse trim. She sits on the old porch swing, legs spraddled in a way that's characteristic. That swing is where we spent most of the summer when we were sixteen. My family's visit back Home that year came when school was out, and I was allowed to remain here and visit relatives, and to date when Carrie Dean did. The swing was the vantage point from which we paid careful attention to the cars on the highway below. To this day I can spot a light blue 1960 Ford Falcon a quarter of a mile away.

"There goes Billy Jim. By himself, no less. He still going with that Evans girl from Big Creek?"

Today Carrie Dean's eyes are trained not on the highway but on the five children playing on a gym-set on the sparse lawn. She shades her eyes and turns to grin in my direction when the car whines over the hill. When I get out, she rises in her loose irresolute way, bending forward as though part of her wanted to remain in the swing but hadn't the courage to argue.

I was raised in the Groves tradition of fierce huggers; Carrie Dean was not. As we hug each other—this day as in many days in our long past—I feel that her force goes to her joints rather than to her muscles. Muscles return value for value; joints give way. When we release each other, I am left feeling off-balance and presumptuous.

This problem is not one that arises up North. Up North hugging is not routine. Up North you aren't called on to hug anybody except in emergencies, such as for a Heimlich Maneuver. Intervention for safety is not to be confused with affection. When I married Larry, it was appropriate to exchange hugs with his immediate family. And I learned that they, too, had a family style of embracing. Theirs is the three-second hug. You clasp each other's arms and/or shoulders, draw your faces near for three seconds and break away in relief.

Probably Carrie Dean would have adapted to it better than I did.

"Can you tell which ones of that bunch belong to me?" She nods her head at the swarm of children now eddying toward us. "Not all of them do, you know. Just the prettiest ones."

The children reach us. They are all blond, freckled and openly curious.

"This is my friend Jeannine," she tells them officially. "She's a real honest-to-goodness Yankee now, but she didn't used to be."

Her pale eyes slide past mine in a knowing tease.

"And she doesn't bite that I know of, so come on up real close and shake her hand like the ladies and gentlemen you know how to be."

As the children twist their fingers and look at one another, Carrie Dean places a hand on the shoulder of the child nearest her.

"This is Victoria. She's mine."

A tiny hand is given and snatched away. Blue eyes stare up briefly.

"This is Garth, Junior. Enough said."

I shake the warm hand and see Garth, Sr.'s, solemn brown eyes in the eight- or nine-year-old face. Has it been that long?

"This is Tommy, that's Harley's oldest—give her your hand, Tommy—and his sister Nell, and the little dickens that just took off like a streak, that's Eliza, Tillis' girl. Three years old and all boy."

All the children turn and follow Eliza's lead, whooping and calling out each others' names as they run.

"Well!" Carrie Dean exclaims as they again cavort at the gym-set. "That's not the end of the show, you know. My little one's in the house taking a nap. Thank goodness. You can see him afterwhile. Save the best for last," she grins, nudging me with a shoulder. There is such authority in the grin—it is the gapped teeth that do it, those marvelous free-standing teeth.

I nudge back. And grin, too. We turn together toward the house.

"I bet that little girl of yours is a sight by now, too. Where is she, again? Off visiting Granmaw?"

"Off visiting *other* Granmaw. A distinction there."

"Uh-huh."

We roll eyes at each other.

"Say, that's a good-looking bunch of kids, by the way, no matter which ones you say aren't yours."

"I already know that," she says. "Now come sit down and tell me what *you* know."

I think she means the porch, but she holds the screen door open for me, and I step up over the threshold and into the living room. The negligent green of our girlhood has been banished. It is by no means the room I remember.

"You can quit looking," she says. "You've seen it all before."

"I have not! You only moved in two years ago, and you've put in this shag, paneled the walls—"

"And this is mine," she declares, collapsing into a rust corduroy sofa and hugging a matching pillow. "I had it ordered when we were still in the trailer. Momma says that's where it looks like it belongs. But I like it in here just fine."

The trailer Carrie Dean and Garth had in Biloxi until their third child was born encroaches on the side yard, some thirty feet from the southeast corner of the porch. I can see part of the aluminum buttress shape through the living room window. It is now the home of Carrie Dean's mother. Old Mrs. Wentworth had insisted upon the exchange, packing her clothes and dishes and announcing that it was time for them to move back Home.

"How much room does an old woman need?" she had put it, and no one had opposed her to her satisfaction. The Wentworth brothers viewed the plan as a matter of course; the house was always to be Carrie's, was it not?

"I liked my trailer house," Carrie Dean says to me pointedly, as though to stare down every pleated armchair and antimacassar in the room that surrounds us. "That was mine. It was on my lot in Biloxi and it was my house and I liked it just fine."

She shrugs a shoulder. "But I couldn't get anybody else to see it like I saw it."

"Was it hard on you, coming back?"

"It's my place to be here since Momma needs me."

"Well, anyway," I offer, unsure which way to go, "I'm glad you're back in Gethsemane so I get to see you."

Her gaze shifts and becomes intent. I pay attention to such looks, but I am unprepared for what comes next.

"Do you remember when we were in the primer together, and they found out you could read and I couldn't? They put you ahead to the first grade, and I felt so awful; I was just miserable. And you wouldn't even play with me when we had recess together. I bet you don't even remember."

And I don't. First grade: I can remember Miss Viola, and Cal threatening to beat up Davie Cahill if he tried to kiss me again. I can remember losing my snub-nosed school scissors and taking Jerry Comfort's. I remember getting restless in class and talking out loud, and being made to write "I will be quiet in school" a hundred times. It was such terrible labor that I quit and threw the paper in the wastebasket the second afternoon. I judged that I had been at it so long that Miss Viola would have forgotten. But the next morning the paper lay on my desk with red pencil in the upper-right corner. The message was succinct. It said "52 times."

I remember being in love with Cameron Wentworth, Carrie Dean's third cousin, who was in fourth grade. I remember the Kits and candy lipsticks we could buy in the school canteen at recess. I remember squatting on the toilet in the girls' bathroom, because my mother told me about germs and never sitting down.

Carrie Dean was not in my life at all. But I had been, she was telling me plainly, in hers.

"It hurt me so bad that you and me had always done everything together. I remember us drawing pictures together at your house."

Yes; we drew pictures of women. Women's faces, principally. For some reason I drew mine with U-shaped faces, the features gathered low in the U underneath a vast deep forehead. I thought my method entirely superior to Carrie Dean's, but when we asked my mother, *she* firmly preferred Carrie Dean's conventional O-shaped women.

"I liked drawing at your house," Carrie Dean resumes, "because you had crayons and I didn't."

Another surprise. I didn't dream that she had no crayons. At her house we played with creamy cool blond dominoes brought by one of her brothers from the war. I had coveted those dominoes with all my soul.

"You used to draw out the alphabet when we played. Your mother taught you all of your letters, but I didn't know what they were. I didn't want you to know it. I was ashamed not to know. I think I liked-to-never got over you not having anything to do with me at school the way you did."

She says this smilingly; her mouth has been smiling for some time, it now occurs to me. What else was there to do with pain so old and hopeless? But I have been looking not at the mouth but into the eyes, where suffering shows its sky-torn blue. I feel I have been spotted. Identified once again as the instrument of someone else's pain.

Something here is my fault, yet how could anything have been my fault? I was six years old and my life was playing jump boards and trying not to lick off my candy lipstick and being hopelessly in love with a fourth-grader. But I am the one in Carrie Dean's memory. Me; my wispy brown hair and baby teeth. If I do not remember, it is another fault of mine, and still more innocence is subtracted. What if I now must go into Jerry Comfort's feed store, and hear about those scissors? What of Davie Cahill, since Carrie Dean has told me he tried to kill himself twice in his teens over unrequited love? Will I meet him after Sunday Evening Prayer Service and hear how in first grade I set the course for his life?

Carrie Dean is saying, "What's your momma doing this afternoon? Why didn't she come with you?"

"She had some things to do. We have a Hinton family supper to go to this evening. You know my aunt Verlie?"

"The only ones of your daddy's people that I know are the ones that come to church. Garth went to school with a cousin of yours though." She goes still. "Drew, I think."

"Drew!" I brighten, anticipating, as ever the case with Drew, a story.

Carrie Dean lifts her tongue to the space between her front teeth, looks as though she will bring something to mind. But then her eyes snap to mine; she brings her spine erect. "Hey!" She shoves aside the cushion she has held. "Come on outside with me a minute. I want to show you something."

I hesitate, and she settles the matter in a tone that is more command than plea.

"Come on."

As girls we were both long-boned and slight, and pretty enough if the looking was kindly. Probably we both look better than we did, or perhaps that is giving style rather than youth its due. We have taken different paths to our looks, however; I am rather too thin these days, whereas I notice that Carrie Dean, when she rises from the sofa ahead of me, has gathered puddles of fat around her hips and belly. Childbearing fat, butter-bean fat.

We walk out of the house and down the porch steps in tandem, and Carrie Dean calls out to the children who have left off their playing to get some signal from her. We walk on up the drive past Mrs. Wentworth's trailer and into the garden.

"I want you to just see," Carrie Dean is saying.

The garden smells of sun beating on tomatoes. The air is heavy as a touch, and it smells of hot okra and bean blossoms. It smells of earth, and it sings with insect voices. The rows of broccoli, zucchini, carrots, peas, potatoes, tomatoes, beans and corn look like the rows of any well-kept garden. It could be the one Larry tends there in the back of the double lot we have in Des Moines. He is proud of it, the way Carrie Dean is. Often when he gets home at night, he leaves his car in the drive and goes directly to inspect his plants for signs of malfeasance in his absence, checking for weeds or worms, conducting a ritual harvest of one tomato or a bunch of scallions for our dinner salad.

Carrie Dean's garden looks like that, except that as we walk along the heady rows of plants, I begin to see that this "garden" extends all the way from the trailer to Tillis Wentworth's fence a quarter of a mile away. This garden is not a hobby; it consumes life. It is Carrie Dean's occupation. She feeds her family with it. She herself, with her hands in hot blanching baths and cold rinses, the kitchen ringing with canning lids and the clank of heat-proof jars on the counters. I know the scene from childhood. I have even echoed it in a fashionable way with a bushel of peaches or plums from a bargain at some rural market. But to live it—to provide for my family in this way!

I am diligent. I compliment Carrie Dean upon the beautiful array of plants. I exclaim over the fat hairy okras, the droop of tiny bell peppers hiding in their dark foliage. An odd look crosses Carrie Dean's face, and I understand how little like real garden talk all that sounds, know I cannot help it, am known for the stranger to country life I have become.

"I canned two hundred quarts of tomatoes last year, and just about that many green beans. And peas! You should have seen the field peas, I liked-to-never seen the end of them."

"Two hundred quarts—you mean your family eats all that?"

Carrie Dean stops and turns a tomato leaf over, exposing a green tomato worm.

"Well," she says with a short laugh, "it sure goes."

She picks up the worm's soft body between her thumb and forefinger, and pulls gently. The worm clings with its myriad feet, and she says, "Hateful things!"

The worm comes free and Carrie Dean grinds it into the loose earth with the toe of her sandal.

She shifts her weight more evenly and squints toward the house and the trailer by its side.

"Well, Momma likes to be able to give the boys something to take home with them every time they stop to see her. Wilson manages to stop about three times a week. 'Carrie Dean,'" she mimics, and the mourning-dove tones are as startlingly soft as her mother's, "'why don't you just find Wilson Earl some of those pole beans we put up last summer? They are the best beans, Wilson, you will love them. Now, Carrie Dean, don't be stingy. I won't be needing my share.'"

The long pause that follows embarrasses both of us. Carrie Dean has said more than she'd intended, more than is proper. This picture of old Mrs. Wentworth melodiously doling out the labor of this garden stuns me into silence. Outrage is out of place here; in the South, family is sacred. I cannot say what I think.

And so, in the hot silence between us, Carrie Dean thinks she hears what she expected to hear.

"Oh, I'm ashamed of myself for feeling the way I do. Don't pay any mind," she finishes flatly.

Turning on her heel to lead the way down the rows back toward the house, she waves one hand loosely at all that surrounds us.

"As you can see, I've got plenty."

There is a way to talk with close friends whom you happen not to have seen for ten years. I am certain that there is a way, and yet shyness or politeness or fear in some other form prevents Carrie Dean and me from finding it. I am sure that each of us keeps a book, and when we meet each other—whether it is a week or an hour or ten years that have come between us—each of us opens her book to the page where we left off. It is probably that simple. If we had the courage to seize the knowledge and proceed, our meetings and our partings would remain orderly. Instead, they are cluttered with overlays of other lives and passages of time and circumstance and the notion that we are somehow changed.

Here we are in Carrie Dean's garden, or on Carrie Dean's front porch or in Carrie Dean's living room sitting on Carrie Dean's mother's furniture, and the things I want to know start from childhood. "Do you still have the ivory dominoes?" I want to know. That is what I care about, not the details of Laura's birth or Victoria's ear operations, or Larry's career or the move to Des Moines.

Clearly Carrie Dean felt the same way. We had settled first grade, and now how about the boyfriends we had in our teens? "How could you marry Garth?" I wanted to ask her. "What did you ever do about the way you felt about Billy Jim?" In that way, on those foundations, we would soon be able to say to each other: "What do you think of this business of being grown up? How do you get through your life every day? How do you stand it, being wife-and-mother? If we could get hold of those books of ours, the recent ones where the marriages jolt and drone along, would you just as soon tear out the last few dozen pages? I would. Would you?"

We don't have that conversation. Perhaps it always works out that people simply don't. Not unless it is two women alone in a kitchen at eleven o'clock at night, the dishes done, the kids in bed, the man of the house gratefully someplace else.

But this is the middle of the afternoon, and life is in process. The garden reeking of it, the throng of children celebrating it. This is not the book but the movie, and we are both studying the ground, trying to find our marks without appearing to look for them.

I follow Carrie Dean down the rows.

"This is the most food I've ever seen in my life," I say, pushing my voice out to be heard over the several yards that now separate us.

"Your memory's failing you, Jeannine," she says over her shoulder.

It is some kind of opening, a lead. But I don't know where it points.

"What do you mean?" I call out.

She stops and faces me, her features open again, teasing.

"Did you grow up on Blue Rise Road? Was Cyrus Hinton your granddaddy? Did he used to sell peas and butter beans and corn to the Bayley markets?"

In an instant I see the old man, see his bald head and tooth-less mouth and the blood veins splayed over the crooked nose, see the rusty green pickup loaded with fruits and vegetables, its flapping tailgate wired shut.

My mother used to say that even the peaches smelled of beer. But she didn't say it when my father, or anybody else, was around.

I laugh.

"Must be this Mississippi sun," I call, as Carrie Dean again turns toward the house. "Must have fried my brains just like it did his."

"I'd be ashamed of myself, Jeannine Hinton." This from over her shoulder again.

"Well—I was supposed to think it; I just wasn't supposed to say it. That's the code, isn't it?"

"You're turning into a Yankee," she warns me.

2

Droplets of sweat are beginning to run down the sides of my neck by the time we reach the porch steps. Carrie Dean motions me into the swing. I settle there heavily while she goes into the house. When I have caught my breath, she reappears, kicking the screen door open ahead of her and carrying two glasses of iced tea. When she is through the door, she pauses and lifts the glasses for me to see.

"You have enough time for this, don't you?"

She takes my motionless body for a reply, and comes to sit down beside me. She hands me the glass, ice cubes rattling.

"That garden is hot, even for half a minute this time of day. I know."

We sit together on the porch swing and sip the cold sweet tea. We cradle the thick-stemmed glasses in our fingers and against our cheeks, exchanging hot sweat for cold. Carrie Dean's fingertips rim the large dimples underneath the bowl of her glass, one after another. Watching her, I begin to do likewise. It has the feeling of a ritual from childhood, and very possibly it is. We have drunk iced tea from glasses like these since time beyond memory.

We look at one another and grin. From the yard the children's voices blend with the drone of an airplane somewhere overhead.

"Tell me," Carrie Dean says. "What brings you back?"

"Are you kidding? You're not supposed to ask me that. My mother lives here."

Her blue eyes are mild. "Now what in the world does that mean?"

"Sorry, Momma and I had dinner today with Aunt Lottie and Eola and the rest. You know."

And, of course, she does know. She sees them every Sunday morning and night for church services, Wednesday nights for prayer meeting.

"None of them wonders why I'm here. They *expect* me to be here. They're wondering where my husband is, where my little girl is, who's taking care of them and how come I haven't been back to see my momma before now."

Carrie Dean chuckles.

"Why, Jeannine! They been making you welcome!" She tucks her chin in and makes the pale eyes large. "They been making you welcome in the only way they know how. When was the last time you were back—your daddy's funeral? That's what I thought. Let me tell you, it wouldn't be a bit different if you were down here every day of your life, tending to your momma. People can always think of a few more things you ought to be doing. Take it from me."

"Well, I don't like it."

Carrie Dean rests an elbow on the arm of the swing and lets her chin drop into the cradle of her palm. Her eyes travel the line of fence posts along the highway below. The words come from between the molars of her immobilized jaw.

"Ain't sposed to like it. Sposed to make you feel bad."

"It does."

"Well, you can quit for now. This here's time off."

"Mom-maaaahhh!" The cry from the yard has a piercing quality we both recognize.

"Time off, my foot," Carrie Dean mutters into the fingers still curled over her jaw. Then, with a practiced lethargy, she pushes herself off the elbow and up out of the swing. She makes her way down the porch steps to tend to Victoria's bloody knee, and to allocate the blame and consequences. Garth, Jr., and one of the others stand back from the little group clustered around Victoria and Carrie Dean in the yard, and hang their heads. They do this as long as Carrie Dean speaks to them. When she turns

toward the house with Victoria, they scamper back to chin themselves with renewed energy.

"I'll be a minute," Carrie Dean says to me as she crosses the
porch with Victoria. "We got us some minor surgery here." Victoria continues to cry all the way into the bathroom for her mer-
curochrome and Band-Aids.

I fish the last ice cube from my glass. I place it in my mouth
and set the empty glass on the floor.

I am here because of my mother. I am here because my father died, I am here because I grew up here. I am here because I
am living my life like a northerner, not troubling about the fact
that the northern part was grafted onto southern root stock. I am
here because my life doesn't work, and in taking the thing apart
and putting it back together again, I don't seem to find enough
pieces. I think it's possible I may have left some of them here. I
think I have come here because this place may have a piece of my
puzzle.

Carrie Dean returns and slides back into the swing with a
sigh. She peers into my face.

"Well, where are you off to? You're not in Gethsemane,
Mississippi, not this minute."

My eyes linger on Victoria, racing off across the grass.

"You wouldn't believe it. I guess I was busy analyzing my
own psychology."

"That's what you studied, isn't it? Psy-chology?"

The word is hyphenated, alien.

"Yep. My father didn't want me to. He told me that the
only people that studied psychology had something wrong with
them in the first place."

"Was he right?"

"He sure was."

We laugh at this, and she shakes her head.

"You are a mess, Jeannine Hinton."

"That accounts for my master's degree," I say, and she
punches my shoulder lightly.

"Are you a psy-chologist, then?" The hyphen still there.

"No. I like to know what kind of trouble people get into, but I don't like to be the one they plan on getting help from."

"I could have sworn your momma told me you worked with mental patients."

"I did research on troubled families for about a year. What I really did was thumb through forms at the children's home. Then I had Laura."

Carrie Dean snorts. "That's about like me. I filled out forms for the telephone company, and then I had Garth, Junior." She pauses and looks at me. "Some way I had the notion you still worked."

I nod. "Part time."

"I was thinking I'd like to do something part time. And then Garth told me I already did *every*thing part time, so I quit thinking about it."

The grin she shows me is brief.

"At least while the baby's so little, and I have Momma," she adds.

She turns to me, the pale eyes suddenly penetrating, as though a series of thoughts has been triggered. "How's your momma getting along without your daddy, Jeannine?"

Southerners keep their skeletons in closets because it's the best place for them. Otherwise they take over the place. You can't have skeletons thumping their heelbones on the polished floors, sitting around the parlor leaving calcium dust on the velvet chairs, making ball-and-socket marks on the divan, biting the rims off china teacups, poking fingerbone holes through your nice silk lampshades.

My father's death two years ago had been unexpected. Unexpected inasmuch as it is difficult to tell just when and how a man who has been the familiar of violence for sixty years will blunder into the right exit. Sumrall Hinton found one underneath a tractor in the dead of night, breathing his presumably alcoholic last into the red clay of the Rise. The same red clay he had plowed into terraces along the slope of the Rise behind a team of his daddy's mean mules. Cyrus Hinton only had mean mules; he bred them that way or bought them that way or they turned mean under his handling. He had that effect on living things.

But it is a mystery, and one that can be counted on, how knowledge can evaporate in the rural South. Or perhaps there is a better word. A mystery has no known explanation. A mystery for which the explanation is withheld is properly termed a secret. Mystery or secret, something must account for the fact that no person alive will tell me that my grandfather was a cruel man. Just as no one will speak to me of my father's drinking. Some things appear not to exist here, or at least they do not exist in public. In this way a man that is drunk, crazy or simply cruel can escape notice. Mysteries, secrets, miracles.

Death, on the other hand, is a public event. And so it is that people in Gethsemane are meticulously routine about speaking to me of my father's death. It is often the first item of conversation, as if to prove that there is no shame attached to his life or to the manner of his passing.

"Why, Jeannine," it goes, "we were so sorry to hear about your daddy passing away. We couldn't hardly believe it. We saw him in town the week before. Your poor mother has been so brave, such a Christian example."

"I always mean to go and see your momma," Carrie Dean says. "I been meaning to and meaning to and that's as far as I get off this hill. You know I always thought the world of your momma."

I nod. I, too, have meant to go and see her more than I do, to see if she needs anything, to see how she is, to see how she fashions a life out of religion and memories and sheer unyielding competence.

"She's a brave woman," I say.

An understatement. But I also think she was mightily relieved to have the weight of my father lifted from her life. At least she must have felt that way at first. Before guilt catapulted her into her present role as revisionist historian. These days my mother's talk of my father works the loamy soil of reclaimed virtues. To do this she has cast aside the jagged rocks of his known character, all the hard truths that I was teethed on.

She herself is the best convert to the new version of their life together. Now it is, "He was so proud of you, Jeannine, so proud he didn't know how to show it. That's why he was so hard on you."

This, in place of the confidences whispered years after some incident, whisperings that left me helpless and enraged: "And then he dragged me out of the house by the heels, and my head bounced on every cement step down to the driveway."

The new father I have acquired so inconveniently late in my life is about as useful to me as the old one. Further, the penalty in this scheme is that I am now to assume my share of guilt and remorse.

"Jeannine, when I think of how you used to get all those telephone calls. He hated it so . . . You were on that telephone all the time! And you knew he couldn't stand it! Why, I guess we all drove the poor man beyond his patience, beyond any mortal man's patience."

This, from the woman—brave even then—who had fought for me during those telephone years, who tried to see that I had lines of escape from the house she was marooned in.

I have not contested this new husband for my mother. She has earned him, I think, this hero who would have shone forth *if only* . . .

Besides, I have telephone stories of my own.

We stand around talking to Momma in the kitchen in Houghton Park. My father opens the front door at 6:40 with that look of prehistoric agate in his eyes. He strips off his tie and drops his change and then his cuff links onto the doily underneath the china lamp in the living room. He says, "Time to eat." Cal and Curtis and I sit down at the table to eat with him while Momma flies at pots and pans on the stove and produces bowls of food for the table. He hangs his suit jacket on the back of his chair. He sits down and folds

*back the cuffs of his white shirt, which is shifted loose at the
broad waist. Momma's eyes give last-minute instructions; I
put out the napkins and the butter. My father serves his
plate, and slaps mashed potatoes, peas and pork chops on
mine. Tears come to my eyes, which I take care not to raise
into view. We eat in this way, forks scraping carefully on
yellow Melmac. And then my father says, "Answer the
phone, Curtis." Curtis looks up from his plate, blue eyes
confused. "It didn't ring," he says. He catches the edge of
my father's stellate glance, and smooths his voice. "It didn't
ring, sir." Curtis is the youngest, and sometimes it takes
more years for the rules to settle than he has available to
him at a given time. He does not read the thrust of the jaw,
nor the way the lips are set in a line. And when the paternal
chair is shoved backward and the tinkle of the belt buckle
rides the air, the snake of leather already drawn from the
loops, it is too late for the frantic "Yes, sir!" Curtis makes it
as far as the china lamp before the belt lashes and the
knuckles to the head overtake him. I lock my eyes into Cal's,
and he says, "What are you looking at? Pass the peas."
Momma picks up her dishcloth and pulls something off the
burner. Curtis learns to answer the telephone when he is
told to.*

Carrie Dean shifts in the swing, sets her foot jiggling. "I see
your momma at church most every Sunday," she muses, "but she
slips out the back before the last hymn, and I never get to say a
word to her. She brings flowers sometimes, and she gave the Father's Day devotional—and you know, nobody can get straight to
people's hearts like your mother can. She had several snuffling
and sniffling right there in the choir. I liked-to bawled myself."

I know the devotional she is talking about. I remember when
it was given in the church we belonged to in Detroit. But these
were soft-spoken, dry-eyed Northern Baptists, long on ideas, short
on Scripture. Sermons were based on popular books like *Secular
City* and popular songs like "Downtown." They were delivered in

a tone that was mannerly and even. Sundays didn't feel much like Sundays to us for a long time after we moved North. But this was a church with stained-glass windows, and eventually I wore a swim cap and a nunlike wimple and white robes into the heated baptistry of Houghton Park Baptist Church. The warm water rose to my neck.

". . . Raised to walk in the newness of life . . ." was what I heard as Reverend Chevalier pushed me up out of the water again, his large hand on my back like a hydraulic lift. Reverend Chevalier was known to be efficacious, and shortly after he left Houghton Park, he got the call to do promotional work for a firm on the West Coast.

Momma overcame her shyness of Reverend Chevalier and Houghton Park Baptist Church after we had lived in Detroit six or seven years. She began to think of doing devotionals as she had back Home. She would if I would do one with her, she said. And so we stood together before the congregation that Father's Day, and recited by turns. I can remember it all, and I repeat the lines to Carrie Dean.

> "And the years passed, and the Father and the Mother
> Grew old together. The little Mother grew weary and
> bent,
> And the Father watched after her, for he was rested in faith,
> And walked with the Lord.
> And when the Path was steep, he bade the children
> Help their Mother and comfort her;
> And when the way was strewn with thorns he bore her up
> In his arms, for she was precious to him."

"Now quit," Carrie Dean says, spanking my knee sharply. "You're going to make me cry sitting right here."

"Okay."

"Besides, I got something else you have to see. You been reminding me."

She leads the way into the house and through the living room, down the dim back hallway to the small bedroom. The room had been hers when the house was new; we slept here that summer we were both sixteen. Carrie Dean places her hand on the doorknob and turns it quietly. She pushes the door open and glances back at me.

I follow her, tiptoeing barefoot across the hardwood floor to stand over the heavy breather in the white crib. Reddish Wentworth ringlets form in the perspiration on his forehead. Violet-shaded eyelids rest peacefully under their burden of copper eyelashes. A thumb discharged from the pink mouth in a slipstream of drool stands poised beside its station. Carrie Dean and I grin at each other as though this miracle infant were the result of some shared triumph.

When the moment is over, she stoops to pick up a small rubber car beside the crib and returns it to a low shelf. We tiptoe out again.

Back on the porch I speak with conviction. "He *is* lovely."

"Well, what'd I tell you?"

We sit down again, the old wooden swing creaking on its chains. I glance up at the ceiling, thinking suddenly of the rusted hooks that hold the thing up. They are there, looking intact.

"How did you ever decide to have a third one?"

Carrie Dean sniffs. She gets a crooked grin in place for the reply.

"It wasn't a matter of deciding, it was what happened."

"Ohhhhhhh," I say.

We nod at each other.

"How does Garth do as a daddy of three?"

"Oh, don't nothing bother Garth. It's me I worry about. I'm the one that gets mad and screams and hollers at the kids. I thought I was bad enough with two." She shakes her head slowly from side to side.

"I know the feeling," I say, but she is not listening. She is looking into the distance.

After a moment she speaks from that distance. "I just pray that my husband will keep on putting up with me."

Pray. Down here, the word is literal. I say nothing. I watch her face. Her eyes are slow in coming to mine.

"The preacher says a woman is to do the will of her husband, who is her master."

I try to give it a beat, but the words are out of my mouth. "I'm sure the preacher says a lot I wouldn't agree with. Me or any other woman that's got her eye on surviving."

"It's not just the preacher, Jeannine. It says so very plainly in the Bible."

And if you cannot question the Bible, where is there for you to hide? This time I do give it a beat.

"The Bible is the Bible. It's the only book Christians have, and it's holy. But it was written down by men, Carrie Dean. And they weren't perfect."

"They were inspired of God."

"They still didn't always get it right."

We find other places to look besides into each other's eyes. The children's activity in the yard suddenly seems restful. We watch them, and allow cars to pass on the road below. After a while we test our smiles on one another.

"Listen," I say. "I've lost track of the time. I guess I'd better get on back to Momma's."

I add, because something still needs to be added, "She's probably home trying to think of some way to work herself to death before I get there."

We stand up together, and Carrie Dean asks, "Does she get scared being all by herself?"

I don't know the answer. I try to think of what I know of how Momma feels as we walk.

"I know how lost *my* momma was when my daddy passed away," Carrie Dean says, swinging her arms and clapping her hands in rhythm with our steps. "She got so scared there for a while, she wouldn't go out the back door if it was past sundown. Not even to the washhouse."

I shake my head. If my mother is scared, she is not scared in that way.

"I know she tends her animals in the dead of night," I say. "She says there's no use in being afraid. But I'm not sure that means she isn't."

"Your momma is a mighty brave woman."

The phrase is beginning to irritate me. "I think she would say she doesn't have much choice."

I climb into the car and she pushes the door shut. With her hands still on the door handle she pauses for a moment, and then leans her weight on her arms on the open window.

"I always thought you were so lucky," she says. "Your mother was so sweet to you. I liked being at your house because she would love me up just like she did you. That wasn't the way it was at my house."

"I guess I didn't notice."

Carrie Dean straightens her back and lets her hands drop to her hips. A heavy sigh allows the bones of shoulders and arms and chest to settle down over one another, and she turns her head to look over her shoulder. Not at the dull silver trailer, but into the past.

"I don't know what it was. I always felt like I was in the way, like Momma was always mad with me. And I wasn't making it up, either. She always *was* mad with me, fussing at me, hissing at me to be quiet, paddling me over just anything. I felt like the best I could do was stay out of the way."

She turns the sky-colored eyes back to me.

"I never felt like that at your house. You were treated like you were somebody. And when I was there, I was too."

She reaches out a finger and makes a mark on the Malibu's dusty side.

"I know you got to go," she says.

We say a little more—that we hope to do better with our own children, that we will see each other in church tomorrow—and I drive away. I wave to the children as I head past them down the road. Children with other things to do than color with crayons and play dominoes.

In the last thirty years I myself have thrown over dominoes for more complicated games. Bridge. Chess. "When I became a man, I put away childish things." But come to think of it, I have in my adult life thrown over at least one chessboard. Childish; a classic of immaturity. But surely it is a sensible move, as sensible as any on the board, when it seems like the only thing worth doing.

For grown-ups, the question arises: Were the circumstances extenuating enough?

Learning chess was one of the things Larry and I attempted to do together last winter. It was a silly choice, far too intense for two people who fear they are already engaged in warfare. But we made the attempt, Larry of course going by the book. I couldn't make sense of it that way. For me the game turned into one more model of social organization.

How uncommonly congruent chess pieces are! Castles with secret passages, hobbled knights, populous pawns. Bishops are merely overgrown pawns, heads split by a swordstroke, so each maintains a separate diagonal. The king: nervous. He paces, keeps himself reined in tight. Setting a good example for the knights, no doubt.

Note: Those who benefit by the rules generally like to play by them.

Thus the queen is a renegade. She gives no quarter, does everything on the board except leap over circumstance as knights do. The skirts must be taken into account. Otherwise she is unbound by the rules, save one: The king must live. The queen's job is not to live but to maintain at all costs the defenses within which the king takes his measured step. If he is taken, all is lost. Game's over.

It occurs to me now, as I settle the Malibu into fourth gear, that some pieces have been left off the chessboard, some continuities dispensed with. What, for example, of the royal offspring? If they existed as pieces, prince and princess, what moves would be assigned them? What limits? Say that the king fell, and none of the pieces were content to be swept from the board. Say the game were to continue. What would be the new object?

These are difficult matters. Nobody has dared approach them, knowing that dynasties regularly founder on the question of succession. In modern life the people who pretend to specialize in human continuities are descended from chessboard bishops. In this new clergy I include psychologists. We who see everything through a sword-cleft in the head.

Well. To return to childish things, let me say that granting our separate approaches to the game of chess, Larry and I played more or less evenly. Until in one of his books Larry learned a trick called "Fool's Mate." I don't know; it was the insult, I guess. *White leads* ... four quick moves into the play and zappo, game's over. And so I turned over the board ... *Black responds by overturning the board.*

This is why men do not approve of women dressed out for soldiering. Women are trained to defend and give no quarter; this is permissible because tradition has it that we bear no arms. An armed woman who has not been trained to halt on the appropriate square is indeed a monster.

The insult of Larry's Fool's Mate was eclipsed when I threw over the board. Insult comes in second to outrage, in the way of things.

So it was I who apologized, I who returned to the battlefield and picked up the pieces.

Larry, officer and gentleman that he is, never again mentioned the incident. But the next night at dinner the conversation took an odd little turn around the family table:

Laura, five-year-old siren, out of the blue: "I have five lovers."

Larry, her father, dropping his fork: "Terrific."

Jeannine, her mother: "Where do you get that language? How about five *friends*?"

Laura: "Did you and Dad be friends?"

Jeannine: "Yes."

Larry: "I thought you were the person who liked truth so much."

Laura: "Dad? Did you and Mom be friends a long time?"

Larry: "About six months. Out of the last eighteen."

At the wide corner of Thorton Wentworth's goat pasture, I take the fork of the road that bears toward the Rise. I am certain that it is a measure of health to remain focused in the present tense, in present surroundings. I make the effort. But I find nothing in Thorton Wentworth's goat pasture to nourish my attention. Thorton. Now there's a name. Gritty, palpable. Unlike *Larry*, a word that lies passive upon the tongue, not a consonant solid enough to set your teeth into. Larry Lewis. "Behold, ye are lukewarm, and I shall spew ye out of my mouth."

And it is no use. How can the present make valid claims when it is the past that exerts such rude pressure? My brain has country-club manners. It allows the past to play through.

That look on Carrie Dean's face, eyes full of feelings she's been hiding for thirty years. Eyes that saw my mother giving out love that she wanted. Someone else's bounty may be painfully shunted aside, but not forgotten. The memory is put by until the time is better, until the perils of wanting are safely gone by. That is, beyond childhood.

The eyes shadow me all the way home, around every blind curve and corner to the Rise. They make me look at a pattern I haven't had cause to remember in the past ten years. People come forward in my mind, childhood friends and even college friends who responded to my mother like thirsty plants. I only half-saw those hooded responses to Momma's oddball playfulness. Her life.

They responded to it, yearned for it. How many of my friends from that long growing-up, bored by their own politeness inquiring after my husband and child, still show that gleam of yearning when they ask, "And what has become of your mother?"

Knowing, of course, that something would.

What I saw, doing my teenage growing-up in Houghton Park, was our family's difference. Our isolation. We were *out of place*. My southern mother could not have taught me otherwise, and yet I blamed her. Oddly, I was the one she looked to—she would have been so relieved, so grateful, to have me open the northern world wide for her. Why would I not seize opportunities?

"You have everything!" she once told me, spreading her fingers and turning out the palms to show the extent. Incomprehensible that I wouldn't join the drama club, try out for debate. Incomprehensible, my dread of being on display and exposed. "If I had your chances," she cried, and I watched the vivid irises stand stark in their pools of white, "I'd be Queen of the World!"

But I had absorbed her suspicion that in our difference there might be something wrong, something to cover and be ashamed of. And so I did not often bring friends home to our split-level to discover what it might be.

The thought reaches me now—now, through Carrie Dean—that my friends saw something I didn't think counted. They saw my mother. Not her bare feet in the kitchen, not the wildly imperfect housekeeping. She outshone it all, made them feel *welcome*. And in my arrogance, I had been blind.

I drive the last stretch of Blue Rise Road awash in sentiment. Sentiment for the mother I have discovered. But when I pull into the drive, the petunias in their white pot are there, and they all but speak aloud. Seeing them, another piece is jarred into place. Seeing them, I remember the rest.

Donna Blanchard is the rich girl at Houghton Park School. She lives in a house situated on eight acres of prime suburban woodland. Tiled swimming pool in the back garden, heated towel racks in the bathrooms, sunken bathtubs, other marvels. I know, as every child in school knows, that her family belongs to the Congregational Church and to the country club and that her mother wears jewelry to the supermarket. And on this day, in one of the accidental harmonies that can sometimes still happen in sixth grade, I have asked her to come home with me and she does. We walk in the front door and Momma calls out a gay welcome. The living room is passable. Momma is busy in the kitchen, and so the clutter there appears functional. My own room is strewn with everything I have to strew, but many suburban kids have this license. The doors to the other bedrooms are closed, which informs me that Momma saw the two of us getting off the school bus together. Donna and I have an hour in my room writing invisible notes with reconstituted lemon juice. Momma brings us a bowl of popcorn, and then it is time for Donna to go home. Yes. Now she must call her mother to pick her up. Yes. The telephone is—the telephone is in my mother's bedroom. We open the door and go in. The bed is unmade, violently so. The dresser is piled with cosmetics, collar tabs, magazines, neckties, matchbooks, lost shirt buttons, used Kleenex in several shades. The unfolded laundry is piled on the chair and drifted onto the floor. The sewing machine is open and stacked with fabrics and good intentions, pattern envelopes and their contents, papers of pins, spools drooling down their threads. Books and cardboard boxes and dustballs protrude from underneath the chest of drawers and the bed. I remove one of my father's limp undershirts from where it lies embracing the telephone, and push the closet door nearly shut. Donna dials her mother, and soon she is gone in the white Thunderbird convertible that briefly blows its smoke over my mother's fledgling thicket hedge beside the drive. I return to my room and Momma follows me as far as her doorway. Moments later she comes to me, convulsed and brilliant-eyed with laughter. "Come here," she snorts out, beckoning with a finger. I follow her and we stand at the door of her room, Momma trying to control her throat. "Did she see that?" she asks. At first I do not see what she sees. And then when I see it, I don't know whether I am supposed to know what it is. But there, deftly tucked into the bedsprings and dangling like an oriole's nest from banded elm branches, is one of my father's used prophylactics.

I remain in the car for a few moments after I have cut the engine, and with my fingers flick the keys that hang from the ignition chain. Some thought that wants to be remembered. And it comes: "Sentiment is what remains of a love that will not recognize its hate." I think I heard that in one of Chevalier's sermons. It sounds a lot like Houghton Park.

3

Momma stands at the kitchen counter assembling a mountainous strawberry affair. Cakes, crisp meringues, strawberries, whipped cream, fresh coconut. Jewel of the kitchen, this oeuvre is beset with pots, pans, colanders, a grater, scrapers, bowls and beaters, knives and spoons on every side. Last night the counter itself was visible. But that was last night.

Since my college days, whenever I stay at home, I follow a routine. I wash the dishes and tidy my mother's kitchen once a day, last thing before bed. That gives us a clean slate to start the next morning with, after which we can forget about clean slates.

"That looks fantastic! What is it?"

"Strawberry Torte New Orleans!" she announces, with a wince of satisfaction.

"When did you bake the meringue part? Never mind. I know when."

"I did it last night after you went to bed. Why?"

"Nothing. You still don't ever sleep, do you?"

"Honey, I haven't had a night's sleep since Daddy died." Daddy. My father.

"That thing looks big enough for Cox's army!"

"Well, that's what we're going to feed with it."

I move close enough to admire the creation and to stick a privileged finger into the makings.

"Why do we always say Cox's army?" I ask her. "Who was Cox, anyway?"

She chuckles without looking up from what she is doing, which is settling graceful daubs of whipped cream on the top layer of meringue.

"I don't know, Jeannine. That's just what we always say."

"And you're going to bring this beauty in and set it before all those *feverishly* trim little people in the Hinton family. And you're going to watch them try and hang on to their diets till their fingernails pop off."

The mischief bubbles out of my mother, and her shoulders shake.

"I can't wait to see Verlie's eyes light up," she admits. "That ole gal's getting to be mud-fat."

The Hintons as a rule are long-boned and slender. But all the brothers put on weight in middle age, a sort of affluent padding. Their wives did not follow suit. Of the women on the Hinton side, only Verlie got fat.

Verlie is my father's only living sister, the only one of three Hinton daughters to survive bouts of whooping cough and croup one winter. The few photographs taken of Verlie in her teens show that she was uncommonly striking. She still is, but over the years she has added pound after pound to her smallish frame. Momma describes her as looking "like a balloon that's been tied at the wrists and ankles."

This makes Verlie an amateur. For Momma speaks of her own sisters and their daughters with less delicacy. She describes any one of them as looking "like a walking refrigerator."

This second family trait of Groves women is the one they are willing to talk about. Obesity is so specific to my mother's family that among themselves they call it "Groves fat." "That ole Groves fat," they will say, laughing, looking at one another. Explaining everything.

Groves bones come heavy and broad, and the weight goes on solid, in slabs. And it goes on to stay. Diets may come and go, but "that ole Groves fat" is with them always.

My mother is the only one in the family rigorous enough to keep the stuff in line, and her success is a sore point with the others. Something like treachery, possibly something learned in all those years up North.

As for me, I am a Hinton.

With her free hand Momma gives her stomach a firm slap.

"I got five pounds I could stand to lose, and I aim to get rid of that stuff. Verlie can have all of this—" and she gestures with a knife over the billowing cake—"that her little heart desires. I don't intend to have a single bite."

"Not even one?"

"Not the first one. I have to fight like a tiger to lose a single ounce these days." With her red-stained fingers she seats the largest and most perfectly shaped strawberries on the crown of the cake. The selection process is vigorous, and one passed-over berry lands with a juicy smack on the linoleum. I stoop for it and head for the sink to find a sponge. But Momma has extended a bare foot to a damp towel that lies in the corner like a limp gray cat. Balanced on one foot, she draws the towel over and swishes it across the brilliant spot. Then, still with her foot, she slides the towel back to its resting place. I shake my head in wonderment and take my own place again, one hip against the counter.

"I thought you always made chicken legs for the Hintons."

"Nope."

"Too easy, eh? No pimento cheese?"

"Honey, nobody eats pimento-cheese sandwiches anymore. You know that."

"We just had some today at Aunt Lottie's. Eola brought them."

"Well, that's Eola. You know Eola."

"I know that pimento-cheese sandwiches were the only things I used to eat at the Hinton get-togethers. Only thing that was safe."

"You knew they were, because I made 'em!"

She laughs—sniggers, actually, is the word. We snigger together. We are remembering the suppers at Grandma Hinton's, the charred sausages floating in greasy water, okra breaded and fried to cardboard, soggy vanilla wafers on congealed banana pudding . . .

Momma wipes tears from her eyes with the back of her hand.

"All I can say is, the men in that family sure were lucky.

They all got to go out and marry themselves some woman that could cook. Verlie just had to keep right on. Bless her heart."

Momma's telephone rings. Telephones in rural Mississippi seem to have been cross-bred with alarm clocks. That grating jangle would appear to make it a point of decency to avoid using the things. When I lived in this house as a child, telephones hadn't invaded the countryside. People just dropped in when they happened to be thinking of you, or simply happened to be out your way. And you were grateful. Your responsibility was to be hospitable, to provide a feeling of welcome. That was all. And that could be manufactured on the spot, unlike a presentable house, which was therefore not expected.

Whenever I am here, I tend to forget that telephones are part of life. I want to jump in the car and take my chances. Using the telephone seems like cheating, a violation of place and time. But very likely the place and time exist only in my memory. For right now, the telephone insists.

Momma sets one more strawberry in position, and breathes out a sigh. Then, in three coordinated motions, she grabs a dish towel, wipes her fingers and snatches the telephone from its wall cradle.

I remove the kingpin strawberry from the center of the cake and, catching her eye, ceremoniously place the entire thing in my mouth.

Momma folds the receiver to her chest and narrows her eyes at me before bringing it to her face.

"Hhhello?"

All mothers have melodious voices for people from the outside.

"Why, hello there!" she sings out, and shoots me a wide glance. "What in the world are you doing up there on a hot day like this? . . . Well, not too much. Trying to keep cool and trying to keep your wife out of the dessert I'm trying to fix. What? Now you listen to me, I did the best job I could. If she doesn't have any manners by now, don't you send her off down here to me. I got enough on my hands. Here, I'll let you talk to the rascal."

She repeats the wide look as she hands me the telephone.

This is the way important calls are treated, and Husbands are always important. As I take the telephone, she moves out of earshot, off toward the bedrooms. She is being hospitable; privacy is a courtesy offered to outsiders.

"Hello, Larry!" I say it with energy, a matter of courtesy. "You don't pay any attention to anything my mother tells you, do you?"

His voice, when it begins, sounds uncannily close. "I have a feeling I should start."

"We're just getting ready to go to Aunt Verlie's for a family supper."

"Which one is that, your dad's sister?"

I hear the door to Momma's bedroom click shut.

"Right."

"Look," Larry says. "The travel agent called me. She has a flight for you back here on the twenty-seventh. Not the later one you wanted, but at seven in the morning. Delta Seven-fifty-three. I told her okay."

"Oh. Thanks."

A long pause. I close my eyes.

"You know," he says, "just talking to you gets me upset again."

I glance down that hall. The door is still closed. I move into the dining room, stretching the coils of the receiver wire.

"Look, Larry. I need the peace. Let me have it. Don't call me."

"And it doesn't matter what I need."

I have no words, none that have not been said. I stare out the dining room windows at the western horizon, the line of pines liquid and bluish, irregular.

"Look," he says. "Okay, I know you need the time. I'm doing fine, using up some of my Saturday in the office. This just threw me, this flight stuff. I know you're doing what you have to do. How's your mom treating you?"

"The same."

"Well"— and at this the familiar laugh breaks through—"I

know that can't be all good. Another week and you'll be delighted to see me."

"Right."

And a smile helps itself to my mouth anyway.

"Take care of yourself," he says. "I love you."

"Thank you." And as I hear the bedroom door open, I return to the kitchen and add in a firmer tone, "Laura and I will see you the twenty-seventh. Bye."

I replace the receiver on the wall hook as Momma comes out of the shadows of the hall. She is still buttoning the blouse that she has not yet tucked into the pants she has not yet zipped.

Her body is muscular and firm. I do not see the five pounds she is "fighting like a tiger." I can see no fat at all on the belly, though the skin slides off the firm contours of her waist. Sixty-five years old, three pregnancies. No, four. The first, a miscarried girl.

"That was a long phone call, long distance," Momma says, "and in the middle of the day."

"Larry has a WATS line in his office."

"He sounded good."

She zips and fastens the waist of her blue cotton pants, and runs her index fingers around the waistband inside, adjusting the tucks of the blouse.

"Yeah, he's fine. We should get gone, shouldn't we? They'll start without us, that bunch."

"I didn't know you were so eager for some of Verlie's sweet-potato pie."

I make the required face at her, but she does not stay to see it. She hurries past me into the kitchen. I gather up our purses and move toward the front door. I can hear Momma saying something as she comes from the kitchen.

". . . gobble up my best strawberry, I'm going to tear you up. One of these days you're going to put out a hand and draw back a nub."

It is something she said to us often while we were growing up. To all three of us premature cake-bowl lickers and icing-daubers as we surrounded her in the kitchen. It used to frighten me, the thought that she would actually take her butcher knife and lop off an offending hand or finger; that I might actually "draw back a nub."

Now it makes me laugh, as she knows. It is a peculiar pass when the things that make you feel most at home are the *familiar* threats.

4

I drive, and Momma puts on her lipstick and rouge. Strawberry Torte New Orleans is wedged between her feet, inside a large lidded Tupperware container.

"Do you need this?" I ask her, pivoting the rearview mirror toward her.

"If I want a mirror, I got this."

She reaches up and flips down the passenger visor. A lighted mirror is set into its underside. When I have seen it, she flips the thing back up again and pushes the rearview mirror back toward me.

"I don't need one for this old prune face," she says.

She caps the lipstick and drops it into her purse, and the tube of cheek color follows. With a sigh she leans back against the seat and its upholstered headrest, and closes her eyes. Her face relaxes instantly. While I reposition the mirror, the relaxation deepens into sleep.

The west section of Blue Rise Road is paved now. The gravel I ground into my knees learning to ride Cal's bicycle has been overlaid with asphalt. The Malibu purrs over this proud shiny black ribbon that leads the way along the ridge past Grandma's, past Serene's pecan trees. Serene and I rode the school bus together those few months both our families lived on the Rise. Both had moved by the time I was eight and Serene was eleven. She married at fourteen. Some boy in the service from Meridian, my mother said. I have not seen her since the last day she saved me a seat on the bus.

Farther along is Great Uncle Delaney's place, Aunt Sophie's house, and so on. This road is so familiar; the road and its landmarks constitute a ritual, a trip around the rosary, if Baptists had a rosary. Which they most emphatically do not.

There is the house with the gray latticework where Aunt Marvelle Hinton lived. The little cabin off to one side of the front lawn is where her husband settled when they separated. That white frame house with the screened porch is where Marvelle's momma was killed by lightning standing at the back door.

My friend Eloise Davis lived in that green house beside the Notmuch sign. Notmuch is the name of the town, the popular account being that after the railroad passed between the filling station and the grocery store on Blue Rise Road a caboose man hollered out one day, "What do you call this town?" Whereupon one of the local wits replied, and the reply stuck.

Eloise's house is overgrown with weeds, the windows broken, the porch collapsed. Deserted. Now, as ever, there is not much to the town: a Western Auto store, a beauty shop, a new grocery and drugstore next to the old filling station.

I slow down for the railroad tracks and try to ease the car over the bumps. Momma's eyes fly open anyway. She straightens in her seat and looks defensively alert.

"Whatever happened to Eloise?" I ask her.

"You know she married her third cousin."

"What does third cousin mean again?"

"Third cousin?" She clears her throat. "I thought you were the expert on families. I thought that's what you got a master's degree for."

"They didn't teach me the part about cousins. I'd have to have a Ph.D. for that. You tell me."

"Eloise's momma's oldest sister, Jeannette was her name, she had two boys, R. D. and James. James married the little old Wilson girl I went to school with, and they had four boys and a girl, and one of the boys made a lawyer. And that was the one Eloise married. Her married name is Jenkins."

"Wait a minute. Wait a minute. That means . . . they had the same great-grandmother."

"Right. Third cousins."

"Well? Isn't that all right? Isn't that legal?"

"Of course it's legal, or they wouldn't be married. But that don't make it right."

She is definite on the point, and I have no reason to argue. For me, all that remains of these school friends are the lineage tracers in my mother's mind. And there are rules for that.

In general Rise people go to church in Bay Springs or Antioch rather than Gethsemane. So the fact that my mother has a line on them at all is a testimony of how tight the rules are, and how important the information is judged to be. The effort of keeping up with who has married whom has always been part of life here. Young people still will meet and marry, and the bloodlines of Groveses, Holloways, Hintons, Drennans, Bynums and Wentworths and the rest must be taken into account. Young lovers may defy the stone tablets of family reputation, and take the consequences. But they are strictly not to meddle in the proliferating garden of known blood relations. Blood is blood, no matter how thin it runs. Its pathways are watched and jealously guarded, because it is ordained to run thinner and thinner. Trying to double back is cheating. Consorting with cousins is cheating, despite the number of genealogists willing to dance on the heads of pins.

I brake for a second set of railroad tracks outside the town. Momma reaches down and peeks under the lid of the Tupperware.

"You better take it easy over those tracks, or we'll have strawberry soup."

I grin at her. She relents and smiles back.

"Well," she says, "how's Larry getting along without anybody to poke their fingers in his dessert?"

"He's doing just fine, Momma."

"How's he liking his new job? Or his promotion, I guess you call it."

I nod. "Just fine."

"I guess he's just fine, then."

I turn to look at her amused blue eyes, still bigger and bluer than mine, set into her head as Groves eyes are. That is, not pop-eyed, as she terms the Hinton characteristic that I bear. These particular Groves eyes, while wide and expressive as a child's, are set in a rubbery sea of wrinkles. She has a term for that, too. "Two fried eggs in a mud puddle."

"He loves his new job, Momma. He loves it just like he did his old job. He doesn't mind working late, and he doesn't even mind working weekends, although he complains about it."

"Why, it sounds like the poor fellow doesn't have a minute to call his own, working so hard. Bless his heart! And now, with no-body there to give him his supper, or take care of him a little bit—"

Actually, it's a kind of relief for him, not having me there. Or Laura, either. Then he doesn't feel he has to leave work for dinner, or that I'm home waiting for him. He can stay till mid-night if he needs to."

"Well, all I can say is, you are a mighty lucky gal. So many men these days, and I mean men with families, they can hardly be made to work. And what little they do seems to make them forget which way home is."

She shakes her head. The eyes, as she turns them to me, are round and commercially sad. I wonder which magazines she has been reading, where she gets this modern stuff.

"Just you talk to your cousins tonight, if you want to hear something."

"Hear what?"

She shakes her head with a tight motion.

"Unh-unh. I'll let them tell you, if they want it told."

Genealogies are one thing. That's information. But this is gossip, and my mother doesn't gossip. It's another reason she is not particularly well thought of among my father's people. My fa-ther and his brothers were raised on a farm, poorer than the red clay they had to grow cotton and corn on. But they got each other through college, and they married women like themselves, women eager not to be poor.

Whenever I begin to think that the South is a place where

time has stopped, I realize that I am leaving out my father's family. Time has not stopped for the Hintons. They do not have the same sense of forward motion resisted. Now for the Groveses—and probably every soul at Gethsemane Baptist Church—here is time ground to a halt as nearly as it can be done. But on the Rise there has always been a sense of drift: new practices, altered rituals. The first tractors in the county, the first Model T, the first soldiers, the first college educations, the first hell-raisers.

Cyrus Hinton sent his oldest boy to college because his cousin Odell Hinton had sent his. And Sumrall Hinton knew better than to let his daddy down. He knew better than to raise hell, too; that was left to the brothers farther down the line.

Being oldest set my father apart from the others. He was in charge of seeing that expectations were met, and never got the gist of being modern. Nor did Verlie. But Verlie because she was the girl and was not sent to college or to the war to learn different ideas than Grandma Hinton taught.

Still, all four younger Hinton boys finished their schooling, and acquitted themselves respectably. Sumrall set the pace, and they followed. Besides, like Sumrall, they all had had enough mornings working a farm without breakfast in the spring, when the flour for biscuits and the cane syrup and the preserves had run out. They had had more than enough of that to take the making of money seriously. As family men, the Hinton brothers were known as good providers. If they had deficiencies in other ways, the knowledge was left at home.

After Vinnie died and Sumrall moved off the Rise, none of the younger brothers attempted farming, or built on Cyrus' land. Their marriages produced ranch homes, city addresses, golf regulars, memberships in the best churches, sons who could not get themselves through college in four years and daughters who married bandleaders. The brothers were embarrassed into impotent anger over such things. Their wives understood them as the hallmarks of middle-class success.

My mother, by such standards, had not been stylish enough. She had raised exemplary children according to the old rules: Cal and Curtis and I were each educated, married and solvent. And this the other Hinton wives had had to suffer. But my mother finally slipped up. She slipped up badly, so that the brothers, too, rounded on her: She allowed my father to die. And in circles where people do gossip, to become a disgrace.

Now, with this treachery revealed, who knew where else she would prove false? Each star in her crown was undergoing inspection for tarnish.

This time, I pass. My credentials are all still good, even down to being married to the same man I started with.

But I think about Marvelle Hinton: How did she arrange that one? How did she get her husband to build himself a separate house on the front lawn? It is an inspired solution: I can see it, a little cottage there on the far side of the double lot in Des Moines. Stonework and shutters, trim and spotless as a ship's cabin. It would be right beside the garden, Larry would love it, Laura could run freely back and forth between the houses ...

The sign beside the bridge says "To Jackson." I put on the turn signal.

Momma sits straight up in her seat and looks around, blinking.

"Don't turn here!" she cries.

"Momma," I whisper, thinking that she may be still dreaming, "this is the way to Verlie's."

"You see that dirt road up on the right? That next one? Take it."

I put on the turn signal again. "Verlie doesn't live in Jackson anymore," I say. I nod my head, as though it makes perfect sense.

She jerks her face toward me, fully awake and fully irritated. "We're going to the cabin, I said."

"You didn't 'said' to me. What cabin?"

"You don't listen. Verlie and Wendell bought some land with an old shanty on it. They made it over, and Wendell put in a pond." She pulls down the visor and glances at herself hurriedly, harshly. She presses her mouth together and clears her brow of frown lines, a last protection against the sisters-in-law. This irritability is for the Hintons. "They come down from Jackson for weekends. Sometimes Verlie stays all week."

She picks up the container of dessert as we make the turn, and holds it in her lap. She closes her vent window; I do the same. We ride up and down over the ruts of the road, with branches of trees slapping at the windows. Dust rises off the road behind us, a longitudinal tornado. After some minutes we see a clearing, freshly mowed and fenced with wire. And then a plain weather-beaten cabin, flanked on two sides with white Oldsmobiles and copper vans.

"Well," Momma says, bracing an arm against the dashboard for one last lurch over the cattle grate, "I guess when you get far enough from the way you grew up, you can go back and call it fashionable. I wouldn't know."

5

The picnic supper has worn the afternoon out. The grown-ups sit in the shade on folding chairs. The remaining Hinton brothers talk softly to each other and to their brother-in-law about business, about politics. Their sons listen, adding an earnest word or two in their turn. They hold cans of beer, the newest erosion of tradition for family gatherings. The wives and daughters and daughters-in-law sit together under a large pine nearer the beach. They are regretting an extra helping of one thing or another while they watch the children in the water. I sit with them while my mother, with her trouser legs rolled to the knees, stands in the shallow lake. She is helping somebody else's grandchild into a bulbous black inner tube.

"Melvinia sure has a way with children," Aunt Lenore comments in my direction. "It's just a shame that all y'all have to live so far away."

I nod, conceding the point. I nod for all of us: Cal in Boston, Curtis in Denver and myself in Des Moines.

"I know she just longs to see her own grandchildren," Lenore persists. It is her grandchild Momma has been helping.

"Well, she's just welcome to practice on some of mine," Verlie proclaims. "Lord knows I get to see enough of them."

"Now, Verlie, you know you just love it," scolds Lenore. "You wouldn't turn those children loose if their mother drove up with an R.N. certificate and a crowbar."

As she speaks, her eyes crawl across everybody else's to make sure we know where the joke is.

Verlie cackles good-naturedly.

"They surely are pretty things, ain't they?" she says, casting her eyes over the children churning the shallow water and patting heaps of sand on the shore. Sand, because Uncle Wendell has dumped truckloads of it, white sand from the Gulf. The sand makes a fine beach, as the women keep remarking. But the children come out of the water with orange legs and bellies and murk-colored swimsuits anyway. The red clay and organic sludge of the lake bed has the final word.

Verlie stands to complete her survey of the grandchildren, and turns beaming at the cluster of her sisters-in-law and nieces under the piney shade.

"Well!" she says. She props her tiny wrists on the expanse of her hips, which, gleaming in the purple swimsuit, do indeed resemble balloons.

"Nobody can say the Hintons don't know how to make 'em good-lookin'!"

The mothers and grandmothers of these good-looking children smile at one another.

Lenore crosses her long legs and sings out, "Well, you can tell Deborah June she's made her share. You better get her big brother Raymond on the job."

"Where is Deborah today?" somebody asks.

"She's got some school doin's—she's sorry not to see all y'all," Verlie explains. With one hand she adjusts the strips of elastic underneath each shining purple cheek.

"Well, it's good her younguns could come and have fun."

"Where is Raymond?" Lenore demands.

"I thought he'd be here by now," Verlie says, looking briefly around at the group of menfolk. They are called menfolk. "But Raymond watches the clock about like his daddy."

"You think you'll ever get that boy married off?"

"He aims to take his time, I reckon," Verlie replies. She lowers her voice and adds, "He told me here the other day that he had some new gal a-scratchin' at his door."

"Well, next time ask him: Was she tryin' to get *in* or was she tryin' to get *out*?"

The entire group giggles and squinches their shoulders at

Lenore's witticism. Lenore herself bites her lip and exchanges naughty glances with the others. She makes sure I am included by reaching over and spanking my thigh.

My cousin Drew has been sitting impassively in the chair next to mine. She has a can of beer in one hand, and she is responsible for the one in mine. Drew is a year younger than I am, and still she was the first human in my wide-eyed history to pronounce the word Kotex. I took the word back with me to Houghton Park that year, a Christmas story from my cousin to the Houghton Park Brownie Troop No. 309.

Drew lifts up her dark glasses and peers at me out of gray Hinton eyes. Hinton eyes are not, of course, pop-eyes. They are merely not as deeply settled into the skull as Groves eyes. Drew's are lushly defined with mascara and lime shadow.

"You about ready to go for a ride with me, Jeannine?"

I nod my head.

She calls over to Lenore, "Momma, look after the kids for me for a little while, okay? Jeannine and me got something to do."

Lenore presses her lips together and nods at her daughter.

We climb into Drew's blue Ford Fairlane, gum wrappers and comic books and a wadded T-shirt in the backseat.

"Damn ill-brought-up kids," she pouts, removing a can of hair spray from beneath my feet.

When we have bounced out of the long road back to the highway, I say, "Do we have something to do?"

Drew throws her head forward and then swivels around to look at me. Her strawberry curls toss in concert. The black lenses are effective above the straight nose and glistening mouth.

"I just thought we'd let my momma and the others cut Verlie into catmeat by themselves."

"What's going on with Deborah June? What is that all about?"

"Honey, you aren't sposed to ask me that." The high teasing tone that Lenore uses, that all southern women adopt when they make the decision to be bitches.

Drew continues in that vein. "You really shouldn't ask me, because I am one of the few people in the family that not only knows but might tell you. But we'll get to all that in a minute. Do you drink beer?"

"I certainly drank the one you gave me."

"But I mean, do you *drink beer*?"

I shrug. "On occasion."

"Well, gooood! We'll just on-occasion ourselves into this little hell-hole."

She turns the car into what my father used to call, with evident disdain, "Tater's Honky-Tonk." The disdain was for people who went there and did their drinking in public. Without shame. The blue and green neon tubes outlining the roof are there like an unlit memory from childhood. But the sign now says, "Your Place."

We park the car next to the door and cross the gravel to the cement stoop. The door actually has a doorknob.

"This isn't much of a scene right now," Drew whispers over her shoulder. She is wearing a black sleeveless blouse and black denims. As we make our way toward the red vinyl booth she swings her hips with a graceful insolence.

Over to our right two lean red-muscled men in T-shirts and dirty jeans smack pool balls together.

"It gets better after dark," Drew says. "When people feel pretty sure the preacher has gone to bed."

As soon as we settle in the booth, she drops the sunglasses into her purse and pulls out cigarettes and a lighter.

"Oho, *all* the vices," I say.

She snaps the head of the lighter shut and directs the stream of smoke my way.

"Honey, we have all got all the vices. What makes the difference is who you show 'em off to." I fan the smoke without comment, while she watches.

The gray eyes light up in the middle of the next drag, and she laughs the smoke out of her mouth.

"Hey. Do you remember the Christmas you were down here

when you were fifteen, and I asked you if you knew what a French kiss was?"

"Yeah, I remember."

"And you said you didn't know for sure, but you *thought* it was 'also known as a French tickler'?" She sputters out a laugh. "Lord, I thought I would die!"

"I thought I would, too, after you told everybody what I said."

"Child, how come you were so dumb at fifteen? Your daddy keep you locked up in a chicken coop up there in Detroit?"

"Close. How did you get to know so much at fourteen?"

Drew props her cigarette on the table edge and leans toward me.

"Practice, darlin'."

She sits up straight again and keeps her eyes on mine while she flashes one of her grins.

"And speakin' of practice, what are you doin' down here without ole—what's his name again, your husband?"

"Larry."

"Larry. Well, don't that boy know anything about southern women?"

I glance over at the men at the pool table. One of them bends to level his cue. The other stands by and vacantly rubs chalk over and over the button of rubber at the tip of his stick. I shrug and turn back to Drew.

"He works, I play."

"Doesn't look to me like you're very damn good at it."

"What in the world are you talking about, Drew Priscilla?" I say, and reach for her cigarettes.

"Hey, what you doing?"

I pick one out of the package and seize her lighter to light it. Filters, thank God.

"It's like you say. We all got all the vices."

In truth, I rarely smoke. I don't do it right. I even hold the thing funny, Larry tells me; he says I'm too tense, I pull too hard. Anyway, I don't enjoy it. It's something I do when I'm drinking enough not to notice how it feels or tastes. Something I do in bad company.

"What I'm talking about, Jeannine Melvinia, is that there hasn't been much of that pretty smile of yours showin' hereabouts."

"Oh?" I say, and exhale smoke.

"You don't smoke like you do it regular, hon."

"So I've been told."

The barman approaches our table, and Drew acknowledges him with a sly pout.

"Why, Drew!" he sings out, slipping an arm around her shoulders and squeezing her to him. "You sweet thang! Where you been?"

He is good-looking. His jeans and knit shirt show off a muscular frame. His blond hair is unnaturally well coiffed.

"Around, Charley, around. Now you keep your greasy hands off that one across the table, that's my cousin."

Charley shoots up his eyebrows in practiced appraisal. "Why, hello there," he swoons.

"You wouldn't like her one bit, that there's my Yankee cousin." She leans forward and coos to me, "Never you mind, honey, he's just going to bring us two tall glasses of Jax. Isn't that right, Charley?"

Charley spins on his heels and calls out over his retreating shoulder, "An-y-thang you *want*."

Drew and I exchange glances, and then our eyes follow Charley as he reaches over the counter for glasses and draws the beers. This male is public property, the way men get to be in service occupations, just like the women who preceded them. Charley brings the tall glasses back to us, foam drifting down the sides. He whistles as he comes, appreciative of our attention. He sets a glass in front of Drew and then me, and he lowers his head to my eye level to say, "I ain't got a thang against Yankees." He pauses his required four seconds too long, and again spins away.

"Isn't he a mess?"

I shake my head in wonderment, and then decide to nod it in response to Drew's question-and-statement.

Drew laughs out loud.

We lift our glasses to one another, drink through the foam and set them down again, making wet rings on the linoleum surface. Drew lets her eyes find me from underneath the green-shaded lids.

"Well, did your momma tell you how I come to be a dee-vor-cee?" She leaves her mouth slack and waggles her head slightly to the three stranded syllables. It is either a joke, or she is imitating Grandma Hinton's palsy.

"What I heard, and this was more than a year ago, was that you and Rusty had split, and got back together."

"Iddn't that just like Aunt Melvinia?" Drew marvels. She is affecting, as she so often does, the trash dialect that transforms "Isn't" into "iddn't," "wasn't" into "waddn't," drops all g's from "ing" and tortures vowels into extra duty.

"Honey, you don't get much news that iddn't good news, do you? Bless your heart, you must not hear much about any of us. Waelll. It is true, strickly speakin'. Rusty and me did get back together—for about thirty seconds. Between you and me, that's about all he's good for, anyway. But listen here, your momma skipped all the good parts, and I aim to do right by you."

She rests one arm on the table, and holds her cigarette aloft.

"I was in the hospital, havin' my surgery—five kids and even I know when to quit some things—and my momma saw my dear husband walkin' down the street with some red-headed woman. She took a good look, and he saw her lookin'. She wasn't goin' to tell me a thing; what she did do was she called up Rusty's daddy. She told him, 'I just saw your son walkin' down Murphy Street with another woman. Now I'm not going to say a thing to Drew, who happens to be in the hospital, and I'm not goin' to say a thing to Rusty. But I'm tellin' you, and I expect you to take care of it.' "

"She called Rusty's *father*?"

"Yeah-she-did. And I'm layin' there in the hospital bed

wonderin' why Rusty's come in ever' day actin' like somebody poked a sharp stick up his butt. He don't know nothin' about the kids, he don't know nothin' about the election, he don't know nothin', period. Finally the day comes that I'm sposed to go home with him, and I ask him, 'Why are you actin' so funny?' He turns about the color of the bathroom door over yonder, and says, 'Your momma been talkin' to you?' I say, 'Not nothin' special, why?' He says, 'She saw me walkin' on the street with another woman. It wasn't nothin',' he says to me, big as life. 'It was just an old gal I knew in school, I met up with her walkin' on Murphy Street, and I told her not to bother you with it.' 'Well, she didn't,' I told him."

Drew pauses to let her eyes and nostrils flare. "And bein' more than half-stupid, I thought that was all there was to it. But the next day when he went off to work, the phone started ringin'. It would ring *all* day long, and if I answered it, some woman would say somethin' real sweet to me. You know what I mean? I mean real sweet. Or there wouldn't be nothin' but music. Or just nothin', period. And this went on all day long, ever' day, from the minute his car left the driveway till it pulled in again ever' evenin'."

I put out my cigarette with care. "That's pretty fair timing," I say.

Drew narrows her eyes to gray-green slits. "I'll say it was. Her timin' was so good because she had got herself a job in the JC Penney buildin' right directly in my front yard. Her timin' was so good because she could see the doorstep and ever' time he laid his foot on it, comin' or goin'. She probably could see right in our bedroom window, though she wouldn't have seen much."

"Did you tell Rusty what was going on?"

"No ma'am. I called the police to put a tracer on my telephone."

"You didn't say a word to Rusty?"

"The first way Rusty got into it was he found the telephone off the hook when he walked in one day. I wouldn't let him hang it up, because that's what the police told me I had to do for them to trace the call. And he figured that one out and he must have told her to quit."

"Lord! Didn't you ever deal with any of this out in the open?"

"Hey, Charley!" Drew calls out, lifting her head. When he looks up from his conversation with the pool players, she shows him two fingers. He brings over the two beers with a minimum of courting behaviors, and goes back to his friends.

"It got wide open before long," Drew resumes. "One Saturday afternoon he left the house without sayin' hello or good-bye or nothin'. To nobody. So I fixed my hair and put on lipstick and high heels and told Nadine, my oldest, to watch the rest of them. I got my girlfriend to pick me up, and we went on downtown to Murphy Street. There's a motel on Murphy Street, if you've ever noticed it."

I shrug.

"By then I knew the name of the 'red-headed ole gal' he knew in school, and I knew she drove a powder-blue Buick Electra with stripin'. I'd seen it go by my house often enough. And there it sat, right in the parking lot of that motel."

She gazes at me, her eyes bright. I don't have a single question. Drew is telling me about real life, as she always has, and I am as many eyes and ears as I have always been around her, trying to catch up. I try, but I can't superimpose Larry over Rusty's burly frame, can't pinpoint all Larry's business travel and late hours as neatly as the motel on Murphy Street. It is not merely the solution that eludes me, but the problem.

And further, I have the notion that people need to communicate. My training in psychology says that people need to talk to each other before they can adequately deal with what is going on. But more and more this notion seems to be some kind of fetish, a set of blinders made to order. Clearly "talking it over" is a useless item in Drew's pantheon: For her there is what is, and what you do about it. And this she is describing to me, rapping it out as she might rap out a business letter on her office typewriter.

"I let the air out of all four of her tires, and I went up to the door of the room and knocked on it. I had my girlfriend there as a witness. There was all kind of scufflin' and scratchin' inside the room, and when Rusty opened the door just a crack, we pushed it on open and went in and had us a look. It was sorry, I can tell you. Rusty was yellin' at her to cover up, and hittin' me across the face and pushin' us out of the room, all at one time. When he got us shoved outside, he slammed the door shut. I knew he would listen to see if we'd go on, so I got right next to the door and said real soft, 'Don't come home, sugar.' "

She picks up the lighter again and tips the cigarette pack toward me. I shake my head. She takes one for herself and lights it, eyeing me over the flame.

"He heard me, all right," she assures me. "But he waddn't goin' much of anywhere, anyway. My girlfriend dropped me off at home, and I called Miss Redhead's mother. She lives in Shady Grove, my momma even knows the family. I said, 'If you want to know where your daughter is, you can find her in the Murphy Street Motel with my husband.'

"She said to me, 'My daughter is no such thang, and I'll thank you not to call me up on my telephone to say such trash.' She was fit to be tied.

"I said, 'You don't have to believe me, you can go look for yourself. She's got four flat tires and she iddn't goin' to be leaving anytime soon.' "

"Drew, you called her *mother?*"

"Well, I didn't know the poor thang had a heart condition, truly I didn't." The laughter bubbles forth. Drew spreads her fingers over her grin. "Somebody said they had to put her back in the hospital the very next day."

I move my jaw from where it has fallen open to say, "When you go into action, you don't leave much the way you found it."

"Unh-unh, honey. Iddn't that the point?"

I work on my beer halfheartedly, while she blows a series of smoke rings.

"Well," I ask, "what about this reconciliation?"

"It's hardly worth tellin'. He begged me and begged me, and

I finally said *all right.* But he couldn't stay away from his redhead. We got a divorce and he married her about three months ago, that's how much sense he's got."

"Was that hard to take?"

She flicks ash into the ashtray.

"Accordin' to the divorce settlement, Rusty gets all five kids every weekend of this wide world. Plus they have the two of hers that she has from her first marriage. If they want to sit around with seven kids in a three-bedroom house while I go out havin' a high old time, it's all right with me."

"Can you have a high old time in a town the size of Bayley?"

"Not hardly. But Hattiesburg is more like it. I'm not goin' to try and tell you that the men are worth much, but when have they ever been? Some have more money than brains, and that's about all you can hope for. There's some that travel. I get to Atlanta and New Orleans when I'm in the mood.

"Hey," she says suddenly. "Hey, do you want to know something? I can tell you that about half the men in Mississippi have hemorrhoids."

"What? What are you . . . ?"

Drew holds up a finger and thumb to make a circle. She closes one eye and looks at me through the circle.

"That's the truth. The rest of them are perfect assholes."

We laugh, hard. I must have heard that one before; no doubt Drew has told it before. But we both laugh till it hurts.

"Hey," Drew says again, straightening up. "Hey. What I've been wonderin' is, you were the one that was runnin' around Detroit and Chicago and Hawaii and God knows where-all, while I was here poppin' babies like some kind of six-shooter. Iddn't that right?"

"Right. And right and right."

"So how come, if you get to play, you can't figure out some better place to do it than goddam-ole-redneck-ole Mississippi?"

"Doesn't make much sense, does it?"

"I'm glad to hear you say so. I was beginnin' to doubt my own senses. I know what work is. Work is doin' what you're doin': Work is bein' sweet as pie to relatives that are trying to get close enough to pick your bones. It's real hard to believe you come here, where there ain't nothing *but* relatives, to *play*."

She cocks a grave eye at me, and waits for me to say something. I am at a familiar place with Drew; I have been here before. Drew has always been full of razzle-dazzle and what my father used to call spunk. She has always been the only one in the family worth telling anything to, and the most dangerous one to know it.

"I don't fit in too well down here anymore, do I, Drew?"

"Nowwwwwww, Jeannine." She stubs her cigarette out in the ashtray.

"Well, I don't fit in too well up yonder, either. Oh, I look all right. God knows I sound all right, after all these years."

Drew's cigarette still hides an orange glow. I hate the smell of a smoldering cigarette, and I pick the wrinkled thing up by the filter and carefully extinguish it. I look up to find Drew's brown-flecked gray eyes still watching me.

"You know how it is," I say. "I know things they don't know up there. I got crawfish and sweet potatoes in my blood. Cold winters are hard on crawfish and sweet potatoes. Sometimes I have to come back down here till my blood gets to feeling southern again."

Drew glances at her watch, and together we drain our glasses. She plunks down money on the table, waving me off as I reach for mine. She tosses a hand at Charley as we head for the red exit sign.

"I tell you one thing," she says to me as we open the door and squint into the orange-sherbet sunset in the global Dixie Cup. "What you got in your blood is nothin' but pure southern bullshit."

In the car she reaches up and slips the last piece of Juicy Fruit from a battered packet on the dash. She twists it in two and offers me half.

"Here, Cousin," she says. "Here's the very thing we need for good ole southern bullshit breath."

She pulls the jangle of keys from her purse and starts the car.

"Hey," I say. "We never got to Deborah June."

"Hey," she mimics. "We never even got to you."

"My life is duller than you seem to think."

Drew throws an arm over the seat, and backs the car up. She glances over at me as we start forward.

"I don't know about your life, Jeannine, but I've seen more spark than you got in a bowl of mashed potatoes."

"Okay, then, let's stick to Deborah June."

She turns to give me a look, but I keep my eyes ahead on the road, on the shadows that are beginning to dominate.

"Well, Deborah June iddn't too high on spark her own self. She mopes around the house, can't stand to see anybody, is scared to death somethin' is goin' to happen to those three babies . . ."

"*Three* kids?"

"You didn't know she had another one? Well, it must have surprised her some, too. Her husband plays in a band four nights a week. He seems to come home long enough in between to change his socks. I guess he's as likely as not to slap her around some if she takes to complainin'. She duddn't do much of that." The gray eyes roll. "But nobody knows anythin' for sure, since she hadn't said more than six words the past year and a half. Verlie talked her into goin' back to nurses' trainin'; I guess that place looks different to her now than when she was a flag-twirler and whatyoumaycallit-her Husband was General Big Deal."

"Does he run around, or what?"

"Or what is right. Nobody has caught him. If somebody did catch him, I feel pretty sure her daddy, your uncle Wendell and mine, would make fairly certain there was one less stud in the county."

"Does she ever talk about divorcing him?"

"Deborah June? Why, honey, she loves him. That's her problem. She *loves him*." Drew caresses the words with her lips and tongue. "Iddn't that what does every one of us in?"

"I imagine it is."

"Besides, don't go talkin' divorce in this family. Lord knows we're all Baptists. We're all so Baptist that don't nobody know Deborah June has any kind of problem. We talk about how *careful* she is about those kids—so careful she threw all the kitchen knives in the trash—and how *shy* she's got over the last year. At least, that's how we talk around Aunt Verlie. You got it straight?"

"Got it."

We bump our way over the rutted gravel road in silence. When we reach the cabin, several of the cars have gone, and Drew pulls into a spot close to the beach. The shade has increased until there is nothing else for the lake and the whole landscape around us. Most of the folding chairs have been taken in, and everyone who is still here is gathered inside the cabin under the ceiling fan. Everyone, that is, except three figures at the water's edge. Drew points them out so that I will notice.

"That's your momma lettin' my two kids get their last licks at the water."

The little group is pulling the last of the inner tubes out of the lake and dragging them up on the beach. Momma waves and starts walking toward us.

"Your momma is the only one in this whole bunch worth more than a nickel. You know that, don't you?"

I do not reply. Momma has reached Drew's door and opens it, grinning like a conspirator. Drew climbs out, and my mother wraps her up in a tight hug. "Now what have you girls been up to?" she says, looking across Drew to me.

"Now, Aunt Melvinia. You know us gals ain't got a thang to do but get older and sourer. And that's just what we been doin'," Drew explains.

6

We are returning home on Blue Rise Road in the relative cool of the evening. The car windows are rolled down, and the sounds and smells of rural Mississippi breathe gently in on us. The crickets, the frogs, even—and this seems a touch theatrical, the South believing in itself again—one lone whippoorwill. Dark shapes slip past the windows, and the changing fragrances carried on the air make the only notations: cool scent of roadside pine, hot tarry smell of baked open roadway, penetrating dank fingers of swamp odor. Evenings here are always the best, so calming after the jangling brilliance of sunlight, the heavy weight of humidity. Even the rain in this part of the country seems too intense by day, ringing down a stubborn gray liquid curtain for days on end, chilly, gusty and thorough. Rain, too, is better in the evenings.

But there is no rain tonight, no clouds, in fact, to blot out the showering of starlight. The moon has not risen from its sluggish daybed, and the only competition offered the stars in this clean night air is from lightning bugs over the ditchwater. They are leisurely about sharing their miracle, never overdoing the effect—one here, then another off in the distance, a fluid interval and then three airborne grace notes of yellow fire.

Momma and I trust each other with this beauty and this quiet. We do not speak until Blue Rise Road delivers us to the driveway that curves in front of the house, this house my father built for us nearly thirty years ago, timbers torn from his father's land, sawed into planks and two-by-fours on his uncle's sawmill, nailed into place one by one on this peak of the Rise.

I remember some of it, Cal and I sitting in the old pecan

tree in the yard and watching the house materialize. In the blue distance we would see Uncle Vinnie watching from his porch or from his bedroom window. We all watched, and my father laid hardwood floors over what seemed an acre of foundation. He notched the timbers for the joists and precut the angles that were to form the roof line—foolhardy stuff, Uncle Vinnie said. But it worked and then both he and my father shared a sheepish joy. For them, as brothers, neither victory nor defeat was worth the shame of having disagreed.

The house stands now as it did then, the wires, the outlets, the pipes, the sheetrock, the insulation, the fixtures, the vents, the doors and windows and sills set in their places by my father's hands. Or his uncle's hands, or his first cousin's, or his brother's. Someone of the blood.

Our house. I turn off the key in the ignition, and let out a ragged sigh.

Momma speaks. "Would you like a cup of tea this evening?"

Some weariness is trying to overtake me here, in this spot. I don't want to go into the house. I say yes.

In the kitchen Mother puts the tea on. I sit in the living room and listen to her moving about, cupboards slamming, water straining toward the boiling point. I am too listless to go in there, though I know she will start on the clutter of the counters and sinks after I go to bed. I know, too, that she will presently stand on a chair and reach back into the top cupboard for the dainty blue and white china cups and saucers that I love. I sit on the sofa in the living room and wait for all these things to take place.

"Here you are." She brings in two cups of tea seated on their fluted saucers. She sets mine on the lamp table beside me, and sits down with me on the sofa. She nudges off her shoes and swings her legs up on the satin cushions to rest them. In the dim greenish light of the china lamp everything takes on a double character of being soothing and also slightly eerie.

I sip the tea and say, "MMmmmm." It is camomile with brown sugar, which is her favorite. She believes it to be my favorite, too, although I stopped taking sugar with my tea years ago. Some things are good because they take their flavor from the past. Set and setting.

"This has been a long day," Momma sighs.

I nod my head, carte blanche agreement.

Presently I say, "Drew seems to have had a rough time of it."

"Drew," Momma repeats. "Drew didn't have a chance in the world of not having a hard time. This divorce thing of hers just makes my heart ache."

"Why?"

"Because it's been so hard on her. And on those children. She is such a fighter. That Rusty ought to be skinned."

"She told me about Deborah June, too."

My mother looks into the shadows across the room, shapes the lamplight fails to define.

"It just makes me sick. What's wrong with people? How can they behave like that with the ones that love them, that need them to be the best they can be? That poor little Deborah has done everything anybody could do—and she is such a sweet little thing, used to be such a pretty little thing—and he does her like he does. I just don't know."

"At least she's back in school."

"Tell me what good it does, her being back in school? Is she going to go out and earn a living? She's got three children, Jeannine. Those two fine girls, and she gave him a son, too. But nothing touches him. What is she going to get out of training to be a nurse when she's got three little children, and one a baby, sitting at home? It's not right. There's another man that ought to be skinned. I'd skin him myself, if I was Verlie."

I cannot believe the way it's falling into place. Cannot believe that my mother's sympathies are so warm and so accessible. I thought it would be much harder than this.

"Momma, listen to me. I want to tell you this now, and not wait till I get on the plane a week from Friday. It's possible that Larry and I will separate."

The round eyes freeze in shock. Frozen fried eggs, fresh frozen mud pies. The voice finds itself half an octave from the point
of impact.

"*Jeannine!* Jeannine, what are you saying? What can you be
thinking of? I don't know what to say or what to do, you knock
the breath right out of me! Honey! Tell me I didn't hear you
right!"

"I'm not going to be able to explain it so that you'll understand it any better, Momma. It's just the way things are."

"Well, tell me what's wrong! What has happened? Has he
got somebody else? What is it?"

She is so stricken, so completely thrown, that somehow I
have the urge to laugh. "Somebody else." Is life so simple? It is
not sorrow or compassion that bubble at the glottal stops of my
windpipe, but the desire, the compulsion, to *laugh.* I am so preoccupied with this bizarre impulse that I am taken still further from
the event at hand. What are these words, this mask of fright that
is my mother's face?

When her mouth stops moving, I take it as a cue. I have
some words ready. "We're not happy together, Momma. There
doesn't seem to be a who or a why involved in it. It's just the
way it is. We have no life together. There doesn't seem to be a
point."

Whatever she says next is contorted at the mouth. Tears
spring up and run down her cheeks. I can almost hear through
the droning sound that fills my head, can almost hear what she is
saying, can isolate the word "children." She is talking about the
children. The children.

"I have one child, Mother. One."

There is another torrent about children, about Laura. As the
odd hysteria of deafness clears, I begin to understand what is
being said, what I am supposed to say back. I begin by shaking
my head.

"One child is all we wanted. We are happy to have a daughter. And she is fine, Mother. She is with Larry's folks having a
wonderful time. When she gets here, you can inspect her for

79

yourself. She is not broken in as many pieces as you may care to think."

"How can you think of taking that little girl away from her father?"

"I don't think for a moment of taking that little girl away from her father. Her father sees her, when he is in town, about five minutes a day. He says good night to her when he comes home from the office, if he gets there while she's still awake. He works on weekends—either in the office or on the golf course with clients. We do quite regularly have Sunday mornings together."

"That man is out working to provide for his family! What do you think life is about?"

My voice cracks somewhere inside my throat. "I think life ought to be about love."

"And don't you recognize love when you see it?"

"No! I don't! I wouldn't know it if it jumped out behind me in the alley! Tell me: What does it feel like to be loved? Does it feel good? Does it grab you by the throat, or does it just feel like the life is draining out of you and you have to keep on anyway?"

"*I said*, don't you recognize love when you see it?"

I give up, let my shoulders go.

"I recognize compulsive behavior when I see it."

"And you think your husband is out killing himself for fun?"

"Killing is a lot closer to what I do see."

"What are you talking about?"

"I think you're right! I think he is out killing himself! I think he's killing me, too. We're not happy, we're not in love, we are just about paralyzed. I know I am."

"Paralyzed? What is wrong with you? That man sacrifices for you and your children, and you—"

"Don't talk to me about sacrifice, Mother. It's no sacrifice for Larry to work. Or to travel, either. It's come to the point that we're both happier when he's gone, anyway. What Larry is *willing* to sacrifice are my feelings. He's got everything else he wants. He can have it all, but he can't have me, too. Not anymore, not on his terms anymore."

"What in heaven's name do you *want* from the man?"

"I want a father for Laura *while she's awake.* I want all the things he promised. I want love I can *feel.* I'm tired of being *grateful* for love."

She sits still, lets the quiet house speak around us. Then she asks it softly: "How can anybody not be grateful for the love of a good man?"

I know where we are going with this, but I cannot stop, cannot say it another way. "I *will not* take love like medicine! I *will not* take it because it's *good for me!*" The sound of my voice, a thin screech like a night animal's, dies away in this empty house.

"Jeannine, you sound like a child! You're supposed to *grow up,* you're not supposed to cry for the moon after you *grow up.*"

"Is that it? Is it the moon I'm crying for? God, Mother, I'd settle for Larry Lewis, by his clock and timetable, if the little time he's home, he was really there. For us. For me. Not for his evening inspection, not for his dinner or his newspaper or the ten o'clock report—Christ, he says he has to unwind. How sick I am of that word. Daddy used to say that, remember? They come home *to unwind.*"

"You happen to be the wife of an executive."

"Yes, I am! But it isn't what I asked for, it isn't anything I want! I'm supposed to think it's a terrific deal, but it's not *for me,* it has nothing to do with me. I am the wife of a company man. What's left over at the end of the day is mine to maintain till death do us part. Parts and service. It's not enough to keep me alive, Mother! Not enough."

"I asked you before, is there someone else? Another woman?"

"I tell you, sometimes I wish that was it. If that's all it was, I would understand what is happening to us."

And now it is her voice risen in despair. "This doesn't make any *sense* to me, Jeannine! Have you talked about it? Have you gotten some guidance?"

"We have talked and talked and talked and talked about it. We have cried and cried and cried. We care about each other—

somewhere in there, we do. Or we did, anyway. We have seen a counselor. We have done everything. It doesn't get better. I am tired. I am so tired of it all. I am exhausted. And I have run out of ideas of what else to do but quit."

The tears begin rolling down my face. Stale tears, used tears with no life of their own. I don't know where they come from, some fetid reservoir I no longer know about.

They are unconvincing, even to me.

My mother reaches out and snatches me to her. She holds me in strong arms, arms that have chopped cotton, dismembered trees, scattered corn for chickens, cradled infants, shaken the daylights out of half-grown upstart teenagers. She holds me and rocks me, and sobs more fervently than I do. My own grief, whatever its nature, is arrested by hers. I am ashamed. I strain out of her grip to reach for Kleenexes. The box rests just far enough beyond me, behind the lamp on the table. I use the tissues to stay free of her. I busy myself, wiping eyes and nose. She wipes hers hastily and pitifully with her large hands.

"I can't believe this is really happening, Jeannine," she says. Her voice is thin, unsteady. The eyes look nearly black now, large, round, but without light.

"Momma, it's been going on for a long time. Years."

"I knew when you brought Laura to me at the airport last Christmas that things weren't right. He looked so unhappy." Her voice creaks open and more tears trickle through the oak hinges. "But I never thought . . ."

"Momma, I just have to go to bed. I am so weary I can't stay awake."

She nods her head, her hands again busy at her eye sockets. I rise to go past her and her arms fly out and seize my waist. I half-turn to face her, and she squeezes me tightly to her, her face pressing into my abdomen. I release a rattly sigh, and settle my hands on her head, on her shoulders. I stroke her gray hair. And when I can do that no longer, I break free and walk down the hall to my room and close the door.

* * *

The night is still quiet, of course, and I lie on the bed with the sheet covering me, listening for the cars that hiss by on Blue Rise Road. They do not come often. They do not make the same sounds. Lights streak the darkness, and they are gone. Vibrations play in their wakes, spreading, spreading, thinning through the night air until only cricket sounds are left again.

I am lying to my mother, of course. Just how it is that I am lying I am not quite sure. Everything I have said is true, more than true, but it is also clear that something is unnatural. I am causing her pain, and I am heavy with guilt and shame. I am also playing to her notions of tragedy, because this sadness I showed her tonight—I must have been faking it. There is no way it could have been mine, my own sadness, because it cost me so much to display it. It was not there ready and aching to be known. I had to find it, maybe I had to manufacture it.

But, dear God, it *is* sad! It is so sad! And shit, here we go. A saltwater bath for wallowing, salt in the wound, my own low-pressure waterworks getting into the act again. My college roommate once remarked that I seemed to cry only from helplessness. Is there another way to cry? When there is nothing left to do, you cry.

But I no longer feel helpless. Principally, these days, I am angry. And I am not helpless, I am doing something about it. I am going to fucking leave this particular good man. Maybe after I do it, I can afford to be sad. Just now it's a luxury I can't support. Not even for my mother's sake.

Although Lord knows I went all out tonight. All those tears. Demonstration tears. Bedtime stories, I guess: Look, Mother, at how helpless I am.

And that is where the lie is. I have been helpless, and hid it. Not fair to collect on the sympathy retroactively. No, the order of the day is decision. And she doesn't want to hear that, has no background to prepare her for it. Well, hell, even I don't want to hear it. Here we go with the Big Nouns again, the ones I count when I can't sleep. First we had Love and then there was Marriage, and then there was Children. TROMP, TROMP, TROMP across the little troll's bridge, every one of them looking like Big Billygoat Gruff. No small ones, no middle-sized ones. Only Big Nouns on the bridge, 350 stress points and greater. And now here come Estrangement and Separation, followed hard on by Divorce. TROMP, TROMP, *TROMP*. Divorce is the really heavy one, the one that's carrying triplets—Separate Maintenance, Child Custody, Failure. *TROMP, TROMP, TROMP!*

7

The church service at Gethsemane begins at eleven, as it always has. And we are scurrying around the house at ten minutes to eleven as we always have, Mother at the ironing board with a dress or in the bathroom with clear nail polish, brush poised over a run that has traveled like albino ants, up one beige-tone ankle. Bobby pins are yet to be yanked from damp hair, the pot roast yet to be turned to low.

I had assumed that all these things would change with my father's death, and with all us children grown and gone away. I thought that we used to be in the house scurrying at ten minutes to eleven because my mother on Sunday mornings had risen early, washed and rolled her hair, made eggs and biscuits and sausages for breakfast, served them, started the pot roast, tied my sash and criticized the droop of my anklets and my hair, inspected my brothers' shoes, put the Jell-O salad with canned pineapple in the refrigerator and set roll dough out to rise. All this while my father sat in his clean shave in his clean white ironed shirt reading the newspaper in the living room, until he went and sat in the car, until he began honking the horn.

But here we are, twenty-five years later, doing the same things on the same timetable. What began so long ago as something compounded of cause and effect now has its own vitality.

I had assumed that so many things would change with my father's death. I had assumed that my mother would sell the farm, join the Peace Corps and send me shocked and aggrieved letters from Ecuador. I had assumed that, at the very least, orderliness would descend like an altar cloth over the end tables piled with old magazines, old letters, old advertising circulars, old telephone directories, old peach pits. I had assumed that, as a point of honor, she would arrive at church precisely on time for the rest of her days.

But things are not so simple as that. And I see that when neither Cal nor Curtis nor I am here to cook Sunday pot roast for, and when there is no one to forget to take the Jell-O salad out of the refrigerator for, Momma still sprints in various stages of disarray from kitchen to bathroom to bedroom at ten minutes to eleven.

We are late for church before we arrive. As we mince across the dusty gravel of the parking lot in our high heels, we hear the singing. In Momma's sigh I hear not only defeat but accusation.

"We'll have to go in behind the ushers," she whispers.

Six men are lined up with their offering baskets just inside the double doors. My uncle Spanner is among them, Groves baby fat rolling up to his cleft chin as he grins at us. He throws me a flirtatious wink. The group is awaiting their signal. They stand tensely alert, with the entry doors cracked open just a little. They fold their baskets solemnly into their chests, like a militia of beggars.

Their signal comes; it is the whine of the organ as it begins the offertory hymn. "Just as I am, without one plea," sings the congregation as the doors behind them fly open. The ushers in their fresh suits and Sunday shoes spontaneously adjust their chests and bellies and chins for the brisk march down the double aisles. When they reach the dais in front, they fan out for an orderly full-field press. "O Lamb of God, I come, I come," sings the congregation, waiting for the baskets with folded bills and change newly settled in their palms.

After a decent interval Momma and I sneak forward into the sanctuary. There is a space for us in the central row of pews about four benches down. Once there, we push past old Mrs. Flowers, who leans into the corner support of the bench with her frail crooked back. We exchange quick smiles and breathy whispers: "Good to see you!" Mrs. Flowers puts her hands forward to grasp my mother's hands. They give each other a reassuring squeeze.

Once into our seats Momma and I rummage quickly in our purses for money. She is ready in time, but I am not. The basket passes. I reach for the green hymnal. Mrs. Flowers tips hers down to show me the number. We beam at one another. I find the page and offer the book to Momma. Her hands remain at her sides resting on the seat. I move the book farther toward her as she looks out over the congregation, and nudge her with my arm. She does not take notice. And she does not sing.

I finish out the hymn with the rest of the congregation. I do not have to wonder much at her behavior. Children know when they are being punished.

"And consecrate my life to thee, O Lamb of God, I come, I come."

I close the book and replace it on the rack. The choir stands for another number, and the rest of us sit back. Momma continues in her rigid posture, which looks more natural now that we are all listeners.

The choir begins. The hymn is not a familiar one, and the voices sound uncertain. But even the congregation's singing sounds anemic to me today. I am listening, I suppose, for the old Gethsemane Baptist Church, the one I grew up in, the original white frame building with its rolling, jouncing piano. That instrument was played by Miss Etta or Glenda Sue or Corrine, depending upon the song or the song leader. The rafters rang with music; there really were rafters and they really rang. The congregation must have funneled their ample sincerity right through the vocal cords and filled the place with their voices.

Maybe they are doing that this morning, but either the sincerity is less ample, or the bricks of this new building don't amplify sound the way the wood did. Perhaps the halfhearted organ now sets the tone that the voices follow. Or perhaps I am just older.

It is at least true that things are organized differently now. People who used to sit fanning themselves with stick-handled fans from Holifield's Funeral Parlor now sit still under air conditioning. There is a glassed-in nursery in the back. And the choir itself: That is new. And the Choir Director. And the Church Organist. And the Church Program, from which I read these things.

The Church Choir persists in singing all three verses of the hymn. I begin to look at the faces for signs of strain, and note with a start that one of them is Carrie Dean's.

I break into a huge grin and nearly laugh aloud at the sight of her. She is not looking at me, of course; she has her eyes firmly set upon the Choir Director. I watch her form words that are lost in the choral effort. I fix on her utterly serious expression.

She is so familiar to me, but the setting, this particular here and now, is off. What I am really seeing is a girl with freckles, a small girl four or five years old. I see her reddish-brown hair escaping the clutches of whatever barrettes her mother has fastened next to her white scalp. I see her full skirts, dotted swiss, aqua blue; she is a kind of pale cloud perspiring on the bench beside me, her pink hands visible underneath her half of the Broadman Hymnal we share. It is Gethsemane Baptist Church, all right, the hot holy place of our childhood. It is the ungainly white frame church the deacons tore down in favor of this red brick one they built across the road.

In this new church they put in greenish-streaked windows something like the fancy ones in town at First Baptist. The windows in the building that Carrie Dean and I knew had clear ordinary panes, and God's house seemed to be built much like anybody else's. But the people at Gethsemane felt that they needed to go and prepare a better place. They had been told, after all, that their God was a jealous God. That was something people could understand—the Old Testament God was always much more comprehensible.

They served Him with a passion, because He demanded it from every Southern Baptist Church within hearing. Passion for God was the only passion not forbidden Baptists. All other rages, cruelties and devotions were things to be ashamed of. "I'd be ashamed!" was a refrain in our lives. It was used to stop a child, or a grown person for that matter, from the pursuit of unsanctioned passions. The phrase would be repeated until the behavior ceased. "I'd be ashamed. I'd be—A-SHAMED!" It would be re-peated with increasing violence, until wisdom came to the wrongdoer. If wisdom were entirely too slow in coming, hands otherwise consecrated to prayer found their way to a switch, a paddle, or direct to bare guilty flesh.

Momma, of course, had her own ways with wisdom. Out in the yard she might snatch the standard limber switch from an ole-ander or peach tree. But in the house we didn't have the institu-tion of the paddle or hairbrush—or belt, unless my father was about. Momma's domain was the kitchen, and when somebody needed a spanking—and that was always how it was put—she would seize from the counter or drainboard her black-handled butcher knife.

This was never a warning. She did not brandish it or excite inappropriate terror. She merely seized the thing and in a flash laid the strokes on, along the backs of knees and thighs, no matter how they danced. She used the flat of the blade.

I don't know that the spankings produced anything in me but anger and outrage. I used to pray, albeit tensely, that she would cut me with that knife just once. But it never happened.

In the old church, when babies cried or toddlers climbed too boldly or complained aloud about being pinched, their fathers or their mothers carried them down the aisle and out one of the two back doors. Sunlight flashed in as the doors opened and closed. To me such an escape seemed dreamlike in its simplicity. But here again my mother took a different approach. With Carrie Dean sitting next to me, and the two of us squirming past any ex-cuse, she would sit calmly with one of my hands trapped in hers. She would firmly press each of my fingers, knuckles, fingertips and joints; she would stroke my palm and the back of my hand. I found this treatment so deliriously soothing that its character of restraint was lost upon me. I would sit raptly staring into Brother Shepherd's jowls quivering over the pulpit. As though he were the one saving me.

Brother Shepherd had a way of parsing out a Bible verse much as if he were spelling a difficult word to children.

" 'For God'—our Father in heaven, the Creator of all that is, was, or ever shall be—'For God so loved'—*love*, now, beloved, I'm talking about pure, sweet, holy, life-giving love. 'For God so loved the world'—the *world!* Think about it! Let your hearts open to it! For God so loved this earth, this creation; for God so loved you, Brother Ollie, and you, Sister Ora, and you, Brother Max, and you, Sister Mary Louise, and me, sinner that I am; for that child in your arms, Sister Lucinda, for every man in this house of God, every woman, every child, and let me tell you more, for every heathen in the dark of Africa—'For God so loved *the world!'*

"... And He loves every one of us, every soul among us, with a tender love, a father's love for his children—'*For God so loved the world that he gave His only begotten Son.'* He loves you! Do you believe it? And He's waiting for you now. Come to Him; He calls you. Can you hear Him? Can you hear Him? Come to Him now while we sing ..."

I saw tears in the old church as a child. I saw men cry, not only women. And at the pulpit I saw the only man I knew to shout in public. Sunday after Sunday, Brother Shepherd would rage at his church, go brilliant red from the shirt collar gripping his throat, and rasp out warnings and pleas-and verses and truths in his cigarette-tarnished voice. The congregation was small; Brother Shepherd also had a job at the lumber mill four nights a week to provide for his family. But there was no question that he had the call for doing the work of the Lord in the daylight hours.

In this particular here and now, the one now playing, the new preacher stands nodding and smiling before the congregation in his featherweight suit jacket, forearms resting eagerly on a lighted lectern.

"Wasn't that an inspiration?" he demands of us.

The choir files down from the small loft beside a curtained baptistry. The women are careful of their high heels on the steps. They hold their flowered skirts and dresses down so they can see their feet as they descend.

"I mean to tell you, that choir of ours here at Gethsemane

Baptist Church, they can uplift your heart, can't they? 'Make a joyful noise before the Lord,' it tells us in Psalms. They can really make you feel like a Junebug in cotton, can't they?"

The congregation murmurs its appreciation of the choir's efforts, and of Brother Percy's deliberate country phrasing.

When it is her turn to step down, Carrie Dean sets modesty aside long enough to flash me a thousand-watt welcome.

Then she crosses the floor to sit with Garth and the children. Victoria's small head bobs into view as she moves to make room for her mother.

"I want y'all to pray for me this morning as I bring you the message," the pastor intones. "I'm going to be bringing you this message as the Lord reveals it to me. And you may not agree with what I have to say, but this is the subject I have been wrestling with in my daily prayers, and it is the subject on my heart this Lord's Day, and—" he brings his hand down sharply on the edge of the lectern, and pumps his head up and down to give himself impetus the prayers may overlook—"I'm really going to shell the corn this morning," he finishes.

"Amen!" The congregation murmurs approval, anticipation. They stir in their seats.

The new preacher—he has been there three years but Momma still calls him the new preacher—is boyish and stocky. He has short-cropped hair. He looks like someone who did everything to play football in high school except grow tall enough. Today he stands elevated in his pulpit, his color high. He has already slapped the object nearest to hand, and now he casts a severe and distrustful eye over those of us in the stands.

Despite his ruddy face and energetic intent, I find this man queerly joyless. But I don't know what it is that I expect. The last time I saw Brother Percy—and the first time—he was presiding over my father's funeral in the same spot he now stands, except that below him was the studied gray of the coffin. He really was new then, and as a consequence he couldn't have known anything about my father. He used the occasion to drill the mourners on the brevity of life and the advisability of salvation. It is possible that he spoke movingly, for I certainly cried. On the other hand, it is possible that I would have cried if he had stood up and delivered two paragraphs from the coach's playbook. But on that day I thought the odds were with me, what with the closed casket (for tractor accidents are rarely inspiring to look upon), my life-long dislike of my father, and Laura at my side busily looking for a pencil and something to write on.

She was three, and when I had found supplies for her in my purse, she sat and drew crude lozenges to which she attached hundreds of pencil-stroke legs. She worked with intense method. The result looked like microbes enlarged to show their ragged cilia.

Presently she looked up from her labors to ask, "Why is my grandpa in that box?"

I put my finger to my lips and bent to whisper in her ear.

"He died, Laura. He's not alive anymore, and we're going to bury him in that box. It's called a casket."

Silence. More drawing, more ciliated microbes. Then: "How can he go to the bathroom in there?"

My finger to my lips again; I should have prepared her better. But how? When?

"He doesn't have to go to the bathroom anymore."

"Why? Is his penis ruined?"

It was too much for me and I shook with laughter and then shook still more as the tears sprouted and ran and my child beside me threatened, "If you cry, then I'm going to cry, too."

"A woman who understands her mission understands that she is a Queen in her household," Percy is saying. "A *Queen*. She is to be *worshiped as a Queen*. She is entrusted with the care of her children. And Young People—" Percy taps the lectern twice with a rigid forefinger. He directs his gaze to the rear quarter of the church where the adolescents have segregated themselves— "I challenge you now to recognize that you owe her your respect and your obedience."

"Amen!" "Praise God." The murmuring comes from the forward sections of the church.

"In my house my wife is worshiped as a Queen. She gives

herself unselfishly to the task before her, and she is worshiped for that. She is honored for that. She is a teacher by her example to our daughters, and our son is made to understand his duties toward her.

"He may have to be reminded, sometimes," Percy throws in, and is rewarded with gentle laughter.

Then he turns on them, shouting as though they have missed the point. *"He is made to understand what is expected of him!"*

When every lamb in his flock has gone still under the lash of his voice, Percy resumes softly, "Now my son is thirteen years old, and he will come and tell me, 'Daddy, I didn't do what you told me to do. I was ugly to my mother. But I love you, and I want you to forgive me.'

" . . . Now, you just can't rare back and smite a child that's asked for forgiveness," he says, rearing back and raising a flushed hand.

The demonstration looks so well practiced that it sends a sickly feeling into the floor of my stomach. My God, this is where they learn it. They learn to beat children in church.

"That boy may be thinking, 'My daddy's gonta whip me all over the countryside!' And I might have. *Except as ye repent, ye shall lose the kingdom!* The wayward child must repent and seek forgiveness of the father.

"My wife is a Queen, and every Christian household needs a Queen that is worshiped and revered. But now listen to me. I want you to look at me. I want every pair of eyes in this congregation on me, because I may not be perfect and I may not even be your pastor long, but while I'm with you—I'm going to love you. I'm going to love you, and I'm going to deliver the gospel and the truth of the gospel the best way I know how, as the Lord helps me to do it."

Brother Percy is leaning forward over the lectern. He speaks in a most reasonable tone.

"Every household has a Queen, but every household also has a King."

"Amen!" "Glory!" "Praise to God."

I hear the rest wash over me. The primacy of kingship, the duties, reverences, fealties, meted out in a hierarchy of virtue. The murmuring periodically resounds. Eddies of conviction set the gray heads nodding throughout the church.

I glance at my mother. She holds her eyes fixedly upon the boy-man in the pulpit, her chin lifted.

Scripture is quoted, chapter and verse. Bibles in a hundred hands riffle to confirm.

I scan the heads before me and find the auburn curls: yes. Carrie Dean, and on one side Garth, and on the other Garth, Jr. Victoria is too small to be seen, though she is there. And listening. But not the baby. Babies are now kept in the church nursery. I turn to glance at the silvery window behind us. Babies under glass, children neither heard nor seen.

"Number One hundred and ten."

It is the rich tenor of the Choir Director. He announces the number and gives no quarter, starting the singing with a drop of his head and the uplifted left hand. His voice, one of those that used to be the familiar of the rafters in the old church, rides up and over the entire congregation.

> *"Are you weary, are you heavy-hearted?*
> *Tell it to Jesus, tell it to Jesus.*
> *Are you grieving over joys departed?*
> *Tell it to Jesus alone.*
> *Tell it to Jesus, tell it to Jesus.*
> *He is a friend that's well known.*
> *You have no other such a friend or brother,*
> *Tell it to Jesus alone."*

The Choir Director looks to the pastor for a sign. Is a second verse required? But Brother Percy is making his last call.

" 'You have no other such a friend or brother.' In this life there are so many false friends, so many people telling you what's right. But you already know what's right, brothers and sisters. You have God's Word on it.

"Now I'm going to ask Brother Randall Holifield to lead us

in the final prayer, but before we do that, is there anybody we should remember?"

A woman produces a thin mumble from somewhere near the front. The preacher cranes his short neck attentively, and announces at last, "Miz Bynum wants us to remember her sister who's in the hospital after a car wreck."

Another voice projects from the rear. " 'Preciate y'allses prayers while we have the care of my mother."

"Thank you, Brother Clarence," the preacher says.

"Pray for my daughter," says old Mrs. Flowers beside me, and my heart pounds cold. Brother Percy says merely, "Miz Flowers' daughter."

Finally, at the preacher's nod, Brother Randall begins to drone away at his prayer while Percy himself escapes down the aisle to intercept the congregation at the double doors. When thought fails Brother Randall, he fills with "Dear God." In this way the prayer proceeds:

"Dear God, bless us Dear God, help us ever' day, Dear God, and Dear God help us to know thy will Dear God and be humble before thee Dear God, and Dear God forgive us and bless us in thy sight Dear God . . . Dear God, Amen."

His labors suffice, and Percy stands in position to receive all, even my mother, who this Sunday has remained for the entire service. I fear it is on my behalf, and take care to slip past them as he earnestly shakes her hand. I can almost feel the brush of her hand reaching out for me. The skin of my back crawls with sensation as I step free.

The congregation streams out of the doors and into the brilliant sunlight. The gray-white sidewalks and the slag of the parking lot are themselves dazzling at first.

"Why, come here to me, you old grown-up thang!" The voice belongs to Miss Dougherty, Carrie Dean's aunt. The arms she slips around me are as dry to the touch as ever, smelling of the same dry powder. Drawing back to arm's length again, she squints at me with pleasure.

"Carrie told me I wouldn't hardly reckonize you."

"Now is that Jeannine?" Mrs. Walters says, and steps up to pat an arm. "We're just so glad to see you, honey."

She steps aside, and Mrs. Hawthorne takes her place, crooking an arm around my waist and squeezing. She addresses Aunt Lottie, who stands to one side smiling and looking on. "You know, I saw somebody come in with Melvinia, and I said, 'Who in the world is that?' It just wouldn't come to me, Jeannine, that's how you get when you get old!"

She gives me another squeeze and departs, saying, "You come by the house, now, when you get a minute."

Cars are already drawing slowly out of the parking lot. They are trying to be considerate of the people standing on the sidewalks in their Sunday clothes, trying not to raise the clouds of whitish dust. One car pulls alongside the main sidewalk and stops, a black car with a chartreuse top. Carrie Dean's car. Carrie Dean herself gets out of the backseat, leaving the door open and three small sets of eyes staring after her. Garth and Mrs. Wentworth are in the front seat, Garth in dark glasses. I wave to them as Carrie Dean comes dashing breathlessly up. Garth lifts a hand in greeting; Mrs. Wentworth gives me a pinched sweet smile.

"Hey there," Carrie Dean says.

"Hey, yourself. I thought I had lost you for good in this crowd."

"I knew you'd be just swamped," she says, grinning her wide loose grin. "But I had to go get my baby from the nursery, and right now I got to get on home and fix Momma's dinner. And Garth's got him a stock car race to get to. Why don't you come on home with us?"

"I think Momma's already cooking dinner for somebody today."

"Well, I knew it, but I didn't want you to think I didn't want you." She runs a finger down my linen lapel. "You look so nice!"

"I didn't know you sang in the choir," I say.

"Shoot, yeah. Did you like our 'sangin'?"

"Like the man said, it was an inspiration. I was so proud to see you up there—you looked just gorgeous!"

"Right. Someday I'll tumble right down them steps, and that'll be a sight."

Garth, Jr., comes running up to his mother, Sunday shoes flatting the sidewalk.

"Momma, Daddy says time to go."

Little grown-up plaid shirt, buttoned to the neck, and a string tie like his daddy's.

"You hush now, go tell your daddy to wait one more minute." Carrie Dean reaches down and lightly swats the wash-pants bottom that scoots behind her and away.

"He's a doll."

"He liked-to drove me crazy today during the service. I wanted to listen, and he had to pick on his sister ever' minute."

"You liked the sermon, then."

"I would have, if I'd been able to pay attention," she says lightly. Then the pale eyes take on a sideways gravity. "I pray to the Lord to make me a better wife."

Garth taps the car horn. Carrie Dean's gaze flickers only slightly.

"Listen, I've got to help my sister-in-law put up her squash the first part of the week, and then I got to run Momma into Jackson for her tests. But I want you to come see us on Thursday evening for sure. If you haven't already got something to do."

"Not a thing."

"I'll call you in between if I get half a minute," she says, backing away. Then she whirls to go and nearly bumps into Aunt Eola.

"Hey, Miz Dwight," she says in passing. "Good to see you this morning."

Eola comes up beside me and grins as she puts index fingers to my rib cage. She jabs the fingers in playfully and then locks her arms about my midriff and squeezes. It is not like being squeezed by a refrigerator as my mother would have me think, but by a large sofa.

"Darlin'," she fairly shouts, "I know women nowadays is supposed to be skinny, but I declare if you ain't plumb *poor*."

The women near us smile at one another in their Sunday

clothes. *Poor* is farm talk; it means not enough meat on the bones. Cows are either poor or purty. Purty means fat and sleek. A cow that is poor is not likely to survive hardships such as birthing and giving milk, let alone winter weather. In farm life, where breeding is occupation and preoccupation, females of any species are evaluated for their hardihood. It is a reflex. I have heard my father talk about my mother's family, with an approving emphasis, as *purty* women.

Eola rocks me from side to side, and plants a kiss on my temple with her hard lips. She is done with me, and pats my hip as she lets me go. Indeed, I am handed about as a child would be. And this fits; it makes sense. As a child I am familiar and known. My uncles and aunts and the church people who once knew us as a family here can make sense of me if I am the child they remember. It is something beside the point that the child is thirty-five and has a life of her own. As a child I still belong here. I am welcome.

A man's arms slip round me from behind. Uncle Spanner. He hugs me till I am oxygen-starved and my feet nearly dangle off the ground.

"You never was much bigger than a minute," he says, resting a shaven cheek next to mine. "You come see us before you get off, hear?" He releases me and turns to talk to Clarence Holloway.

"Now where's that man of yours?" It is Miss Dougherty returning. "And that sweet little one?"

"Larry's in Iowa, working, and Laura is traveling with her other grandmother and granddaddy in South Carolina for a week. But she's coming. They'll put her on the airplane next Saturday afternoon."

The wrinkles push back from her old eyes as she tries to contain her astonishment.

"All by herself?"

"All by herself. She's five now, and the airlines will take them at five and escort them. She's quite the young lady, you know."

"Five years old!" The worried look does not depart. "I guess I forget how they grow. Listen here, I'm going to go find your mother and see about you two coming for dinner." She pats my hand and walks off toward the church building, where Momma stands talking with the preacher's wife in the shade.

A hand is placed underneath my bent elbow.

"I just wanted to say hi there," the voice whispers. "Do you remember me?"

"Sure, Mrs. Taylor. It's nice to see you."

"How long you going to be with us, Jeannine?"

"About two weeks."

"Well, I know your momma's happy. Your family didn't come?"

"My little girl's coming. End of the week."

"Your husband couldn't get away?"

"Not this time."

"Good to see you."

There is a failed sweetness about the way the patterns repeat and repeat. The same questions, the same answers. The same smiles, wearing thinner by the minute. But there are conventions to be observed. If you are a man, people ask you about your livelihood. If you are a woman, people ask about your husband and children. If you have a broken leg, total strangers in elevators will ask about that. There are certain conditions of life that seem to reduce you to a single dimension. When I was pregnant with Laura, it occurred to me that I could have cards printed and avoid all conversation. The cards would read:

Fine, thanks.
April first.
Either one.

When Momma and I wave our last wave and start across the slag to the car, both of us are strained. Difficult to pinpoint, as nothing has gone well all morning. But my mother, being my mother, has been answering the same questions I have. And the day has become insufferably hot.

The Malibu's chrome door handles are blistering to the touch. Its doors swing open to invite us into a red plush oven. I sigh and drape my arms over the top of the door, unwilling to get in.

Momma sits down heavily in the driver's seat, but leaves her legs outside. She says, "Well, I've had all I can stand."

She drops off her tan pumps in the gravel, and proceeds to pull her flowered skirt up to her hips.

I look fully around the parking lot to see that we are indeed by ourselves.

She wriggles in the seat, lifts her hips, and down come the panty hose. She jerks them swiftly off her toes and wads them into her hands. She pokes the shriveled mass into her purse, then reaches out and picks up her shoes with a groan.

"Let's go," she says.

I get in and pull my door shut, and we lurch out of the parking lot.

"What are we doing?" I ask.

"Going home for dinner."

Her tone is such that I ask no more questions, and we drive in silence all the way to the front door. When she stops the car, she takes her purse and hurries into the house barefoot. The pot roast, for one thing. I reach in the backseat for her shoes and then go around the car to shut both doors before I go into the house.

I carry the shoes to the kitchen doorway and drop them. She does not look up. She continues placing little balls of dough in muffin pans. The whole place smells of cooked meat.

"You can set the table," she says.

"Is anybody coming?"

"No."

"Then I'm going to change clothes first."

"Just take your time."

I wheel about to look at her.

"Look, what is this? How come you're so unpleasant?"

"Well! You noticed something."

"Yeah, I notice a lot. I notice that you're cooking this huge meal, and there's only two of us. I notice we're not going to Miss Dougherty's. I notice you're acting like a really pissed-off person and at my expense."

Eyes full of wild lights lift the head to find me.

"You will not use language like that in this house."

"Sure. Okay."

"This is Sunday. This is the Lord's Day. It's not over because church is out."

"Right, Mom. Say, it's really too bad Daddy isn't around. He could help you out, whip me with his belt or something."

"Don't you talk that way to me about your daddy!" She starts toward me, and I know the look, know by the way her hands are positioned. I throw up an elbow to take the blow from her palm, work both my forearms in front of my face and head to take the next four or five attempts. Suddenly something happens in my brain, something opens like a spout of cold water. I drop my arms to my side. She whacks the open side of my face soundly. I stare at her through the cold water in my eyes as the flash of heat spreads up my face. Her face looks at one time both fierce and terribly frightened.

"Feel better?" I say.

I can't sustain the eye-hold, and as the tears brim up, I turn. I lead myself in the direction of my room by the searing glow in the right half of my face. I don't quite make the first turn; the love seat catches me at the hip. I spin and stumble backward into its velvet lap. When I know where I am, I turn my face into the seam at the wing shoulder and still my breathing, try to destroy the need to cry. Within moments I am overwhelmed with sleepiness. I want to go to sleep. I close my eyes and breathe velvet.

"Jeannine." Mother's voice, sodden with tears. Her arms slip around my knees, her face presses my leg. I do not want to open my eyes. I can feel that she is kneeling beside my feet. I don't want to go on with the rest, with the apologies, with the tears, with the rest.

"I'm sorry," she says. "I'm sorry for losing my temper like that."

"I'm sorry too, Mom. It's okay."

"I don't know what happened to me."

"It's okay. Really."

"It's just that I love you so much, Jeannine. You just don't know. I love you more than anybody in this world, more than my own life. I would do anything to help you. You have always been the joy of my life, and this . . . this tragedy with you and Larry, it just hurts so much!" Her voice catches on a sob.

"It's painful," I say.

"I don't know, I can't understand . . . Tell me what I did wrong! Tell me what I can do, how I can make it right!"

"Mother." The words whirl. "There's . . . It has nothing to do with you."

"Oh, I know you don't need me, I know I'm useless to you. I'm an old woman, and I don't understand the way you live, or what it is that you want. You grew up different from the way I did, you had people that loved you and cared for you, and you learned different ways."

"Mother."

"But Jeannine, honey, don't throw it all away! Don't let this thing, whatever it is, just ruin your life and Larry's! And Laura! Have you even *thought* about that little girl? I mean, really *thought* about her? Do you want that little child to grow up in a broken home?"

"Mother, what are you saying? Are you telling me that I haven't thought about anything? That I—"

"I'm not telling you anything." Words through the teeth. "I'm asking you. I'm asking you if you have thought about anybody except *self.*"

"Goddammit," I say. I try to yell, but my voice lurches through as a screech. And now here it comes. That flood I've been carrying around with me.

"Goddammit, Mother, you don't know a *thing.* You don't have a single piece of real information, and you load me up with this crap. Where do you get your stuff? From the goddam preacher?"

And that's it for the defense, because the tears take over. They roll like hot rain, down the cheeks, out the nose. I grope for another box of Kleenex.

My mother, for her part, brings a scorching anger to dry them with. Spine straightened from the postures of supplication, eyes transformed into cooked marbles, she sits back on her heels.

"The preacher would be here for dinner right now if you hadn't been so rude! And if I weren't so ashamed of you. I know that whatever is wrong with your marriage is your doing, Jeannine Hinton. Any woman can hold on to her marriage, and you can make yours what it should be if you want to bad enough. Larry loves you. That man has bent over backward for you. He let you have a career when it was nothing but more trouble for him, somebody worn out to come home to, baby-sitters with his children. He is a good man. He works hard, and he's responsible, and he's a provider. He earns a living to try and make you happy! You don't know how to be grateful. You are ungrateful, and spoiled, and you are about to ruin three lives.

"I have listened and listened to you, and I still haven't heard what it is that you're after. What is it, something more for you? For *self*? Something for your *career*?"

The word extrudes itself from between her tightened lips with fourteen e's in it. It is a foul thing, not to be entertained on the tongue.

"You are ungrateful, and spoiled, and I expect that's my fault. One I will take with me to my grave. You think I'm going to sit here and sympathize with your little tears?"

Abruptly she drops the tone of disgust and begins to reason with her child, the wayward child for whom there remains some hope of repentance.

"I always loved you and catered to you, and I guess you got to thinking that you had to be *It*. You didn't ever learn how to do for others, how to let somebody else be most important. That husband of yours is an executive, and he needs a wife that understands him. He needs somebody that knows how to make him feel like the King of the World!"

And then her thread of hope snaps again, and she narrows her eyes.

"You think I'm going to say, 'Sure, darlin', do whatever you need to do, you know best.' But let me tell you something. You have a child, and you have to think of her. You don't have a life anymore, you have her. And you ought to lick the dust from Larry's shoes, my lady. I would, if I had a man like that. Any woman would be proud to."

Her uplifted chin pulls the band of skin that connects chin to collarbone taut. A fury carried cobra-cold.

"Mother, I have spent the last year working at unlearning everything you have just told me."

"Who have you been working with?"

"Myself."

"*Myself*—" she shakes as though she holds the word captive between her teeth—"is subject to the devil. And you had better at least find yourself a Christian counselor."

"No thanks. I have learned all I want to know about self-sacrifice. I learned it all from you."

"You didn't learn a thing from me. You are not in the least way my daughter. You belong to your father's family. All you think about is Self. Ever since you were a little girl, you have put Jeannine first. You didn't help me in the kitchen, you had to be dragged in to wash the dishes, you didn't clean, you didn't cook. You left it all to me. And not, 'Thank you, Mother,' or 'I appreciate all you do, Mother,' but those cold snake-eyes. Like two pieces of ice."

"Do you love me, Mother?"

The face before me tries on four new contour maps. The last one has ragged blue twin lakes offset to the right of center.

"Why, Jeannine, when you were a baby, I loved you, I played with you, I held you, squeezed the life out of you. I don't know how I got anything else done. I would play with you all day long and then jump up and try to put supper on the table when your daddy walked in the door."

The lakes mist over.

"You were my whole life. No child could have been loved more than the way I loved you."

My voice is having to force its way through rock caverns. "But, Momma, I'm grown up now."

Blue lakes. Blue lakes flooding.

"And I don't think you love me, Momma. I don't think you even like me."

Ice chips melting.

And what more is there to say? Now that the echoes have taken over the stillness.

Momma releases a shaky breath between the fingers that have risen to cover her mouth.

"Jeannine, it's just that you're not like me. You don't act the way I would act. I can't see how you're the same little girl I loved."

I nod. My eyes search out some place in the room to rest.

Momma takes several tissues from the box I have forgotten in my lap. She blows her nose. I watch her as though she were a thousand miles away, a stranger.

But then she lifts the eyes to me and I recognize them.

"I know what's wrong with you, Jeannine. I know what it is that you have lost, and it's your faith in God. I know you and Larry don't go to church. I know—"

"Let's drop it about here, okay? We've got no place to go with this."

"How can I help you if you won't listen to me?" she cries.

"This is a dead end, Momma." I push myself up out of the deep cushions. The box I have been holding tumbles to the floor. Where will I go? A walk. Need other shoes on, other clothes. I leave her sitting on the floor beside the love seat. I go down the dim hall to my room.

The dark mahogany four-poster stands out against the white walls. My bed from age five. I was given a choice, I recall, between this bed and another, a blond maple. I chose the blond maple.

A breeze floats through the open window and distends the

heavy satin of the curtains beside the bed. A relief, no doubt, from the persistence of gravity.

My stomach hurts. I am hungry, I remember.

I sit on the pink chenille spread and remove my navy heels, then stand again and peel down the panty hose. My jeans hang from the footrail; I pull them up before unbuttoning the gray linen dress and slipping it over my head. I find a shirt in the drawer and lay it out ready to put on before I take off my slip. It is not cool in the room, but I do not want to expose my skin to the air, not more than the few seconds absolutely necessary. I have one of those angular bodies that looks much better without clothes, or so Larry tells me. But today there is no comfort in nakedness.

I button my shirt and find my shoes and decide to ignore the disheveled hair that the mirror on the back of the door tries to show me. I focus instead on the hand that reaches for the glass knob.

Going toward the front door, I must pass behind the love seat. She is no longer sitting there, but her voice catches me before I get to the door. A quaver passes through my chest.

"Jeannine." She speaks my name softly and then closes the distance between us over the soft gold carpet. She still looks dressed for church, except for the bare feet. And the face.

"You haven't eaten."

"I can't eat." My hand on the door.

"I know what you're really doing, Jeannine. You may not realize it, but you are rejecting Larry because you hated your own daddy all your life. You're trying to make him pay for all the things that *in your mind* you think your daddy did to you."

I close my eyes. "I read that book, too, Mother."

"I know. I know. You have your own notions, and you won't listen to anybody. Larry has been so patient with you, to help you arrive at decisions that were right. And this is how you act."

I yank the front door open. She steps between me and the screen and seizes my shoulders.

"Look at this face, Jeannine. I am an old woman, but my

face has been old since I was thirty. Since I had children. I have given my life to being the best mother I knew how to be to my kids. You don't know what I went through to get you through college, to get you married to a good man."

I shake my shoulders violently free of her grip.

"You want me to be like you, right? You want me to make my life a sacrifice to somebody else, so that I can be like you. I can look like you, too. That's how you got all those lines on your face, not from being a mother but from twisting things enough to get through your life believing what you want to believe. And now you deny everything you really know—you spout that Bible crap about men having the Word of God and women supposed to be subservient. You buy that after telling me how you were forced to have sex right there on that carpet, Daddy's skull crushing your windpipe to make you stay still. You got that face by trying to believe anything but the truth, that you were sacrificing yourself to a cripple. And now Daddy has conveniently knocked himself off, you can really do it. You can believe anything you want to."

I push past her onto the columned porch. I am down the steps onto the gravel before she cries out through the screen, "Spitfire! Your father—*your father was worth ten of me!*"

8

I take the old road that winds behind the barn. We used to keep calves there, feed them soybean meal from our hands. Great warm woolly tongues. Nothing in the barn now, probably the loft is rotten. Probably rats.

The road is not used at all now, either. Couldn't be used, the way it's overgrown with weeds and young trees. Farther down, erosion has taken the whole thing. Saw it happening year by year on those Christmas visits: First the end of the log bridge over the creek washed sideways. Daddy could still ease the pickup across that first time. But there was nothing left to ease it over the next year, and the next year there was no sign that anything had ever been there at all. Every year after that was the same, changing only in matters of degree. The red gully gobbled up the road chunk by chunk.

Renters cannot be expected to care for much. Even in the house, gaping holes in the wallboard underneath old calendars. Not a hand turned to the land—probably didn't matter. The land takes care of its own business. Given an even chance, the mother—and did the Indians have this in mind?—would throw us all off her back.

Milkweed. Pokeweed. Blackberry vines, wild huckleberry bushes. A discarded stove, rusting bed springs, water oak sparkling in the breeze. Pine trees growing great mops of lush needles, sighing, sighing.

There are places to hide on this farm when you need one. That was something I loved as a child, something I have missed in city life, life on the Iowa prairie, married life.

Off in the east pasture there is the big gully, layered with

thick nets of kudzu vine, grown into a deep canyon from the red
slash it was when Daddy first found it. There are woods, the
pond, the steep meanders of the spring. Along its moist slopes jug
plants hide their traps for insects—hairy-mouthed little brown
jugs, fleshy and cool beneath the leaves. Y'all come.

There are also cotton shacks, tool sheds, the barn and empty
sharecropper cabins strewn about the acreage. But these are for
adventure, not safe hiding. Such places can attract other kinds of
wanderers. They feel abandoned rather than safe.

But not the long-needled pines. Not inside the circle of
heavy boughs that droop all the way to the ground. These are
shelters to be entered. In there the wind soughs gently, making
sounds that could have come from inside your head. Fallen needles form a smooth mat from the trunk outward, so thick and so
acid that nothing can push up and grow between them. Winter
and summer these green tepees stand, their brown mats covering
the ground. Quiet shelters to be entered. A child's haven.

Since Laura was born, I've been back to the farm a few
times. Glancing visits, never long enough to let the place take
hold. I don't know: For so long I didn't feel safe being with my
parents without Larry. As though without him I could be reab-
sorbed. In the past five years he has been too busy to come with
me, and yet I've felt drawn back by Laura, have felt that I owed
my mother her grandchild. A Rumpelstiltskin bargain.

We brought her once while Daddy was alive. She was eighteen months old, and Larry had a business trip to New Orleans.
And once for the funeral, those few streaky mottled days. Into the
air, into the ground and home again. A blur of thinking, feeling,
seeing.

And then last Christmas we brought Laura to stay by herself
with Momma for a few days. Larry and I handed her over in the
airport at New Orleans. We had a flight to Hawaii, and didn't go
beyond the boarding gate. I could have stayed and visited the
farm when we picked her up again. But I didn't.

The fence here is a grid of rectangles, and fairly new. I cross
the road and climb the clayey bank. One of the long-needled

pines stands just at the pasture's edge. I lean on the fence wire and peer between the boughs. It is as inviting as ever: cool, private, safe. And I do not want to go inside. Something in me resists. I don't know if it is the adult or the child, and maybe it doesn't matter. Whichever is in charge is content to stay at the fence line. Content to observe that things remain the same.

The boughs bob up and down with a sporadic breeze. The same breeze cools the back of my neck. It makes its faint whistling sounds among the green needles. Sighing, sighing. And shit: Why do I get into these things with her? She's crazy, she's an absolute lunatic. Alone on this big place, nothing but TV and lunatics all around—

I reel and clamber down the bank again, scudding on the moss beside the roadbed.

Okay, okay. What did you learn today, Jeannine?

One. Your mother is crazy. You knew that. Still, a good place to start.

Two. Your mother is dangerous. That one you keep forgetting. She doesn't know she hates you, and you keep forgetting.

Three. Do not go into the enemy camp and expect sympathy.

Four. Dealing with your mother, expect the worst. And then get ready to be blown away by how bad it really is.

You used to understand these things better. When your father was alive, you were more careful. Imagine being thirty-five years old and not knowing which parent is the dangerous one. Or not knowing all the time, all those long years, it was both, both, both, both.

Can't think and cry at the same time. All right, then, one at a time. Sit down. First get through with the crying part.

I sink to my heels and fall the rest of the way to the ground. The crying part seems to take some time.

Christ. I just want it all to go away. I don't want any of it to be true. I am afraid! Scared to death I could be making the biggest mistake, I could blow it all, the husband, the kid, the mother, the whole fucking family. She's probably at home on the phone, giving my name to sixteen prayer groups. God. I need to get out of here.

I sit up, brush the sand from my hands and forearms. Work on my face with the backs of my hands.

There is a stick on the ground, an open space of sand. I pick up the stick and draw. Circles around the rain dimples in the sand, circles and maps around the grayish anthills, around the chips of bark and half-buried stones. Nothing square, nothing constructed, nothing inorganic. Make everything connect, twine it all together.

A mockingbird sings a complicated warble. The imitation, if it is one, is lost on me.

And for one clear instant I miss Larry. Well, why not? I picked him out to save me from all this. I miss his sweetness, his straightness. He can always see it when other people are out of line. I want to talk to him, want to be held and comforted, want to be told I'm sane and she's crazy.

With her simple ideas, simple solutions: Let God into your life. All the energy goes into enforcement. Into snuffing out the contradictory evidence, shifting the blame. Riding with the vigilantes.

If I am the sane one, why do I feel so cut off? The only person in the known world who would think of such a thing: a life for myself.

The line of the old fence runs along the small rise just opposite the roadbed. From Cyrus' time, it is not much of a fence: two strands of rusty barbed wire pinned to posts that lean and stagger into the undergrowth. Used to be cows in there. Grandpa turned the field into pasture after he gave up on cotton. And something else is gone: the sound I associate with this place. The periodic whine and creak of the old windmill, metal complaining against metal, singing against its will.

I turn to look, but the windmill is gone. It used to stand next to the barn inside the west pasture. That windmill and the big old dead tree that just now gleams silver-white in the field—these always were the two landmarks of Cyrus Hinton's place.

The windmill must have gone in the last two years. For Cal
and I walked this road the evening of Daddy's funeral, and neither of us remarked that it was gone. We did talk about the dead
tree. Or Cal did. About having to plow the whole field around
that thing, working behind one of Grandpa's mules.

I hadn't remembered the plowing until we stood there talking together. And then I could smell it, feel it. Cal was twelve
then, to my seven. I would walk barefoot over soft new furrows
until I caught up with him, or met him coming up the row,
sweating and squinting and clucking to the mule. I was carrying
jars of water to him.

"Whoa-up," he would gasp, and the mule and the harness
and plow would come to a clanking, squeaking stop. Cal's nose
and ears glowed red in the sun. He would pull a sleeve, already
dark and rank with sweat, across his face. With his other hand he
reached for the water. I would quickly unscrew the top, something his fingers couldn't manage after their hours of gripping
plow handles. I didn't know that then. I was doing what I had
been ungently told.

"Hand it to me," he would mutter. I did. We had no further
conversation, since my brother had become another person out
there in the field. I would watch him drink the water down like a
thirsty, irritable mule himself.

We walked together beside that field in the peace of the evening, our father lying in the fragmented peace he had achieved.
We faced into the light as it faded into the west over Blue Rise.
Cal's brown-flecked Hinton eyes looked off toward the big tree
receding into the twilight.

"I tell you what, Jeannine. You know when I think about
this place the most? I think about it when life gets to looking too
complicated to put up with. Sometimes when I've been punch-
ing buttons and pushing pencils and listening to people talk pale
shit for too long, I sit back in my chair and all I can think of
is, 'By damn, I used to plow the goddamnedest straightest
furrow...!'"

He lifted his arm and held it out straight over the field. He followed it with his eyes, as if in earnest. But the face he turned to me was brimming with gaiety.

I have never understood Cal. I feel close to him, but probably in ways he has never guessed. Or it could be that he guessed long before I did; I have never been able to fathom what he does and doesn't know. But sometime when he was in his teens, I made him my father.

Momma is not the only one to tamper with history.

Cal was older, bigger and shrewder than I was. He was relatively friendly, and more or less reliable as an ally. He was the one who blazed all trails before me, more trails than I would have need of. He was arrogant, underhanded, rebellious—probably a middle-grade punk. But he had the facility to imagine other ways to do things.

He pioneered our alliance with Momma, the one that afforded enough margin to live and to make choices. That is, to get around Daddy. But Cal also pushed everything too far.

When he paid, he paid in thumpings and slappings and whippings and low grades and scrapes with cars and the other tennis teams. He paid in dress and haircut regulations, in disciplinary dismissals, in mothers who wouldn't let daughters go out with him. He paid in at-home algebra lessons, with knuckle-chops to the temples for each wrong guess, each unknown unknown.

I watched and listened and learned. Principally I learned how dangerous it was to try anything. But there was one other lesson before Cal finished high school.

The first incident blazed across my cosmology like the Bethlehem star.

We were at the dinner table, and something Cal said sent Daddy jolting to his feet. He already had one hand to the belt buckle and was halfway around the table. Then Cal leaned back in his chair and gave his soft laugh.

"Daddy," he said, "you can knock me right through that wall if you want to."

Which was more than obvious. Which was standard practice. And I believed Cal to be at that moment utterly insane. But instead of knocking Cal right through the wall, Daddy turned on his heel and sat down in his chair again. Not one word was spoken.

Something had happened that changed everything, and I didn't know what it was.

Cal managed to finish college in one piece and then he left home. He got a job and an apartment and a wife, and then another job, and another. And then he was a sought-after young executive. Suddenly he had approval by the armload, Daddy's arm included. He could afford to unhook himself from Mother. He could step back from our pitiful confederacy and take his punk's-eye view of the whole show. He could sit on any side he pleased.

Perhaps it is that all men who marry bring a new sympathy home to their fathers. The same fathers who once made their lives a misery. How else to explain Cal? The son becomes another dreaded husband and father. One cannot hate one's own kind and survive.

With my stockings at risk, I pick my way through the bramble-strewn road beside my brother. At nightfall we are still dressed in the clothes we wore to the funeral. I can still make out Cal's dark pinstripes. I cannot see the shoes, but it strikes me that their soft leather could have been dyed to match the deep blue of the suit. Probably not, though. Cal's perfectionism never bears the stain of effort.

He is looking west, where the last light is reflected off low clouds and is caught closer to the earth by the dead tree.

He says, "You know what, Jeannine? I used to think that old tree out there was the biggest thing I would ever see in this world. Man, I knew that tree was it."

He chuckles softly to himself as we stop to gaze at the jagged old monument. The tree had been blasted by lightning before we were born. Blasted silver. As we watch, it all but glows in the roiling dusk.

When the clouds have blotted everything on the landscape into dull blue, we start back to the house. Cal sighs.

"Every time I come back to this place, that old tree gets to looking littler and littler," he says.

Cal now is vice-president of a firm that manufactures safety equipment for water sports. Flotation vests, rings, belts and a line of children's items. A leisure business, as he himself likes to say.

He is a moderately tall man, once keenly competitive at tennis. He still carries himself well, though his weight is fast gaining on the carriage.

"Groves fat," as he is in the habit of accusing Momma. With his usual glittering grin. He says he now keeps himself "mobilized for doubles."

He will add, "If I'm going to sweat these days, it's going to be country-club sweat."

He and his wife and teenage daughters live in a suburb of Boston. I'm sure these women can no more credit Cal's stories of plowing behind a mule than Larry can conceive of me carrying water barefoot. And why should they? As cocktail talk such stories are diverting. If they are the truth, they must appear no less irrelevant.

Cal is one of those people who can handle problems of any kind. I often try to incorporate such problem-solvers into my thinking, put them to work for me.

"What would Larry say?" "What would Momma do?"

I have never been able to do this with Cal. He has always been too dangerous to emulate. His trick probably has less to do with solving problems than in making them seem to disappear.

Besides, I have never been able to predict what would come out of his mouth next.

When we all flew home for Daddy's funeral, I believed that all of us were heaving simple sighs of relief. It had gone on too long. Curtis and I had been certain for years that one of our parents would finally kill the other. Cal used to laugh about our future as wards of the state. But well past midnight on the night of the funeral, the night before the three of us would depart this grim reunion, it was Cal who still sat in the shadows of the living room. I walked past him, unable to sleep myself. At first I didn't realize he was there. He sat on the wing chair in the corner, my mother's reading chair. Or so it is used when the light is on; Cal sat there in the dark with his hands over his face. He was crying.

And saying, between the breaths that shook him, "What a waste."

In the morning before we leave for the airport, I take a close look at my brothers. Curtis and I are friendly. We inhabit the same world. He is the lawyer from Denver, attuned to ecology and the politics of oppressed groups. Unlike Cal, he does not think his wife's job is to pick up his socks wherever he may drop them. His blue eyes are earnest. He presents them for my approval when we talk, which is something we do easily, even over the spread of years. Curtis seems to understand it all, to be unmarked—no hatred, no displaced energies racketing round. Of the three of us, the healthy one.

And so it is Cal, who lies sleeping on the couch, his bulk in ungainly repose, who seizes my heart. I am happy he is here. We do not and cannot talk; there is no exchange to substantiate any of the feeling I have for him. But it is there. This is Cal. He is who he is, and I adore him as simply as I adore my child. He is not my mother, not my husband. I do not have to live with him, feint by joust. There is nothing to become complex. In daylight, without the benefit of tailoring, it is clear that he is fat. He is bloated from the failure of his liver to cope with the daily drenchings in scotch and vodka. He colors the first of the clean morning air with cigarettes that replace each other like bored soldiers all day long. His mottled eyes water in the light, even interior light, and that is the reason for the sunglasses indoors. And my heart swells when he is there, crushes like a caterpillar when it is time for him to go. There is too much feeling, more than I know what to do with. I look at him, laugh with him, try to

crystallize in memory his every manifestation. He has always
been at cross-purpose with the greater logic of life. The pat-
terns he generates are at odds with the primary ones. And
where the ripples meet and form their dissolving ridges, he
laughs. His laughter is a gift. I have not heard another like
it. And nonetheless, he is dying. He will die violently, like
Daddy. But not the big bang, not the desperate intention.
There will be one risk too many, one laugh out of sync, and
Cal will pay the tab he has run up.

A crow has settled on the uppermost shard of the dead tree,
where lightning has created a fork. Its mate follows, and the two
flap their wings for a time, as if to make the place more homelike.
Their cries easily reach me from the distance.

And Cal's daughters, his wife: I wonder, do they despise
him? Will they be relieved?

I myself could not have been more than five when affection
for my father had been crowded out by fear and dislike. I could
not have been more than five for the glimpse that suddenly goes
alight in my mind.

I can pick up the scene, can see it—Christmas night,
lights in the tree, the little frame house where Curtis was
born. I stand beside my crib in the living room, showing
how I can tie my shoes. My father is smiling and offering me
a disc of pink frosting—the best part of my favorite cookies,
the bothersome cookie part nibbled away.

I take the oval from his fingers—hard, pink, damp from
his mouth. I give it back, push it away. Merely because he
has touched it.

My stomach churns. I return to my stick and my patterns in
the sand. They are now traveled by ants, tiny reddish creatures
nearly translucent in the strong afternoon light. Ants are streaming over the blazes I have made, and indeed over the tip of the
stick itself. These are not black ants from the small gray cone-
heaps. I look about, and finally see the foot-square truncated pad

of an anthill several yards from where I sit. It is seated in the sand like some mushy, porous orange-colored scab. These are fire ants. Come up from South America, Momma said, in the years since we lived here. I move out of their traffic lanes and squat to watch them work their hill. They are merely about their business, it seems, moving particles of sand from the dim red interior to the passageways outward.

"Fire ants, and it only takes one bite till you know where they got the name." But one bite is the dream. Like Adam and Eve with the apple. Like monogamy. "By the time you feel the first one, you already got a dozen on you." These light-struck beings, distracted from their industry, quietly set pincers, quietly seed the flesh with miniature boils that itch and infect. "And you will burn like fire."

Fire. For the fall from the light.

It is Christmas afternoon, the white frame house. In the front yard. We play in the grass in the patch of sand beside the porch. We have new toys. A doll bed for my big doll with the soft baby ears, and real shoes for her that I can tie. A metal drum with metal heads for Curtis. Cal has already been slapped for scoring it with his new pocket knife. And now Curtis has done something. What could it have been? Something. Because Daddy slaps Curtis. His face? His head? And then yanks his pants down. Pants, not diapers, so Curtis is three. And I am five, Cal eleven. Daddy throws Curtis across his knees and beats the naked buttocks with his hand. I see blood streaming from Curtis' nose and mouth. He screams and blubbers mucus and blood. These dribble into the sand. Daddy keeps on beating. He does not see. I stand and watch. No doubt Cal watches, too, no doubt my mother watches. We must do this a lot, this standing back and watching. We are getting in practice, for algebra lessons, for telephones that don't ring, for the checking account out of balance, too much money spent at Christmas.

And is it the same day? Is this the man who will offer me the pink icing from the last Christmas cookie?

Is this the man worth ten of my mother?

These pictures that run in my head are the ones that do me in, tie me to her. The same ones, Curtis squalling through blood, Cal having high school algebra rung into his skull, the scarves I wore to school to cover the belt marks at my neck, the rest.

Knowing my mother was there watching. Knowing she, too, was powerless. Was there ever a beginning? Can the clock be turned back far enough to find a beginning?

From my room I hear the shouting. My father's voice, loud and repetitive. A trick of his: to repeat the same phrase over and over and over and over, whipping himself incrementally into a blind rage. "What did you think you were doing? What did you think you were doing? What did you think you were doing? What did you think you were doing? What did you think you were doing?"

The questions had no meaning, were unanswerable, surely; were a litany. Still, the hope of answering swam through your head and over your tongue. If you could say the right thing, touch the balance spring somehow, if—But every utterance would be cut short by the same question, repeated. The question soon came to have a blow for punctuation. And then nothing was possible. The answers, the reasons, the explanations, the apologies, swam in a maelstrom, a percussion of pain ringing in the head and ears.

I hear the shouting, and come awake in my bed— Houghton Park. Can it have been the first time? His voice, shouting. Then hers, offering something. What? Offering words, useless little end-stopped phrases. Whack. I come out of my room, come into the living room, fuzz-balled nylon carpeting under pajama feet. Standing just outside the butterfly of light, the kitchen doorway and its light path that stretches into the dark living room. I see her. She sits at the kitchen table, stacks of checks before her. She sits with her face in her hands, in Curtis' chair. Seeing, if anything, the drifted aqua piles on the stained oilcloth. Not seeing me. He bellows and gestures, striding back and forth behind her chair. White workshirt open at the neck and chest. He reads aloud from the book of check-stubs, bringing down knuckles on the top of her head, then the heel of his hand against her temple. Numbers and punctuation. She rights herself after each thump. Twice she gets as far as, "Daddy, I—"

How long does it take me to see this much? Half a minute? One and a half? But for some things you get more than value. For me that particular moment has lasted over thirty years. It is still going on, if I close my eyes and let it. No wonder he rode tractors at night. All that shouting and hitting, thirty years and more? I'd be tired, too. I am tired. Tired of seeing it, tired of knowing what I know. Maybe he was, too.

All right. Half a minute, let us say, beside the doorway. And then my hand is seized. From the other side I am yanked back away from the light. Cal's voice in my ear.

"Come on. We'll play Monopoly. You can play with me in my room."

I pull my hand back with the urgency I feel, but it does not come free. "Cal, let go. Daddy's—"

"You can be banker. Come on."

"Cal."

"I said, come on."

I go with him. Inside the room he lets go of my hand and closes the door. He turns on the light and I watch him push his bedspread into the crack underneath the door. We play Monopoly. I am the banker. I get to use the racing car as my piece, and under Cal's stern eye I count out the bank bills—orange, yellow, blue, green, pink, white.

And that is all there is of that night.

Except, of course, for the questions. More unanswerable ones to go with that half-minute of kitchen footage. What if I had tried to stop them? Had Cal ever tried? Could I have changed everything?

Suddenly there is a pinpoint of fire at my ankle. I make a grab, and jerk my pants-leg up to get at my skin. Four, five—a half-dozen or more of the ants beat me to it. They have curled into their stinging postures before I can brush them off. I see them; I feel the singe as they bite. I jump to my feet brushing frantically, slapping at my jeans and canvas shoes. The prickling sensations up my back and neck make me think they are all over me. I dance about in a frenzy of rubbing and patting and brushing at my clothes and body. I stand in the road and scratch myself hard all over—that, at least, is a known sensation. It makes me feel solid and sound. But for a long time I continue to overreact, jumping at every twinge.

I think about going back to the house.

Could I have changed everything?

That is the question that returns, and something moves me to laugh out loud. For the answer is yes. Yes! I could have changed everything. I *would* have changed everything. Maybe not for her, but certainly for me. If I had tried to stop him that night, that first time, then I would know something.

I would know whether or not I had failed her. I would know whether being silent and afraid was my only real choice.

"Hell, Jeannine, what is the difference? You'll never get the world put back together and fixed. It was never together in the first place."

I can hear Cal's voice, can hear it because I don't have to imagine it. Don't have to imagine words into his mouth because he has already said them. I could telephone him this minute— part of me wants to run and do just that, run and tell Cal. But I would only hear it again, replayed from all the other times. The lesson I can never learn, *to keep things light.*

For the love of Christ, what the hell you expect? You've known the woman all your life, Jeannine. You live in a different world from the one she lives in. She's doing the

*best she can. You think you're doing somebody a favor, tell-
ing her the way you see things? Just who are you doing the
favor for? You and Curtis, you got those stiff necks. You
think it matters what you know? You know how to behave
around Momma. You know what she's going to say before
she says it. Laugh it off! You don't have to say anything
back. What good does it do anybody?"*

Yes, Cal, yes. You are telling me how to get along, how to
survive, how to be somebody's daughter. You are telling me what
you and I have known forever: Keep what you know to yourself.

I would, Cal, I would; I have. But I don't have many places
left to keep it. It wants to spill out of all the cracks, Cal. Of which
there are many, many, many, many.

9

The sun tilts a degree lower in the sky, lighting up the sawgrass that rags the fence line. A hot chlorophyll odor is brought by the breeze for sampling. The pine boughs over my head dip and sway. A dog yelps somewhere in the woods—an odd sound, it seems to me, even with the echo taken into account.

I have a harder time getting to my feet than I expected. Sticks have their uses, and it is a good thing I have held on to mine. I lean on it to take the strain off my unwilling knees for a moment. And then I crawl out from under the drooping boughs of the pine tree. My back aches where I have leaned against the craggy bark.

That sound. That first afternoon in the front yard. Momma said she was having trouble with wild dogs trying to get into the hen houses at night.

"Wild dogs? On the farm?"

Somehow it was an idea I associated with other places. New Guinea. Uganda.

Momma stooped to pull a weed from the base of an azalea bush beside the front steps.

"Yes, wild dogs. And they get at my chickens, and they mess in the garbage dump. That's why I keep Juno tied in the back. I want my terrier pups for watchdogs. And if I'm not careful, she'll go off and have her pups in the woods, too."

"Is that how you get wild ones?"

"Well, of course. The females go off and hide when their time is close. And if they don't bring the little puppies back here while they're young, the blame things just run wild. The SPCA won't do a thing with the wild ones. So if I see one around my hen houses, I shoot it."

While she was close to the azalea, she pinched off several new shoots that would disturb the symmetry of the bush.

To me there was something striking about the notion of ordinary farm dogs being wild things. I wondered what they looked like. If they had never been tamed, would they look the same, walk the same, carry themselves the way we think dogs just happen to? Would the look in their eyes be the same? Or would there be that element of strangeness, something of what I heard in that single bark from the woods?

"Momma, if the wild dogs are whelps of your own yard dogs—say one of Juno's puppies—how do you know from a distance that you're shooting a wild dog?"

"Because my dogs know better than to be where they're not supposed to be."

"But how can you be sure?"

She turns her back to me as she reaches for the next weed.

"I just know," she said.

From where I stand I can see the roof of one of the old cabins on the place. It's just beyond the tops of the bushes and young trees that are rapidly taking over what was a front yard. Vines climb all over the gray logs and through the empty window frames. The timbers of the roof sag, and the wooden shingles have been torn away in great patches. But Momma says it's a sound structure. She says it could be turned into a summerhouse, if one of us children would just take over and do it.

Even as I move toward the cabin, I am amazed at the power of such veiled reproaches. My head knows better, while the rest of me is drawn on. But before long I am stumbling, all but tripping in the briars and undergrowth. My feet and ankles are scratched and raw. The ant bites itch, and are already inflamed. I am oddly exhausted, maybe just hungry. Very hungry indeed, I decide, and turn to pick my way back through the way I have come.

After a hundred yards or so, I can cut through the trees and across the garden to the driveway. Momma's dogs run to meet me in a rowdy pack. They sniff and nuzzle the one hand I will offer—curiously, I withhold the other. A kind of stubbornness, I guess, reflecting my divided mind. I am feeling that I should not approach the house without armor, an attitude of some kind at least. But I am too weary to think what it might be.

The dogs abandon me at the front steps. They are not allowed on the porch.

I push open the front door and let the screen bang shut. The house is cool and quiet. It has the distinct feel of an empty house.

"Momma?" I call, unsure which way I wish to be convinced.

I walk through the living room. There is no answer. She is not in the kitchen, and no sound comes from the rest of the house. From the kitchen windows I can see the path and the barn, but no movement. Which means little. She could be inside, tending to equipment, replumbing the place, anything.

I open the refrigerator and take out the jar of pimento cheese. Momma makes it in the blender now, stores it in wide-mouthed canning jars.

I make my sandwich and get a glass of milk. I feel uneasy about being in the kitchen. As though I might be surprised and embarrassed to be found stealing food. Something else for Self. I pull a napkin out of the package on the counter and decide to take the things to my room.

Down the hall, the door to Momma's bedroom is standing open. I look in, needing to be certain that she is not in there. As the door swings back, the mirror of the vanity against the opposite wall shows me an image of myself that is certainly furtive enough.

In any case, I step inside.

The furniture in this room holds no surprises. Dear God: Was it ever new? Of course it was. It was new before Cal was born, new when she bought it with the savings from her job at Kress's candy counter, going home half sick at five o'clock from candy orange slices. Her favorites, then. But then so was the furniture. In my memory it has always been exactly as I see it now, maple-colored varnish gone sticky and opaque in the Mississippi heat. The entire finish must have been steamed loose from the wood one sweltering summer, then gone solid again when the weather changed. The slippage stayed as wrinkles in the varnish, like an ill-fitted balloon skin. Momma would appreciate that.

Over between the north windows, her own four-poster bed. Not the sort of four-poster that soars and imposes, inviting canopies and drapes, but a stunted, half-hopeful sort. Lots of lathework to show that energy was expended, in concentration if not in sweep. The bed sits squarely on the floor on its stubby pineapple legs, justifying the chest of drawers on the other side of the window.

The classic domestic chest of drawers. Broad-waisted, a suggestion of hips. This is the masculine piece of the set, for some reason in better shape than its partner, the vanity-styled dresser.

And here we arrive at the true epicenter of my childhood. That dresser, with its nicked and wrinkled finish, bald corners and club feet. The tilting mirror upheld on two slim versions of the bedposts. The fittings and drawer pulls matched to those of the chest of drawers. I must have stared at these drawer pulls from infancy. Looking at them now, I seem to know them better than any other articles on this earth. I cannot hold them in my gaze without translating the black metal hardware into images my child's mind must have invented: profiles of twin children separated by a Christmas tree.

My adult mind intervenes and classifies the design as Early American. Then the child goes back to work, and the U-shaped drawer pulls are really telephones connecting the children.

I cover my eyes with my hands so that I can see other things.

In my mother's bedroom the dressertop and its wadded scarf always appeared to be the scene of some geological upheaval. But there were certainties, too: the amber-tinted glass fawn, mounted on a dish that once contained face powder but had come to hold rusted bobby pins and single earrings. And there was the small colored hat, made of my Aunt Lottie's fine crochetwork. The hat was meant to be a pincushion, but in fact the pastel blue and ochre and pink and lime and purple variegations in the thread were quite pristine.

Pins would have rusted and marred the fancywork, and besides, Momma kept her pins and needles elsewhere. She kept them tucked in the vicinity of their last employment—embedded in the cording on the back of the sofa, or stuck in the heel of the ironing board, or woven into a ratty band of green fabric mounted on the barrel of the sewing machine. Needles often flew their thin banners of thread down the length of the kitchen doorframe or the living room curtains.

The little hat had a pink satin ribbon threaded around its crown which could be tied and retied as often as I cared to practice. Which, according to the way the ribbon sagged in its starched crochet braces, must have been often.

Though I had other business: lipsticks and eyebrow pencils to locate underneath the debris of old envelopes and matchbooks, tweezers to lift the envelopes and matchbooks with, the rectangular blue bottle of Jergen's lotion to smell, the cake of Tangee Natural Heather Rouge that I could open at my peril. For a mere touch to the surface inside colored my fingertips as unforgivingly as it did Momma's face. I would watch as she rubbed the skin of her cheeks as forcibly as she kneaded bread.

When Momma put on her makeup or brushed her hair in front of the mirror, she knelt on the floor. The seat of the vanity seems never to have existed. Kneeling was as natural to her as her bare feet. I see her kneeling there, her wavy brown hair held back against the nape of her neck, head swiveling proudly.

"This is how I shall wear my hair when it is silver like my mother's hair," she told me. "All the Groveses have pretty silver hair."

She does have pretty silver hair now. She keeps it cropped short so that it is easier to wash. She washes it often, to keep out the smell of the barn.

I see her kneeling there, tears streaming, streaming as she examines the upper plate of dentures in her mouth. The new teeth, the ones that are too white and too long for her mouth, ugly. "I hate them, I just hate them," she sobs, choking on the words or the teeth; it is difficult to tell

*which. She is forty years old. I am ten. I have never seen my
mother crying or helpless or so dim in that mirror. The teeth
have been going, two at a time, for weeks now. She goes to
the dentist in the afternoon and gets home before I have
come home from school. On those days she is gaunt-faced
and cooks supper in silence. My father has got tired of paying dental bills for filling her teeth, has said she can just
have them pulled. She has been obedient, and now these
teeth. She has tried going back to the dentist, and he has
turned a professionally deaf ear. The vanity of women. So
she has come home again with the hateful things, and cries
for days—the afternoons, anyway, when I am home and
Daddy is at work—and then for several more afternoons she
works before the mirror with a steel file on the teeth. After
school I stand in the doorway of her bedroom and watch her
kneeling before the dresser. I watch her file, file, file, my new
ugly mother with the collapsed upper lip and gray, gray face,
eyes almost brown, or so they seem without their light. By
Sunday she has taken the front four teeth down, shaped
them sufficiently that she can wear them to church. But not
proudly. Not proudly.*

I open my eyes and check the yellowish face that I present to
my mother's mirror, and take my sandwich and milk into my own
room.

"When we were first married," Momma was fond of saying
to me during my adolescence, "your daddy loved me so much he
could have eaten me up. Now he wisht he had."

It was her notion of something humorous. So important,
knowing when to laugh.

I place the napkin on the antique sewing table next to my
bed, and set the sandwich and the milk on it. I stretch out on top
of the pink and white spread. I can wait to eat until I am hungry
again.

So. It has always been easy enough to find my mother's position in life unappealing. I did not intend to be like her. I would

not have only one car which was "his" car, would not rely on "his" gasoline to save "my" grocery money comparison-shopping between Piggly Wiggly, the Jewel, the A & P. I would not penny-shop the discount stores to exhaustion, then fly home to have dinner on the table at 5:30 and pretend that I had been nowhere, spent nothing. Sitting on the passenger seat of my father's black 1955 Buick Super, looking with disdain at my mother's tense and—yes!—wrinkled face, her body straining forward over the wheel to make us be home that much sooner, I was able to develop a good deal of resolve of that sort.

It served me well into my twenties. Marriage simply was not appealing. And then when I felt safer, when I had one degree from the University of Chicago in hand and prospects of another, when I thought marriage could be worked without the contingency of total surrender, I took pains not to marry my father.

Larry was gentle. He did not raise his voice. In fact, he did not ever show the slightest sign of anger. He handled waiters and menus with ease. He was neat and orderly, the only son of a naval commander. A house and a family mattered to him. His hair was beginning to thin, and he wanted to marry me.

He had an apartment on Lake Shore Drive overlooking the city. Student housing at the University of Chicago could not compare. I spent evenings studying there, feeling like a privileged truant. He'd pick me up at the library when he finished work, tie and jacket folded in the minimal backseat of his MG. A quick dinner somewhere downtown, and then I would sit on the white carpet of his apartment, my books and notebooks on the coffee table, the city view opening before me.

Larry sat in a puffy cream-colored chair across the room skimming newspapers and trade journals. Or he might spill an accordion of computer printout over the kitchen table. This latter impressed me mightily. I thought of him as The Man Who Knew Computers.

I liked to try to impress him in turn.

"Larry, listen to this." I waited for him to finish a paragraph or a column.

"Hmmmm?"

"I want you to hear what Jung says here. 'Logically, the opposite of love is hate, and ... fear; but psychologically it is the will to power. Where love reigns, there is no will to power; and where the will to power is paramount, love is lacking. The one is but the shadow of the other—' "

"You're captivating," Larry interrupted me to say. "I especially like the red and yellow pencils behind each ear."

I blushed and removed the pencils. And said, "You're supposed to be paying attention."

"I am paying attention. Do you use them for coding, red for major concepts, yellow for interesting miscellany—?"

"Larry! You're supposed to be listening."

"I was listening."

"Well, then, what did you think?"

"I wasn't listening to the stuff about the will to power, I was listening to the sound of your voice. I'm always amazed at what a soft voice you have."

By this time I was moving toward him, utterly won, but shaking my head.

"I never hear anything you say at all," he insisted as I put my arms around him, nestling my face into the soap-fragrant curls at the nape of his neck. "I'm sure you're a very intelligent person, and sometime we should have a serious conversation."

"I'm ready."

"Okay, I think I've got an idea. How are you at Morse Code?" He stepped back a couple of feet and turned to stare blankly into my face while his fingers drummed dots and dashes on the tabletop. I stared back until his narrow boy's face split wide into a grin, and we both began to laugh. Then he patted me heartily on the shoulder, and sent me back to the coffee table.

"No study break yet," he said. This was indeed code. "I've got two more sets to do. You need to study for your exam."

His sweetness was overwhelming to me. I would sit over my notebooks and doodle flowers and orifices over the ringbinder holes, my heart melting. The *kindness* was what I couldn't get over. I could not seem to learn to expect kindness.

And even then, it struck me as unnatural. I wrote it down in one of the notebooks that rested blurrily beneath my hand: *What kind of marred creature is surprised by kindness?*

And in this way it came to pass that The Creature Surprised by Kindness fell in love with The Man Who Knew Computers.

It is well established that marriage is hard on surprises. And people are notoriously short on gratitude for what they come to feel is theirs by right. Parents have been complaining about this trait in children for centuries. And sharper indeed than a serpent's tooth is the marriage of The Man Who Knew Computers to The Creature No Longer Surprised by Kindness—the Creature who, in point of fact, would rather be heard.

10

"You can be some help with this trash," she calls out from the back porch. By the time I get there, she has hoisted two of the four sacks lined up beside the back door, and is on her way out with them.

Since Sunday afternoon our tacit agreement has been: We have nothing to discuss. Certainly there is no ground safe enough to begin from. This is Wednesday morning, and our interactions still buckle and roll, glance off some buried and invisible object.

Since we have nothing to discuss, there has to be some other basis for my being home. It seems to be that I have come to help.

So: Hauled back to the farm by my love, my guilt and my lack of imagination, I come as a dutiful child. I come to help, then, and am immediately trivialized by her competence. I rise at eight of the clock, full of purpose, to see her come striding from the barn in her ripped sweat shirt and hip boots. Her physical motion has forgotten how to be tentative as she does her work, strikes her path.

Tentativeness is reserved for society, in which milieu this rocky assurance collapses like a paper Christmas ornament. Out of doors she is at home, pitting truculence and determination and resilient physical strength against what stands in her way.

I lift my two sacks and hurtle down the back steps to follow her. She chooses a path through the underbrush and kicks a branch violently aside—a rapid, definitive slash at obstruction which wastes neither motion nor thought. She is headed across the field toward the gully. She steps over the electric wire—dead since she got rid of the bull, but still in place, an obstacle—and follows the path that emerges through the undergrowth.

After the morning's light rain the field has the look of a win-

try Scottish moor. Mist rises from the ground in places, and there
is low vegetation turned ochre and brown, colors of resistance.

Small briars tug my jeans and canvas shoes. When we kids
were growing up, the gully was a red slash in the ground, not
more than two or three feet wide at the base. We used it as a
hideout. Now the thing is huge, a canyon that spans perhaps half
an acre. There is an accumulation of household garbage and
chicken carcasses littering the slopes. This is supposed to be fill.
But on this scale it is little more than a clinging plaque. I stand
on the rim of the canyon and look for a place to toss the two grocery bags I hold in my arms.

"Come on, throw it in," Momma directs, a little short of
breath herself. She has heaved her sacks over the edge and has
turned to go back. A tinny rattling sound is all that is returned
from below.

"I'm just looking for a spot," I say, moving off the path and
stepping over ridges of weeds. As I jump clear, a long briar whips
through the air and catches in the sleeve of my knit shirt. I hesitate. I want to stop and free my sleeve, but Momma is waiting
and I know I should throw the bags over the edge with haste. I
move to do that but the briar constricts and digs into the skin of
my arm, settling the question. I let the bags slide to the ground.

"Now what in the world are you doing?"

"I'm caught, Momma. Just a minute."

Gingerly I work the threads of the shirt over the thorns.
Momma expels a sigh. I hear her approach the spot where I left
the path.

"Just tear it loose and come on. If you aim to help me before
the sun gets high."

"I'm working on it," I say. I have freed perhaps an inch of
the three-inch snag.

"Here," she says, her exasperation dragging r's from the gut-
ter. "Heerrrrre." With her boot she tromps down on the base of
the briar strand, and it leaps again. It tears through the flesh of
my fingers and through the yarn of the shirt, leaving both in ragged shreds.

"MOTHER!" The word tears from my throat, a roar of

pain and fury. The look I turn upon her would undo an entire herd of water buffalo. The look on her face is withered and stricken. We stare at one another as the canyon finds its hollow voice: Motherrrrr.

Momma lifts her chin.

"I'm sorry," she says. She turns and hastens up the path.

I watch her go, my eyes stinging. And when I bend to pick up the bags I have let fall, tears drop on them, a silly and superfluous irony. I hurl the whole business over the side. When I finally turn to follow my mother back up the path, she is no longer in sight.

I go back to the house and make breakfast for myself and do the dishes and sweep the kitchen floor. And then, because I do not know what else I am expected to do, I walk down the path to the barn.

It takes a few minutes of standing and looking at the door to remember how it works. It is a cross-barred plank of unfinished lumber. There is no handle, no sliding bar. The tangle of hemp trailing in the breeze at first means nothing. Then I remember, and pull on this length of bailing twine that is threaded through a hole drilled in the wood frame. The twine lifts a latch on the inside of the door, and the door can be pushed open. My father's design, crude but effective, his usual parameters.

I step inside and pull the door to. The heavy ammoniated manure odor is overpowering. But the barn floor is clear; she has used the tractor to rake the place out. The dirt is smooth and lightly patterned where the rake has traveled, and flattened down again where she has walked on it.

As my eyes adjust to the gloom, I look down the length of the interior and find my mother atop a thirty-foot ladder. One leg is hooked back into the rungs to guarantee her perch. She is repairing one of the ceiling supports attached to the steel girder her ladder rests against.

She sees me coming in the dim light, and calls out.

"Hand me those needle-nose pliers over there on the ledge. No, farther down, past that winch. You see that winch? Right there."

I locate the pliers and bring them to the foot of the ladder. I climb up slowly, placing my feet in the center of each grooved aluminum rung. The ladder vibrates with each step. I pause until the shaking stops and take the next rung.

"What's wrong with you? You're moving like a blind man toting a sack of eggs."

"I'm trying not to shake you off this thing."

"You let me worry about that. I want you to get those pliers up here before my arm gets tired holding this thing. I can't wait all day."

I deliver the pliers, and then a few more tools. I learn to race up the ladder in a steady rhythm. But when she has everything she needs up there, I stand about below with nothing to do.

"What needs doing down here?" I finally ask.

"I'm too busy to tell you," she says, taking the screwdriver from between her teeth and looking down at me. "Just go on back to the house. Do something you *can* do."

I turn to go, stung by her tone.

"It's too filthy down here for you, anyway," she adds.

But not too filthy for her. I am the princess, the peasant's burden. Exempt and beloved and despised.

I go back to the house and begin cleaning, the morning's bitterness hanging on me like swimmer's weights. I open the refrigerator and slam it shut again. Chaos is chaos, but does it have to be disgusting chaos?

I lean my back and shoulders and then the back of my head against the cool enamel of the Kelvinator. What is happening here? Our battle stations are pitched. She is the weary, impatient laborer, and I the ungrateful wife to a slob I detest.

I have become the person I least wanted to be: my mother, as seen by my father. She has become the person she least wanted to be: my father, as seen by herself.

Or could I be wrong about this? Maybe she likes it, the prison-camp reversal Bettelheim talks about: identification with the oppressor.

Oppressors are where you find them, these days. Or where you create them. Momma started with the unloved childhood,

Grandma Groves too busy plowing fields and milking cows and looking after her brood of eleven to bother very specifically over one of the willful, wistful ones in the middle.

But Momma never gave up. When Grandma was still alive, living with her younger sister in a blister of peace—manless, childless peace—Momma would ask her to come and stay on the Rise for a few days. For one day. For an afternoon. And then sooner or later, Grandma would let Momma come and get her. And for a few hours she would sit in the wing chair in the living room, shy over her deafness. She would let herself be cooked for, fussed over, patted and hugged, her thin silver hair rolled and curled. Then she would not be talked into staying for supper but would insist on going home again. I would hear these stories over the telephone, Momma gay with her success over getting some time with Grandma, and jealous over not having gotten more.

And then there was the story of the thundershower when Grandma was visiting and the telephone rang. Momma answered it; no doubt Granny didn't know the thing had even sounded. But when Momma put the receiver to her ear, an electrical charge traveled down the wire and knocked her to the floor.

"It knocked me clean out," she told me. "I mean, cold. I don't have any notion how long I was lying there. But when I came to, my head felt like it would bust wide open. My ear hurt so bad, I didn't think I could stand it. I crawled on my hands and knees to the living room where my mother sat just a-goin' with her crochet hook, and I put my head in her lap and said, 'Momma, that ole lightnin' came through the telephone and about killed me!"

"And do you know what my mother said? She said, 'Hmp. I guess that'll teach you to answer the telephone in a thunder-shower.'

"I just crawled over to the sofa and pulled the afghan down. I covered myself up right there on the floor, face and all, and just cried myself to sleep."

When my mother told me that story, my heart was wrung with pity. In a way, it still is. But standing here in the kitchen today, I side with my grandmother. How little peace she must have felt in my mother's loving. Like trying to rest in an antbed. The same stinging contact, the burn afterward. What did the child want from her? What was it that she was supposed to be giving this one? And why such a confusion of injury no matter what was given or done?

Suddenly it seems to me that Grandma had every right to fend Momma off. To keep her at arm's length and better. But then Momma overcorrected and held me so close that we drew one breath. And I, not the end product of this cycle but one of the endless perpetrators, do I now overcorrect the other way? Do I push Laura from me? Brush aside the tendrils that would cling?

I imagine I do.

Nobody ever told me that children changed everything. That they bring out the underside of all you hoped to skim over.

With my marriage I had determined to bury my experience of family life. Larry was what I wanted. He was sweet, clean and generous. He was also funny, and we laughed our way through the first years of our marriage. We disputed such issues as who would follow whom to which end of the earth. I finished my master's degree, and Larry made money. The thinner his hair got, the tighter he clung to me. I thought that was a fine arrangement. I thought so for quite a while. And then I got a job. And then he felt it was time we had a baby.

I was thirty, he reminded me.

Birth defects, he reminded me.

We always liked children, he reminded me.

You said, he said.

In the critical junctures of my life I have never had enough imagination to invent. My approach has been to obtain information on what is normal, and then perform to spec. With motherhood I was in trouble. Nothing I saw looked possible, let alone normal. If I went to visit a friend with children, I might find the children playing in the house, and the friend sitting in the family car with all four doors locked. This is how mothers got to read books.

None of the available role models looked like people I wanted to be. With this one even Cal was no use. His wife was already living my mother's life, Cal a stopped-down version of my father's.

With Larry I felt that I had escaped my father. But when Laura was born, it became clear that I would not escape my mother. The percolating hum of the old Kelvinator resounds inside my skull.

I had no place to go except deeper into her experience.

That was easily done. I quit work. Then housekeeping, which had been a playground of enlightened chore-swapping, became my job. Cooking and incidental errands became my job. Being home became my job. And then, of course, there was Laura, with whom I was privileged to spend my time. Larry's own baby girl. She even looked like him. I felt I had been used.

His eager fatherhood made me ashamed. He overflowed with pride, and my soul crinkled in its cellophane shroud. I was prickly, short, paltry, ungrateful. I thought I was an inadequate mother.

Larry concurred.

"You aren't adjusting," he would explain. "You have to give yourself to it, or you won't be happy. Besides, it's only for a few years. Then you can go back to work, whatever you want. You should make an effort to enjoy yourself."

Larry was right. So reasonable, so gentle. So earnest, so stupid. I despised him, and tortured myself over my vicious character. My selfishness.

I was on my mother's turf, all right. Selfish is the worst thing a woman can be called. If you don't sacrifice the self, you are evil. Lost. Wrong. Blind. Selfish.

How has such a word acquired such charge? Selfish, shellfish. When it doesn't roll off the tongue like an automatic oyster, it's quite a harmless word. Nearly inconsequential. Elevenish, brownish, bluish, English, blandish, selfish. Of the self.

A really unselfish woman, a Christian woman, gives of herself for others. She wouldn't take so much as a breath of air that others might care to have. And soon we arrive at the place where we see that the only truly unselfish woman is a dead one. And all for love.

Maybe I should have taken the trouble to learn from my father. His ideas were simpler. He didn't talk about love. His conviction was that showing respect was equivalent. A father showed respect by providing a home, clothing, food and a college education. A son or daughter or wife showed respect by doing what they were told, by not having opinions of their own and by deferring promptly.

It was, in any event, what was required.

My father also had the virtue of not talking about his unloved childhood. Cyrus Hinton had been an intelligent man but a mean farmer, a proud man reduced to filling his pickup with farm produce needed for his family and selling it on the roads of Bayley. And further reduced to spending the proceeds in honky-tonks. He beat his wife with regularity, his children with imagination. Verlie told Momma that she once saw Cyrus pull a long root up out of the ground and whip Sumrall "like a dog."

If this was a father a child could not love, the child could nevertheless show respect. And that was the lesson that my father passed on to us children. It is certainly clearer than anything my mother has ever said to me about love.

I push myself off from the refrigerator and start out of the kitchen. As I pass the telephone, I give the receiver a rattle in its wall cradle.

Love. My mother traffics in the stuff.

In the bathroom I gather up the combs and brushes scattered on the countertop and stand them in a jar. They can be cleaned later. I open the storage drawers and make space for the jars of night cream and liquid makeup. I do not wipe them off. I gather up the bobby pins, white ones she uses now, and find a box for them. The rusted ones I throw away, and scrub each brown hieroglyph from the pink Formica. I throw away loose Q-tips and cosmetic boxes and soap wrappers, and collect the assortment of lipsticks in a shallow dish I bring from the kitchen. I put the steam iron in the linen cupboard, the curlers in a plastic bag, the prescription pills in the kitchen cabinet alongside the vitamins. I replace the matted puff inside the box of dusting powder and move the whole ensemble from the top of the toilet tank to the vanity cupboard. I throw away the paper matchbooks, matches with their red heads run together in the damp, which are tucked in the bunches of decorative plastic grapes. I submerge the grapes in soapy water in their own bowl.

I know that Momma will be furious. She will understand that each of these acts is an insult, will know that I do not clean her house out of love but out of revulsion.

No one would ever say that my mother is lazy. Everyone knows she works harder than any two people, and this may have some foundation in fact. Grandma Groves always said that when she was carrying Melvinia, she thought she was carrying twins. It is my personal opinion that she was right. My mother seen as two people rolled into one would begin to make sense of things.

On this farm chickens thrive, bread is expertly baked, flowers bloom. More than that: Flowers bloom inside the sixty-five pounds of concrete borders my mother has formed and poured for them. Two mammoth fans for the house are rewired, twenty sections of burst pipe replaced, the thermostat mechanism repaired, the upstairs bedroom Sheetrocked, the fire in the meadow put out. For holidays the doorways of the house are lined with borders of plastic poinsettias and tiny lights, pinecone wreaths adorn the fireplace, a crèche is assembled while four fruitcakes bake in the oven.

It is just that the interior of a house cannot sustain her attention on a day-to-day basis.

I scrub at the lime stains in the toilet bowl for some time before I remember that they are permanent. I ought to remember; my father explained the whole problem to me, the type of hard water the Rise has, the calcifying interaction of the molecules, et cetera, et cetera. He explained it to me the last time I knelt here on the tiles cleaning the toilet. That was the first time I brought Laura here, the only time he saw her.

He also explained to me, after I had cleaned the bathroom,

about all the hard work that had gone into preparing for my visit. He beamed with pride. Had I noticed that the yard was mowed and weeded, the garden plowed? The Japanese fruitcake Momma had made and persimmon pudding and the dresses for Laura?

They had been ready, and I couldn't see it. I saw the inside of the house standing in litter and grime, the kitchen sticky with his experiments on feed mash, the bathroom detritus, the spider webs with their abandoned flies, the dozen dirt-smudged pumpkins sitting on newspapers in the bedroom where Laura and I were to sleep.

"We worked like slaves for two days before you got here," he told me. "Mother was sewing on those dresses for Laura and I don't like to bother her when she's involved in one of her projects. I got out and hoed my garden. Got strawberries blooming and onions Verlie stops here for, tries to trade me out of my onions, she thinks I don't know it, but I got plenty." He winked happily. "You notice how clean and neat the garden looks? Mother makes a dish with my onions, I like it and she showed me how to do it so I don't bother her, creamed onions. It makes the best! Hit's fattening, but you don't have to worry about that *ever'* day. You'll have to get you some before you get away. Your ole daddy'll have to cook for you."

As I remember him in this way, the tears rush forward and surprise me. Same old surprise. But I could never make this side of him fit with the rest, the sweet-natured shy charm with the rages, the eruptions of a vast brutality.

It was my mother who taught me to see the sweetness. She insisted upon it, conditioning me after some terrible scene or other to remember that Daddy loved us. He worked hard. He made us a living. When he talked about me in particular, she would tell me, he "lit up like a Christmas tree."

I wipe my tears on pink toilet paper and toss the wad into an overflowing wastebasket.

These talks with my mother didn't do much for me except confuse my feelings. But they worked for her, it seemed she could use them to make herself fall gratefully in love with him again.

As for me, I hated him. I hated him because I had no rights

and was afraid. I showed him respect because I had no choice. I loved him against my will because I was taught to see that he meant well. I stayed away from him because I could never integrate what I felt with what I was supposed to remember to feel.

Staying away is still the only solution I can imagine.

But there are others. Because the fact is that sometimes you have to go on living with somebody you hate. Grandma Hinton did that. After Cyrus had his strokes, she had the care of him and continued to show him respect. She kept his clothes and his bedding and his body clean. But she could not bear to feed the man she loathed. In one of Momma's rare revelatory moments she told me how the old man died. Daddy and Verlie stopped in to visit their parents after a month of cold winter rain, when the only contact had been by telephone. They found the old man lying on the bed, skin sunken and bones pushing shapes in it like knobs in a croker sack. He was begging Grandma for a soda cracker. He was so far gone that he didn't recognize his children. They took him to a nursing home and he lived for several days; the old woman was simply unable to care for him, is what the case worker said.

But Grandma Hinton cared for herself and her garden for several more years before she, too, passed on. During those last years she refused to hear Cyrus' name mentioned.

No one in the Hinton family speaks of this. Daddy and Verlie never told any of the others about the starvation. They knew, of course, that she had killed him, and it is truly frightening when someone else does the terrible thing you have caught yourself wishing.

I straighten my back and turn to work on the bathtub. I gather up the partially used containers of shampoo and creme rinse and pour certain of them together. I store the spares in the vanity cupboard.

I have learned from my in-laws that people who keep their houses impeccable have just one secret: They do not consider horizontal surfaces to be functional. Countertops, dressertops, tabletops, TV consoles, toilet tanks, tub rims and open shelving are not to be used for stationary objects. These places are reserved for the activity of dusting, and they are to be kept strictly clear. A house is to be kept the way one keeps a ship's cabin, the assumption being that at any moment the room—indeed the world—could come to rest at a 45-degree angle. Everything battened down, all decks cleared and swabbed. You are in the navy of domesticity but never at sea.

My mother takes for her model something more akin to the primeval rain forest. If you leave things about, lying where they fall in their native soil in their natural habitat, something good will happen. Loam, or humus, or perhaps one day coal, diamonds, petrodollars.

The South cooperates generously with this model. Each day there is a fresh layer of dust to be bound by humidity. These two form a scum that is the perfect embedding medium for thousands of small insects that take their leave of this life every night.

Once having expired, they lie there as they do now on the floor of the tub and around its rim, their tiny legs crimped, their antennae extended. They lie perfectly, as though they had prepared themselves for an afterlife in clear amber. Ancient bug religion, and I suppose they have every right. But it is I with my yellow Excello sponge who do the sweeping up here. I explain this with my regrets as I flush them down the drain with plenty of water.

I am a great believer in the influence of family life. That is of course why I am so worried about what will become of me. In my life I have come to feel that without Larry to save me, I will become like my mother. Whenever I leave her house, I leave with fresh resolve to be permanently neat and tidy, to put more effort into housenitkeeppicking.

Larry wishes I would visit my mother once a week.

Momma is still in the barn when the phone rings at just past noon. It is ringing, or buzzing, or grating, or whatever it is that it does. And I will have to answer it and convince the person on the line, and it will be some relative, there is no doubt of that, that I

am suitably clear, cogent, friendly and cheerful. I am very tired of
the effort to be convincing. I set the dustmop down on the
kitchen floor and lean on the long handle for support.

"Hello."

Telephone hellos are a lot like signatures. And students of
handwriting are instructed to note that signatures often bear no
relation to the body of writing. They can be distinctly larger or
smaller, slanted to another purpose entirely, or bear little
flourishes and elaborations that a person might use to shore up
identity.

"Aunt Melvinia?"

I recognize the voice, but then I recognize all the voices.
There is only the matter of pinning down which voice it is that I
recognize.

"No, this is Jeannine. Momma's out at the barn."

"Well, hey, Jeannine. This is your cousin speaking. Now tell
me quick, which cousin?"

"God, Drew, don't torture me. It's tough enough."

Gay laughter, bright clothes fluttering on a line.

"Don't feel bad. I thought you were your momma when you
answered the phone."

"I could be, by now."

"Unh-hunh. I thought you might be getting a touch tired of
being your momma's good girl."

"It wouldn't be so bad, if I was any good at it."

"Well, don't depend on me for advice. You're the only one
in the family with any idea of how it's done."

"What are you trying to do, depress me?"

The laughter again.

"No, lamb, I'm tryin' to save your neck. Think you can get
yourself a passkey for a night on the town, such as it is?"

I laugh. Volunteer laughter, and suddenly I feel relaxed, a
person again.

"If I'm tricky," I answer. "Maybe you could bring me a rope
ladder concealed in a Bible. Hey, Drew, how come I say such
things to you?"

"Cause you're plumb rotten, and you know I am, too."

"How old are we again?"

"I make it thirty-four and thirty-five, honey. 'Less you got some new way of counting."

"Not fifteen and sixteen?"

"Not ten and 'leb'n, neither."

"Well then. Things being what they are, I believe I can get myself sprung for one evening. You talking about tonight?"

"I can do a lot, but I can't make Bayley look like a town on a Wednesday night. How about Friday?"

"It'll have to do."

"Good. I tell you what let's do. If Cousin Raymond's around, that'll give us at least one to hold on to. We can take turns dancing with him if nothing better shows up."

Suddenly I realize that the picture of Raymond I carry in my head shows a wide-eyed subteen. "You mean to tell me Raymond has grown up?"

"Raymond? Why, you haven't see him? You wouldn't have to ask twice. He bosses construction for his daddy now. We may have to beat the other gals off him with a stick, but otherwise it should work out. Have you handled a stick lately?"

"Uh. Not lately." I pull my hand away from the handle of the dustmop, just to stay consistent.

"You'll get the knack of it. Why don't you meet us at the Holiday Lounge at nine? They got a band now that can just about half make some music, and if they manage we can half-dance to it. How's that sound?"

"Sounds distinctly wonderful."

"Well, distinctly gooooood. You better bring along a scrap for your momma's dogs so they'll let you back in the house without raisin' Cain that hour of the morning."

"Good Lord, the dogs. How can life be so complicated?"

"Life ain't a bit complicated, Jeannine. It's just survivin' that can get to lookin' tricky."

"I'll have to think about that."

"Lord, honey, don't do it! I don't want to be the cause for none of that thinkin' you do."

"Has this conversation taken a nasty turn?"

"Listen, you go ahead and think yourself blue. Just get done with it by Friday, so we can go out and have ourselves a time. Okayyyy?"

"Okay."

"See you afterwhile, then. Bye!"

I hang up slowly several seconds after the line has busied itself with clicks and buzzes. Who was it that said people affect you like a touch? And you could classify them, warm fuzzies and cold pricklies? Well, he missed it by a little. There are not only warm fuzzies and cold pricklies in this world, there are warm pricklies to be taken into account. I am thinking, of course, about my cousin Drew.

And, as long as I'm THINKING ABOUT IT—and here I surprise myself with theatrics, whirling and throwing the dustmop the length of the hall like the javelin it is. It strikes the tapestry at the end of the long hall with a sound that is more muffle than thump. AS LONG AS I'M THINKING ABOUT IT, the existence of warm pricklies argues the existence of cold fuzzies. Do I know any cold fuzzies?

Of course I do.

I produce a shallow theatrical laugh. I explain it aloud to my audience, treating them to authentic nigger-loving jive rhythms in speech, head and hand gestures.

"O' coarse Ah dew! Ah be *married* to wun!"

A freeze on the gestures. The audience is unresponsive, antiracist, very likely. Southerners have been in bad taste for some time.

And now there is the mop to be seen to. Stagehand, upstage. But when I arrive on my flap-feet, it seems useless to pick the thing up. So instead I squat down on the floor of the hall beside the disheveled mophead. What else do I know? I know there are two kinds of people in the world, those who divide people into two kinds of people and those who don't.

I know, too, that it is a virtue to make order. I set about the task of grooming the dustmop, making each strand of limp dust-fuzzed yarn lie with the others, straight and uniform. I do my work with efficiency. Something about the way I am pushing each piece into place makes me think of Larry. Of Larry's fingers, of a certain inflexibility in the way he uses them, something I am repeating now. Pushing, pushing. Pushing is effective even with a mophead, but there are alternatives.

Name one.

The alternative would be to smooth things into place. A motion that follows the texture, the grain.

Larry and his blind, bald fingertips. The baldness I had decided not to mind. Many people bite their fingernails; the habit in general imparts a certain softness to the flesh. Besides, I grew accustomed to Larry's touch in the dark. So one way or another, the baldness has been accepted. But not the blindness. And perhaps blindness is the wrong word, but what word is there to account for it?

I said to him once, in one of those late-night exasperations that can occur in the dark, no faces in the bargain, "You seem to get no information at all from your fingertips when you touch me."

One of those spontaneous offerings that chill the molecules in the air, turn the sheets into impassable frozen tundra.

I pulled my blanket of guilt up over my head and found little comfort. Never let the truth just fall out of your mouth like that.

"It would help a good deal if there were something there to get information from."

Ah, this was better. There was at least some warmth in embarrassment, in anger. Besides, here was something familiar being offered, something for me to pursue. If I had provoked him into saying something terrible, I could make up for it by being understanding.

"Larry, I didn't mean that the way it sounded."

"Yeah, I know. I'm sorry, too, Jeannine, you know I didn't mean it."

Reconciliation was underway, and before long so were the rubber-glove manikin fingers.

"Mmmmmm," I said.

147

Both of us know the sound of a formal retraction when we hear one.

The back door slams and I jump to my feet. The now-smooth coif of the mophead rests ridiculously in my hands. I right the thing in a haste my mother could have been proud of and present myself briskly in the family room. As Momma reaches the kitchen doorway, I stretch for a cobweb above the bookcase and set my face to look grim and inconvenienced. In my experience these are the hallmarks of a hardworking person. I notice that Momma herself is wearing a matching expression, with the addition of a generous sweat. So she wins.

"Did you find something to make for lunch?" she asks shortly.

"Not a thing, Momma." Lightness is usually worth a try.

"I don't *see* a thing."

No sale.

"Oh," I say, "I just thought we'd open the refrigerator and have whatever falls out."

"That sounds like some of your thinking."

"Oh, Momma, let's not make a big deal out of lunch. There's cottage cheese and peanut butter and leftover fruit salad."

"I'm not making a big deal. I'm just looking at those ribs of yours and wondering why you don't eat enough to make yourself look like something worth having."

Opening the overburdened refrigerator, she begins taking things out. Hatboxes of Tupperware, china bowls covered with saucers for lids, casseroles with tinfoil. Cal's formula for lunch at Momma's house: meat, potatoes, lightbread, fruit salad and fourteen vegetables.

I watch her in dismay. All those dishes. All that mess.

"I hope you take the trouble to cook something for that husband of yours, much less your growing child. You do feed them, don't you?"

"They eat."

"They eat." The repetition is maggoty with disgust.

11

It is late at night. Very late, and Mother's party is over. I am to drive some people home. City people. I do not know them, although they, of course, know my name and use it. But this is the situation, the reason I am outside the house in this night air, and because of the danger I try to keep them all together and get them into the car without incident. They seem not to understand, and are stupidly slow. I am as pleasant as possible. I shut them inside the car on the passenger side and start around the car in relief. These are the last of them; the front door of the house is closed and Mother has even turned off the lights. I am reminding myself to breathe and am placing a hand on the driver's door when the upstairs window slides open, and my Laura in her pale blue nightgown floats through the air and over the lawn into the daffodil pool. Her small body slips into the water silently, she and the daffodils recede from sight, the water in the pool begins to churn. I run to the edge of the pool, my heart a freight train in agony. I am afraid to put even a hand into that water, and I can still see her. She is under the surface with the daffodils, sinking further and further from my hands, looking up at me with solemn brown eyes.

My screams bring me bolt upright in the bed, bring my mother stumbling into the room. I am awake and know it now. She is holding me, rocking me, smoothing, smoothing my hair away from my face. And still the terror does not lose its hold. I grip the arm she holds me with, needing to hold on to her and hating her for being there at all, hating this torrent of grief and fear.

"I'm all right, Mother."

Still she sits, knowing better.

"I'm okay. Really."

"You want to tell me about it?" she asks gently.

I shake my head and clasp the covers around me. Finally she gets up and leaves me, a kiss prickling the crown of my head.

I will sleep. I will wake in the morning and try to work it out. Nightmares! How long has it been?

And in the morning, knowing it was only a dream, I will still need to be with Laura. Know that she is all right. Talk to her, at least. She is in a dream of her own right now, something about clowns probably; the child actually laughs in her sleep. In the morning it will be a wonder to hear that little bird voice, so feverishly alert. I will say, "Kisses on your tummy," and she will burble laughter, and then I will say, because I have to say it, have to disarm the merest casual possibility, "Stay away from daffodil pools."

I am awake very early. I lie in bed and let the night movies play through my head, trying to fit this piece and that piece into some kind of rational framework. I cannot concentrate. Things don't bear looking at too closely. They begin to move, layer after layer wriggling spreading apart to reveal the atomic structure, all those careering protons, fickle electrons whizzing by. Too little framework, too many odd pieces. I wait until I hear Momma moving in her bedroom, in the bathroom. I wait until I hear the slam of the back door. I get up and walk quickly through the house in my bare feet. I find the number in my purse. South Carolina is an hour ahead; the time will be right. I bill the call to Des Moines, and then Mother Lewis answers on the third ring. She is mildly surprised by the early call, but knows as I do that seven A.M. is a reasonable hour to call people with young children.

"I wanted to catch you before you headed for the beach this morning," I say. "I dreamed about Laura and just needed to talk with her today." I make my voice cheery. The truth can be risked if people don't realize how deep it goes, how much bedrock has been shaken loose.

"It's pleasant to hear from you," I am reassured. "Let me

get Laura for you. We were planning a walk on the beach this morning, and she's just having her breakfast."

The line is quiet as the receiver is put down. All the silence of a thousand miles rushes over the wires. Next comes a series of scraping and shuffling noises, and then my daughter's voice.

"Hi, Mommy." A little silver shook the bell.

"Hi." I am emphatic. I convey solidity.

"Know what, Mom? I get to have sugar with my cereal. Grandma says I can."

"Grandmas have special rules, I guess."

"I like bananas now, but not blueberries. Grandpa has blueberries every day, but I don't."

We have more conversation in this vein, and the normalcy seeps over me, soothes the nerve endings. Synapse by synapse the fear is chased out of my system, down the friable ropes of my courage. I feel slightly silly, sheepish. I know that this is a good sign. It is a comfort to find the hysteria so useless.

All the same, I manage to throw in a mention of daffodil pools. Laura hears but does not respond, choosing instead something that makes sense.

"Know what, Mom? Davy lives next door. A different Davy. Not the Davy that comes to my nursery school."

And so on.

I hang up the phone and remain sitting on the kitchen chair next to it. Not thinking, but engaged somewhere, some healing modality. Resting. Expanding the iron cage around my heart.

And thus I am startled by the rattle of the back door. While the sound of booted feet being wiped on the mat gives me the needed margin, I dash back to my bedroom and jump between the sheets. I pull the quilts and coverlet up, all the way up. A cool heavy envelope that seems to magnify sound.

When my heartbeat slows, I hear the kitchen noises and house noises, and then Momma's bare feet on the carpet. She enters the room with a resounding push of the door, as if to disqualify as evidence the cup of tea she bears in one hand. One cup, not two.

She sits on the bed and hands it to me. Camomile tea with

brown sugar in my favorite china cup. I sit up and take it as she unhooks her own finger from the handle and releases it to mine. I am touched by the gesture, and smile fondly into the face that still disowns the kindness, still looks haggard and defensive, still has not found reason enough for softness.

"Thank you, Momma."

The tea is still too hot to drink, the thin china too hot to cradle in my hands. I hold the cup stiffly aloft by the handle.

Momma sits in silence and examines my face. With my left hand I trace the precise scallops of the warm cup rim with my finger and feel sane.

"Did you get back to sleep last night?" she asks.

"Yes. Eventually."

"Well, I didn't. What was all that hollering about?"

"Bad dreams."

"Well? Tell me."

This is a demand, but one that comes of genuine feeling. The face at last is congruent.

In my head I see Laura again, sailing through the air, the blue nightgown billowing. The cold clamp screws down over my heart again, and I look at my mother's face. What is in that face for me?

I try to sip at the tea. It's still too hot, but the business of reacting gives me enough delay to remember something. One thing, but the right thing: Intimacy with my mother means I draw near enough for her to tell me what's wrong with me.

No malice. But how else to make me malleable enough so that she can save me?

"Jeannine, honey, tell me."

I take a breath and let it go.

"I dreamed I was in the car with Larry. He was driving, because he always drives, even though I was the only one who knew the way. A bunch of people were in the backseat, and there was a baby that absolutely insisted on sitting on Larry's lap. Larry didn't like it, but there didn't seem to be any choice. In fact, Larry didn't like any of it, but the rest of us were cheerful and happy. Anyhow, we were driving down the highway when the truck in front of us suddenly stopped. No warning at all. Larry was looking at me, trying to let me know how miserable he was, and he didn't see the truck. I grabbed the steering wheel and we shot around it."

Momma's face is set. The dream I am telling her is a true one. It is merely the *other* dream I had last night. One that didn't wake me up screaming, one that simply felt like real life. This one she can have. It doesn't cost me so much to tell her again what I have already told her.

I sip at my tea.

"Is that all?" she asks.

"No. Then a truck in the opposite lane started to pass another truck. But it never went back in its own lane; it stayed in ours just like we weren't there. Larry didn't see this either, and I got the wheel again and steered us between those two trucks. But as soon as we got through, up came *three* trucks across both lanes. I couldn't believe it, and Larry was looking out the side window or something. I threaded us through those three trucks and then pulled off on the shoulder. It was too crazy to go on, and I couldn't figure out what was the matter with Larry."

"And what were you hollering about?"

I feel the blood flush into my liar's face.

"I guess I was trying to get him to stop."

"Mmmm-hmmmm," she says, as though satisfied.

I drink the tea down while she watches me. She takes the cup from my hand. She is wearing her zealot look, the one that promises to burn citadels full of selfish women and ungrateful children and miscellaneous infidel pagans in the name of Jesus.

"Well," she says, "I can tell you the meaning of your dream."

A long severe look, full of promises to keep. My mother, too, knows theater.

"You may have thought you'd get sympathy, but you don't get it from me. I've been *pretending* to be sympathetic, listening to you and asking questions, and I don't have it all figured out about what you're doing, but I *can* tell you the meaning of your dream, Miss Lady. Do you want to know?"

"Sure thing."

"You were in control because you *are* in control. Larry can't do anything; it's *you.* You are the one trying to break up your marriage, leave your husband and your children."

"Child."

"Child," she concedes.

"So now I'm leaving Laura. Where did you get that one?" But despite myself, cold fear tentacles its way into my heart. The terror of the real dream, losing Laura.

"I know how much you care about your youngun, flying off without her the way you do. Not only one time, either. You went off and left that child to spend Christmas with me so you could go have yourself a high time in Hawaii. What kind of a mother would leave a youngun at Christmas?"

"I don't know. The kind that was trying to hang on to her marriage?"

My mother blinks rapidly, recalculating. She had not thought of this, and besides, she had put that time with Laura to good use. She told her about Jesus and God and taught her Bible verses and took her to Gethsemane's Little Angels Sunday school class.

On the airplane going back to Des Moines, Laura asked me, "Who do you love best, Mommy?"

"You and Daddy."

"Unh-unh, you're not sposed to, Mom. You're sposed to love God the best."

"Who told you that?"

"The lady at my Sunday school."

"What else did the lady at your Sunday school tell you?"

Laura concentrated. "She said if you don't love God the best, you go to a bad place."

"Even little children like you?"

"Yes."

"Where did she say you would go?"

"She said I would go to the devil." She paused. "Or to the foster home."

Larry and I looked at each other, and laughed. Larry elbowed me as Laura showed us the severe frown she had also learned from the lady at her Sunday school.

"Do you know what a foster home is, Laura?" I asked.

"No," she confessed without concern. "Why don't you believe God, Mom?"

"I sort of do, Laura, I just don't believe the way your lady does."

"You know what happens to people that don't believe God? They get all fired up. It's not funny, Mom."

"I just know *you*," my own mother is saying, having found her theme again. "You think life ought to be a party, with no responsibility! You with your friends partying in the backseat, being backseat drivers. You're not cleaving to your husband, you're just *using* him! And he knows it!"

"You know what, Momma, I think you probably had that speech all ready to go no matter what I said."

"You won't listen to me. You won't let God in. Why don't you let me help you, Jeannine? You think I'm an old woman raised in the country, you don't need me. None of you children need me. I know that."

"What is this, another nightmare? Stop it, Mother." I throw the covers back and hurl myself out of bed the way Larry does every morning of our life. It makes a decisive break with whatever was in bed holding you back. I spring off the far side of the bed, away from her. I grab yesterday's blue jeans and shirt from the chair in the corner. I begin shoving myself into the clothes.

"You're just like your father. You think you know it all."

"Seems like that should be a compliment, since my father is so well thought of here lately."

"It would be, if you were a man! But you don't know there's a difference, do you?"

"No, Momma, I guess I don't."

"Well, then, let me tell you something, if you don't know

it." She stands and squares her body, the chin aimed toward me arrow-sharp. "You are not a man, you are a woman. A wife, and a mother. No daughter of mine is going to leave her husband and ruin her children. You *won't* do it. I would kill you first."

My fingers leave off buttoning, and I look at the face that blazes at me across the room. My voice is numb when it tries the phrase. "Kill me . . . ?"

"*I would kill you first.*"

"Christ," I whisper. "Mother, what are you talking about?"

"I brought you into this world, and I can take you out."

"What do you have in mind, Mother? A gun? A knife? An ax? Poison?"

"That's not your concern. You only have to know that I will take care of you. Wherever you are, whatever you do, I'll find you." A finger jabs the air. "Vengeance is mine, saith the Lord." And He has His anointed that carry our His will."

"And you love me that much."

"Yes, I do! I love you so much I'd give my life to make things right."

"But it's my life we're talking about."

"And it's mine. You are my child. And I didn't bring you into this world to have something like this happen."

"Mother—" I stop. This is horrifying, not even possible. And yet it goes on, will not be derailed. "Never mind. It doesn't make any difference, doesn't matter. I will remember what you've said. Now please get out."

In a splitting of seconds the door of my room slams shut. Tears scald the rims of my eyes, but I am not having any. Will not. This is fucking ridiculous, a waste of good water.

I pull the suitcase from underneath the bed. I find clean panties, clean shirts. Too late. Socks, where the hell are my socks? It's like a bloody morgue in here. I pull on a sweat shirt.

The hairbrush is on the dresser, and I use it to work over my head. A hundred strokes, like the old days. All right.

When Laura was being born and the LaMaze breathing didn't work anymore, I panicked. Up until then I had been a

model primaparturient, fourteen hours with Larry sitting beside
me with his thin-lead pencil and graph paper recording con-
traction intervals. And then the pain started coming from
everywhere. My abdomen and all it carried felt like a collection of
dinosaur bones that were taking life and trying to walk away. The
nurses whispered outside the white curtain that the baby was
"stuck," and I knew what I had known from the beginning:
There was no way a baby was coming out of me. Not my body,
not these narrow Hinton hips. The doctor stepped in again for
another examination and announced with his cheerful pink face
showing between my knees that the baby would be coming
"sunny side up." Wrong side up, that meant: I had seen the dia-
grams, knew which way the bone structures conformed during
the birth process and which way they didn't. I began to hyper-
ventilate and then to cry, and then it was Larry's face over mine,
his breath heavy, modeling the correct techniques. I screamed
and struck at him and he moved his face. I clutched the bed and
screamed through the next contractions. And then when I had
quieted down enough to lie panting between pains, I heard his
whisper near my left ear.

"If the other stuff doesn't work," he said, "you could try
contemplating my navel."

A laugh broke through the tears. And for a crazy moment I
did it, stopped the tears and replaced the circular fixture in the
ceiling with the image of my husband's navel. I saw its counter-
clockwise knot and the dark thatching of curly hair. And then
there was his voice near my ear again, a low steady count for the
breathing.

I push the bristles into my scalp and continue stroking. Cal
is right: I've heard all this before. Practically textbook stuff, right
out of family systems theory. When the rulebook says that children have no rights except to conform, then parents handle violations in one of two ways. They can say, "If you don't do what I
say, I'll kill myself. Then you'll be sorry." Or they can say, "If you
don't do what I say, I'll kill you. Then you'll be sorry."

This is conducted in varying degrees of metaphor, naturally.

But it's just like my mother to cut through the metaphor and offer to do the thing direct.

Both things, as a matter of fact.

And the tears spring out again, despite my efforts at discipline.

All right, resume: A child who tries to create a choice that is not in the family's repertoire of choices will receive no support. Threat of abandonment, trump card in the game. What did I expect? I'm pushing the woman's Number-1 button, trying to get out from under my husband, trying to get his foot off my neck. She stuck with that bastard for forty years, and I'm telling her her life was wasted?

I tumble to it with a shock. I have come here to ask my mother if it's all right for me to leave Larry. She is busy specializing in the past, and I come to her bearing the future and say, "Tell me I have a right to save myself. Tell me you know what I'm talking about. Admit that your life and all that pain were for nothing."

She is aghast. I was always supposed to live a better life than she did. "Don't do what I did," she has said. But the catch was, "If you don't do what I did, how will I know you as my daughter?"

The way I am to better myself is clear. I am to stay married *and like it*. The dream is, *marriage with the right man*. And she has certified Larry as Mr. Right. Father of my plural children.

I put the brush down, suddenly tired, my anger spent. The handle clacks on the glass dressertop.

It has nothing to do with choosing the right man. Marriage is the woman-killer, the long train of little deaths. Marriage by the rules. Innovators come in and try to open them up, redistribute the tasks. But marriage simply does not work. Not with two people who are alive. If there is one live person and one dead person, it will work. My mother has demonstrated that.

I have demonstrated that you can make do with half a dead person. One live one, and one who is half dead and half alive.

I lean into the speckled mirror and examine my face. For

what? For a sign. But there is merely my face, looking gray and yellow. *It is the rare face that is beautiful in repose.* I don't know where I read that, but I am tired of hearing myself repeat it in front of this gray and yellow face.

Before you go, mottled lady, one more point from the catechism: The child who tries to create a choice that is outside the family's repertoire can expect to be exhausted for at least two years. So the family counselors say. It's that tough.

"Child," I say to this dim face that mouths speckled words to me through the glass, "you are in what's generally known as deep shit. Better get fired up. You are either going to hell or to the foster home."

12

The evening sky is just getting that hollow glassy look of the first hour after sundown. The yellowish glow and the black shadows through the woods are queerly affecting. In such stillness I would go transparent if I could. Even breathing is an intrusion.

I drive slowly over the clay road toward Gethsemane, easing the Malibu into the two deepest washouts and out again. These places have been cut deeper by the rain since I was through here just days ago. They will continue to get worse until the road is all but impassable, and then the county's road-grader will push its way through, scraping the clay down to a smooth track once again.

I have seen the road-grader at work in this spot two or three times in my life. The presence of other traffic on this road always seems a coincidence worth noting. But the road-grader is in a class by itself, more marvel than coincidence. So great is the authority vested in that great yellow dirt-moving machine—all the power and majesty and businesslike intent of the adult world—that *you* become the coincidence.

The first sign is the nasal snockering that ricochets through the trees; the second is the look of alert recognition on my father's face. He slows the car. When we round the next curve and see it, we pull to the side and stop. We are careful not to intrude in any way. The enameled cab is mounted high above a great silver blade, which is carried in front as a predator carries a smile. One man sits at the controls in the cab; he is The County Man. He sees us and completes two or three more maneuvers, the machine barreling its noise angrily through the quiet of the woods. Then

he throws levers to lift the blade, and twists the wheel to
bring the machine lurching to one side of the road and half-
way up the bank. He waves our car through. My father has
been waiting with geniune patience at the wheel. He returns
the wave as we start up again and pass. He has a kind of
tender respect for men who do roadwork, and indeed for any
fellow passengers on this road. The wave is not automatic.
Intelligence is exchanged, information given and received.
Whose car? Whose boy at the wheel? How many with him
and who do they belong to? Going where at this time of
day? The County Man, in his course, sees it all.

Two years ago, driving this road on the way back to the Rise after
my father's funeral, we came up behind a cart pulled by a farmer
on an ancient tractor. The cart had high wooden sides and a low
slatted tailgate. Inside was a small thin woman, standing with her
back to us and holding on to the front wall of the cart. She wore a
loose faded pink dress and a grayish figured sunbonnet, and her
hands were placed on the top rail. She stood much as a docile
child might stand in a playpen. She did not look behind her. Cal
and Curtis and Momma and I followed this odd processional for
over a mile, my father's rare patience visited upon us. We said
nothing at all to one another. The old couple turned off onto one
of the smaller dirt tracks. Neither of them ever turned to acknowledge us. The scene could have been a dream. But then, fu-
nerals can have that effect.

I pull the Malibu behind Carrie Dean's Ford, which is
parked in the chartreuse carport next to Garth's big Harley. Mo-
torcycles have a way of taking up all the space they occupy. Their
presence is decisive, and somehow the look of them challenges
my notion of comfort. The black leather saddlebags catch my
eye, with their silver skull and crossbones emblazoned beneath
the name Parrish, which is set out in semicircular type. Is it supposed to be a pun, I wonder?

Carrie Dean has heard the car on the gravel and is at the
screen door of the kitchen, the light behind her.

"Come on in!" her silhouette calls.

I resolve to put away the sudden distaste I feel for Garth and return to the peace of the evening.

"Coming," I say.

She swings out the door for me as I start up the back steps. At the top she slings a loose arm around my waist and draws me into the kitchen, letting the screen door slam to. The kitchen has a smell of frying. Garth and little Michael are still seated at the overhung Formica counter—the kitchen, too, has been re-modeled. They are finishing their supper of pork chops, green beans, mashed potatoes and squash patties. I stop to say hello, and Carrie Dean moves to the range top to remove the last pan and to turn off the fire.

A blond beard rakes across Garth's cheeks and crimps into uneasy curls behind each pink earlobe. The skin of his face and neck is ruddy, with sunburn or windburn; his lips as brightly col-ored as his young son's. He greets me with soft-spoken politeness. We do not know each other, really, and southern men have little to say to women who visit. He returns his attention to the child beside him.

"Finish what you got on your plate, and then we'll have some ice cream," he tells Michael.

This gentleness and domesticity encourage me, ease my dis-trust of the man. I have needed some sign, something to offset the dark glasses in the car after church and the Harley.

Carrie Dean wipes her hands on a kitchen towel and asks me, "Have you ever been to Mexico?"

"Nope."

"I thought you hadn't. Garth and me went there on our honeymoon, and I thought if you hadn't been, we'd look at the slides we took. We haven't seen them in a long time ourselves, and I borrowed a machine from Uncle Wesley. Now you have to tell me right off if that sounds like the worst idea you ever heard."

"No. I'd like to see them." Carrie Dean's animation easily carries me. Besides, nobody is obliged to tell the truth about other people's slide shows.

Carrie Dean hangs the towel on the refrigerator door handle

and starts off through the dining room, "Garth is going to finish giving Michael his supper, and then he'll come watch some with us. He's already had to promise not to say anything about how skinny I used to be. And don't you say it, either."

In the living room Garth, Jr., and Victoria are seated on the floor some two feet from the television, which is on loud. Carrie Dean switches it off and raises a finger to the yowls of protest.

"I told y'all before you started that you couldn't finish watching that show. And I also told you not to mess things up in here. Now say good evening to Jeannine and take your things to the bedroom, if you still want to play."

"Evenin, ma'am," they both mourn in my direction. Garth, Jr., troops balefully out of the room. Victoria stays long enough to show me the picture she has been coloring, a large grinning head with legs and arms attached without benefit of shoulders, torso, hips.

"Look at all those bright colors," I say, in the nonjudgmental way I have been trained to appraise children's art.

Victoria continues to hold the page out, looking at me. She does this until I say, "That's really pretty!" Then she scoops up crayons and paper and two naked Barbie dolls and scampers toward the hall.

"Those are sweet kids," I say to Carrie Dean, who is taping a white sheet to the wall.

"They do all right, in general," she replies and glances after her daughter.

I follow her eyes and remark, "I hate to see kids running with Barbie dolls in their hands, though. They could fall down and break a tooth on one of those breasts."

Carrie Dean is delighted, despite the look she throws me.

"Or poke an eye out," she concedes, and lets the grin spread over her face.

Before long we get the lights out and the slides clicking away. What we have before us is a kind of newlywed period piece: photos of Garth, unsmiling in the Elvis Presley-Ricky Nelson mode that was still popular in the early sixties. Photos of Carrie

Dean, sheepishly sexy in her two-piece bathing suit. Photos of the two of them, arms tensely intertwined and eyes watching their camera in some stranger's hands. Blank wide shots of the ocean and beach, of the famous Johnny Weismuller cliff at Acapulco, of Mexican plazas and sidewalk markets, of the hotel where they stayed, of the wrought-iron balcony that signified the window of their room as seen from the street, of the hotel across the street which represented the view from that window.

We laugh and hoot over the clothes Carrie Dean is wearing, and she claims she still has some of them in her closet. We laugh at the way her slip shows when she is regally posed for the camera, and at a series of shots of Garth trying to do trick dives into the hotel pool—particularly the shot that shows only his feet protruding above water.

Garth joins us after an interval. He sits with Michael firmly implanted in his lap, and Carrie Dean elicits factual husbandly comments from him.

"No, that little marketplace was in between the hotel and that big square. It wasn't anywheres near the water."

"Yeah, we got it for under five dollars American money."

Garth, Jr., and Victoria lurk in various doorways in their pajamas until they are told they can come in and watch. Then they giggle and dash in front of the screen and hold wiggly fingers in the lantern light until they are told they cannot.

Carrie Dean holds a slide on the screen showing a bespiked and bleeding Jesus being carried in a religious processional. She cues Michael, who duly removes a thumb from his mouth and offers a breathy solo of "Jesus loves me, this I know."

When the last slide clicks past and the machine light glares on the sheet, Garth, Jr., immediately moves to the piano and plays a song meant to be as impressive as Michael's singing. Victoria switches the television on again, and from the armchair Garth tells her which channel to turn to.

"Let me just move these pictures before something happens to them," Carrie Dean whispers to me. "No, you stay right where you are."

And so I sit as she moves about with the trays and projector. Garth and the children are absorbed in the television program. Garth, Jr., watches from the piano bench, for a time his fingers still on the keyboard. Michael struggles up from his daddy's lap and waddles noisily in his paper and plastic diaper across the room to Victoria. He crumples down next to her on the floor in front of the TV.

Carrie Dean returns and sits beside me on the rust sofa. The television program is about a high-powered medical team, and Carrie Dean begins to talk openly about the troubles they are having with Garth's mother, who has been diagnosed as having "bi-polar syndrome." I listen and offer what little information I've come across. I address some of this to Garth, since it is his mother we are discussing. But I am not certain whether or not he is listening. I try to stay balanced between them with eye contact until it becomes clear that Garth is reserving his eye contact for the television program.

"When Miz Parrish gets to feeling extra good like she does," Carrie Dean says, "can't nobody stand to be around her. She just goes like a buzz saw. And when she's kindly low with the bad feeling, she can't hardly stand anybody herself. It's hard to know how to be around her. Mr. Parrish says he's had about all he intends to put up with. I don't know what's going to happen to that poor woman."

Garth continues to watch television and to ignore us. Or to pretend to ignore us. I really don't understand what is supposed to go on here. Does this represent privacy? Are Carrie Dean and I supposed to go ahead and talk about whatever it is that we have been saving up to talk about? Are we all staying in the same room out of politeness?

Carrie Dean makes no move to "slip off into the kitchen," as my mother would put it, and before long I am too numb to think that it is even a possibility. This is the way life is, then. Conducted in the bosom of the family, no secrets. The television as hearth, all gathered round.

At nearly ten o'clock Carrie Dean checks her watch and says

with a sharp sigh, "Well. It's time for me to go and take care of Momma. I hate to have to send you off like this, but it's really no use for you to wait. By the time I get her her little pills and get her settled in for the night, it takes right at an hour."

She stands up meaningfully, and Garth snaps his gaze away from the program and says, "Time to put your mother to bed?"

"Unh-hunh. It's a little more than ten minutes to."

"I was thinking," he says, stealing one more quick glance at the TV, "about taking a little ride myself."

"Well, go on then."

Garth stands up, straightening his pants over his knees.

"All right, you kids, bedtime!" he growls. "I mean now, this minute. Y'all be some help to your mother, and get gone. That program is over with, and I want you in bed before I have to make the dust fly off them butts."

He whacks the back of the armchair with his red hand, and dust cooperatively flies. Garth, Jr., and Victoria dash from the room, leaving Michael asleep where he lies on the rug.

Victoria's voice comes from the hall. "Tell Granny I said good night, sleep tight, Momma."

"I will," Carrie Dean calls. "Leave the light on for her, but you better be asleep by the time I bring her in there."

"Yes, ma'am," comes the voice, more distant yet.

"I'm on my way," Garth calls from the back door.

I look through the dining room to see him standing in the doorway, silver and black helmet in his hands. He looks up and sees me and says, "Good seeing you, Jeannine, come back."

"Nice seeing you."

He pushes the screen door open and it swings to behind him with a loud whack. The next sound is of the Harley's starter being kicked, and then the roar of the engine. The carport serves as a kind of resonating chamber.

When I turn back to Carrie Dean, she is nearly out of the living room with the sleeping Michael sprawled over her arms. The child has one leg extended as though he were trying to touch something with his toes.

I follow them down the uncarpeted hall, and into the bedroom that used to be her brother Wally's. She tucks Michael securely into the lower of the two bunk beds. Then she straightens and gives Garth, Jr., a pat on his blanketed bottom.

"Good night, Buster."

"Good night, Momma."

When we are out in the hall again, she whispers, "I've been putting him to bed with little Garth ever since Momma started sleeping over here. Victoria is still little enough to sleep in the baby crib, and Momma would rather have her for a roommate than Michael. He's too much of a monkey."

"Your mother sleeps over here?"

"Well, we had to start doing it when her kidneys got so bad. She's just plumb scared to be by herself all night long, and I guess she's got a right to feel that way."

"My God."

"It works out all right. Or it would, if Michael would stay put. He'll sleep there in the bunk bed for about an hour, and then he's up again. And he won't go to sleep anywheres but in our bed. It's lucky we got a king-size bed, I reckon."

"How long have you been doing it like this?"

"About a year, a little more than a year."

We pass back through the living room on the way to the back door. The television is still on, apparently unnoticed. A thought manages to make its way through the dimness that is my brain: For a year and more, Garth and Carrie Dean have not slept alone together in their king-size bed.

"Where was Garth off to, just now?" I ask.

"Oh, riding. He likes to get away from the house and ride some, especially about this time of night when I have to be taking care of Momma. Can't say that I blame him even a little bit."

"Do you ever go with him?"

Carrie Dean's eyes pop wide. "Me? Get on that thing? No-thank-you-kindly, unh-unh! I don't disapprove or nothin', it just scares me half to death. Now my brothers, they don't seem to like it too well that Garth rides. But that would be anybody on a motorcycle, to them. Well. None of them has Momma on their back doorstep like he does, and I tell you, Jeannine, I'm right proud of Garth. There's not many men would put up with everything he has to in his own home. And I want to tell you something else: He hadn't never said one word about it."

"Amazing," I lie.

"I mean, not the first one."

"But then, you're the one that takes care of it all."

"She's my momma, not his."

"But if it ever gets to be his momma, let's say his daddy won't put up with her anymore—you'll be the one taking care of her, too."

"I'd sure do the best I can."

"And it's your house and your land in the first place."

"Jeannine! He's my husband, and he earns the living."

"And you feed and house your family."

"He's my *Husband*."

Both of us have been speaking as though we were explaining simple things to a halfwit. There is no anger, merely astonishment at the other's dangerous failure to grasp the essential facts of life. Obvious things. We both stop and look at each other tenderly, because neither holds any further hope for the other.

With a fingernail Carrie Dean scratches a spot of grime from the door handle.

"You know I wasn't head over heels with Garth when I married him, and couldn't have been. I was always so messed up over Billy Jim. Lord, Lord. But I thank my lucky stars that I finally had the sense to marry Garth."

"I have been wanting to ask you. Whatever happened to Billy Jim?"

"Billy Jim *Musgrove*?" There is a brief sparkle in the pale eyes—the heart of the question recognized—and then she shifts her gaze.

"Oh, him and his wife have about five little kids, I reckon. He married that girl from Collins—oh. You wouldn't know which one. Anyhow, a girl from Collins. He works in a dry goods store. They've done right well, by some standards. They had a fire in the old Musgrove house shortly after they married, and collected insurance. And about two years ago they had another one in the new house. And collected the insurance."

The eyes that she turns to me are mild. Blue blanks that refuse to comment.

"Two fires," I say. I hold up two fingers.

"Two fires."

"And insurance."

"And insurance." Her grin breaks through, and she throws both hands up, a loose gesture that disavows everything, anything. "I don't know a thing about it. But Billy Jim had the claims adjustors or whatever you call them swarming like ants."

"That rascal. Is he still good-looking?"

"I haven't seen him for quite a while, but he *was* getting pretty heavy. He still has that head of hair, though."

"Do you ever think what you would be doing if you had married him?"

"I think I'd be keepin' a close eye on my kitchen matches."

We laugh immoderately over this. When we have both wiped our eyes, Carrie Dean adds, "I'd also keep an ear tuned to which way the back door was slammin'."

"Ohhhh. Not really."

"Really. So I hear tell."

"Well, it's just like him, isn't it?"

"A lot just like him." She shakes her head slowly. "I've had a lot of dumb luck in my life, but marrying Garth was some of the best. Jeannine, I have come to love him and respect him more than I ever thought it was possible to love and respect anybody. And ever' day that goes by, I am less and less able to think how I would ever have got through my life without him."

I say nothing.

"Besides," she says, giving me a shoulder nudge, "ain't nobody else that would put up with me."

I pull away as though she'd slapped me. "Goddammit, that's just it. You aren't somebody just to be put up with. You deserve better, we all do. You deserve somebody that really loves you."

"Jeannine, honey, what are you talking about? Garth has loved me all his life. You know that."

She pauses for the obvious clarity of this to sink in. And then she begins again. "I was only saying that, something dumb to say. I know you and me don't think the same way anymore. I don't have even the slightest idea what kind of man you married. *Larry.*" She says the name with a shrug. "And I never can remember your married name, Lord have mercy."

"Lewis," I tell her.

"But Jeannine: Garth and I have known each other all our lives. The Parrishes are hardworking and honest, and I know that Garth is always going to take the best care he can of me and our kids. I know him the way I know my own soul. And in these times, with divorced men and women running around like they do, it's a comfort to know just who it is I'm married to, and till death do us part. I worry about it sometimes. I get to thinking, 'Why would any man want to hang around here with me and the kids and Momma?'"

I roll my eyes at this. It is like talking to my mother. The same categories.

"No, listen. I am so close to Garth in my heart that I would know it the minute his heart looked any other way but at me. I would know it the very second he looked at another woman. Do you know what I'm talking about? Do you feel that way about your husband?"

"No." It is the truth. I would, of course, have no way of knowing whether Larry had been looking at another woman, or merely at another account. And the thought of it makes me smile.

"You're fooling me," Carrie Dean concludes.

"No. I'm not."

"Well—do you love him?"

I take a breath. "Look, I don't even know how to talk about it. It seems like that's a question I would know the answer to—do

I love him? But I don't even really know. Not the way you think of love, not the way my mother does. Does he love me? Isn't that the next question? I think it ought to be. And yes, he loves me just the way you think of love coming from a man to a woman. He works hard, he earns money, he comes home at night. Eventually. But I tell you, Carrie Dean, I don't think love has much to do with it. I think it's more like brainwashing."

We look steadily into each other's eyes for a long moment.

"Have you prayed about it?"

Why is comedy so inconvenient? I try to force my smile into something that will look more like a grimace. I follow it with a sigh that is thoroughly genuine.

"In my fashion," I answer.

"Look," Carrie Dean says suddenly, grasping my arm, "I hate to leave you like this, but I really do have to see about Momma. She gets to worrying, and then she won't get to sleep the rest of the night."

"It's all right. I'm glad we had some time together."

We embrace for a moment, and then I, too, am out the back door and down the steps. As I walk round the front of the car and stand by the driver's door in the darkness, Carrie Dean leans out the back door.

"I'll pray for you," she calls softly. I see the silhouette of a final wave.

I get into the Malibu. Here I could afford a whole raft of wide-open smiles, but they are gone. Temporarily out of stock, as my husband might put it.

On the way home I leave the windows rolled down and speed down the blacktop with the night air rushing in.

The television in the other room suddenly blares to the point of pain. I come down the hall and through the doorway of the family room. I see Laura, just eighteen months old, staring wide-eyed a bare two feet from the screen. A tremor of ancient anger and fear shoot through me. I say, trying for a calm voice but one loud enough to be heard over or through the deafening noise, "Can't we turn this thing down?"

The man in coveralls, sitting with his back to me, jerks erect. With a sudden startled grating of chair and table, he jumps to his feet and whirls to face me. Features contorted in rage, knife in hand. "You may yell at your own husband, but don't you yell at me like that. The very idea! Not in my house!" Behind him the onions roll off the table and tumble to the floor in confusion.

"Daddy, I—the televison is so loud! I didn't mean to startle you. I was trying to be heard over the television!"

"You can talk ugly to your husband, but don't you try it with your daddy. The very idea." The teeth clenched, chin forward, lower lip drawn upward in a hairline of control. Familiar from my childhood. Had he been drinking? Would he strike me? The knife? "The very idea." The fury is receding into disgust. Arms twitching with blows not given, head turning to inflict short glances of violence still cherished.

The crisis is past. But there is still the blame. To contradict is to show lack of respect.

My father kneels to adjust the volume on the TV set with the point of his knife. The knob has somehow fallen lost and will never be replaced; instead, erratic piles of table knives and screwdrivers appear upon the console and nearby. Because his hands still tremble, the television continues to roar unabated. "I turned it up," he yells above the noise, his face a blotch of reflected reds and greens, "because that child was sitting so close. Her ears are bad. She couldn't hear it."

"Her ears are fine." My own anger flares. "She just has to be reminded to sit farther back."

The television is drowned out in the tide of his resurging fury. "Then you remind her. You train that child, that's your job. Don't you come here and holler like that at your daddy when your child can't hear. You can do that to your husband at home. Don't you try it here." He jabs inside the console and the volume goes down. He gets to his feet and his voice switches keys, now a wheedling taunt. "It made you mad, didn't it? You came running in here mad as hell and lit into your old daddy. It made you mad, didn't it?"

"I deliberately took the time to keep my voice calm."

"You're perfect, aren't you? Miss Perfect. You're just perfect. You were mad, Jeannine; be big enough to admit it. Come in here screaming like a banshee. Tell me, are you perfect?" Eyes glistening, darting again.

I leave the room, leave Laura watching television, leave the house. Outside, the warm Mississippi night blesses and soothes. I walk in the grass, walk the gravel path, take off my shoes and feel the fine fine cold dirt of the driveway, stand under the pecan tree, gape upward at the bright stars in vaporous southern velvet, try to recall how awesome it all used to be. I stop shaking, stop trying to regulate the gusts of sobbing that open and shut like doors in a cheap hotel corridor at night.

And what was he doing at the table? Peeling onions. His prize onions. "Your old daddy will have to cook for you."

I go back into the house, past my daughter watching television in peace, head for my bedroom. I am thinking of Larry, that he will be through with his business in New Orleans tomorrow. Tomorrow we can leave. I do not remember until I walk into the room that my mother is sewing in here tonight. She sits at the sewing machine before the window, hand-stitching a hem in a blue cotton jump suit for Laura. She has overheard everything, of course. The yelling, certainly; probably my crying outside, too.

And there is a word for the way she greets me, that southern word: sniggering. The woman is absolutely awash in suppressed giggles. Her face is pink with effort, her eyes merry and conspiratorial. They insist that I know what is so

*funny and why. She wipes tears from them. She motions me
to sit down on the sewing machine console, and I do. Then
she lays her head in my lap and puts her arms around me
and laughs a little more noisily. The sounds move from her
sinuses into her throat. Her body shakes with laughter.*

*I sit and hold her, rigid as an iron bedpost. I under-
stand by now: It is I who am so funny. So foolish. To go up
against that frightening man, to think I could hold my own.*

Something took place in that room on that night, with the
laughter, the embrace. A welcome into the sisterhood at last, the
sorority of the hopelessly oppressed. I was being instructed once
again: I had better learn to find things funny.

How much time I have wasted. Looking for the connection
with my mother, with Carrie Dean. With Larry. They see me, of
course, exactly as I see them. They observe that there is a part of
my experience which I refuse to integrate.

Clouds have blanked out the moon and stars over the Rise. I
drive the highway alone at this hour, with the sky above me black
and unadorned.

How is it that life gets so badly arranged? What is manifestly
needed here is a competent casting director. Carrie Dean is so
obviously the daughter my mother longs for—dedicated mother,
submissive wife, churchgoer, sings in the choir, for heavensake.
Carrie Dean would adore having my mother right there in the
trailer; why, Momma would have that garden put shipshape in a
minute. And in the evenings they could raise chickens and devour
the grandchildren who would be so conveniently nearby. And
Larry? Larry is the husband Momma would have wished for herself. How is it that I have got myself wedged in between all the
things my mother, who insists that she loves me to the point of
killing me for my own good, wants for herself?

13

I have a history of non-escapes. Given the French Foreign Legion, I will hedge my bets and fly into the outposts of the Regular Army every time.

I sit up in bed and look around. This is my mother's house, all right. I have done it again. Another stunt in the tradition of Wrong-Way Corrigan.

The light shimmers in, announcing that another day is out there waiting. I lie back down on the pillows.

Incredibly enough, the last time I wanted to run away, I ended up visiting Larry's parents. A winter home off Hilton Head *sounds* like a vacation. But it was in fact just one more bivouac. And as I recall my military terminology, a bivouac is not merely a temporary encampment, but most specifically one that is "without shelter or protection from enemy fire." But a change of scene is a change of scene.

Q: How can you run away without looking like you're leaving?

A: Visit relatives.

I was again not adjusting, as Larry diagnosed. He was right. I wasn't adjusting, but I hadn't turned all the lights off upstairs, either. I still had a few pieces of furniture left up there, and no intention of checking out early. That is to say, I had an idea what was wrong with me, and it amounted to the design of our life.

That design has been that Larry has a job in which he travels. I have a job in which I take up the slack. When he is gone, I have the furnace repaired, the snow shoveled, the grass cut, the bills out on time. I get myself to work, Laura to school and back home again. I book the weekends with social engagements and baby-sitters. I pick up Larry's check and sometimes Larry himself from the office or airport. Larry-himself is tired and overworked. I am not adjusting.

The travel began in earnest about the time Laura was born. He would fly away every week for one night or two or three. Uninspiring places: Cleveland, Detroit, Buffalo. But he was gone. He would return late at night, exhausted, complaining about airline food. I waited up for him, milk and cookies, a joke between us.

"Thanks, Mom."

He hated the travel, he said. He missed me; he hated missing a single day of Laura's growing and changing. I hated it, too. I hated the way my life stood still for the time he was away. I hated worrying about whether his flights would arrive, hated worrying that he would fall asleep driving from the airport to hotel or hotel to airport or airport to home. I began to hate the way he traveled during the week and used the nights and weekends home to rest from traveling.

I began to doubt that he hated it.

I began to defend airline food.

Larry began to grow weary of the searching conversations that I would start just at bedtime on the nights he was home. He didn't like such conversations, fell asleep in the middle of them. I felt guilty when he woke in the morning tired, and guiltier when he slogged off to work at 6:45. He suggested that I get away. He suggested that I take Laura and get away.

By that time it was winter, and Laura nearly a year old. What I needed, he decided, was someplace warm, away from the Iowa snows. And with his parents wintering in South Carolina and my mother lifing it in Mississippi, the Sun Belt was a shoo-in. I could take my choice, and do a little maintenance on the family network to justify the trip. I was abashed at Larry's kindness and understanding. I was ashamed of myself.

I was also ashamed of the way I made the choice between his mother and mine. I said to myself, "Who runs the best hotel?" And since to my knowledge the best hotels are not conspicuously strewn with dead-bug carcasses, I chose his mother.

In South Carolina with Grandma and Grandpa Lewis, Laura and I walked the beach, dabbled feet and ankles in the cold waves, and searched in vain for seashells. We swam in the heated pool and sunned on chaises. We drank tall iced drinks in our bathing suits, orange pop for Laura, rum and tonic for the grown-ups—rum, since it is still the daytime beverage of choice for sailors, even retired commmanders. Evenings we had red snapper and bluefish and Gulf shrimp on the patio along with our coastal sunsets and triple martinis.

There was one night, after I had three of Father Lewis' martinis and the sun had blazed recklessly down into the nearest ocean, when I thought: "I'm warming to these chilly folks. I'm ready to talk turkey. I can adjust as well as the next person." And sure enough, right there over the hors d'oeuvres I burbled, "Let's tell secrets! I'm ready! What do you want to know?"

Mother Lewis' reply was prompt and dry, served up like the best of her husband's oversize cocktails.

"Not a thing," she said.

I thought about it in the morning. When my head had come back together. When it became clear that the small face next to my ear possessed a disproportionately loud voice, and was not going away until I got up. And so I got up, and found the cereal and orange juice and milk for Laura's breakfast. I stood leaning on the kitchen counter with my arms clasped over my stomach and my eyes closed while she munched and chattered. And I thought about it.

This is why I had married into this family, wasn't it? I liked it that they were impersonal. They didn't crowd you. They didn't assume that they had all the answers as well as a line on your every sordid motive. That was *my* family. The Lewises were different. They didn't want anything to do with your personal stuff. You name it—questions, answers, comments, grievances, joys, sorrows, worries, triumphs, failures, plus or minus points on the adjustment scale. If it was personal, it was your business.

I found these attitudes so appealing in Larry because to me they looked like generosity. Imagine! Someone who didn't pretend to know you like a dime-store religious tract.

I took it that my feelings and my individuality would be respected. I failed to anticipate that they would be ignored.

It's very difficult to read somebody else's rulebook. It took me the better part of ten years to figure out that the Lewises had one. During those years I would have said that Larry never criticized me. True, he never spoke an unkind word. But whether or not I had been criticized is a matter of how you read the rules.

Or more precisely, whose rules you're reading. Sometimes there's a translation problem. After I got to know Larry's family better and had begun to notice the unusual energy Larry would put into reminding me to lock the door, buckle my seat belt, put plastic ties on the garbage bags and keep the lint filter on the clothes dryer empty, I began to get a clearer picture.

When Laura was born and Larry's mother came to help, she washed and folded clothes, made underwear white and made closets appear to consist of 90 percent space.

Larry joked, "So this is what it's like to be married!"

Another clue.

Another: In Mother Lewis' kitchen Larry's father would appear like the spirit of the Spanish Inquisition. Commanderlike, he would bark a series of questions to his wife. Is the roast set? Is the oven preheated? Is the meat thermometer inserted to the proper point? Is the serving platter warmed? The electric carving knife plugged in? The Bordeaux at room temperature?

Larry's mother would meet such assaults with an answering volley. I told you to buy sirloin tip, not tenderloin. You haven't started the charcoal. The handle on this knife is loose. The leaf still isn't in the dining room table, and I can't put the cloth on until you bring the table pads up from the basement.

For some time I assumed that they were pilot and copilot, an efficient team beamed in on running a tight ship. Finally it struck me: *This was fighting!* This was marital conflict without benefit of threats, accusations, slurs on family, raised voices, sound effects of flesh on flesh.

In the Lewis family you do not get personal with people. If you have a grievance, you set aside your precious reactions. What you do is, you wait until you catch them in some infraction of the rules. Then you take your shot under cover.

Decoding this set of signals was of some help to me. I began to understand that Larry possessed such a thing as anger, and that seat belts, garbage bags, and so forth were his vocabulary for it. What wasn't so clear was how I was to fight back. I, and not Larry, would always be the one with keys left dangling in the lock, Tupperware stowed in the wrong dishwasher rack, a full lint filter.

In time I decoded other things. First to tumble was the Lewis Reflex. That was almost too easy. The Lewis Reflex is: *Keep It Clean.* When I applied myself to Keeping It Clean, I stumbled across something bigger: the Lewis Family Rule. Translated, this one reads: *If you're functioning, you're okay.*

This is the kingpin rule. It is notably efficient for dealing with distractions that might interfere with Keeping It Clean. Distractions such as mood, preference, inclination, desire, illness or physical disability. Such things can be swept aside in a trice.

"You're awake, so you must be ready to get up."

"You've played eighteen holes of golf, so you must have plenty of energy."

If you are functioning—if a flicker of life can be espied or deduced in any way, shape or form—you are accountable. You must perform to standard.

On the other hand, should you find yourself in ambiguous circumstances, the family rule comes in handy. All you have to do to put yourself above suspicion is cite a recently completed function.

"Of course I like being retired. I just reorganized the basement crawl space."

"Of course we love having the grandchildren visit. I Scotch-garded the guest towels just this morning."

An *impending* function will do nearly as well.

"I'm delighted that we'll be having so much time together. I'll just edge the sidewalk and repot these plants first."

If you're functioning, you're okay. As a family rule this has real versatility in addition to being practically airtight. But just in case, it paves the way for another clincher, in the form of the Lewis Therapeutic Code: *If you just get up and function, you'll be okay.*

Here is a tidy fallback, in the unlikely event that a person is managing to suppress all vital signs.

Now these rules are writ fairly large. I can't think of what took me so long to see them. It must have been the translating, or perhaps just the absence of fine print, that threw me.

One thing for sure: This kind of thinking didn't go well with a hangover. But the Lewis rule is: You only drink what you can handle. Therefore I didn't have a hangover. Not that morning or any other.

Still wincing at the day's uncommon brilliance, I rinsed Laura's breakfast dishes over the disposal and wiped away the excess water, which would leave spots. I put the dishes in the correct rack of the dishwasher, and went to help Laura into her swimsuit. Eight o'clock in the morning is the time to walk the beach, and I would, of course, walk with the family.

I had got up and functioned, therefore I was okay.

As for my offer of confidence the night before, I decided to stop feeling robbed. My mother-in-law made perfect sense. A family with no fine print in the rulebook would have no traffic with secrets.

The heat and humidity begin to rise. I lie here in my bed in my mother's house, neither up nor functioning. Why should I bother, when the house is so busy around me, fomenting in its primal soup? Not only dust and dead bugs, but secrets in the very air, secrets and subtexts and covert reasons and hidden agendas and all the rest that remains unspoken, all these things nudging at the closet doors.

I am, as I have said, a great believer in the influence of family life. I know just why my husband, The Man Who Knew Computers, became the joker in his family. I know why he chose me. He needed somebody with lower standards, some way to sidestep the pressure.

For, as many sons are, my husband is the star of his family.

With his mother and father he is unruly and impertinent. He insults his father's genes, his mother's quicksand memory. He behaves exactly as he is expected to behave. For, as many stars are, my husband is a star on somebody else's terms. Not his own.

If the terms were his, he would advance at the Lewis family table such subjects as the trade-offs between profits and sales strategies, the viability of investments in industrial real estate, the ethics of bribery in Third World economic bargaining. These are the subjects in which he is expert, in which he is in his own right a star. But a son has no honor at his father's dinner table. At his father's table my husband discusses his father's genes, his mother's memory.

They love him for it. They love him for it the way I love him for it, and for many of the same reasons. Even for the Lewises, the rules are too much burden. They are weary of being right all the time. They cannot give up the lash, but they have raised up a son who can take away the sting.

Father Lewis: "I see you're showing more forehead than you used to."

Larry: "It's because I inherited defective genes."

Mother Lewis: "I didn't remember you being quite so thin on top myself."

Larry: "That's okay, Mom, I'm just glad when you remember my name."

Mother Lewis: "Oh, honey . . . "

Larry: "Honey's good. That'll do."

Father Lewis: "My father had a full head of hair till the day he died. But your mother's father was bald. You probably take after him."

Larry: "Why did you marry this man, Mother? Can you remember that?"

Countless family dinners are passed in this way. Well: Probably they could be counted, since we are together so seldom, but it would be a cruel exercise. These exchanges over dinner are not meant as conversations, anyway; they are merely rituals. Rituals are meant to extend the past into a present that might appear to have little relevance. They provide a form when the content might be threatening or simply too much trouble. Rituals, like the family, provide continuity. They fall together like Sodom and Gomorrah.

And so they rarely fall. Sons do their part by remaining sons in their fathers' houses. In their own it is a different matter.

There is a decisive point when a son becomes the father in his own house. I watched Cal do it, and could not believe my eyes. When Larry did it, I shut them.

I stopped hating it when he flew away on his business junkets. I began hating it when he came back home. There were months on end when every time he got near an airplane I'd find myself half-thinking: Maybe it'll crash.

I had married a son and was now wedded to the father. I found myself living, like Grandma Hinton, with the enemy. And starving this one was out of the question. Larry took half his meals in hotel restaurants and airplanes.

Well: How did it start? Things never start. They just materialize out of some secret you've been keeping from yourself. You know and you don't know, and doing both at once takes a good deal of energy. So you are a little spacy, walking around trying not to decide whether to know or not know. Meanwhile the library sends you the second overdue notice, this one on yellow paper signifying bureaucratic alert. The nursery school matriarch points out sweetly once again that your child is becoming anxious about being the last to be retrieved every day. You get used to the yellow parking violations envelope, same shade of yellow, tucked under the windshield wiper the way you get used to lines in supermarkets and urine on the sheets.

I was having one of those periods last fall. Fall is in any case the time people have picked out to let you know that your life isn't your own. So when fall arrives and you haven't worked out a ride pool for nursery school and your kid's dresser drawers are still full of swimsuits and belly-peeker tops, you know they've got you.

Even I knew they had me. But instead of bustling about righting things in the football-inspired Iowa weather, I found myself drifting through the days trimming split ends from my hair, and evenings quite content to lie on the carpet in Laura's room while she slept.

What I was doing was listening to the thwang and thunk of acorns pelting the rain gutters. A sign of a severe winter, all those acorns. But most things that happen in Iowa in the fall are signs of a severe winter.

As often as not I fell asleep on Laura's soft green carpet, the most peaceful sleep imaginable. The child's heavy, regular breath was comfort against the war of acorns going on in the night. But I would wake when Larry pushed open the back door downstairs.

I have always had the ability to come fully awake in seconds. It's not always needed. Larry's routine, for example, is dependable. He shuts the door with a bang and locks it, throws his keys on the kitchen counter and walks through the living room to the front closet, where he prefers to hang his jackets. He glances at the mail as he pulls the newspaper from underneath it on the hall table and heads for the bathroom.

A peculiarity he has maintained since childhood: The determination to use his own bathroom, and only his own bathroom, for what must have always been for him the most intimate moment of the day. He admitted to me that, as a kindergartener, he raced home at noon with his empty black construction-worker's lunch box banging against his knickered knees. Home, to his own bathroom.

Presumably the newspaper was a later refinement.

With this sequence being set in motion downstairs, I had plenty of leisure to pull on the light cord in Laura's closet and set about digging through the box of her winter clothes. My object was to come up with some items for school the next day, some long-sleeved shirt, some pair of pants not too badly wrinkled. I pulled out a green jersey in fair shape and, with my hand forced down into the nether recesses of the box, located the coordinating corduroys by feel.

By the dim bulb light I judged both items presentable, though the pants would be as short on her as the pair she wore that day. Well. She had to have new ones, that was all. This week for sure.

I smoothed the outfit on the carpet in the rectangle of light, and set two of Laura's large storybooks on the jersey for an overnight press. I reached again for the light cord, but something about the arrangement on the floor arrested my attention. The clothing as I had laid it out on the floor looked like a flattened child, the rib cage crushed in. Books are an unusual weapon. Fired from an unseen catapult, an invasion of Mongol Jesuits.

I pulled the cord and sat in the dark.

It wasn't that I didn't hear Larry come up the stairs, but that it seemed irrelevant. I was utterly startled when he flipped on the overhead light in the room.

"Where is everybody tonight? What's going on in here, how come the place looks deserted?" Larry's habit, questions fired in volleys. One was, after all, accountable.

"I'm setting out Laura's clothes," I whispered. "Turn out that light, she's asleep."

"What do you mean? The light doesn't bother her. That kid could sleep through an explosion." He crossed the carpet to Laura's bed to demonstrate his point.

Can it be mere ignorance, after ten years of marriage, that lets this man think I do not mind this assault of the light? If I were to mention it, he would say: "I'm *sorry*. I didn't realize you felt so strongly about it." And he would be injured, disapproving. Pressed to the point, he would say he finds me hypercritical, and what defense have I? If I say nothing, he does not know the difference.

Or am I wrong? Is there a small thrill of victory with each unacknowledged violation? Can there be any equality, finally, if I know his preferences down to his preferred weight of fly rod, and he will not learn how I like to use my wits to see in the dark? It is a willful act, surely, not to learn. It is a willful act to inflict one's own version of order upon another, one's own brand of approach.

How many times has he tried to find me in a dark room, not by adjusting his own eyes to see as I do, but by inflicting the light? If I am in a room without light, is it not presumptuous for him to enter it and throw the switch?

When he has exposed me to his satisfaction, he runs a crowd of chatter into the room. Not my silence but his noise fills the air, chokes the atmosphere. I am crowded out. Under his questioning, I no longer possess even myself. How can this fail to be harassment?

And these matters are all so trivial, so beyond discussion. How to argue with my husband about whether the light belongs on or off? It may be that marriages do not break in the crush of events but collapse under the weight of accumulation. Yes. Layer upon layer, built up like lacquer boxes to a hard sheen and brittleness. Fragility.

I watched my husband across the room, feeling porcelain-fragile, lacquer-box brittle.

"Look at this kid!" he exclaimed, and turned on the bedside lamp to show her more clearly. "Sound asleep, prettiest little thing I ever saw." He bent over to kiss her cheek, noisily. It was true that she did not even stir. She has slept like this since she was born. It has seemed a kind of feat, not only to Larry and me but to friends of ours who routinely suffered the nighttime tyrannies of their small children.

Larry lifted the covers to settle them around her, and said sharply, "How come she's not wearing warm pajamas? She'll freeze her little tail off if she kicks the covers off tonight. It's supposed to be the first frost, didn't you know that? Haven't you been listening to the radio?"

I didn't and hadn't. I had given up reading the newspaper, and lately even the FM station had seemed irritating and artificial. When I had the choice, I preferred silence. In the house, and even in the car, I preferred silence, darkness, isolation and warmth. All these had become scarce that fall. At least I had come to terms with the acorns.

From my position on the floor I turned back to the box in

the closet and rummaged for Laura's winter sleepers. Her fuzzies, she called them. I located one set deep in the box by its plastic sole. I extracted it and tossed it to Larry.

He loved to dress Laura while she slept her impossible, imperturbable sleep. He propped her up against his pinstriped chest and lifted the blue summer nightgown efficiently up and over her head. Her small arms swung down loosely out of the armholes. The eyelids didn't even flutter. Larry hugged and kissed her in delight, and then stuffed her slack limbs, one after another, into the cozy red sleeper suit and zipped it from toe to neck. When the neck snap proved difficult, he examined the feet, where her toes made the plastic swell tight.

"These things are too small!" he said. "Look at that! Do you see that?"

"Yeah."

"They'll cut off the circulation in her feet!"

"Okay."

I rose and looked on top of Laura's chest of drawers for the nail scissors. I had used them to cut her small fingernails just before bed. The snippets were still heaped on the doily; I hadn't gotten around to throwing them away. The sharp little scissors had slid underneath the cloth, but I retrieved them by feel. You can get the kind of nail scissors with blunt knobs on the ends to use with children, but I have never needed them with Laura. From babyhood she has been content to sit perfectly still and watch my scissors peel away the transparent tips of her fingernails.

I lifted one of the pajamaed feet from her father's grasp. Holding it firmly, I inserted one point of the scissors into a wrinkle of the plastic at the small toe. I snipped a jagged line across to the opposite seam where the plastic met fabric, and did the same to the other foot. Laura's toes slid through the openings like schools of slow minnows.

Ignoring Larry's exaggerated noises of astonishment, I tucked the small legs back under the covers and dropped the nail scissors on top of the chest of drawers. Larry finished settling her roughly back into her pillows, and I heard him land several more loud kisses. I put out the bedside light and shut off the overhead switch beside the door.

"I just love manhandling her like that while she's sleeping," he exclaimed happily, catching up with me in the hall and throwing an arm about my neck. "It doesn't matter what you do, she never wakes up. I really treat her roughly, too. It's the most amazing thing."

He squeezed me so that my face was near his, and kissed me.

Larry's exuberance often has the effect of making me feel dead. I was in the habit of admiring his fondness for Laura, his fatherly and husbandly devotions. His sense of order has always complemented mine. He gives his attention to what I think of as necessary maintenance—to the environment, to all the external machinery of our complicated and quite ordinary suburban lives. Without him, I know none of it would work. Without him, I would fail to notice something essential—that the basement had flooded, that Laura had no shoes. The days would fail to mesh into units of weeks and months, the solar system would slip into geocentricity. I was in the habit of being grateful.

The fact that I suddenly hated everything he did made me feel irrational, more than slightly crazy. I thought about this while I got our supper, listening to his stories of the day with the front part of my brain but keeping something logged in the back. I wasn't even sure what it was. Only one thought came through clearly, and this was not until we sat in the dining room while Larry had dessert. I had become aware of the sound of his chewing and his fork scraping the ribbed china plate. The thought that came to me was: Turning on a light switch in a dark room is probably not grounds for divorce.

On the other hand, denying a husband his connubial rights is. Of this legality concerning marriage, Larry reminded me. Jokingly, of course.

The power of a joke should never be underestimated. In fact, the two, joking and power, go together like Bob Hope and

Uncle Sam. In any situation you can tell who is in power by who is getting the laughs.

In his family career as son and joker, Larry had developed a specialty of turning a given issue inside out. He could state the truth in such a way that it became ludicrous.

Jeannine: "Larry, my folks called and said they may come visit us some weekend this spring."

Larry: "Did you tell them we're already going to the movies that night?"

This particular gift of his held a powerful attraction for me. My understanding of life was that if you recognized a problem, you were stuck with it. You had to worry a lot and feel helpless. Naturally I would be attracted to someone who could show me that all you had to do was restate the problem and laugh at it, and it disappeared. Anything you can laugh at has no power. At least not while you're laughing.

With Larry I got the chance to laugh at my mother, my father, higher education, finding a job, earning a living, cooking, pregnancy, giving birth, motherhood, car pools, chicken pox and feminism. I got many chances to laugh at myself. But somehow the skill proved not to be transferable. If I meant to laugh my way through life, I would have to depend on him. A formula, then. The key to a lock I have been fumbling at for years: Two things are capable of binding a woman to a man. Sex is the first. Laughter is the second.

Every now and again some visiting businessman at a dinner party is naive enough or drunk enough to complain aloud that his wife has no sense of humor. Specifically, that she never thinks his jokes are funny. I am embarrassed the way you are always embarrassed for people who display their sympathy bids without being able to read the message printed on the other side. The message invariably reads, "Look, chump, there's a war on."

It comes down to this: You can only laugh with someone who is on your side. Or more precisely, with someone you believe to be on your side. There is a shade of difference. Early in our marriage, when we were still sorting out shower schedules, elec-

tric blanket privileges and other issues that people who live together must sort out, Larry developed a habit of slipping an arm
around me at parties and making funny remarks to friends. The
remarks would have to do with our progress with the rules, and
they would go like this: "Jeannine and I can't agree on what to do
with leftovers. She wants to keep everything. I want to throw
everything out. So we compromise. We keep everything for three
weeks, and then we throw it out."

The arm fooled me for a long time, and I laughed along with
everyone else.

When I understood things better, I tried to defend myself.
"Larry! That's not fair!"

That way I learned what I must have forgotten since grade
school: You can't convince people not to laugh. Sincerity and
rectitude are losing moves against a good laugh. And so I tried
topping him.

"Oh, yeah? I notice that you save things. You save your shit
all day long for the home bathroom."

A deeply inappropriate and unfunny remark. I was not adjusting.

After I tried that, Larry remained with his arm around me
after the embarrassed circle had dispersed. He spoke kindly.

"You need a coaster for that glass, Jeannine."

And he was right. As far as I could see, I had two ways to
"adjust": I could be one of those wives who dimpled prettily and
responded with, "Oh, *you!*" Or I could be one of those wives who
pretended patience, or pretended deafness, or pretended to be
single and living on another planet. The last one came to me
most naturally, and now I think of it, I am certain that there have
been dinner parties this last year or so during which Larry has remarked to some giggling person that his wife has no sense of
humor.

Sex and laughter. I didn't take the formula far enough,
didn't show that when one goes, the other is bound to follow.
That would have saved me a lot of trouble.

* * *

I believe I could have gone on indefinitely having stomachaches or finding a spot of mending to do until two A.M. Larry and I had never had anything like "a sexual problem." Sex was a matter of convenience. If I lay in bed beside Larry and he felt like "a little roll in the hay"—it was Richard Benjamin's line in some movie, the joke being that Larry utterly detests Richard Benjamin—then we had "a little roll in the hay." Sex was not something Larry needed to plan ahead of time, or come looking for. He had always found me rather too keen.

"It isn't very exciting for me when you're so willing," he told me early on. But for years I could never quite manage to be elusive enough. Not convincingly. Not on Larry's schedule of conquest, let alone on his schedule of appearances at home in our bed.

In my new mode of feeling about him rather as he felt about Richard Benjamin, I found that if I merely absented myself at bedtime, the subject had no way of being addressed.

And this new mode, too, must have had a beginning, must have materialized from something. Some germinal episode, and I can only think of one, the time last fall when I came upon Larry—a very drunken Larry to be sure—kissing a woman at a lawn party. It was nothing, he insisted, he was drunk; I had never had any reason to suspect his behavior and he would not accept any accusations. He was drunk; it happened. He would not apologize, he said; he was merely under the influence, too much booze, too much flirtation, he was only human after all. He hadn't meant to cause me pain, but he couldn't say he was sorry, either. It happened! It was nothing! It wasn't as though he had slept with her. It wasn't as though it was anything but harmless.

I tried to take it as that. I had to, since Larry refused to have me belabor the incident. But my husband was clearly in the wrong, was he not? And in a way that caused me, his beloved, searing pain and a roiling humiliation. Yet such feelings of mine did not have sufficient weight with him to call for an apology. How had I become this person of no account? How, when by Larry's own impatient assurance, I was "loved"?

I could not make the pieces fit. In ten years of marriage the rules had changed. In my understanding of the way we were to go through life together, I didn't have the freedom to embrace another man in that way. Was I wrong? Such a naive picture of marriage—but not one I had dredged up from a hope chest to carry on our wedding day. No. I feared marriage, the trap it presented. That was my experience of my parents' killing contract, my only notion of what marriage meant, apart from Larry's assurances. It was Larry, with his legacy of orderly kitchens and predictable cocktail hours and meals produced in well-meshed tandem, Larry who told me over and over that we could make it work. We two.

If I carried that dated picture with me on our wedding day, it was my something borrowed. Borrowed from the bridegroom, the picture he said he wanted.

In our early married years, with all the commerce at graduate school and no child at home, I had turned down any number of appealing young men on the strength of what Larry wanted. What Larry insisted he needed: a two-party marriage. No men under the bed. He could not bear to share me ever, he said, and he meant past, present or future. On the one occasion early in our dating when I ventured to discuss other lovers, he stopped me mid-sentence. We were at dinner; we had to leave the restaurant.

"I can't be that modern," he said, once we were safely back in his apartment. "It makes me want to throw up. I can't put that any more nicely. It's just a physical fact. I can't stand to think of you with anyone else."

I was moved beyond words. I had seen how affected he was, and was convinced. I kept my knowledge to myself to save him pain.

A big mistake; a classic of its kind. Never give up any part of the truth about yourself for someone else's convenience—that is what I have learned. I was years catching up with all I gave away in that single early act of compassion. I saw it as compassion at the time; actually, it was robbery.

And it set precedents. In later years I kept quiet when he

would say, "I trust myself to handle an affair, but I don't trust you."

I would hear this whenever some friend's marriage would seize up over infidelity. And I was complimented. I took the statement as a measure of Larry's touching vulnerability. In that way I missed the whole other operative range of what he was saying: that since he was more trustworthy, he should have more privileges.

And less to answer for.

It surprises me how the memory returns so easily. So familiar and so unwanted, a return like the return of nausea with each morning of pregnancy. It was nothing; that is what I was told. It was nothing, then. It was nothing that my husband could have too much to drink at a party, nothing that he could make a serious and most physically materialized pass at a woman, a quasi-friend. And it might have been nothing, except that I had come upon them halfway along, this woman's shoulders and breasts shining in the full September moonlight behind McGaffrey's hedge, my husband bent over them. A German beer garden, the theme had been, outdoors and in September rather than October, for it is Iowa after all, and one does not rely on October moonlight for a garden party. One does not rely on much.

It was nothing and I was not to dwell on it and truly I do not wish to remember as well as I do but my stomach, like Larry's, is a slow learner. It begins to stir at the merest whiff of memory. I stood there, damp privet prickling at my arm—the hour was late enough to invite the dew—for the eternity it took my eyes to decide to recognize that back, that shirt, that bend of the neck. I must have closed my eyes to steady myself from the swoon, the swan song of my rising stomach, just as the woman—Clara Condon, it was, or does it matter?—opened hers. For she was the one who breathed my name stark in that moonlight before I had the sense to turn and run.

There can be no quarrel with the fact that Larry was drunk. I myself saw him shift and stagger at the turn of events, slur out my name in a foggy echo of Clara's alarm. Days afterward, weeks, I heard that tone each time he said my name The sound sent a fresh shiver of disgust coiling upward into my throat, and I could not help it.

We came home to the same house that night; it is the bitter condition of married couples in small communities to know the name, and to have to come home to the same house at one time if not at another. And there came a time days later when we talked, when I sat sobbing and listening to him tell me earnestly that he had not meant anything; he was drunk, had I ever seen him drunk before as he was that night? Had I ever a reason before to think he would betray me? He was drunk; he didn't even think of Clara; he didn't know what he was doing, but he wasn't going to bed with her—that he knew.

"I saw enough to know that if I hadn't come along—"

"I know what you saw. I went too far, I admit, but you have no cause to jump to conclusions. You have no right to assume."

"I saw enough . . ." I wanted to say more but could not, because of the activity of my stomach. "I saw enough."

Larry stood up, his eyes focused sharp. "I wish I'd never tried to explain things to you. It never ends. All right then, I'm not sorry. I did what I did, and I'm not ashamed of myself. I was feeling what I was feeling, sex between us has been a chore for years as far as I'm concerned, I did what I did, but I won't spend my life apologizing. As far as I'm concerned, the subject is closed."

" 'Sex between us has been a chore for years?' " I repeated, but the words now played to an empty room. Larry had turned on his heel and left.

"Wait a minute," I yelled at him, running to the hall. "You son of a bitch, you don't just dump something like that and walk away!"

I reached him at the back entry hall. He was pulling his jacket on with his back to me, his shoulders hunched more deeply than usual. I had to walk around him to see his face, but the face I saw was set and rigid. For the first time Larry's face scared me. I

sensed he would as soon strike me as look at me, and I was immediately sorry to have placed myself so emphatically within range.

I must have pulled back, for when he reached for the door,
he opened it in the place where I had stood.

"I've never stooped to names, Jeannine." Words short and
bitter. "I've never spoken to you in anything like that tone."

"Where are you going?"

"For a drive. Seems like we both could cool off." He turned
from the open doorway and finished zipping his jacket. He
reached for car keys on the key rack. Nylon rustled briskly. "I
want you to figure out how you're going to handle yourself. I've
said all I intend to say." He paused. "I love you, and I've never
been unfaithful to you. You have no reason to doubt my word
and you know it." He turned to go.

"You said sex between us—"

He spun, his fists knotted, eyes as though under arrest. "I
didn't *mean* that. See? These long discussions"—he jerked his
head, stamped his feet on the mat—"they drive me nuts. I'm a
simpler person than that. I've told you how it was." His expression, which had softened with misery, regained the hard ground it
had lost. "Now I expect to forget about it. I am for sure done
talking about it."

He pushed open the door and went through it, letting a
smart breath of late September into the hallway. He closed the
door, closed it so that the latch clicked into place as it normally
does. He did nothing like slam the door.

We spent a few hollow and awkward days, and then the routines
of fall began to smooth out the silences, the small lapses. We
functioned, and the world was remarkably well behaved. We ate,
we slept, we went to work and took care of Laura and soon were
able to chat about one thing and another, very much as though
nothing indeed had happened. It was only in the privacy—no,
the isolation—of my mind that things went unruly and ragged,
untidy. Larry could not endure talking but I could not master his
trick of forgetting, his talent for the seamless join. Too many

things jabbed at me in the dark. Why does a person suddenly *happen* to do things he has never done? For nothing? Things do not materialize from nothing: they materialize from something. What something? If not Clara, then what? From doing chores? For years?

The known universe began to rearrange itself. Nothing noticeable at first, nothing like an overnight change. But change there was, a change that went all the way in and reorganized the molecules of the way I felt about my husband and about our marriage. I could not put words to it. But part of me fell away inside, some critical support for being married in the way that I had thought we were married. For being in love the way I had thought we were in love.

By default, I was a woman trained up in the offices of pleasing a husband. I had been so willing to please that, among other things, I had offered up my body for Larry's convenience, when and if he wanted it. I thought that was generosity. I didn't grasp that under such terms, a gift is rendered paltry, that the receiver cannot choose but become ungrateful. A motive to please propels nothing by itself. It must act against a known quantity, must find the friction outside itself, and it leads—Oh, and Oh yes—directly to martyrdom. "I have found my love, and now let me lay myself down and die before him." How should Larry be anything but ungrateful? What moral person could accept such a gift? A paltry gift, and tainted with such gore?

The result should not have been a surprise. "It's not so exciting for me when you're so willing . . ." But it was. And so I set out to remodel my habits. I became nothing like so openhanded in my efforts to please.

The universe changed further. The germ of change spread and found conditions ripe and moist and rotten. Without the impetus to please, I found no accountable motive for much that I did. The meals I cooked, the company I entertained, the clothes I wore, the movies I saw, the colors I chose for the bathroom, the price of the shoes I bought for Laura. . . . I was embarrassed and aghast. I put the brakes on hard.

From a systems point of view, of course, it was predictable that such a change in my behavior would produce a corresponding change in Larry's. And it certainly did. My disinterested, sex-with-a-yawn husband who routinely fell asleep on top of me suddenly became avid and lusty. I had never turned him down for sex in my life. And to start now was to feed the very thing he had lacked: the challenge of conquest. Friction, obstacle, difficulty—these were exciting to him. Overcoming me was exciting. Never mind that my resistance was as genuine as my willingness had been. And, to an inquiring mind, as suspect. But Larry was not inquiring.

I no longer entertained a systems point of view. I was busy discovering what pleased me. And what didn't. As a product of this new selfishness, I found there were things in my life that I didn't actively want. And one of them was sex. Top of the list.

The results were astonishing. Here I had stopped wanting to please my husband, and suddenly he wanted to please me. He wanted to please me with sex. He was becoming insistent about giving me for my pleasure the last thing in the world I wanted.

And so I kept finding occupations elsewhere in the house when the hour for bed arrived.

A time or two he called nasally from the bedroom, "Ja-neeeeeeeen! Ja-neeeeeeeeeeeen!" This was a further reference to Richard Benjamin, a sort of Richard Benjamin love call. And in the Lewis book of personal encounter, it translated as a hint, if not a seduction outright. But I was busy downstairs practicing invisible weaving on frayed Handi-Wipes, or discovering that the rocks in the aquarium were in need of bleaching.

And so life was orderly. We Kept It Clean. We Functioned. And we were okay.

Meanwhile I was beginning to understand some things about the way I was loved. I was loved as long as I didn't get in the way of something Larry wanted. If he wanted sex as conquest, if he wanted sex as a casual and juicy and harmless flirtation, if he wanted a particular idea of himself—innocent, uncomplicated, in the right—then I was not to interfere.

196

If I interfered, if I intruded my own feelings or desires or witness, I was in danger of not being loved. I certainly wouldn't be talked to.

"Do you love me, or do you love the way your life goes when I do what I'm supposed to do?" I asked him late one night. Larry had taken to reading the newspaper in bed, and there were times when I failed to outwait him.

"Oh, Jesus God, help," he moaned. He folded the newspaper, shoved it in the wastebasket and turned out the light. "Look, I love you for your mind. We've established that, haven't we? Now bring your mind over here. Have I told you lately how I admire the depth of your thought?"

Part of me knew what was going on. Part of me always does. But not necessarily the dominant part, not the part with credibility or any authority. I could recognize that Larry not only wanted to please me but was trying. But he wouldn't risk anything, wouldn't say, I know things aren't right between us. No; he would do the opposite of what might have touched me. He would joke. Or he would be angry, short, fault-finding, and when all else failed, pitiable. A kamikaze display—see, I will destroy it all if you don't do what I want you to do.

And the part of me that knows things for what they are recognized this as insecurity. A frightened demand: We will do things the usual way. Or else.

Extortion, blackmail, with no way of communicating across the criminal gap. Despite the part of me—yet another part—that knew love was still there and would perish. And what then? What of Laura? The risk scared me so greatly that I began to practice again at my mother's recipe for peace: keeping quiet.

It's not as easy as it sounds. Sometimes you can think a difficult matter through, and decide in six separate policy meetings with yourself not to say a single word. You take counsel; you hold your tongue. And then comes the surprise, the thing that you suddenly blurt out like a speech out of one of those talking dollies with its string caught like a noose around your finger.

I did my talking-dolly routine with Larry just after the Hawaii trip, the one I'd insisted upon. I had pulled myself together and paid up at the library and at the traffic bureau and at the nursery school, where they had begun to charge me for the extra half hours Laura spent there waiting to be picked up. I had sized up the situation with our marriage, listened to Larry's jokes about connubial rights of cohabitation, and decided to stage another of my flights to freedom. This time *with* Larry—for I was at that time still under the delusion that it takes two live people to make a marriage work.

I chose the only time of the year that Larry would with certainty be able to get away from his office and rounds: Christmas. I arranged for us to drop Laura with Momma. I implanted a picture in my mind, a picture with its edges somewhat curled, it's true, but a real picture. I found it buried in memory banks underneath the stack of studio shots of Laura and snaps of the three of us and eight-by-ten glossies from the company publication showing Larry shaking hands with his latest sale. The picture in question was one I'd seen many times in the early years of our marriage: no captions, just Larry looking at me across a restaurant table with an inarticulate hunger. And me looking back. It was a look that hadn't gone away after coffee and dessert. This was the picture I wanted to see again. I thought maybe if we took it from there, I could reconstruct the whole thing. I would like him again, want him again, we could start over. In a new place, no overlays: grass huts and thatched roofs and body-surfing in a warm ocean, nights under the stars, rainbows and halos over a new foundation of well-being.

The traffic from the airport to the beach choked the freeway like a carbon monoxide *lei*, even at eleven o'clock at night. Our room in Waikiki turned out to be an incongruous Mexican-style hacienda a mile from the beach. The only roar to be heard was the roar of traffic.

"It's okay," Larry had reassured me when the taxi pulled up in front of all that stucco and all those oval portals. "This way we don't have to go through the culture shock of being in Hawaii."

I woke in the morning with the feeling that things were yet

going to go my way. The hotel was massively quiet, and all was peaceful and paradisiacal save for the smell of onions frying somewhere. The window was open; perhaps the kitchen was downstairs. I lay in bed, half dreaming and elaborating on my picture of Larry, whom I now saw as gazing burningly at me over a table heaped with pineapples, guavas, mangoes and bananas, one finger forgetfully trailing *poi*.

I had not yet opened my eyes, and was basking in visions of Larry and me as the only persons alive in paradise, except perhaps for whoever was up and going at the onions at this hour. I was beginning to develop an appetite for *huevos rancheros* when the door to the room burst open and Larry came briskly through it. He wore his bathrobe and a white hotel towel slung over one shoulder. I saw that he had used all that silence to be first into the bathroom to shower and shave.

"You're up," I bleated, blinking at him weakly.

"Yep, me and four couples on the tennis court and three joggers on the terrazzo and a kid with a shoeshine operation outside our door. And an executive from GE running in place in the shower."

The effect of all this reportage was stunning. I wanted to curl up again inside my dreams, but I now felt lazy instead of leisured. I got up contritely while Larry moved about the room hanging jackets and pants in the closet and tucking underwear in drawers and snapping and stowing our suitcases.

"Feel like a swim before breakfast?" he asked.

It was out of the question. I had discovered I was nearly starved, and besides, I wanted to get on with my tableside scenario.

"Unh-unh," I said, yawning as gracefully as I could manage. "I'm really hungry. I've got to have something. Aren't you hungry?"

"Big warm ocean out there, the kind you don't see much of in Iowa."

"I know."

"Beach is beautiful, I saw it from the *lanai*."

"Won't it be there after breakfast?" I was getting anxious.
"No promises."

"Larry, I'm starving. I can't remember when I've been so hungry."

"First things first, then," he smiled.

When I had brushed my hair and pulled a cotton dress over my head, I turned to look for my sandals and noticed that Larry was standing behind me wearing his swimming trunks. And his salesman's smile.

"You go ahead to breakfast," he said, putting an arm around my shoulders. "I'll catch up with you later. Must be the Sirens I hear calling me. Do you think that's it? Do you think it's possible for an ordinary executive to hear the Sirens calling all that way? From Crete all the way to Mexico?"

I could tell I was going to hear a lot about Mexico over the next five days, and I was right. At breakfast downstairs in the hotel dining room that morning, I got food poisoning. Or dysentery, or *la turista*. It was my last supper in paradise, that breakfast, but whatever it was, it was meant to last. The next four mornings of our time in Hawaii, of our attempted second honeymoon, I woke in the silence of the room fearing death and the smell of onions.

Larry functioned without me. He brought me newspapers and reports of the people he met on the beach and the restaurants they tried. I began boiling cabbages in my heart, the stench filling my head and puffing out my intestines, and my husband faithfully brought me Enterovioform and bouillon from downstairs. Every morning he returned from his breakfast of pineapples, guavas, mangoes and bananas, and sat on my bed engagingly. For four days straight he led off with, "Listen, I've got it figured out. You don't have to do this. See, this isn't really Mexico, it's Hawaii. You can get up!"

We had collected Laura from Momma at the New Orleans airport and were back in Des Moines before I said anything to him. I had recovered and the suitcases had been unpacked and the vacation clothes washed and put away in boxes marked "summer" and Laura's Christmas toys had been put on the shelves with the others and she was back in nursery school and being picked up on time for godsake and none of it worked. I had got up and functioned, and I was not okay. Larry was okay; Larry had gone off to Cincinnati and San Diego and come back again.

Or so it appeared. I had come awake and sat up in bed in the dark to find myself watching him put his shaving kit back into the bathroom cupboard.

I shaded my eyes from the glare of the bathroom light. I knew rather than saw that his motion was rapid and efficient, even at that hour, whatever it was. The payoff of a well-established routine—my father also had touted it, for what man of the world wishes to decide afresh every day whether or not he will shower-and-shave? The payoff was just this: no rough edges. No choices. No break in stride. No slack, even for exhaustion.

The bedside clock showed one-thirty in the morning. The bathroom light showed my husband bent to his honed routine.

O beware the slim stoop-shouldered men, the ones who carry the head provisionally forward on a graceful neck, like a bellflower upon a stem. Beware the long openhanded arms that advertise no weapons, no lethal instruments. Be watchful; go round and see that there is no force stored up along the shoulder blades, no accumulation of angers not displayed in the face, defeats not acknowledged. Beware the burdens carried where they cannot be frankly espied, the determination not to show what wares have been hoarded. For these are the men who train themselves for the eye of the needle: They will narrowly pass. They will mildly bear what must be borne. And they will give up nothing.

At the routine sight of the neck bowed over the bathroom cupboard, sympathy began to spread through me. Sympathy, too, is the product of routine. Of habit, like a long history of vasodilation. In this culture men are sympathy objects. I bring myself up short. This man is happy, I tell myself. Do not waste time feeling sorry for long hours and dogged performance. It is still zero-based arithmetic: You subtract where you can afford it. He subtracts from his body, from his life, from Laura, from me.

No more waiting up. No more milk and cookies.

Larry moved into the bedroom and flicked on the light. I lunged for the pillow and buried my face.

"Sorry," he offered after a pause. "I didn't think I'd wake you." Cheerfulness and a strained vigor in his voice.

"You have me mixed up with Laura," I muttered.

"Sorry," he laughed. "Oh, boy, I didn't think I'd make it to-night. Flight delayed, three hours drinking coffee in the Denver airport. I am really wiped out."

"You sound fine," I said from the pillow. "Your garden sprouting or something?"

"As a matter of fact, I was noticing that the birch clump still looks unhealthy—you didn't get that guy out here to look at it, I guess. And then, in the nick of time, I spotted Laura's tricycle in my headlights as I swung in."

"Sorry."

"I got out and moved it. It should be kept in the garage at night, you know. Laura should be taught to put it away." Larry's voice came from various directions as he moved about the room unpacking.

I began to be able to open my eyes again. I looked up to see him zipping his hanging overnight case and hooking it on its closet peg. He turned and saw me and walked quickly over to his side of the bed. He leaned partway over, bracing his hand on the headboard, and waited for me to stretch forward to be kissed. Obediently I did so. To resist would seem so completely unrea-sonable. He patted me on the shoulder with his free hand before he pushed off to finish undressing.

It took effort to avoid seeming unreasonable. Expectation sweeps honesty aside, and to resist makes one stick out. It is so unfeminine to stick out. I didn't want to be touched, which was unreasonable, and I didn't want to feel that way, because every-thing then required such effort. And I knew what this meant, I recognized the signs—the resistance, the cover-up, the effort to seem normal. The signature of depression is effort. And the cry is: Leave me alone. As though one could be insulated from abrasion, when the very current of life is abrasive; anything is abrasive that moves, grows, breathes, changes, uses time and space and substance. There was a moment, but it is long gone, a point when I should have been able to address Larry the talker and mover and say: "Your energy works on me like a steamroller; your heat and weight and pressure are one part vitality and three parts denial and when you get things smoothed over the way you like them, you have flattened all the textures I need for my life."

But that moment required effort and I let it go and now I did not think of myself as being reasonable but as being cornered; I thought I had one corner left that might be mine, one last privacy, and that was the preserve of my body: I thought it was a place to which I could retreat and be still, I thought it should not be touched. I was unreasonable.

"The ashtray was in the bathroom. I emptied it. Are you smoking again?"

"I had one tonight after supper."

"And a couple yesterday?"

"Yes."

"Not with Laura around, I hope."

"No."

"So what have you been up to, besides the usual pining away for me?" he said, unsnapping his wristband and dropping the watch on the bedside table.

"Just the usual pining," I said, covering with a yawn. These jokes bracketed everything. Made it impossible to say all that fell outside them. Keep It Clean.

A flash of anger incinerated the drowsiness. I was alive and functioning and could prove it. "I've been doing more work on family ordinal theory," I told him.

"More first-born, second-born stuff?"

"Right. Some interesting things: If I count my mother's first child that didn't come to term, that makes me the third child in my family, not the second. The third-born stuff sounds a lot more like me. It sure would explain a lot."

Larry hung his pants on a wooden clip-hanger, by the cuffs. After a moment he said, "Mm-hmm."

"Anyway. The profile for third-borns is they think their job is to keep the parents together. Because of this long training they will never make any kind of decision where a relationship might be at stake. In a crisis they just dither around and hope to outwait it. I wonder if that's why I feel paralyzed half the time."

Larry, first and last-born and the quintessence of decision, stood in his T-shirt and junior boxer shorts looking slender and preoccupied. Thin arms, long thin legs. Lean and hungry would just about cover it, until he smiles. Then the small boy's head atop that length of bone offers the reminder: Something has been forced here, some element of growth. Manhood fitted down too early over this narrow frame?

Larry dropped the shirt he had just unbuttoned into the hamper. He turned off the light and tumbled into bed, heaving the covers up and over himself. He put his arms around me and pulled me to him.

"I'm interested in the half that isn't paralyzed," he said.

He kissed me rapidly some half-dozen times, as a preface for what we liked to call his "welcome home." It was the tag line from some traveling-salesman joke I can no longer remember. I must have found it funny once.

But there I was, tired of laughing. Now I wanted things to have their own weight, to *count*. No practice runs, no concealed probes. I wanted things *to be what they were*.

His fingers poked at my breast. I twisted away from him, rolling my shoulder into his hand where my breast had been.

"Tell me more about third children," Larry said, grasping the shoulder and whispering into my ear. "How do they feel about married men? Do they think it's their job to keep married couples together?"

The remarkable thing about Larry is that he picks up information when he appears not to be paying the slightest attention.

He picks it up and uses it to facilitate some other piece of business. It is another of his maintenance tasks, performed as routinely as he mails out baskets of fruit to good customers at Christmas. Charm and personal currency. Part of the deal, no big deal. The price of admission for a welcome home.

When I didn't reply, he began to slide the hand down my upper arm. It may have been the gooseflesh, more palpable than I would have guessed, that made him stop.

And that is when I said what I thought I wouldn't say. With my eyes toward the wall some two feet from my head, I mumbled, "I don't want you to think of me as your wife anymore."

I felt him relax. He laughed softly and resumed stroking my arm. "MMMmmmm, exciting. Whose wife do I get to think of you as?"

I whirled, inasmuch as it is possible to whirl lying down. *"It's not a joke. I don't want you to think of me as your wife anymore!"*

Saying it the first time had scared me. Now it had become the easiest and most obvious point, the point from which everything else must follow.

"I will be your friend, I will be your partner, I will be your dinner companion, I will be your roommate, I will be your lover on occasion, but I will not be your wife."

He swung his body away and lay flat on his back. "The class wars, is it? What have you been reading, again?"

"Are you being hard of hearing on purpose?"

He reached over and switched on the bedside lamp and squinted at me. His eyes focused like radar scanners. They swept my face for clues, for some evidence of faulty alignment that could be righted. For indicators of how pitch strategy would have to be adjusted.

"Look," he said. "Just tell me what you want. Sometimes I'm a little slow, and you may have to spell it out. We *did* just put out two grand for a so-called second honeymoon. Okay. You don't want me to think of you as my wife. How should I think?"

I sat up and looked at his face, which was not the face of a person ready to hear anything.

"Oh, no," I said. "I've been here before. Larry, the corporate strategist. You say, just tell me what you want. You set me up so that I make the policy, I draw up the job descriptions, I police the violations. You'll cooperate, as long as it doesn't require your time and effort. You'll wish me a lot of good luck with this relationship project of mine."

He kept a sullen silence. Then he said, "Well, we're not going to get anywhere tonight. Not with that tone in your voice. I can't handle it."

"I can't handle it either! It's there because I'm fucking desperate!" Angry tears cropped out of my eyes, and I wiped my face with the sheet. Larry handed me tissues from the table beside him. Keep It Clean.

"Look," he said. "If you want something from me, you have to show some patience."

"I've shown patience. Nothing happens!"

"You're not making sense. This wasn't my idea; I was happy just being married to you. If you want some other deal, I'm willing to listen, but you have to be patient."

In another context, "all deliberate speed." It is an inoffensive way of saying "Never," and preferred by politicians everywhere.

"You're right," I concluded. "We won't get anywhere." I slid back under the covers.

"The first thing you have to do," he said reasonably, reaching up to turn off the light, "is decide on a program. You have to know what you want."

After that we lay there breathing in the dark. My throat and eyewells ached with tears I didn't see the point of. Larry reached for my hand, and I was grateful for the touch. Then the sheets lifted as with his other hand he began to stroke my arm. I felt my limbs go cool as what was alive in me contracted, fell back. A rushing sound came into my ears. This is what it must be like to die, I thought, letting more and more of that part of me drift away. Larry's fingers rubbed circles on my collarbone.

Suddenly I shivered and turned over on my stomach. I drew my arms in to hug myself back into being. Larry went very still. I couldn't even hear his breathing. Yet a question like What's wrong? is not one he can ask. Nothing is wrong. A person carries on. Functions.

I distilled all that I understood of us both into a clear quiet voice. "I can tell you what I want. I can be very specific."

"What is it?"

"No sex unless I initiate."

He waited for a moment.

"That's it?"

"That's it." I moved away from him, leaving a space between us, and turned my back.

"This is a little unfriendly, isn't it? You act like I'm some kind of criminal. Does no sex mean I'm not supposed to touch you at all? No kissing? Should I avert my eyes, should your undies mingle with mine in the clothes hamper?"

Extrapolating into the ridiculous—effective against people who pride themselves on being reasonable. An invitation to temporize, something all third-born children do well. Or more simply, an invitation to laugh, something that used to be quite as dependable.

"We'll see," I said. That was one from Larry's own repertoire, but I said it without the smile that he generally liked to use with it.

I had taken a stand, and for a time it felt like winning. Maybe that should have been warning enough. But I hadn't ever taken a stand before, and I thought the disorientation was natural. Disoriented is how you feel when the opposition seems to fall back like magic as you continue sprinting for the wrong goal post.

If what I was doing was winning, I was relatively unskilled. Like most women, what I knew how to do best was understand. I could understand in several modalities: silently, approvingly, warmly, painfully, patiently. I could do it clearly, feelingly, perceptively and "only too well." I could switch from participatory to nonparticipatory, directive to nondirective, without dropping a sympathetic half-tone.

But winning? Was that what it was called when you introduced change unilaterally? When you no longer asked for cooperation but demanded it? When you went hard-ass on the rulebook because you owned it? Or thought you did?

I demanded change. I got change. For one thing, Larry and I no longer had a common language. Words didn't mean the same things to him as they meant to me. We had long conversations, and I didn't know what we had said. And he didn't do any of the things I expected him to do in consequence of what I thought we had agreed on. Misunderstandings didn't clear up. It wasn't as though I could simply check matters out with him. The clarifying questions also came back turned to gibberish.

"You aren't being at all clear," he would tell me. "I think you are often intentionally vague." At other times, "You obviously have developed some very specialized meanings to the words you use. Can you put that another way?" Or, "Now say that so that someone like myself can understand it."

I was impressed. I didn't know how I had so rapidly passed from being a lovable incompetent into such a bundle of coded ciphers. But the evidence was before me.

The day I brought my car into town for a tune-up, I waited at the garage for Larry to pick me up on his way out to lunch. We'd said 12:30. At just past two o'clock he drove up to the body shop. I'd given up calling his office; I had begun to feel like a fixture in the dusty yellow plate-glass window.

"I can't believe you're still here!" he exclaimed as I climbed in and slammed the door.

"What do you mean, you can't believe I'm still here? This is where I was supposed to be, except I wasn't supposed to be here quite this long."

"I've been looking all over for you. I was so late getting out of the office, I figured you would've just walked downtown to the Creperie."

I sat stonily and he continued.

"I parked at the Creperie and you weren't there, so I waited for half an hour. I even walked down the block and checked Luigi's and the Café and the Spaghetti House." His irritation showed as he ticked off the places on his fingers, all the places I hadn't been. "I even looked into Ballanteen's."

"Larry, stop acting like I'm the one who is behaving irrationally."

He turned to give me an accusing look. "You said you wanted to have lunch at the Creperie."

"Right. I did. But I said I'd meet you here."

He shook his head in disgust.

"I couldn't imagine you would hang around a body shop for two hours."

"I hadn't planned to, myself," I said hotly. "And if I said the Creperie, and I wasn't in the Creperie, why would you think I'd be in any of those other places?"

"I don't know." He shrugged. "Obviously I can't understand the way you think."

The way I thought and the things I believed on account of the way I thought were becoming a real problem for us.

In bed at night:

"Look, Jeannine, I see your point about not acting like I owned you. Don't you agree I've changed?"

"How?"

"What do you mean, how? Don't you believe in me at all anymore?"

"What does it matter what I believe?"

"How can we go on if you don't even believe in me? I really care about you, and I want the things you want. I want you to be happy. But I have to feel that you care about me, too."

"Larry, stop climbing on top of me."

"I'm not climbing on top of you! What kind of remark is that?"

"Okay, what do you call it then? Your leg is on top of my leg, your arm is across the other side of me."

"I'm not climbing on top of you," he said heatedly, climbing off. "You make it sound like I'm some kind of animal. I don't even know how to act around you anymore."

"We agreed that I would do any sexual initiating."

"I don't see you doing any."

"Maybe after all these years I've come over to your point of view. Sex is something I can take or leave, mostly leave."

"I don't feel that way anymore."

"Odd how things work out. How do *you* like it?"

"I don't like it, Jeannine. I miss loving you."

"You miss fucking me."

"I don't like you using that word about me."

"I don't like you doing that word to me."

"Jesus," he said, smacking his forehead. "How did we get into this? Do you feel love for me at all anymore?"

"I used to. Lately I feel—used up."

"I mean, do you *feel* anything for me?" he said wistfully, running his bald fingers over my collarbones.

I drew a sharp breath. "Get your hand off me."

He muttered as he turned away, "I don't know how I find out anything anymore."

"You *ask*, goddammit! You *wait* for an answer! You keep your goddam hands off me!" I was half-shouting, but hoarsely. The tears poured down my face, molten lead from the castle keep.

"You'll wake Laura," he said, handing me the box of tissues.

"Since when are you worried about waking Laura?" The nose-blowing and snuffling were humiliating. I wanted to apologize for the mess. I seized the Kleenex box and grabbed at several, a handful. Maddened by having to take them one at a time, I wanted suddenly to rip open the box and smother him with the contents. How children must hate us! We hand out first the torment and then the comfort. I hated Larry for being there at all, for seeing me vulnerable. I hated him for the way he lay like some predator in the dark, waiting to make the next flanking move.

"I feel like I have no rights," he said. "You make me feel like I can't be myself. I have no right to express myself."

"What does that mean?"

"I don't even feel I can express happiness around you."

"Why? I don't want to see you in pain. I just don't want you to cause me pain." More tears. More mucus.

"God, you twist everything around. I'm not trying to cause you pain. I don't know what the hell you are asking me to do. What do you want from me? You want me to go slow. You want me to stop. You want me to listen to what you've been reading lately. You want me to do anything but be myself, and goddammit, Jeannine, I have to be me. I am the person I am. It's not my style to go slow, it's not my style to analyze things to death. Part of what I need is the chance to be spontaneous, and you won't let me."

"Spontaneous. Meaning you want what you want when you want it?"

"That's not it! When I'm happy or when I feel close to you, I want to touch you or hug you or make love to you. And you make me feel like I have to have *permission*."

"You *need* permission to touch another person! Otherwise—" I drew a breath. "There's a word for what you're talking about, for 'making love' without permission. It's called rape."

He shut his eyes. His shoulders collapsed, and he looked at me through colorless eyes that expanded and contracted strangely in the light of the bedside lamp. What I saw was resignation changing places with hatred, and back again. These I knew were the hallmarks of defeat, and yet I did not want to defeat him, I wanted—what did I want?

"*It's called rape,*" he repeated. "You make everything so ugly, Jeannine. You're unwilling to help me with my needs, and I'm sick of the way you throw words around like sledgehammers. *Rape.* I'm supposed to see that your needs are different from mine right now. I'm trying to understand, and I'm changing, goddammit, whether you believe in me or not. I love you. But there's only so much I can take."

I heard all his words, not vague, not incomprehensible, not seamed with specialized meanings. I heard them all having their specific rational intent, all intending themselves in different directions: the understanding, the pleading, the fear, the disgust, the warning. I heard the emotion in his voice, knew him to be as desperate as I was, knew that he meant each of the things he had said. I took his words to heart, where they squirmed over themselves like nests of baby snakes. I lay on my back and made choking sounds. The bloody tears.

We lay there side by side, stiffly, until I had stopped shaking and making ungulate noises. Then I felt Larry's foot move over next to mine. When can one be sure of comfort, free of doubt? That warm, somewhat damp foot that he offered felt like a demand, a threat. And there I was, hauling my sledgehammer words around again. What was there that I could say? How had all the polarities got turned around? I had loved Larry for his jokes, for his orderliness, for his dedication to task. These were the things I had now come to hate him for. I had married a man who was physically remote, believing I could change that by loving him freely and ardently. Now I had finally done it by hating his very touch.

Nothing had its established value. Nothing could be counted on for plus or minus. All had become negotiable, subject to some new politics that neither of us felt we had voted for.

And so I tightened my jaw and said nothing. Larry's foot remained. My muscles gathered like springs while I practiced a grim tact. Tact, I disciplined myself to consider, is always a lie. But a lie is not always tactful. It can insulate people from consequences. Tact is then a subset of lying. Tact is a lie, with time off for good behavior.

And goddam, is this as far as I will ever get? This mind-prattle, the effort to control myself from feeling what I feel? And what is that? Confusion, revulsion, nobody's fault, nothing to be done, whirlwinds in a dark wood. But there is something there, some kernel, some trail of pebbles to be followed out. The politics switched too violently. Sex! How could sex be the issue? Sex never pleased Larry before.

If I become available for the sex he now demands, I'll be no nearer to pleasing him than before.

Pleasing him. As if I could! And certainly he is no better at pleasing me. His efforts that way amount to clumsy props for seduction. A bottle of wine after dinner, a shave. He is ignorant of what I want, of what I have wanted all along. In those long years of abject availability, not sex, but connection with him—your now-famous cliché of intimacy. Intimacy does not equal sex. Sex is not a foreplay for intimacy. More words, more analysis. My husband is simpler than that.

I shut my eyes. Reset.

My husband's foot remains beside mine. Dormant, but it remains. How do the collections-agency people put it on the first round? "Just a small reminder." Larry means to work on me. To win me. To defeat me.

To defeat me. The sudden force of it strikes hard. Hard. Much harder than that wayward kiss-with-amenities I witnessed last fall. My stomach churns in confirmation, and I turn in the dark to look at the man who "loves me." Our struggle has not been over sex. Our struggle has been over control. Who would get to define what was what, what we could say and what we could not, what could count as real and what could not.

I lie still beside the familiar form of the stranger I have been living with. This married man who has no need to learn who I am or what I want. A businessman, a student of chess, this one moves only from strength. His strength lies in knowing what he wants and insisting on it. Sex, certainly. As a bargaining concession. Because the object is control.

This man means to have it.

Larry's foot began to move alongside mine. Changing from dormant to pupa phase, it began to crimp itself and rub against my foot. A test: Did this count or not? I ripped the covers back. Tact notwithstanding, I leapt out of bed screaming, "*STOP IT!*"

My first earthquake.

"Jesus God!" I shouted. "We are in conflict! We both want *my* life!"

Even in the dim light I could see how frightened, how confused the man was. I could see him as a small boy, with the urgencies of a child.

"Jesus-fucking-Christ, Larry." Not the language you use with a child, but the tone. The resignation pulled over the anger like a tight rubber surgeon's cap. I seized the hair of my head in both fists and pulled, pulled hard, for the relief of some simple immediate pain.

Then I let go. "I am going to take a shower," I said. "A shower. Let me make that clear. Let there be no misunderstanding. I am going to take a shower, and I'm talking about that little metal gadget in the bathroom. Up high? With the holes?"

The eyes gave back nothing.

It was a very long shower, that one, a marathon shower. I lay down in the bathtub, and let the spray riddle my body. I nearly fell asleep. But as the hot water gave out, I thought of something quite amazing.

For once I had not been the last to exit from the scene of the crime. I was not still in there, trying to explain, trying to give Larry enough information so that he would *understand*. No: I had walked out. That must be halfway to control right there. Think of it! I had walked out . . . and with a joke.

What did I need Larry for? I had become him.

But it is never easy to hold on to what you know against the undertow of what you hope to believe. Not all nights of my impersonation of my husband ended as nights of comedy, however grim the laughter. There were still nights of attempted lovemaking, nights when enough of the doors in the maze had opened and shut in the right order to get us there. But in our marital lovers' lane awaited the newest and cruelest changeling: If there were enough trust and enough safety and enough feeling to begin, there would not be enough to make it through to the end.

In the worst times, no sooner would I signal willingness and the bargain be sealed than I would experience a terror of being wrongly and dangerously exposed. Larry's mouth and body were gelatin and wood. I wanted nothing more than to be through with them, done, finished. I rushed everything as he had always done. I hated him for any gesture that was not essential, any motion that meant that this intolerable joining would be prolonged.

And so we learned not to begin. For the most part, anyway. Those last months of a painfully early Iowa spring, there were still times when stubbornness or disbelief or some other atavism led us on. One of these was the night in June before Laura left for South Carolina and I for Mississippi. In June, and this the same month? The same life? Larry and I had clung to one another that night, frightened and trembling and silent. A last time, then. A last blind agony in honor of our pain.

And when it was over, when the obscenely hopeful ritual was again over and again failed, we both burst into tears. In each others' arms. But separately, separately.

14

It is early afternoon when the phone sounds off again. I am in my room, putting my suitcase in order. An exercise. A discipline. Today is Friday, Laura arrives tomorrow. I am once again marveling that I have taken this week, this one week when I did not have to serve as wife or mother, and come here to put my time in as daughter. Why is it that you can't understand that you can't go home again until you get there? And then, of course, it's too late. Bankroll and options shot.

The ringing stops. Moments later Momma's feet come padding down the hall carpet. Her head cranes through my doorway and she says with a studied neutrality, "Your cousin Raymond wants you on the telephone."

I say, "Oh." And slide the suitcase back under my bed. It occurs to me that I am behaving like a guilty person.

In the kitchen I pick up the receiver and say into it heartily, "Well, Raymond! How are you?"

"I—I'm just fine, Jeannine. How about your own self?" The voice is thoroughly unfamiliar, a strange masculine voice draped around the shy stammer that *is* familiar.

"Not bad. Just playing suitcase jockey."

"Whut?"

"Oh, just messing around with my suitcase. You know. Women that travel always carry them, and we keep them full of brickbats and lead weights. Nobody normal can lift one."

"Shoot, I know just what you're talking about. My—my momma brings one like that home from Baton Rouge ever' dang time."

I decide I had better slow up some for my cousin Raymond.

216

Before too very long we get through the logistics for the evening ahead, and I hang up. I'm aware of Momma's back as she
stands at the sink running hot water into the dishpan. She is
wearing one of my father's shirts, the sleeves rolled up, the shirt-
tails nearly to her knees. I address my speech to that blatantly
turned back.

"I'm going to meet Drew at the Holiday Lounge tonight.
Raymond's picking me up."

She doesn't reply. But when I move to leave the kitchen, she
says to the sink, "That boy is nothing. And Drew ought to know
better."

I look at her back, her busy hands. "Yeah. Well. Is it all
right with you if I take the car this afternoon?"

A moment's pause. The hands still.

"Where are you going?"

"I don't know yet."

A few more of those moments, like blanks in a Luger.

"You know where the keys are."

I do indeed. They are on one of the magnetic hooks on the
side of the refrigerator, beside the five-year-old calendar with all
the family phone numbers written on it. I take the keys and get
my wallet from the bedroom. As I go out the front door, I hear
the sound I used to do my homework to, the sound of pots being
scraped, abraded, scoured.

For their own good, of course. There has never been much
doubt of that.

Motion is soothing. No one who has ever raised an infant could
doubt it. Toymakers and baby-furniture manufacturers know
whereof they reap; they put their ingenuity into faking babies out,
making them think they're back in the womb and going somewhere. And here is General Motors on down the line, collecting
on its bucket seats, red velour upholstery, lullabyes beside your
ear with a rocking beat: "Mother and Child Reunion." Cal's
company car has a driver's seat that heats up when the temperature drops. He says it feels exactly like he's wet his pants.

And what does all this mean? It means your synapses are still present and accounted for, Jeannine. Going clickety-click in the same old rhythms, Polly want a cracker?

Given a choice between Larry and my mother, I'd take Larry every time. He isn't trying to kill me, after all. He may not have noticed that his foot is pressing on my windpipe, but he's not actively trying to kill me. That he knows of.

Given a choice between Larry and my mother, I'd better invent another choice.

That's the hard part, God knows. The family repertoire is a closed shop, and where are the lovers waiting in the wings when you really need one? What I need right now, what I could really use, is a sign. A dove, out of the parted ruby curtains over the Gethsemane baptistry, say, which flutters to my shoulder while the sound effects go: "This is my daughter, in whom I am well pleased."

It is half in my mind to go over to Carrie Dean's, but when I reach the turnoff I don't take it. She will not be home, or worse, she will be home but will have an aged mother, a sister-in-law and an aunt sitting on homemade chairs on the porch. They will be shelling peas together, thumbnails turning into pale green jellyfish, peapod carcasses up to their ankles. Today I don't have it to be made welcome. Can't crank up all the energy that I would have to run into keeping my shields up.

I press down on the accelerator. Warp five, Mr. Sulu.

Speed has always felt good on this road, rocky blacktop humming under the wheels. The yellow sign comes too soon, as it must have done some forty years ago when a farmer and his truckload of alfalfa plowed into a dairy truck at the intersection. Thus, Buttermilk Crossing. Except forty years ago there was no yellow sign.

From the crossing it is six miles into Bayley, six miles of two-lane highway past the Robert E. Lee School, where Miss Viola still teaches first grade but where the jump boards have been replaced with jungle gyms. Past vegetable stands and shrimp trucks from New Orleans, past the Frost-Top and Dalloway's

Sof-Freeze, past Bob's Café, the same black and white sign flailing the breeze since my mother and father had premarital Coney Islands there. Or so I was told. There are antique shops along the highway now, since local people have learned how quaint their culture is. Antique shops don't belong in my remembered geography, and it takes effort not to see them.

I still have no clear destination, and merely take the Bayley stoplights as they come. The route into town has been redone. The broadening streams of traffic are unfamiliar, guided by five-story traffic signals. The afternoon has turned steamy after this morning's cloud cover gave up the siege. Waiting at a red light, I notice that I am driving the only car with windows rolled down. All? I had not known air conditioning had undone so many.

I follow the streams of cars over the grid of streets without prejudice, when Murphy Street presents itself. Murphy Street, site of Drew's last maneuver. Full of family feeling, the kind of inspiration that launched a thousand genealogists, I turn to search out the Murphy Street Motel. Stop sign after stop sign interrupts progress, and I begin to see why the Murphy Street Motel was the motel of choice. Murphy Street itself is not heavily traveled. The tiny houses lining the street would not have curtain-peekers of any consequence. Even the azaleas here appear to be disadvantaged.

Soon I see it, blue wood trim over shoe-polish white stucco, the shrubbed and shaded parking lot nicely concealed from casual inspection. I pull in and try to decide just where it was that Drew did her work, where the blue Oldsmobile must have slowly sunk on its black gumshoe feet. I feel happy and proud sitting here in the parking lot of the Murphy Street Motel, which I have come to regard as the Alamo of Bayley. But before very long, or so it seems, the screen door of the office, as announced in blue letters painted next to it, squeaks open and slams flatly on its mechanical slammer. Through it has emerged a sloshingly fat woman. I am pleased to observe her as part of this scene, but she doesn't see me that way. She stands and stares with her ham-sized forearms crossed over her floral polyester bosom. I begin to catch her drift:

The place has standards. I can't just show up here to borrow drama or history. I will have to let the air out of some tires or leave.

Regretfully I start the car and depart the grounds, an unworthy pilgrim. Again I follow the cars as the traffic flow dumps them like salmon into the ocean of a new shopping center. I do not resist. Today I wish to be anonymously mainstream. I circle the parking lot and pick out a shop. Clothes, I decide. I find one with manikins emaciated enough to suggest a fit.

I park the car and enter the silvered glass door to the tinkle of a bell. The door shuts itself. Air conditioners work at lowering body temperature to the point that shoppers buy to save themselves. Even I start scanning the sale rack. Some recess of my mind has begun playing with the notion of what I will wear tonight, and also how much of a hard hat Raymond is going to turn out to be. And so it is that I nearly stumble over his mother without recognizing her.

"Jeannine, hey!"

"Why, Aunt Verlie! My mind must have been a million miles away."

Verlie would be unexpected anywhere. Just because she generally sports the same polyester fare as my motel lady is not a reason she would not be found here, trying on a see-through black tunic shot with metallic rose and silver.

"Why, it's a lucky thing! You know, it's a lucky thing, because here I was just thinking this morning what a shame, I mean, you being here so infrequent and all, what a shame you couldn't get to see all your cousins. I was just tickled, I was at the house this morning when Drew called up for Raymond, here he's just staying the night, some business over in Moselle with a supplier, and I'm just so glad y'all can get together. But listen here, it's just lucky, like I tell you—Hey!"

Verlie suddenly jerks her head beyond the eye-lock she has on me. She secures the attention of a little girl in a red taffeta dress. The girl must be about nine, and the ample skirt of her red dress is held aloft as though her long slender legs are the shaft of an open umbrella. Her brown hair is loose down her back, but the front section is done up in elaborate braids affixed to her crown. I have ample opportunity to observe the arrangement of ribbons and matching barrettes. Verlie beckons, and the girl comes nearer and chews her gum midway between us.

"Now stop chewing that gum so big or I'll make you spit it out. You're supposed to be a lady. Go tell your momma I said come here. There's somebody wants to see her."

The child throws me a look over her shoulder and runs off. Her ruffled white panties show as the red taffeta bobs on its layer of crinoline.

I add up all the signs and say, "You don't mean that's one of Deborah's?"

Verlie looks startled. "Why, law, why, I didn't stop to think, why, of course you wouldn't know Angela. Not any more than you saw her the other day at the swimhole. Angela, you know, that was my momma's name. Deborah's Angela doesn't look a thing like the Hinton side of the family, of course, but it's a pretty name anyway, I always said. Here she comes, here she comes."

A thin pale young woman moves toward us with an unsteady smile. She gives up glancing from Verlie to me, from me to Verlie, and comes the rest of the way down the aisle to us with her eyes fixed on my feet. This is Deborah June, and she bears no possible relation to the chubby, rollicking and, yes, gum-chewing co-ed I saw ten years ago.

"Baby, look who's here in the store! I bet you don't even recognize her. This is Jeannine, your cousin Jeannine! Sumrall's girl!"

Verlie speaks to her as though she is a little hard of hearing. But Deborah June looks at me with a wide bright smile, and drags up what is left of the flag twirler she was to exclaim, "Why, Jeannine! Why, I just can't hardly believe it!"

She offers those frail arms and frames me inside them. An angular, a rectangular, embrace.

I begin to say what a surprise it is to see her, but words start to fly out of her mouth, out of that face so suddenly and unnaturally bright, like a cloud of partridges startled under fluorescent light.

"Why you look so good, where's your husband? Oh, that's right, Momma told me you came by yourself, well, we're proud you did, we're so sorry about your daddy, of course, I don't have to tell you. We don't get to see Aunt Melvinia enough, just busy, I guess, like everybody else. Well, my goodness, that's a pretty necklace, and those earrings! Where do you find such pretty things? Up North, I reckon."

She talks like her mother, I think at first. But it is worse, far more desperate. She is using the words and the brilliant amperage behind her face to divert attention. I know the feeling too well, know she is spending more of this brightness than she can afford. My God, she'll be exhausted for a week.

"These are silver and enamelwork, an artist friend of mine does the work in Des Moines. She sells them from her house, and hopes to get some commercial accounts before too long."

I chatter on like this in confusion. Deborah June nods brightly. Her alertness is focused and intense, it seems, but the eyes dart sideways. The pressure on her increases with each moment. Each moment demands that she demonstrate convincingly that she is Deborah June, still that old vivacious girl, still absolutely okay.

I don't know which part of her to address, least of all in front of her mother, who looks on beaming happily.

"I wouldn't have known Angela," I say, breaking the eye contact and pretending to search for that red taffeta and crinoline package. "I could hardly believe she was yours! I think she's disappeared into the dressing room."

Deborah June scurries off in relief to locate her, and I am left nodding at Verlie. I can't see how this can possibly end quickly enough. I can't see how I am going to get out of Deborah June's way in time for us both to leave looking all right. I feel myself beginning to crack under Verlie's manic expectation.

"It's been such a long time. I can't believe it's been so long. You must be proud," I finally remember to say.

"Oh, my, yes, we love all our grandchildren, every one of them just as sweet as the other. We keep hoping Raymond will find him a gal and get settled into family life, but he just wants to make him some money and go get an MBA, he says. One college degree just not good enough, but I expect you know how that is. I say to his daddy, 'Reckon Deborah getting married and not finishing her training made Raymond want to do it this way?' But he says I bother my head too much about it, and well, he may be right, maybe I do. You modern kids got lots different thinking than us old ones, my children let me know that much. Anyway, Deborah is finishing her LPN now, did she mention? Anyway, here she comes, and Angela with her."

Verlie drops her voice as though their arrival were a secret. Meanwhile Deborah June flashes me another of her expensive smiles. She eyes me coquettishly as she directs a speech to her mother.

"Momma, Angela has just *reminded* me that we have to go on *home* so that she can go to her *skatin' party* tonight. She is just about to have a *fit*, she's afraid we're going to make her *late* again. Jeannine, I'm *sorry* we have to rush off like this. Gettin' ready to go *skatin'* takes *more time!*" She rolls her eyes and shows a knowing pout. "You can't *imagine!*"

The singsong that has come from her mouth is worthy of Aunt Lenore. Still, it is an exit line that will serve, and I smile to ease the way.

But Verlie's eyes glitter, reminding me suddenly of my father.

"You don't have to go and do up that child's hair a different way for every hour in the day and night," she fumes.

Angela cracks her gum and complains, "You gonna fix my hair, ain'cha, Momma?"

"We'll fix it up just the way you like it, darlin'," Deborah coos to her. "You'll be the prettiest girl there." She winks at me elaborately, and seizes the child's hand. "Come on now, le's go. Say bye to Aunt Jeannine."

"Bah."

"You have to bring that *husband* of yours down to *see* us!" Deborah sings, backing toward the exit.

"Tell him to come with you next time. We're just about to forget what he looks like!" They go for the door then. I am left wondering whether a fish without a bicycle has ever been seen in these parts. Verlie tarries long enough to stage-whisper, "I don't hold with all this fussin' with clothes and hair-dos, but don't nobody listen to me. You come see us, Jeannine. Don't judge our manners by Deborah June." She hustles her plump body toward the door, a low-volume cacophony of polyester on polyester. She stops and turns as she remembers one more thing. "Now Raymond is a more sensible child. But, of course, don't judge us by Raymond, neither." She throws her head back and laughs. "That boy's his daddy's son, I declare. Y'all have a good time this evenin'."

And they are gone. And I am, oh, so grateful. I am also sick of myself. Sick of my stock of sentimental pity. Wasted on Deborah June. She is a touch dysfunctional, to be sure, but a dysfunctional what? A dysfunctional Southern Belle. A touch of paint, a little repair, and we have ourselves a genuine slimline sternwheeler, paddling along like a ghost. All that latticed fancywork on the outside, all that emptiness echoing around inside. All aboard. A charming remembrance of days gone by, ladies and gents.

It has all happened to her, and yet she insists on her ignorance. In her dreams she is still out there on the football field at halftime, stomping around in her white tasseled boots, flag whirling like the angel's sword.

The seductress is an angry woman, goes the feminist line. A sister in search of a piece of male power. Well. More power to you, Deborah June. And to you, too, Angela. There's a long road ahead, a lot of football fields to be crossed. I won't be there cheering and I don't trust the aim on that anger of yours.

Love thine enemies. Now which one of the patriarchs thought that one up? In my experience the only way you *get* enemies is by having people say they love you. All the rest follows.

15

The music in the Holiday Lounge is loud and professional. Drew seems to have these identical characteristics as she stands up in her crystal drop earrings and Lurex décolletage and hails us to her table. When Raymond and I get there, she shouts introductions over the music to a woman who sits at the table laughing to the man beside her.

"Meet my best friend, Rochelle. Rochelle, my first cousin, Jeannine. You know Raymond."

Rochelle lifts her cigarette in greeting, and returns to her companion.

"Rochelle has attracted her some oil-field trash," Drew announces, her voice still carrying above the music. She indicates with her eyes the two men seated on either side of Rochelle. One of them is sloshing about in his late forties or early fifties, and either he is too drunk to hear or the music has carried Drew's voice away from his ears. The other is young and pinched-looking, and if he has not heard, it is a case of hysterical deafness on his part. If he is drunk, he is the kind that goes rigid, looking sober until accidentally felled by a stray table leg.

Raymond, in his beefy courteous way, finds me a chair, and I sit down on it while he finds himself one. I am glad to sit down. The noise and the cigarette smoke and the tension of gaiety have a disorienting effect. I have a sudden fear that I will pass out.

I know that I have returned to my senses when Hershell, the elder of the oil-field men, turns to be sure I have caught his name. "Hershell," he repeats in a whoosh of alcoholic odor. He smiles and claps a hand to his chest. I nod in appreciation.

There is a rustle of red taffeta beside my ear, and then the frilly rear end of a waitress extends over our table. She is bending over in her microscopic skirt to hear the drinks being ordered at the next table.

Hershell whoops and wheels himself around in his chair.

"Hey, Ro-chelle!" he shouts. "You see what I see? I swear, looks to me like she got herself a chaw of tobacco in that thang!"

Raucous unshared laughter. The younger man continues to appear to be hard of hearing.

Raymond stops the waitress and orders drinks for our table. He points a finger in my direction and I lean over the table to mouth the syllables mar-ti-ni. Raymond picks it up on the second try. He cups his hand around her ear and speaks into it and she nods. Then she is gone, only to return on the downbeat of the next rock number. She unloads her tray as I realize that no intervals between the songs could keep you pinned on the dance floor for hours.

Everyone at the table appears too overcome to do anything but drink. We do that, and I find myself drumming my fingers on the cocktail napkin in rhythm with my own nervousness. I check Drew's face for a clue, but Drew is ignoring everyone in present company, her eyes lightly scanning the dance floor.

Hershell places a heavy hand on Rochelle's shoulder. She turns and scowls at him and shrugs free, and then catches my eye. She leans across the table to speak, and her heavy breasts in a velour scoop-neck rest on the tabletop just short of the ashtray. She is about my age and very attractive, with well-cut short hair, perfect smile, perfect eggplant-lacquered nails. She pushes several glasses aside to have a clear line of vision.

"Hey," she says to me cheerfully. "Don't daince with this one." She jerks a thumb toward the bleary-eyed man between us, whose face and iron-gray mane are now half hidden by the outspread fingers he is laughing into.

"The old fart'll slobber all over you, and I ain't kiddin'."

She tilts her head toward the dark-haired silent one, who sits on the other side of her staring into the air. "This one's not too bad, but he's so young that when he blows in your ear, he goes 'wwwhhuhhhh!'"

Rochelle puffs out her cheeks and blows the way a three-year-old blows out birthday candles, launching perhaps half the volume of spit.

The young man suddenly stands and stalks away on his uncommonly long legs. The joke is cruel, and of course very funny. Drew and Rochelle and Raymond and I laugh. Hershell lifts his head and lets the fingers slide down from his eyes, and belatedly joins us. Then we are laughing at him.

Suddenly the band stops playing and our laughter becomes audible. We subside as the band members leave their platform for a break. Rochelle seizes the moment and slaps a hand down on Hershell's knee. She says, "Hey, you better go see what happened to your buddy. He just kinda up and took off."

"Aw, he's awright."

"Naw, he ain't! I mean it now, you better go find him and take care of him. I mean it. You go on now. Find him."

"Ro-chelle, sugar—"

"Don't you sugar me. Go on. Shoo. And don't you come back without him, hear?"

Hershell sits eyeing Rochelle helplessly. Raymond rises. He stammers softly, "Come—come on, pardner. You and me'll go see where he went."

Raymond remains standing, all six feet five or so towering over the table. He rests there at his ease while Hershell gathers the resolve to get to his feet. With a show of effort Hershell shoves himself off his chair and waddles sideways away from the table. Raymond reaches out and hooks his fingers into the sagging belt loops, and makes it plain that he will be a patient escort. The two of them disappear into the network of tables.

"You *mean* thang!" Drew teases Rochelle, pouting. "Now just look what you done. You got rid of all our play-purties."

Rochelle drags jauntily on her cigarette.

"Tell you what," she replies. "I'll get you another one. Just like it. They all just alike anyway."

The three of us bite our lips and giggle.

"But let me tell you something right now," Rochelle goes

on. "I want that cousin of y'allses to come right on back. He's mighty fine, and I wouldn't mind taking him on just to keep in practice. To tell you the truth, just lookin' at him makes my tongue get hard."

Drew slaps the table and checks me out to see if I've fainted away. She grins, and gives her head a half-turn toward her friend.

"Now, Rochelle, he's just a baby."

"Mmmmmm-mmmm, and I know just how to treat a baby like that."

"Rochelle, that's my first cousin."

"Unh-hunh, we got two of 'em here tonight. And I'm just grateful to you, but one thang I for sure ain't, and that's a lesbian. No offense, honey. My goodness, who would want to be a lesbian? How do you suppose they stand it?" she asks, wrinkling her perfect nose. "I don't know how men stand it, either, for that matter, but they sure do, they just *love* it."

She demonstrates briskly, moving her head from side to side. Imaginary thighs are nosed apart by the zigzag of kissing sounds.

Drew throws back her head and laughs. But she is still keeping one eye fastened on me, gauging my responses.

My responses are peculiar. I always warm to people who go around breaking the rules in what I consider charming ways. A hangover from the sixties, I guess. And Rochelle definitely classifies, a solid outrageous original. But there is another feeling, not so charming, that Drew has trotted Rochelle out as a test. I don't feel invited to throw back my head and laugh. I wonder if I am invited to disapprove, be embarrassed, stand up for my ridiculous principles. Behind the warmth and sparkle of Drew's attentiveness, a cool inquiry.

I reach out and take one of Drew's cigarettes. Always best to go out with your boots on, I reason. I light up and consider the quickest route to outrageousness.

"By the way," I address my cousin, "I've been meaning to ask: Where did you get something like that?" I indicate the glistening expanse of Drew's half-exposed breasts. "I didn't think the Hinton catalog carried such things."

"It don't, sugar." Drew pulls a breath in and preens. "You got to have yourself some outside blood. My momma may be crazy as a coot, but she's a Holifield."

Rochelle looks down at her own ample chest. "Mine was a Bush. They never did know when to quit."

"Shoot, Jeannine, your momma is a Groves!" Drew reminds me. "Why didn't you get some of that good juicy Groves stuff? You didn't have to take everything that comes with it. You must be tiny as you are out of plain meanness."

I laugh. "I've been told that's what it is. Pure Hinton meanness."

Rochelle leans over the table again. "Honey, you can give a feller some help, you know. Ain't no law. You can just holler out Eu-reka when he hits on the right spot."

Drew rolls her eyes. "Lord, Rochelle," she sighs. "You got a mouth on you."

Rochelle lifts her glass. "Hey," she says. "Here's to the man that invented the Braille system. I just know it was a man, too."

Raymond returns, bringing the waitress in tow with more drinks for the four of us. He lowers himself into a chair, and grins at Rochelle.

"Sweet pea, next time do me a favor and be more—more careful who you let fall in love with you."

"If ole crazy men just haul off and fall in love with a gal, ain't nothin' she can do about it."

"Come on, we both know better 'n that."

"What you want me to do, put a stopper in it?"

We all look at one another, and Raymond lifts his glass to Rochelle.

"Here's to it," he says.

We drink to Rochelle, who parodies a series of orgasmic wiggles. When the winking and hooting is over, I can't help myself. I ask Raymond, quietly, "What did you do with that old guy, anyway?"

Raymond smiles at me, a kind smile. Throwing his eyes over at Drew and Rochelle, he leans down and says softly, "Why, I—

I think ole Hershell just decided he could sit this next one out."

Drew and Rochelle snicker, and Rochelle adds, "And the next one, and the next one after that . . ."

"Well!" Raymond declares. "Looks to me like I'm settin' with—with the best-looking three women in this hell-hole. I reckon this'll last about another minute and a half."

"Oh, now Raymond, you fixin' to leave?" pouts Drew.

"We sure as heck settin' on it as long as you do," Rochelle puts in.

"Well, I'm just lookin' across the room there, and who do I see but ole Marvin Greene."

"Oh, Mar-vin," Drew and Rochelle say to each other.

"Better watch out for *yourself*," Rochelle tells me.

"Why?"

" 'Cause that boy got a nose for anything new. He don't like to see nothing that he don't recognize as bein' a little bit used."

"Now, Rochelle, don't you go scaring my cousin. He's harmless, Jeannine. Little ole married man that likes to dance. Just don't leave the room with him, hear?"

Raymond begins to scold. "Would y'all hush up long enough for me to finish sayin' what I was tryin' to say? Or is this jabberin' and clackin' going to go on the whole night?"

"Shhhhhhh," Drew hisses to Rochelle and me.

"Well, I'm just settin' here, like I said, and lookin' across the room, and I see not only ole Marvin Greene, but Talmadge Wheelock."

"Talmadge?" Drew fairly shrieks. "Where?"

"Quiet, woman, and pay attention. I figure I have to revise my original estimate of a minute and a half—Evenin', Talmadge. I—I was just estimatin' how long it would take you to get over here. How you gettin' along?"

A tall lean man in a red satin cowboy shirt stands behind Drew's chair. He distributes his weight evenly between his two polished cowboy boots and places smooth hands on both her shoulders. Drew tilts her head back and gazes up at him, her long white throat exposed along with the rest.

"Hey, Drew," Talmadge Wheelock says to her. And to Raymond, "I'm doin' just fine. How you, Raymond?"

"Well, as you can see, I got myself ever'thing worth havin' right here."

"You mind if I borry a little of it?"

"Not atall. Just don't forget where to bring it back."

Talmadge winks at Raymond, and slips an arm around Drew's waist as she rises.

"Now I don't know nothin' about what you got your hands on, Talmadge, but these other two here, they got names. Meet Rochelle, and Cousin Jeannine."

Talmadge gives a small nod of his head toward each of us, and murmurs, "Pleased to meet you."

Drew sticks her tongue out at Raymond. The band resumes as abruptly as it left off, announcing itself with a siege of trumpets and drums. Drew and Talmadge walk arm in arm to volunteer on the dance floor.

I am good and tired of Marvin Greene's bourbon breath and his casual hands on my ass during the slow numbers, and I head for the bathroom. I finish off my drink and grab Drew's cigarettes from the table as I pass it; Raymond and Rochelle have disappeared long since.

The Holiday Lounge cowgirls' room has one of those antechambers with mirrors and hot-air dryers for hands and a vinyl-covered divan. After I have peed, I stretch out on that, thinking what a handy place for mothers to change diapers. I light up. From in here the music is faint. Even so, it mixes unpleasantly with the sweetened odor of disinfectant. The cigarette smells good to me.

I have been lying here for about half a cigarette's-worth when Drew comes in and groans, and sits down beside my feet. She drops her evening bag beside her hip, then leans over me to reach the cigarettes. I toss her the matches.

"Lost my gold lighter in this very spot about a month ago," she says between her teeth. She holds the match to the tip of her cigarette.

"You with Talmadge then?"

"Naw, somebody else. Hey. How you doin'?" she asks, letting her hand drop to clasp my ankle.

"Not so bad. I actually got a conversation started with Marvin."

"Go on. Tell me another one."

"I did, truly. I said to him, 'Well, Marvin, what do you think of married life?' " I bring the cigarette to my lips and draw. Stage business. Drew waits.

"And Marvin said to me, 'Oh, hit's all right, I reckon. Long as she gives it to me reg'lar.' "

Drew shuts her eyes and shakes her head. "Scratch any man," she says, "and his ole peter'll stand right up."

"Well, anyway, that cured me of conversation. How are you and Talmadge getting along?"

"Aw, he's crazy. Crazy as they come. Talk your right arm off, and make sense about half the time. But I wouldn't hardly say you can have a conversation with him, if that's what you set store by."

"Doesn't it get discouraging?"

"It would if I gave a damn."

"And you haven't since Rusty?"

Drew flicks ash onto the floor.

"One time. It didn't work out. His wife left him with babies to raise, youngest one not even in the first grade. I knew I didn't have it in me to raise two more younguns."

She shrugs. She brings her eyes to meet mine, remembers something and bursts out laughing.

"You couldn't talk to that one, either. Lord *knows!*" She pushes herself off the orange divan and heads for the other room where the stalls are. "I got to pee," she sighs. Her high heels echo off the tiles.

Sometimes I think it is no more than a fetish. *A man you can talk to!* A dream, and such a persistent one. In college it was what we said to each other in the dorms at night every time we fell truly in love: "And we can talk about *anything.*"

What were we thinking of? What kind of talking? *Who* were we thinking of—our silent fathers? Those men who spoke only in anger?

I chose a man who talked to me. Nobody could say Larry doesn't talk. He bursts in the door at night a geyser of chatter: the garden, his green onions, the sales quota, the contract, the tricycle in the driveway.

There was a night last spring, Larry and I were going out. The baby-sitter was already there when Larry got home, and Laura was sullen. When she shouted, "I don't *like* Cindy!" Larry engaged her in conversation on the spot.

"You don't like Cindy? Well, I don't like you."

Laura was shocked. "How come?" she demanded.

"Oh, because you're too old," Larry said.

"I'm not too old."

"Then because you're too young."

"I'm not too young."

"Then because you're wearing a red dress."

"I'm not wearing a red dress."

"Oh," Larry said.

"Dads are supposed to *like* little childs," Laura persisted.

"Okay, I like you," her father conceded.

"How come?"

"I like you because you're too old."

"I'm not too old."

"Because you're too young?"

"I'm not too young."

"Then because you're not wearing a red dress."

"Oh," Laura said.

With the child thus bewildered into quiescence, we left the house. Larry was buoyant. I admired his sleight-of-tongue and his success, and yet my heart was wrung. Is it really all right to cheat your way out the door?

Laws govern everything. The universe is orderly. Behavior that is successful tends to be repeated. Demand regulates supply. Women have demanded men we can talk to, and that is what we

233

have got. We must specify more carefully. We must demand men who will listen, men who don't do all the talking or none of it, men who reciprocate the language without cheating.

Supply and demand. I have demanded Larry's spontaneity and now am overstocked. My own has been getting dusty on warehouse shelves, taking up space somebody has to pay for.

I take a last drag on my cigarette, and stub it out.

My sodden brain reels. What was the point again? Which laws apply? Human behavior under conditions of threat takes two standard forms: fight or flight. I am under threat. Larry is under threat. People do not have energy available for change when they are busy defending themselves.

Fight or flight. But a third term can be found for any dualism. Thus one can fight while fleeing, flee while fighting. Thus withdrawal can be a form of combat. But I am weary of combat, weary of the effort even to pay attention.

Flight. As the other end of a dualism, it can't be more than half bad.

"You going to hide in here all night?"

I open my eyes and find Drew standing over me. I blink, embarrassed to have dropped off like that. "Thinking about it," I say.

Drew clicks over and picks up the little black purse she has left beside my feet. She takes it to the mirror, and pulls out lipstick, comb, teasing pick, compact. She works on her appearance, standing hipshot in her trim black slacks.

"You awake?" she asks.

"Mostly."

"You alive?"

"Mostly." I sit up, a gesture of good faith. I watch Drew lift her strawberry blond pouf with the teasing pick. Strawberry blond is not in the Hinton catalog, not in the Holifield catalog, either.

"Listen here," she says. "You can't spend all your time bein' sensitive to what a shitpile life is. Same old shitpile, honey, goin' to be there when you're eighty-five."

Her eyes hold mine in the mirror. "You just about fed up with ole Larry?"

"Yeah. Just about."

"Then you better pay attention. You already heard me say it once: Ain't nothin' down the road for us except being old women. One man is pretty much the same as another, and in a few more years I'll pick me out one. The words you got to remember are 'meal ticket.' Old women do still like to eat, from what I can tell."

"Meal ticket. What a trap. Deborah June has a meal ticket. I saw her today. I saw how much good it does her to eat."

"Deborah June's problem is she hangs around like an old dog waitin' to be petted. Keepin' yourself married don't mean you have to lay down and die. You got to keep your spark up. You got to give a man some hell, or he don't know he's alive. There's some lines you can't cross over. But once you find out where they are, you play like hell in between 'em."

"Sure. Anybody can learn to live in a cage."

"You can think of it that way. Or some other way. But you better make up your mind to put up with it."

"You sound like my mother."

"She outlived your daddy, didn't she? And she's still eatin', isn't she?" Drew uses a small finger to wipe lipstick from a front tooth.

"God, Drew. Are we chalking that up as a successful marriage?"

"Sugar, you come up with something better and I'll be right behind you. Maybe you figure you can eat those college degrees of yours. But in the meantime you better plant yourself a row of butter beans and two of squash."

She snaps the little purse shut and clicks over to the divan. She sits down and takes my hand in both of hers. Her perfume envelops us.

"You don't especially trust me, and maybe that's right. But you don't have many secrets, Jeannine, so don't waste your time tryin' to fool yourself *and* me. If you're halfway thinkin' about gettin' a divorce, I got some advice from the other side. What Marvin told you about married life ain't stupid. It may be crude, but it ain't stupid. This is how it works: Married life is okay as long as *some*body gives it to 'em regular. It don't have to be you, puddin', if it's too much trouble. Believe you me, if they're gettin' it anywhere, it usually turns out to be too much effort to tear up the stump."

Drew's expression is absolutely matter-of-fact. I can't help but laugh.

"You're telling me how to stay married without screwing, is that it?"

Drew turns my hand over in hers and studies it. "Then you got different worries, of course, but maybe you think you'd like them better."

"I don't think Larry would cooperate."

She pushes my cuticles back with her frosted-pink oval nails.

"Married men that haven't screwed around before can tend to be a little shy at first. They hang on to the little woman for dear life, 'cause they're scared as chipmunks to find out whether their ole thang will even work with somebody else. But it just takes once. When they find out it works, they're off like a shot."

I am quietly in shock. I feel a little giddy, much as Hansel and Gretel must have felt discovering a house made of gingerbread.

"Well? Ain't you got the sense to ask me what happened to ole Rusty if I'm so smart?"

"No, I haven't, and what happened?"

Drew drops my hand and swings her eyes briefly to the ceiling.

"I flat don't know. That's God's truth. I think he got tired of me knowin' ever' last move he made before he thought of makin' it. That's another thang I can tell you—you don't want to let on too much. They just can't hardly stand it."

"Goddam, I don't want to live like that!"

"Darlin', you don't appear to be livin' atall."

The silver laugh, so fluid, as she stands and pulls me to my feet. Two women with long ash-blond curls and perfume to match Drew's come through the bathroom door, letting a blast of music in with them. Drew and I let them pass, and step outside.

The music hits in a solid wave. As we walk into the lounge, Drew speaks over it.

"You may be movin' a lot of furniture around upstairs, but don't nothin' show on the outside but sweat. I couldn't put up with it myself. Why don't you haul off and do *some*thin'?"

"I don't know how."

Raymond, who has reappeared at the table, catches sight of us and stands up to wave.

"Well, shit," Drew says, throwing me her coquette look over one sparkling shoulder. "I'd rather at least be fuckin'. And I bet you a dollar, so would ole Larry."

Drew seemed to understand old Larry quite well.

"Proud you two could make it!" Raymond shouts, holding out chairs with each arm. "While you were gone, things—things have changed. Marvin took off, and Rochelle started beatin' your time with Talmadge. I told her she better look out, but you know Rochelle."

"I know her, all right," Drew says. "I know I told her she could have him at midnight, when the second string comes in."

"Second string?" I ask.

"Never mind," Drew replies shortly. "Did you bring my cigarettes? Hand me one. Raymond, these new drinks for us?"

"All yours," Raymond says. "If they aren't all water by now."

Drew lifts her glass and gestures toward mine.

"Down the hatch, Jeannine. All the way down the hatch. We're celebratin' a pledge to action. Raymond, you can join in, too."

"I'm with you-all!" Raymond assures us, and we finish our drinks in a breath. Drew tosses the plastic glass happily over her head. It lands on an adjacent table and bounces off. The two couples seated there look up in irritation, and Drew salutes them.

"Here's to the action, folks!" she calls.

"We ain't seen none," one of the women calls back. Everybody grins. There must be only one joke in the whole wide world.

"Well, which two of us is going to leave which one of us sittin' down while there's dance music?" Drew wonders.

"Why don't we split up the duty? You and Raymond take the first cut at it, and I'll guard the cigarettes."

"You got yourself a deal."

"We got some drinks on the way, Jeannine," Raymond says, bending to rub my shoulders before he follows Drew toward the dance floor. "So make yourself to home."

I do just that. When Raymond and Drew don't make it back to the table in good time, being held on the dance floor by the machine-gun spray of rock numbers, I start on their drinks. I don't mind sitting here in the least. There is plenty to think about. For one thing, it still astonishes me how routinely women lie to men, how much the common ideas of who wives and husbands are depend on women lying to men. We are persuaded to lie by economic necessity, by religious training, but also by our men, who use their anger and their vulnerability as strategies to keep us from telling them the truth. A collaboration of lies. A conspiracy of ignorance.

If I were to actually "haul off and do something," as my cousin recommends, I have figures I need to run over in my head. Dollar amounts, the cost of heating and maintaining a home. Mortgage, insurance, tax base. Clothing costs, child care. Food. A meal ticket. Can I convert education into money? Enough money? Other people can, so I can.

Then there is Drew's notion of how things work. There is this notion that Larry could change in ways I hadn't really thought about. From her data base Drew is every bit as good a scientist as I am. She has pointed out the gap in my thinking: When you break out of one pattern, you don't get freedom. You get to be part of a new pattern.

When the music comes to a screaming brass halt, Raymond and Drew come back to the table breathless and flushed. Raymond sizes up my situation, and clamps a large hand on my shoulder as Drew slumps into her chair.

"Jeannine, you're doing just all right, aren't you? I better see if I can't go get us all something to quench thirst." He winks at me, and I watch his purposive zigzags through the tables over to the red-suited waitress. He throws an arm around her and they appear to be having a conversation. Imagine that.

"Hey?" Drew says, nudging me with her elbow.

My head swivels easily.

"I didn't mean to get personal back there about your home sex life."

"You might as well be," I burble. "Nobody else is."

Her eyes narrow. "Child, you gettin' any at all?"

"It's not the point. I'm *delighted* to do without."

"Mm-hmm. How does *he* take it?"

"He's pissed. Real pissed. He likes life orderly, you know? Likes things to run smooth." I find my hands floundering and realize that I am drunk. Still, it doesn't seem to matter too greatly that I am not being coherent on the outside, when everything is quite clear on the inside. I am grinning over this irony when I hear Drew repeating something.

"Tell me what he says."

"He says"— I search for it, and it comes— "he says I don't let him be spontaneous."

"Spon-taneous!" Drew marvels. "Boy, you two really go at it hammer and tongs, don't you! Real ole nitty-gritty. Does he ever get rough with you?"

"Rough with me? God, no. He wouldn't touch me. He *pushes* me around," I amend, pushing a finger in her direction. "He sure *pushes* me around when he wants . . . a little roll in the hay."

"Roll in the hay?" Drew hoots. "Is that what he calls it?"

I nod.

"And is that how he gets it?"

I keep nodding. The problem is so complex. We train men for sports, for competition, for aggressiveness. And then we expect them to be good lovers. A complicated mess. Hopeless.

"Hell," Drew exclaims. "A man's got to dance to my tune a little bit if he aims to get very damn close."

I look at her and reconsider. "My problem is," I explain as the notion comes to flower, "I never learned there was any kind but unconditional love."

"What?"

"You know, like Jesus and God and all good mothers." The hand, my hand, floats into the air again. "Unconditional love. Anytime, anyhow."

"Even if they come at you smelling like a he-goat?"

I wave the argument away. "Larry smells exactly like Dial soap. At all times." I squint at her through the cigarette smoke. "Shit, Drew, how can he be such a problem? He's such a gentle person."

"Dial soap, hell; you're talkin' Ivory. I got one more piece of good advice for you. You got your ears on? Let me tell you: give-away is not the name of any game in *this* world. Jesus and God and all good mothers can do their trade in the next one."

This seems to be hilarious. We laugh hilariously.

Then Drew says, "What do you want from him, anyway?"

I had not known they would be there, but the words tumble from my lips. "A room of my own and a lock on the door."

That, too, seems to be hilarious.

The men you feel safe with are always the dangerous ones. Now there's a motto that ought to be carved into the headboard of every cradle in existence. Think of the trouble it would save in matters of incest alone.

Sometimes I think my guardian angel—and I was told by a part-time tea-leaf reader once that I had one—probably succeeded in getting that particular legend on my cradle. Her intentions were good; she probably got it sketched on in pencil. But my mother, who feels you do something thoroughly or not at all, took the trouble to erase it. So I never got the message, but I have known always that there had been an erasure. The smudged finish was a giveaway, the trouble taken to obliterate. It's the erasure that has been on my mind all these years.

And here I am in the parking lot of the Holiday Lounge with

Raymond, sweet old comfortable old protective old teddy-bear
Raymond, and while Raymond proceeds to give me a sweet old
comfortable old protective old teddy-bear hug, that blank spot is
revolving in my head like an unlit police bubble.

After Rochelle left the place with what's-his-name and Drew
came and whispered in my ear all giggle and perfume and insin-
uation about having a late heavy date and then poof disappeared,
Raymond and I were left to sit and talk and laugh about whatever
it was we sat and talked and laughed about, and to dance to whatever it was the band was playing. Mostly slow numbers, I guess,
toward two o'clock in the morning, which is probably about what
time it is now. And I am still feeling a little funny about being
held so close by my baby boy cousin even if this is just friendly,
even if everybody does seem to be so persistently familiar down
here. And I am still feeling silly out here in the warm night air,
having to convince myself that a light kiss on the cheek is okay,
two are okay, a brush on the lips is okay. And then when Raymond's not-so-familiar but quite comfortably warm tongue is
rammed into my mouth, I begin to realize that it's probably not
okay. There are probably limitations to this cousin thing. Probably he has gone too far, and probably I should do something
about it. So I do. It seems like a good deal of trouble, probably
making something out of nothing, but I pull back. I say, because
a light touch is essential at times like this, "Hey. Raymond? You
aren't into incest, are you?"

He tilts back his big head and laughs a kind of soft laugh. He
keeps his arms locked around me. He's not offended, then. But
soon a new worry flashes over my mind: Does he know what incest means?

He tilts his head back down again, his complexion going
green, pink, white, green-pink-white under the flashing lights that
point the way to the Holiday Lounge. I see his teeth light up; he
is smiling. Then I am staring into blackness, very close blackness,
Raymond's face it is, and the tongue is all over the inside of my
mouth.

This is beginning to seem unpleasant to me. Stubborn, on

Raymond's part. I not only have to pull back, I have to push him away. Once, twice.

"Come on, Raymond, knock it off. Stop. Let's get in the car, okay? Let's go. I mean it." I am trying not to sound unreasonable, but everything I say begins to sound bitchy. Or whining. It's embarrassing. But I am also the only one saying anything. Raymond merely waits for me to stop talking and then dives in again. This maneuver, I believe, often passes for listening.

Finally I begin to understand the fine points of what is happening. The fact is, this person I'm with is a man. I have not been out with a man alone, other than Larry, for ten years. This is what it used to be like, and this is what it is still like. I am taking uncommonly long to realize: This man is not on my side. He is not trying to understand what I want. He doesn't care what I want. Next he'll be telling me that I have to have more patience, and trust him.

I stiff-arm Raymond, the heel of my palm in his big throat. I speak clearly, in my best Yankee: "I think they castrate boy cousins for less than this down here. Now take me to Drew's house. I don't intend to drive home with anybody this drunk."

I wonder about the construction of that last statement of mine, but Raymond freezes. He drops his heavy arms from around my body and shrugs himself free. He doesn't look angry. He looks, even in green and pink and white lights, completely nonchalant.

"Okeydokey," he says.

Courteously he opens the car door for me.

So. So, we are still playing the rules. Part of what he expected. It cost him nothing to try, nothing to get turned down. I am the only one who takes things too seriously, who must sit here with my anger and my silliness coiling and uncoiling like two resilient snakes.

It is always the ones you trust! Of course! Who else could come so near? The handbook must read, *Get near enough to foster trust.* Then you can say, "She was wanting it. She was hot for it, believe-you-me."

With a shock I realize that I am drunk enough to start crying. So I say nothing. It doesn't matter, for as Raymond guides his white Toronado over the deserted streets of Bayley, he punches music into the cassette deck, and we listen to Rita Coolidge and Willie Nelson instead of to my knotted silence.

Drew's house is in the first residential block behind the shopping center, right in back of JC Penney's, as she pointed out. There are no lights on anywhere on the block as we approach the little frame house, but I am relieved to see Drew's blue Fairlane in the driveway, parked halfway under the carport.

Raymond slows the Toronado down to a crawl, and considerately turns the music down when he turns to ask me, "You sure—?"

"Absolutely sure."

He eases the car into the gravel driveway, and slides the humming transmission into "park" with the headlights illuminating Drew's back doorstep. The kindness is disarming. But I prefer my anger to the opportunity to be disarmed again. I say good night. I get out my door and shut it, being careful not to overplay the gesture. I cross in front of the car, feeling the blaze of Raymond's headlights on my back, and walk into my own shadow alongside Drew's car toward the door. I feel the way I used to feel in a new swimsuit in high school, as though I am practicing walking, trying not to do it imperfectly. I am so taken up with this self-consciousness that I nearly do not notice the black-and-chrome thing in the shadows of the carport, the motorcycle that Drew has concealed from the street with her car. I stand and stare at the death's-head insignia set in the black leather saddlebag under a spray of silver letters. I look at it as though I have never seen it before.

And then of course I turn back into those obliterating headlights, retreating from one front of friendly fire to another.

16

I pull the car door shut and let go of a breath. I avoid looking at Raymond, though I am aware how calmly he sits gazing in my direction, awaiting some word. At the periphery of my vision I see that he nods his head with what must be a sudden broad comprehension. He switches off the car lights, and we back slowly out of the drive by the light of the streetlamp. When we are in forward gear and several blocks beyond Drew's house, he switches the lights on and turns to me again.

"Home, I guess?"

I am grateful that Raymond knows the ropes, but they are, after all, such sleazy ropes. He reads the stiff nod and slips a cassette into the tape deck. He turns the volume up so that conversation is again politely displaced, and we speed on our way.

I take in the blur of lights and traffic, and do not allow thoughts to form. I let the evening, the whole bloody occasion, play through me in the form of light. Strings and strings of tiny Christmas bulbs blinking and winking throughout my body, igniting in random fashion: delight, anger, fear, anger, disbelief, anger, outrage, anger, disbelief, fear, anger, anger, anger. White, red, blue, red, yellow, red, green, red, yellow, blue, red, red, red.

Should Raymond speak to me, I know the lights will freeze into a single hard clear crystal of rage. I armor myself and let the lights stream by. Inside lights, outside lights. Before long we are on the highway heading into the country. Into the darkness and the stillness of the hour. Darkness and stillness easily envelop this moving capsule of glass and white metal.

Raymond begins to sing softly with the music. I haven't noticed the music, which I now hear as a wistful country and western complaint. I haven't noticed that the air conditioner is blowing a cold spread of frost, or so it now feels, on my left arm. Raymond has joined in harmony with the ballad, and his voice is a clear and sensuous tenor. The very relaxation of the notes he sings brings me to a pinpoint of irritation. But it is not the crystallization I have feared. I pull my left arm across my body, and rub it with my right hand.

Raymond stops his singing and reaches to turn down the volume control. His hand rests there while he asks, "Is this air too cold on you?"

I shake my head in the negative without turning. His hand hesitates the merest moment and then punches one of the steel buttons on the dash. A loud mechanical sigh dies away as the air stops playing on the gooseflesh of my arm.

"I reckon we can do without it," he says.

Without the competition of the air conditioner the music plays sweetly—a very clean violin dressing up an instrumental break. Raymond now hums rather than sings with the verse as it resumes.

> "Out searchin' for love
> Not just seeming . . ."

And soon he is singing the words again:

> "On my sleeve there's a weary heart
> Tired of scheming;
> Finding some someone
> Hoping and dreaming
> This time is the last time I run
> Out searchin' for love."

The music and the lyrics have a sincerity. Raymond's voice has the same sound, and I wonder if he actually hears what he is singing with such expression. Typists can type manuscripts without any idea of content; they can process what is before them with part of their minds asleep, and when the job is done, they know nothing. Singing can surely be done the same way. The lives of poets, philosophers and psychologists argue that art is not easily transferred into life.

"My singing bother you?"

So the man understands that his voice can melt ice. What woman could continue to be rude or wayward under the caress of such a voice?

"Is that something you do, sing your way out of awkward situations?"

"Whaat?" He pulls on the vowels in mild comfortable surprise. It is the sound that makes him seem stupid over the telephone, and which in person gives him a boyish innocence.

Pointless not to meet his eyes, since resistance, too, takes energy.

"No, I don't mind your singing."

He gives one quick nod, and we both look away.

I have noticed this before: The charm of southern men does not stand any kind of translation. There is so much done with the warmth that can shine from the eyes, even if it shines falsely; there is so much done with the bashfulness that plays about the mouth, with the soft tones and slurred shaded speech. It is a complex language they speak, certainly not English.

This elusive manner is one of the reasons there is no way to explain what my father was like. The telling of what he did, what he said, is a hopeless fragment. It leaves out what actually happened. Mere telling leaves out why, in the face of atrocities acted out, it is impossible to despise him thoroughly enough to be free. To not be led back, led back, led back . . .

Or do parents always loom so large in life that their characteristics appear infinite, unbounded by normal definitions and ordinary notions of behavior, pattern selection, cause and effect?

"I know I ought to quit while I'm ahead," Raymond says, "but why don't you tell me what *is* botherin' you?"

I register the way my fingernails are biting into the flesh of my left wrist. It seems to help.

"Shoot, Jeannine, I know I acted the fool, and I apologize. Sincerely. But something else has got hold of you."

His words hang like a speech in a balloon. An accusation, an invitation. Soon he adds, by way of parenthesis, a soft chuckle.

"What's the matter, Jeannine, Drew and her friend drop their clothes on the back step, or what?"

I turn to him now, my eyes shooting darts handed down by my brain.

"You think it's so goddam *amusing.* One more dirty joke. I'm sick of it, sick of you all. Fucking *men.* You think with your pricks."

Raymond whistles. He turns the tape player off.

"You can pure lay it out when you get ready."

"Come off it, Raymond. Women *do* pure lay it out, and routinely. It doesn't make us—"

"Doesn't make you what?"

"I don't know. You tell me. One thing for sure, women aren't supposed to *let on.* We have to keep things secret, so folks don't call us crazy."

Raymond laughs his easy laugh. "I know one thing, didn't nobody have to drag Drew off kicking and screaming. You didn't see signs of a struggle, did you? That isn't why you come runnin', is it?"

"So what does that make Drew in your book, Raymond?"

He takes his time, completing the turn onto Blue Rise Road.

"I reckon it makes her a divorcee."

"It's so easy, isn't it? All the right words, everything fits. And Rochelle?"

"Rochelle?"

He grins, adjusts the cruise-control lever. "Rochelle is known hereabouts as a good ole girl."

"Right. A good ole girl. And who could object to that? No wonder men find a woman's anger in such bad taste. Nothing more unnatural than an angry woman. Unless it's an ungrateful one."

"Which brings us to you?"

247

"Which brings us to any number of women in your acquaintance. Which brings us to conclude that a woman, if she is to survive, had best practice up at not looking angry and not looking ungrateful."

"Is this women's lib stuff?"

"No, Raymond. We're just talking about keeping secrets. We're talking about your sister."

The ease leaves Raymond's body. He sits upright in his seat and frames the steering wheel with his arms.

"You saw her today, didn't you," he says, turning partway to look at me.

"Yes. With your mother."

He rubs the back of his hand and returns his eyes to the road. "If you're right, Debbie June doesn't know which secret she's supposed to be hanging onto anymore. Or whose it is. You saw how she's changed?"

"How could anybody not see it?"

Raymond leans back in the seat again and sighs. He slaps the steering wheel with his palm.

"You'd be surprised. My momma and my daddy like to carry on like everything's just dandy. It all but breaks my heart to look at her, and I don't see how they act like—like it's the same."

I say nothing. I look out the window again, watch the round shapes of pecan trees glide by along the roadside. What is the point of talk when the data keeps proving itself?

"Hell, what am I supposed to do?" Raymond exclaims. "I sneak her out every now and then, take her up to Jackson for a party. She goes right back home and acts like she ain't been noplace. She's in love with him, she says she is. And three fine kids? Hell, maybe she's happy. How would I know?"

"She looks happy, all right. Acts like it, too."

Raymond pulls a deep breath, fills his cheeks, expels it.

"Yeah," he says.

"Do you know how Grandpa Cyrus died?"

Raymond looks at me warily. "Your daddy tell you that?"

"He told my mother."

"Well." He sends a hand through his wavy hair and clamps the hand back on the steering wheel. "Some men is worth the killin'. That I would agree with."

We smile then. Few people, I think to myself, could agree so innocently over homicide. But here we are, the two of us like brother and sister, sharing the family secrets. It is possible, because Raymond is still a son. He is not one of the fathers. Not yet.

We have come to the driveway. The headlights shine on the barricade at the rear end. The sections of trunk with their shorn limbs cast shadows that rear up, or so it seems.

"Boy, I remember playing in that old tree," Raymond says. "Seeing it cut up like that makes me feel all of thirty years old."

He slows for the turn and switches off the lights before they hit the house. When we are on the gravel, he eases the car to a stop and turns the engine off, setting the key so that the music plays. Aside from the music, everything is suddenly quiet. The dogs have decided not to bark. The house is dark, even the porch light is off. The sky has a blank cloudy look, leaving the red and green button lights of the tape player illuminating the interior of the car.

Raymond scratches the side of his neck.

"This may not be the right time—in fact, I'm sure it isn't, this whole night has been one dadgum circus after another—but I been wanting to tell you how sorry I am about your daddy. It tore me up when he got killed. I always liked Uncle Sumrall, and I believe he liked me."

"He did like you. A lot." True. Raymond "helped his daddy." My father always admired that in a son.

"He came down to New Orleans one time for a ball game when I was still in school. Me and some boys was giving a party—we had steaks and about four kegs of beer. There was just going to be a bunch of us, and I didn't think Uncle Sumrall would enjoy it. But he came, and I tell you the truth, I think he

really did enjoy himself. He told me he did, and I believe he truly
did."

"If you had steaks and beer, he probably thought he was in
heaven."

Raymond glances at me and laughs.

"Well, there wasn't anybody in that crowd to look down on
a man because he had a beer in his hand, that's for damn sure."

He shifts in the seat and hangs his shoulders over the steering wheel for a moment. When he looks at me, his face is half
hidden by the shoulder.

"I thought I took it hard," he says quietly. "But you should
have seen my momma carry on. And Debbie June. You would
have thought it was their own daddy that passed away. Well, you
know . . ." His hand turns in the air uncertainly, then drops to
the seat in failure. "In some ways that's what it was."

He shrugs and pushes himself back upright into the seat. He
has finished speaking. Death has a way of making people fumble
with words, and what the hell. I look out the window again. The
Rise is beautiful, always beautiful to me, and at night . . .

"Look," I say. "You were telling me something. What was
it?" And I am amazed at the tears that introduce themselves
around my eyes.

"Oh," he says. "It's just something I always knew, something Momma probably told us, even. But she always looked up
to your daddy like he was *her* daddy. Grandpa Cyrus being such a
rough customer, you know, and your daddy the oldest and
Momma the youngest. She felt like Uncle Sumrall was her daddy.
She just always felt that way. So, for us kids, Uncle Sumrall was
somebody—extra special, I guess. Like he belonged to our family.
I guess that's why we all took it so hard."

Something in this stops my heart. My father's real family.
The family that really did love him, honor him. The family that
really did grieve for him. I did not, after all, deprive him of a
daughter's love. He did not die for lack of love.

A sound comes out of my mouth, and I put my face in my
hands.

"I'm sorry, Jeannine, I didn't mean—I'm sorry."

A box of Kleenex appears on the seat beside me. But I am all right. I take a few breaths through my mouth.

"I had a hard time loving my father. All my life. I couldn't get over . . . some things."

"What things?"

"Oh—they don't really matter. It's just, I couldn't forgive him for one part of who he was, and couldn't forgive myself because of the other part. I needed to hear what you told me. About your mother and my daddy. I'm glad somebody else loved him straight through."

"I think I know what you're talking about," Raymond says after a moment. We sit in silence for a number of minutes more.

Then Raymond clears his throat. "You know what?" he begins, and when I turn to face him, I can see the outlines of his features in the dim red and green lights. "I can remember looking up to you when I was a little kid. You were like some kind of celebrity coming down from Detroit every Christmas. The big city of Detroit. Boy, was I impressed! You probably don't remember the way I used to follow you around."

"I remember you as all eyes. Big brown eyes set like headlights."

"That was me, all right. You and Drew used to go off in Granny's back bedroom and close the door to keep me out. I used to listen at the crack."

"We probably didn't want you to tell Granny we were jumping on her bed."

"Nope. You were talking. Telling secrets."

"Drew was telling the secrets. I was listening as hard as I could listen, just like you."

"That's what I thought. You've always been the same, haven't you?"

He places a hand on the back of my neck. It feels good, it feels like a friendly and knowing hand, it feels like I am at home with someone who knows me.

"Still the same," he repeats in his kind way, and the hand

stays in place as he brings his head toward mine, finds my mouth with his.

It is a nice kiss. I enjoy its sweetness. When it is over, I look for the brown eyes that must be inches from mine, but the little red and green lights have disappeared behind Raymond's wide shoulders. They no longer illumine the face before me. And suddenly the black shape that is his head moves into me, mouth crashing on mine once again, tongue thrusting through like a rolling Confederate cannon.

Before I can respond in any other way, tears spring to my eyes and I choke. Raymond pulls back in alarm, and I hold my throat and then my face and let the tears pour through me. I shake and sob while Raymond, murmuring apologies, again offers tissues. For some reason the sight of the Kleenex box makes me burst out laughing. If I am not drunk, I am still too vulnerable, too hungry for kindness, to withstand all this. I have been too long with my mother; I am worn down. Too much energy has been run to my shields. I can still fight destruction head on, but not when it comes disguised and slips in the side pocket. I am fighting my own hopes, my own needs, and there is not enough of me: I break, I break, I break. The pieces fly apart and shatter. O, I will die of too much knowing.

How can you love part of a man? How can you partly trust? Things are so clear when they can be divided tidily. I can understand the pieces but I cannot be responsible for the whole. I cannot make the parts match. Part of me loved part of my father. Part of my mother still loves part of me. Parts of Larry and me hang on to each other like crazy, watching in horror as the other parts change and divide like cells in a frenzy of mass mitosis.

When the innocence is lost, you can't get back into the garden. Try to rush the gate and the sword is there to chop you into pieces.

"Jeannine, I'm just as sorry as I can be," Raymond is saying. And what am I doing still sitting here? I find the door handle and open the door, flooding the intimate space with light. Raymond's arm shoots across me and pulls the door shut.

"Jeannine, I don't want you to run off like this. I'll behave myself, I give you my word. I promise," he says, pulling the arm back and moving away. "Really and truly. Please trust me."

And then suddenly I relax. I am as relaxed as Raymond. I recognize this place: I have been here before.

"You know what I'm learning, Raymond? The only way to really screw up is to expect things not to be the way they are. Like I have been doing. So good night. No hard feelings. But good night."

And truly, there is no anger left. No confusion. I get out and shut the car door softly on the sound of my name.

When you don't want to play the game anymore, you give up trying to get signals in to the quarterback.

When you can't stand the heat, you get out of the kitchen.

One kitchen down, nine to go.

Once I am out of the car, the dogs run to investigate. I can hear their rapid feet thudding on the sand. I walk toward them, speak to them, cluck to them, snap my fingers so they will come to me and hush. Four canine heads find my hands in the dark. They nuzzle and push against me. The only bark is a single low gruff note from one of the older, slower dogs.

I walk to the front porch and see that Raymond still waits. I wave him on in the moonlight, for the moon has finally shown itself, has finally come from under the clouds and opened up a fresh patch of stars. Raymond starts his car. Normally I suppose it would be considered a quiet noise, but it shoots through this pre-dawn stillness like an electric needle. Then he pulls slowly out of the driveway. When he is back on Blue Rise Road, his lights go back on, and he drives away.

I decide to sit where I am and enjoy the stars—the sky is indeed beautiful, Old Testament clouds rolling away, defined in moonlight, and Orion up there glittering. Okay. Bring on the male sky-gods. I no longer feel anything except the deliciously subtle play of warm-cool air on my skin and the calm of the hour. What hour? Nearly four.

I think about my father, and I think it is not my fault that he was a man I could not wholly love. If a piecemeal love is all that is possible and the pieces will not divide, then it is an honorable thing to save oneself. It is also honorable to destroy oneself, which was the way my father chose.

There is comfort in what I learned about Verlie tonight. Again I am not alone in my methods. Verlie, too, transposed brother into father. How many other displaced fathers wander this world?

Cal is the man I learned to love in my childhood. I loved him because he struggled so to be free of Daddy. His struggle carried mine. I loved Larry because, when we laughed together, I again felt free.

But Daddy has double-crossed us all. He has superseded the stand-ins, has offered the final freedom, and now for what do I need the others? From what do I need to be free? From this childhood, which is long over? Which ought to be as dead as he is?

I have the feeling of it now, Daddy: It must have been a night much like this one, a lot to drink and then it could have been that the stars hung over the Rise a little too brightly, a little too silently. You could change all that, the clanging rattle and diesel snorts of the tractor barging into the stillness. And you must have felt it when the machine heaved up over the terrace, sensed the shade of difference: world spinning anyway, but this one had a feel to it, consequences defied at last. Then the payoff, the acid taste of Rise clay in your mouth before the stars were put out, put in their place at last and you at last in yours, O Daddy—

The tears pour freely, the sobbing finds its rhythms. I am good at this for a change. My breath comes and goes as though it belongs here, recognizes this grief and makes no protest. It is finally mine.

The moon is nearly full where it shows itself sinking in a clear space toward the western horizon. It is near dawn now, and I am suddenly moved to find a spot on the east side of the house. I will see it all, see the balance of light played out, moon and stars and rising sun.

Dew soaks my toes and heels as I walk through the grass in my sandals. The wet is cold and unpleasant; it is interfering with my lofty visions, my resolve to serve as fair witness to the changing of the light. As I round the corner of the house, a terrier starts yapping its brains out. Juno. The pregnant one Momma keeps tied beside the back door at night—I had forgotten.

In a panic which is automatic I hiss at the dog and run for the porch. When I reach the first step, Momma yanks open the back door. It shudders in her hand. She is wearing one of my father's old T-shirts for a nightgown, and she stands there blinking at me as though I am the one who looks like some kind of ghost.

"Hi, Mom."

More blinking. She is old, this woman; she is old, after all, when she is not in motion, when she is merely inside her body. The body is, all of it, everything about it, fully sixty-five years old at four o'clock in the morning. And she is still inside it, eyes squinting, looking at her married daughter who has stayed out more than half the night.

"What are you doing back here?" she mumbles at last.

"I just wanted to walk around some, but what's-her-name didn't like it."

My mother turns on her heel unsteadily and returns to her bed through the dark house. It is like her to do these things without lights to guide the way, and I am at least in this respect her daughter.

The telephone is sounding, sounding, sounding. When I tumble to the fact that it is doing so in real life, not merely in my dream, I leap from the bed and run for the kitchen. I pull the thing off its hook and find with my eyes the clock on the stove—the only reliable clock in the house, and it is well to know what time it is when you answer a telephone, that is something I have learned in my life. Eight-thirty. In the—yes, morning. I force out a thick hello.

"Jeannine?"

The voice is far-off, tentative. It sends spirals into my stomach. Larry's voice.

"Larry." Pronounced as one would a verdict. My head pounds.

"Listen, I'm sorry to get you out of bed. But I needed to talk to you. Are you awake yet? Are you tracking?"

"Yes. I'm awake. I—it's good to hear your voice."

A pause.

"I'm glad to hear your voice, too."

"Larry, something's wrong. I can hear it. What's wrong?"

"Take it easy for a minute. Can you talk?"

"Yes."

"Jeannine, your mother called me early this morning. About six. I was just out of the shower. She was whispering, so I could hardly understand her. She didn't want you to hear—she made me promise I wouldn't tell you. You know your mother."

My stomach drops twenty-seven stories.

"I thought I did. What did she say?"

He exhales into the receiver. "I had a terrible time understanding her, but one thing she said over and over till I got it." He expels another breath. " 'Larry, can this marriage be saved?' "

" 'Can this marriage be saved.' " I groan. And then the play of hysteria flows through me, and I laugh. I keep laughing.

"Can you stop?" he asks. "You're scaring the shit out of me."

"I'm sorry," I laugh. And then the compulsion is gone. "It's just so painful," I add.

"Yeah. It bothered me, too—in lots of ways. But in the first place I was afraid something horrible had happened to you."

"What else did she say to you?"

"She wanted to know what kind of friends you had and whether we would see a Christian counselor. She wanted to know *what she could do.* Christ!"

"What did you tell her?"

"I told her to lay off you. I said it was our business. I told her you didn't need any more pressure from anybody, and for her to lay off you. Now what I need to know is, are you really all right?"

But of course I am crying by now. There is a long silence over the wires while I do my crying with the receiver held away.

"It's not so bad," are the words I finally produce for him. "It's just the usual stuff." The rest comes out in a squeak. "Worse because I don't know what to do about us."

"Jeannine, there's no reason for you to stay there."

"I wouldn't, for myself. But Laura gets here this afternoon—"

"We can always change those plans. Or you could let Laura visit your mother by herself."

"What reason could I possibly give?" I ask. "Everybody's involved!" I am seeing faces, Larry's mother, my mother, Aunt Lottie, the preacher. This was supposed to be a quiet little trial separation, no fuss. My mind jumps to the conversation I had with Drew. My stomach churns. What did I tell her? Did I say we were going to separate? Did I say I wanted a separation? A divorce? If I said any of those, it will be all through the Hinton family by today. Drew to Lenore to Verlie to . . . No. I didn't say it. What I said was, I want a room of my own and a lock on the door.

I'm sure that's what I said.

Is that what I want?

"I thought the whole idea," Larry is saying, "was for you to take care of just yourself for a while."

"Jesus. I'm not very good at it."

"Like you say: You need practice."

"Christ, Larry, how am I supposed to take it when you suddenly turn up on my side?"

His voice, when it comes, is steady and earnest. "I want to be on your side. More than anything. It's clear to me that I need some practice, too."

There is a silence. I work at not crying again, until I can say it: "Well, listen: I'm not handling things well here. But I'm not sure I can handle being with you, either."

Another silence; a breath.

"You know," he says, "the thing that bothers me the most is the way I never feel wholly *loved* by you anymore."

What is there to say? "You got that straight."

"I'm real glad I called to hear it."

"Look, Larry, don't do me favors. And don't expect me to keep on believing that you only have my best interests at heart. You don't."

"Jeannine, that's not true. That's unfair."

"No, that is *normal!* I get to be the one with my best interests at heart. And I intend to *be* that person."

"Look. I want you to do what you need to do to feel better. Don't worry about leaving Laura with your mother. To hell with everybody. Go wherever you need to go. Go to your brother's, go to Los Angeles, go back to Hawaii if that will help."

"Wait a minute," I say. "This is not some imaginary problem I have. The problem is real, and it belongs to both of us. I can't go somewhere and solve it, and you can't stand there waiting for me to stop imagining things and come home."

"I wasn't saying that. That's not what I meant."

"What did you mean, then? What was that go-away-and-feel-better stuff?"

A long pause.

"Honest to God, I think we'll be better off if we just hang up."

"No! Every time we get to this point, you walk out on me!"

"I don't know how to straighten this out. And I'm not the one walking out. I was concerned about you. I called to see if everything was under control."

"Okay. Everything is under control."

"Jeannine, your mother called me this morning. Remember?"

"She frightened you. Were you frightened for me or frightened for yourself?"

"Both," he says at last. "Both."

The hum of the long-distance wires stands in for silence.

"My God," he breathes. "What is happening to us?"

"I don't know." The tears flow helplessly. "Maybe you were right all along. Talking doesn't help. Maybe we ought to hang up."

When we do, I am trembling. Crouched on the floor and

nestled into the wallboard of the kitchen corner. How many feelings? I count off on my mental fingers: anger, sorrow, fear, vulnerability, tenderness, gratitude, regret.

I love this man. But he cannot protect me, least of all from himself, cannot give me what I need. That is left for me to do, and I don't know that I am strong enough.

And this woman, this interfering woman who is out there cleaning the barn, this brokenhearted and sleepless and aged mother who is fighting, like Medea, for what she loves—what of her?

17

I have the leisure to look at all the faces that appear and stream past me at the concourse gate because what I am looking for is so easy, will make its presence known, will be heralded by a showering of golden light. Or so I imagine, and feel no need to trim the sails of this expectation that billows up through me from my chest.

Momma stands beside me wearing the same expectant glow. I turn to look at her, and see the great blue eyes ignite.

"I see her! Isn't that her? Look yonder."

I am expecting two people, Laura and the steward assigned to my unaccompanied child. But emerging into the light and now through the ramp doorway is a child alone, an ordinary brown-haired child wearing a red sweater and lugging a child-size red suitcase. It is my child, however, and the tears nearly burst out from behind my smile.

Laura sees us and smiles shyly. I drop to one knee just outside the barrier, and she flings herself into my arms, suitcase and all. Before the first "Know what, Mom?" flies out of her perfect red mouth, I stand up with her so that she can give Grandma a hug, too.

"Know what, Grandma?"

"What?"

"This is my own suitcase! Grandma Lewis gave it to me!"

"She did? Why, how lucky you are to have such a sweet grandmother! I bet you miss her already!"

"Want to see what's inside?"

Laura throws the suitcase to the floor and leaps for the zipper closing.

"Sorry," I murmur to the pedestrians who must shift and stream around us.

"Let's take it over here to one side, honey," Momma croons to Laura, seizing the red suitcase and removing it from the floor and from Laura's grip.

"It's mine!" Laura screams, struggling for the red case.

"Hang on, Laura." I say this quietly, meaning to be soothing. But Laura is paying no attention, and Momma shoots me a hard look.

We struggle into an empty waiting area, Laura carrying the new red suitcase with both arms wrapped around it, my mother emollient and explaining, explaining, explaining.

On one of the empty chairs, with the stench of stumped-out cigarette butts in our noses, Laura proceeds with her objective. Her stocky little legs are braced for effort, her head tucked down in concentration as the fingers work at the zipper catch. She knows what she is about; probably she has opened and closed the thing fifty times in the two-hour flight from Savannah. Still, the hasp is difficult.

"Want Grandma to help you with that old zipper? Here."

But Laura moves to block Momma's fingers with her small stubborn back.

"Here, darlin', let Grandma show you. Here—well! My goodness! You did that old thing all by yourself. We're just a-growing up, aren't we? Let's show that mommy of yours what it is we've got in here. Ooooo-eeee, a pretty pink robe, and slippers—!"

Laura snatches the things and holds them aloft, beaming. In her triumphant grip dangle a pink nightgown trimmed in rosebuds and lace and a matching pink negligee. The slippers are clutched by their pink terry toes in the other hand.

"See, Mom? See, Grandma?"

The gifts have been well chosen. The conspicuous luxury, the implied attention to the niceties of daily living—these will show whose grandchild Laura is.

"What *lovely* things for a *lovely* little girl!" Momma rhapsodizes.

Laura turns her birdlike look to me and, overcome, I can only grin back at her. She whirls and crams the pink stuff into the open suitcase with both hands, and whirls again to throw her arms around my knees. It is nearly a completed tackle, and I laugh aloud as I stumble backward. When I regain my balance, there is still a rapturous little face grinning up at me from between my thighs.

"You are a dangerous person!" I tell her.

She giggles and releases me.

Momma is refolding the little garments and laying them carefully into Laura's suitcase. She brushes the soft fabric straight with her hands, examines the labels and then zips and fastens the closure.

"Here you go, darlin'," she says, handing the case to Laura. Laura seizes it and starts off briskly, catching my hand. Momma and I smile and shake our heads at each other in wonderment.

Whenever I am being swept along in the adoration of the child, there is a question that persists: Was I loved like this? Is it possible that my mother looked at me in this way?

I look at my mother now in her surrender to Laura, and know that it was absolutely so. I am in her way now; I stand between her and the child she wants to reach. But it was that way between us when I was little. I can remember my part of it: longing to wear the dresses she wore, yearning for a necklace of blue drop crystals like hers. Suffering jealousies over things that she could bake or sing or draw. And later, erupting into a blistering rage over the fact that she walked in the garden with Curtis and not me.

What a ferocious, possessive love we bore her! I remember it. And I am embarrassed, as one always is after spent passion. I do not remember her part, the adoration. She says it was so, and when she looks at Laura, I can believe that she did feel just like that about me. Once. There is an old joke that applies: The real reason grandparents get along so well with grandchildren is that they have a common enemy.

Now that Laura is here, there seems to be another question:

If I am in her way now, if I stand between her and the child she
wants to reach, which child is that? My child, or hers?

I stand and wait for the luggage to be set out on the trolleys,
and Momma sits with Laura. I watch them together, each pair of
eyes absorbing the other. Momma tells her about the chickens,
the kitties and Juno's puppies that will be born while she is here.
She gives Laura a piece of Juicy Fruit and shows her how to peel
the foil from its paper liner. She tells her about Sunday School
and what a Revival is. The two of them transact their business
with the utmost gravity.

At the house Momma insists that I spend time with Laura while
she fixes dinner. It is the same kind of struggle we had at the airport about who would drive the car and who would sit in the
backseat with Laura. Since we are women, the competition is not
for the honors but for the degree of abnegation. I am already tired
of it, especially of the tone in which she says, "Now you take time
to be with your daughter. Let me do that much for you."

To protest does no good. It merely raises the stakes.

As a matter of plain fact, I already feel "reconnected," as we
say in the trade, to my daughter. It takes about five minutes of
Laura's unshakeable normalcy to make me feel like her mother
again. In five minutes I reach the same pitch of devotion and re-
sentment that I recognize as my usual brand of parenting—as we
say in the trade.

Nor have I built up the same child-hunger that Momma
has, and with Laura so near, the woman is nearly delirious with it.

I said to myself after I talked to Larry, "I need to stay to see
that Laura gets some kind of rest stop between all the carni-
vores."

But it seems to me that I am oversolicitous. Nobody could
suck this kid dry. She could be Dracula's fountain of youth.

She lies beside me on the rug and colors in one of the books
Grandma Lewis sent along on the airplane. I am coloring, too. I
am allowed to use the brown and the purple. Laura's tyranny has
an enviable consistency, that same value that parents are advised

to acquire for themselves. "Be consistent." Emerson said that
consistency was the hobgoblin of small minds, and the psychology of parenting was born.

"Don't color that little girl's socks purple, Mom!"

"No? Why not?"

"Because I'm coloring her dress red!" Such indignation,
tempered by a little winning clemency: "Purple doesn't go with
red."

"Pupple doesn't go with wed," I repeat.

"RRRRrrrr-w-wed!"

I am instantly contrite. I see that the Lewises have been
drilling Laura on her r's.

"I'm sorry for making fun of you. I like the way you talk."

"RRRRrrrr-w-wed!"

"I think you are a terrific kid."

Unimpressed with my sincerity, Laura goes on coloring.
When she is finished, she flips the book shut and says, "I colored
the whole book. You can keep it, Mom. But you have to share
with Daddy."

This is a clause that has accompanied nearly every piece of
work Laura has done over the past year. The kid knows, that is for
sure. And she continues to state her position: Don't make me
choose.

"Daddy and I sure love you a lot," I say, the tears rising in
spite of everything."

"I know," Laura says, replacing each of her eight new crayons in the box.

Laura has finished picking the icing off her chocolate cake, and
slips off her chair out of sight, underneath the table. Momma and
I smile at one another. I feel something pinching my toes under
the table, and I cry, "Ouch! Momma, there's something under
this table."

A quiet giggle from Laura.

"I know it!" Momma fairly shouts. "It's my pet bulldog.
You better watch out, she bites!"

Suddenly Momma throws her arms back in the chair and howls. "Eeyow! She bit me on the leg!"

Laura cackles, and makes her way back to my leg. Small teeth push on my skin.

"You know what?" Momma calls. "I think I better go see about that thing. Ain't no dog of mine sposed to be under my supper table."

And before my wondering eyes she, too, disappears underneath the table. She growls and yelps like something four-legged and hydrophobic. Laura screams in terror and delight. And then the two of them scramble through the table legs and chair legs in a frenzy of sound and fury and one more related thing: glee.

I slide my chair back from the table and put my head underneath to see. Laura spots me and scuttles into my lap out of breath. Her face is flushed and shining. Momma crawls over to us and she and Laura laugh at each other.

"Did you see that little thing climb between those chair rungs over there?" Momma pants. "Like a rabbit in a briar patch."

"I saw a big old rabbit in there, too," I say. "Didn't know she could still move like that."

"Shooooot!" Momma puffs. "I was after me a little bulldog. Is this it? It sure got funny ribs." She pokes Laura in the ribs, and Laura squirms and giggles and holds on to me.

"You better hold on to that mommy! You better hold on tight!" Momma says, and with that the fun is over. She stands up and says, "Well. I got to go finish laying out my pans. You leave the dishes and I'll do 'em when I get back."

"I'll do them."

"Leave them, I said." This with heat and intention. "You want to help Grandma in the barn?" she says to Laura, holding out her hand. Laura springs away into her arms.

When they are out the back door, I clear the dining room table and rinse the dishes and stack them. From the kitchen window I can still see the two of them lingering on the path down to the barn. In the bluish dusk Momma is bending over Laura, showing her something on the ground. Skunk cabbage, I would guess, or perhaps a hill of fire ants.

When the dishes are piled next to the sink, I take the dishcloth and rinse it in warm water and use it in the dining room to wipe the table. I do this first, because it encourages me in this house to have at least one room in order. The vinyl cloth has a raised pattern that simulates lace; it is distinctly unpleasant to the touch. I bought it because it looks formal enough so that Momma would consent to use it. I bought it so I wouldn't have to continue looking at years of food stains and tea rings on the old damask cloth.

I have systematized things in the kitchen so that the day's dishes are soaking in the sink. The counter now stacked with supper dishes is otherwise clean. Items that mysteriously appear there throughout the day—a wrench, a plastic-tipped ballpeen hammer, a greasy rubber gasket, a peanut butter jar containing an oily yellow solution—these I place on one of the other two counters. I display them as prominently as possible in the jumble of old jars and plastic lids and paper napkins, feeling that such recent leavings may be needed sooner than the stock items. Sometimes I am right.

Another part of my system is never to go onto the back porch. The concept of limiting the number of fronts you are fighting applies here.

And everywhere.

It could be, for example, that Carrie Dean would prefer not to know particular things. She may feel she has enough to do already.

I shake this thought off and entertain another: Could it be environment rather than heredity that produced the nearsightedness Cal and Curtis and I share? Have we trained ourselves not to see more chaos than we can stand?

In any case, within these limits I enjoy doing the dishes, making this pocket of order in my life. With a fork I fish in the cold scummy soaking water for the drain basket. I catch its stem and succeed in tipping it. The gray water runs out. I replace the basket upright in the slot and fill the sink with hot water and suds.

Laura does very well with her grandmother, I decide. There is no need for me to stay. And I am ready to leave.

I am lying on the sofa in the family room half asleep or more, when the kitchen light snaps on.

"Shhhh! Your mommy is asleep. Let's be real quiet."

"It's okay," I say, but perhaps not loudly enough.

Laura comes and stands quietly beside me, and when I open my eyes she gives me a prim smile and reaches out both hands to pat and smooth my face. I open my arms and she climbs up on the sofa and stretches out beside me. I fold my arms around the tender little body. I can hear Momma washing her hands at the kitchen sink.

"Did you see the hen house?" I ask Laura.

"No baby chicks got born yet, Mom. They come in three or two more days on top of this day. Grandma told me."

"Oh."

"I saw a baby frog, but it hopped away."

"Oh."

"Are you going to sleep now?"

"I'm just waking up. How about you? Are you sleepy?"

She props herself up on one elbow in order to inspect the person who would suggest such a thing.

"I'm not tired!" she says.

I look at the set little face and laugh. "You know," I say to her as Momma comes to wipe her hands at the kitchen doorway, "I think there are people in this world whose children get tired. I'm not sure, but I think so."

"That gal's my little helper!" Momma puts in. "Tell your mommy what we did, Laura. Say, 'Mother, I've been helping Grandma, and I set some feed out where Grandma told me to, and I helped her count how many pans she needed.' Tell her that."

"Mother," Laura dutifully begins. "I been helping

Grandma—" Then she pulls her head down and buries her face in my neck.

"Come on, tell her," Momma urges. "Tell her about the hens and the cows and the pans you counted."

Laura stays quite still.

"You can tell me another time," I say. "I like to hear about what you do, but it doesn't have to be right now. Okay?"

Laura pops her head up. "Should I turn the light on, Mom?"

"Sure, if you want to."

Momma, who stands next to the light switch, reaches over and flips it on.

"No!" Laura shouts. "She said I could!" She jumps off the sofa and hurls herself at the switch. She jumps once, twice, to reach it. On the third jump she manages to flip the switch back to the off position.

"Good heavenly days," Momma says to me, meaning Laura's manners.

Laura jumps again to turn the switch back on. She succeeds on the second try. But as she falls back, she strikes the corner of the sofa. She wails loudly and angrily.

"Here, doll, let Grandma see," Momma croons, kneeling and lifting Laura upright. "That bad ole sofa. We'll just have to throw it away, won't we? We can't have an ole sofa hurting my helper, can we?"

Laura's crying continues, though the angry quality is gone.

"Looka here! Look at the funny face Grandma can make!"

Laura looks, and a giggle bursts from her before the next sob catches up.

"Look, see here? Look at Grandma's ugly ole face. BRRRRRRRDDRRDDTT!!"

The sudden loud trill startles Laura into silence. It startles me as well.

"Ha, ha-*ha!*" Momma cackles brightly. "That's *funny!*"

Laura turns to me, her face puckering to cry. I open my hands and she pushes past Momma and flings herself into my arms. I hold her and try to keep from clutching her, try to keep the anger at my mother from stiffening in my arms. I cannot look at Momma for fear I will turn her to stone.

"Well, I guess we're going to have us an ole crybaby around the house."

"Mother, the child is exhausted. Let her cry."

"If you encourage her like that, she'll keep on being a crybaby. She's five years old, Jeannine, if you hadn't thought about it lately."

"Right. She's five years old."

"She won't learn better if you don't teach her."

"Mother, that's enough." Words with the weight and taste of granite. Momma pushes herself up from her knees with a grunt, and leaves the room. The set of her shoulders advertises injury. I smooth the damp curls off Laura's forehead and feel the small body relax, the breathing deepen. Soon she is asleep. The tenderness I feel for her is almost unbearable. I savor it until the anger, the jagged crystal in my chest, dissolves.

The sandals slip off Laura's feet easily. I admire the rosy heels, the curve and texture of the soles of her feet, the niblet toes. Slipping an arm underneath the bend of the knees and getting to my feet as smoothly as I can, I carry her to the crib we have set up in my room. I let her lie on top of the coverlet and pull the light blanket from the foot of my bed and cover her. She remains peacefully asleep.

Momma sits in the living room in the wing chair, the reading lamp on over her head. She has her glasses on, the large Bible in her lap is turned to one of its three satin ribbons. Blue, red, white. First, second and third prize.

She goes on reading until I have stood in front of her chair for fully a minute. Then she looks up, her eyes huge behind the lenses. They regard me as though I am someone selling vegetable slicers door-to-door.

"Momma, I think we need to talk about this."

"I don't need to talk about anything."

"I do."

"I already said what I had to say, and you chose not to pay any attention to me, as usual, so what is there to say?"

"I think children need to be allowed to have their own feelings. I don't think it's right to shut them up or distract them, so they lose track of what's real."

"You think it's all right for their mothers to lose their tempers. I certainly noticed that."

"I'm sorry. But I wanted you—"

"Oh, I get the message, all right. Don't worry. I just feel sorry for you, ashamed for you, losing your temper like that."

Wrong for being angry, wrong for showing it.

"I have raised three children and I know something about it. I know that child never cries when she's here with just me. The Bible says, 'Train up a child in the way he should go, and when he is old he will not depart from it.' "

"Could we stick to Laura?"

"You want to tell me about *feelings*, something you got out of one of your psychology books."

"Yeah. I did. I learned about feelings in books the way other people learn about geometry. I would like Laura to have a chance at the real thing."

Momma's voice finds a high singsong note. "Pore little thang, her mother was so mean she didn't let her have any feelings."

She turns her face back to her Bible to resume reading.

"Everything seems to turn into some kind of struggle between us," I say. "I wish we could find some other way."

She does not look up. After a moment I walk out into the darkened kitchen.

There is no hope for me here. No mother and child reunion on the ticket. Last night before I fell asleep I remembered something, one more piece of that night—three years ago—the night of onions and Laura's TV, the night my mother laughed. Later that evening my father and I met in the kitchen. An accident; I had thought to avoid him, hopefully for the rest of my life. But for the first and only time in thirty years I faced him. I talked to him about what had happened. I told him how scared I had been.

He settled his weight on the kitchen chair, his face turned from mine. I leaned against the stove, braced myself for the explosion that would come. Instead, the face that he turned to me was puffy, vulnerable, the eyes brimming. He tried to talk, his voice grating with emotion, the words finally coming in a hoarse whisper.

"It's something, I don't know how to stop it. I never have, all my life. My temper. I lose my head—I don't know. I'm so ashamed. I would bite my tongue off if it would do any good. Please don't turn against your daddy—I know it doesn't look like it but—I don't know how to make it show—but I love you."

"I know," I told him. "I've always understood how you meant to show me. But, Daddy, I was always too scared of you to love you back."

We both cried then. I believe I loved him at that moment more purely than at any moment in my life. We did not embrace; both of us bound as we were by awkwardness and guilt. Not a perfect moment, but a truthful one, the words and the feelings in the right places for once.

All my life I hated and feared this man except for one moment in my mother's kitchen. All my life I loved and admired my mother, and yet such a moment eludes us. For us the kitchen holds knives and unwashed silver, egg yolk growing more stubborn on mismatched plates, a surfeit of leftovers.

I look at the kitchen clock, which glows. Ten o'clock on a Saturday night.

I walk through the house; the living room is now empty, the lamp over the wing chair switched off. I go outside and sit on the smooth front steps. It is dark, but the concrete is still cooling from the heat of the day. Cars pass on the road, sending the shadow of the nearest pillar crawling over me. People in the cars could pick me out if they were looking; as they pass, there is enough light thrown across the yards that I can distinguish the pink of the day lilies. If my father sat here, he would know even in the dark whose cars these were and who was driving.

"That's B. L. Bynum's youngest boy, driving his daddy's

pickup. He thinks he has to put it in low and pop the clutch ever' time he finds a curve in the road."

My father. My *father*. When did I start using that language? When I grew up down here, it was Daddy and Momma; up North it was Dad and Mom. At some point—I can almost remember!—I began calling them my mother and father. There was a certain edge to it. It made them sound more formidable but less personally connected to me. Not my momma and my daddy; my mother and my father.

The whine of these cars that pass is a modern sound. It goes with the rolled-up windows and the faceless drivers spilling their headlights over the Rise.

My mother's bedroom window is dark behind me, but that means little. She reads the Bible in the wing chair in the living room, but she can be awake anywhere. More than once I have come into a room well after sunset to discover her kneeling before a west window, seeing whatever it is that women see in the dark.

If she is awake now, she knows I am out here. And she is staying away out of delicacy, the late-blooming delicacy that comes between people when they have given up. When harmony is no longer possible and disharmony no longer a means to any end. I am grateful for this delicacy, and pained by it. I would like a lap to rest my head in, a mother's warm fingers massaging mine, a mother to rock away the hurt of the next steps I need to take. But it will not be this mother. And that is that.

"What are you doing sitting there on that cold cement?" The voice comes harshly, from behind me. I turn to look for her and make out a whiteness behind the front door screen. "You'll have yourself a bad cold in the morning, I know. I've done it too many times myself."

One of the last romantic dreams: that love will manifest in the form we need. But when she is dead, will I come again to sit here and mourn for all that has been lost? And find the sword still whirling at the gate?

I search for neutral ground.

"Momma, is that Buford Holloway's grave close to Daddy's? The one with the telephone?"

She pushes open the door and comes to stand beside me. Her bare feet are grooved and shadowed in the starlight.

"Lord, yes. And I remember the day that man died. We didn't have telephones up here then—do you remember?

I nod.

"I was looking out my kitchen window out over the valley, and there were cars parked all around Gethsemane Church. I said, just like that, 'Somebody died.' And I skinned out of my clothes and got in the car and went. Sure enough, Buford Holloway. Heart attack, and him not but forty-two years old. A wife and two younguns."

"I remember Delores. Whatever happened to her?"

"She married a boy out of high school. They had a little boy about three years old when—well, her husband went to the preacher and told him she was runnin' around." She pauses, and I wait for the rest.

"They went to her and asked her to stop, the preacher and the board of deacons—"

"They all went? Does the whole church have to get into the act?"

"Anyhow, she told them she wouldn't quit. And she didn't. She aimed to get a divorce, she said, she didn't intend to be treated that way. When she got it, the deacons voted to remove her letter."

"They took her off the church rolls?"

"They flat booted her out."

"That's a little strong, isn't it?"

Momma groans and sits on the steps beside me. "They should *not* have done it," she pronounces. "The Bible says you don't prune the bad roots lest ye loosen the good ones. And that's exactly what happened. Her mother and her grandmother removed their memberships, too. Hilaree said, 'If you're throwing my daughter out, I go, too.'"

"And Delores?"

"She married the one she was runnin' with. And then left him a year later. Delores was just about as smart as your cousin Serene up the road. You remember, she eloped with that boy out

273

of the army when she was just fourteen years old. She went out the window in the middle of the night and left her momma and stepdaddy a note on the pillow that said"— and here she lifts her voice again to mock—"We know this is what God wants us to do."

We laugh about this. I say, "And they lived happily ever after?"

Momma turns to me and leans away as though I have lost my senses. "They had four little boys, and he got himself killed on a motorcycle joy ride, that's what." After a moment she murmurs, "It *is* possible to jump from the frying pan into the fire."

"Dear God. I'm afraid there must be a moral in here someplace."

"You bet there is."

"And now I'm afraid you're going to tell me what it is."

"No, I'm not, either," she laughs, getting to her feet. "I'm going to bed. Church is tomorrow. I've told you enough stories for one night."

18

The women are dressed in pink, coral, green, ivory, navy blue. Men sit with their pale shirt-sleeved arms over the backs of pews. Within their reach are tucked the women and the bobbing heads of children. Where women sit alone, and these are widows or the wives of ushers, their arms are the ones slung over the pew. Carrie Dean sits well forward in the congregation; that is where people sit who have things to say during the service, such as "Praise God!" and "Amen." It is Garth, of course, who will say these things; his arm is hung behind her shoulders and extends as far as Garth, Junior. Virginia's small head is within tapping distance. Laura, too, is sitting near the front; occasionally her bright face peers over the barricade of Aunt Lottie's dimpled arm. Just checking.

Revival Sunday, and my mother loves me today, me dressed in my flowered Italian silk print, my hair up. Today it is not "You look like an old woman," or "That hair looks like a rat's nest." Today I have provided a grandchild for her to show off, even if Aunt Lottie is cutting in at the moment, and a beautiful silk dress that leaves her breathless with admiration.

"Will you send that dress to me when it wears out?"

She is sweet to me, humble, even fawning. Is this something I want, something I used to expect? Is this a good thing, having her cowed by her pride in me? It hardly seems so, and yet now that I feel it again, I know it for the way it used to be between us, on the occasions when I appeared to be what she hoped I was. What is changed from yesterday is my dress, my hairstyle, my presentation to the outside world from whom all blessings flow. I feel from her what passed for love all those years.

The little dog-faced preacher is introducing a soloist, a member of the congregation. He points out that some churchgoers who find time to play cards under the influence of Satan might learn from her example.

I lean next to my mother's shoulder and say, "No more Rook games."

She returns stiffly, "I don't. I promised God I wouldn't after Daddy died."

Not ready to give up a thread of alliance, I insist, "No more Old Maid with Laura. No more Go Fishing." But she looks ahead and aloof.

The soloist rises from her place in the congregation, gives one suspect rotation of the jaw and then walks down the long aisle to the dais. She sings sweetly and soulfully through the verses of "Sweet Hour of Prayer." She even keeps a straight face, which is more than I can do, through the third verse:

"... Till from Mt. Pisgah's lofty height I view my home and take my flight,
This robe of flesh I'll drop and rise to seize the everlasting prize;
And shout, while passing through the air, Farewell, farewell, Sweet hour of prayer."

This done, she returns to her seat, slowly chewing gum all the way down the aisle. I think of those clear soprano notes rolled out over Wrigley's, and wonder if Satan has his hooks into gum-chewing.

Revival Sunday, so Pastor Percy is obliged to bring in a specialist, some thunderous spokesman for the Old Testament God who will not hesitate to lash this congregation into a froth of guilt and humility. This man, Brother Kingsley, takes the pulpit, smoothing his silver hair and composing the red bloated face from which bastion he scours every eye in the house.

A hush falls, and this man's first words are gratifyingly hoarse. This is the mark of a man of God, a man who has spent

years spewing forth the same brand of fire and brimstone adver-
tised in hell. The gentleness of his tone deceives no one.

"Are you saved?"

The congregation settles back defensively, and even the
"Amens" sound wary. The deacons of Gethsemane are saved, of
course, but all the same, could this be one of the preachers who
occasionally turn and rend amen-sayers?

But no. This one draws them on, incorporates them into a
trusting choral rhythm.

"You have to ask yourself, am I part of America's health or
part of America's sickness?"

"Amen."

"You can't be of this world and a Christian, too."

"Amen!"

"Show me one of your cocktail-drinking, flipper-flapper
women, and I'll have to show you the difference between her religion and mine!"

"Amen! Praise be!"

I am thinking that "a difference between her religion and
mine" sounds like a weak punch line. But then it dawns: There is,
of course, only one religion. That's what makes the difference so
terrible.

"We got nine perverse old men on the Supreme Court of
this nation, and if they're telling me I'm going to have the ERA
and homosexuals teaching my children, I'm going to have to tell
them the difference between their religion and mine."

"Amen, glory to God."

Having disposed of all uncertainty, Kingsley moves off safe
subjects and on to the big nouns. Regeneration. Salvation. Trust.
Obedience. Obligation. Redemption. Consecration. Sacrifice.
Transformation. He shrewdly works in a business-management
theme to catch the new generation: cost benefit, plea bargaining,
merit increase, union dues, promotion day. When the Amens do
not come fast enough, he punctuates himself with foot thumps.
He shouts and scrapes down the residue on his vocal cords. He
knows his work; these so-called Christians will feel *alive* if he will

flay them mercilessly enough. If he can abrade them deeply
enough, cut through the sinful flesh, through the dullness and in-
dolence of their wallowing in sin.

The congregation have heard it all before. They come here
every week to have their sinfulness celebrated in this way. They
hope to be redeemed through the violence in his throat. And, of
course, by the tie-in to supply and demand.

I look at my watch. Old Puff-and-Toot is hitting fever pitch
too early. Twenty minutes in is too early; there are too few moves
left on the board. On the bedboard. We have here a premature
ejaculator for Christ.

"Must Christ bear the cross alone, and all the world go free?
NO!" he reassures them. "There is a cross for *everyone!*"

His roaring brings Laura threading through the pews back to
where Momma and I sit.

Kingsley returns to his theme at full volume. "*Are you
saved?*"

"Is he talking to me?" Laura asks. She looks over her shoulder at the man hunkered over the microphone.

I nod an affirmative.

She peers back at the man whose baleful eye accuses the
congregation.

"Then why is he shouting?"

I give Laura pen and paper, and she draws crude lozenges.
The lozenges now have eyes and two-hole noses and great gaping
smiles. I return my attention to the sermon. This man has a
problem, as I see it, for he has at least seven minutes to fill before the Invitation can be issued. And indeed he begins a new
tack.

"Tell me something. Are you a Bryl-Creem Christian? A little dab'll do ya? Are you an Alka-Seltzer Baptist? Put him in the
water and he'll fizz for half a minute? Are you a C & E Christian—Christmas and Easter?"

And so on with On and Off, Hot and Cold, Lost and Found,
Mini and Maxi, Before and After, Sweet and Low, Short and
Sweet, Brown and Serve. The attendant bouquet of Gethsemane

Christians smile and murmur their laughter at one another, and Kingsley finishes the series with an upbeat appreciation.

"With all your faults and blemishes, I contend that you are the best crowd. God's crowd is the in-crowd, the only crowd that will make it in heaven. God's crowd is the best crowd on earth, too. He guarantees the highest promotions. What it costs, He can pay. And my friends, graduation day, promotion day, is coming. Will you be there? Are you saved?"

This, then, is the Invitation. He stands red-faced before the baptistry curtain, his meaty hands extended. The Choir Director gives the signal, and "Are You Washed in the Blood of the Lamb?" plays weakly on the organ. But Kingsley plainly has made no sales today. He stands empty-handed through another verse.

His mistake, of course, was letting these people off the hook with laughter. When the politics are fear and self-loathing, laughter is the enemy. You don't tickle your fish and then invite them to pierce themselves on the hook. Laughter is not in keeping with sacrifice or repentance. Different muscle groups are required for chuckling and breast-beating; you simply don't mix them. Not when you're after blood.

My own particular blood runs cold at the power wielded by these men, these preachers with their combinations of emotion and ignorance, their willingness to combine the seduction with the hunt.

I understand seduction, of course. I am a woman, and I will sit here calmly in my bordered silk print. I will sit here and do my best to seduce my mother, seduce the preachers and the congregation.

The seductress is an angry woman.

An angry, cocktail-drinking, flipper-flapper woman.

I look through the rows of heads and see that Garth still wears his arm hung patriarchically over the pew behind Carrie Dean's shoulders. I wonder: Is he careful about Drew's perfume? Is it even conceivable that the stuff would wash off? Who attends to such details? Men? With their hunter's instinct for the spoor?

The Other Woman, with her instinct for proofs? Or is it the *other* Other Woman, the one at home with her addiction to self-preservation?

Carrie Dean *does not know.* She is doing her job, and her job is not to know. That is her part of the conspiracy of ignorance that preserves her marriage. She does not know because it is her business not to know, and surely goodness and mercy will follow her, and her lord shall dwell in her house till promotion day, Amen. No matter what he smells of, or whom.

Pastor Percy steps in and speaks to Kingsley so that the congregation hears. "Lost people just sometimes won't come voluntarily," he explains. Then he turns to his flock.

"Now I want you to come on down today, if you're lost. If you're saved but haven't joined, come on down. Whoever is burdened, come on down and unburden your heart to me. I think we all want to start this revival meeting off with a bang, so come on down."

Kingsley's seduction has failed, and here comes Percy with the prod: A flock that won't prove their love to the shepherd is no damn good. A pastor tease.

But Percy does not realize the extent of the damage Kingsley has done. Kingsley let the congregation laugh, and laughter is a glimpse of the truth. The truth always gets in the way of a seduction. These people have remembered that besides being hopeless sinners, something they come here every week to hear about, they've got stock at the water-tanks and feedlines in the chickenhouse that tend to get plugged by midday. So despite Percy's commands, no one moves to obey.

Laura looks up from her drawing to see what the stillness is about.

Percy stretches forth his arms to all the heads bowed stolidly before him. He is determined to play this one into overtime.

"I feel like somebody has resisted the spirit of the Lord this morning," he warns. "I know some of you, I know there are four people here today who need to put their lives in the hands of Christ. Are you going to be part of America's health, or part of

America's sickness? Why don't you come on down and surrender to the Lord?"

By now the organ has begun bleating verse after verse of "What Will You Do with Jesus?"

"I want to ask you this today," Percy intones. "I want you to ponder it in your hearts. How many of you here with us today are not saved?"

He pauses a moment, and asks, "Would you just stand where you are and put up your hand? Just show me your hand."

Keeping my head and of course my hand down, I wall my eyes from left to right, but detect no movement.

"All right, just show me now, how many of you are married to a loved one who hasn't accepted Christ? Just raise your hand where you are."

The merest rustle, somewhere forward.

"Thank you. How many of you have a son or a daughter that's not saved, that hasn't accepted Christ as their Lord and Redeemer?"

To my horror there is movement all around me, people raising hands forward, and behind, to the left and right. My mother with her hand in the air? The waters swirl over me. I remember not Percy but another implacable man: "Buried in faith, raised to walk in the newness of life, saved for all eternity." I turn my head to acknowledge my mother's raised hand. But she stands there next to me, arms at her sides head bowed, eyes closed, mouth tight.

So. There is at least that much between us. I had not been sure.

"Well, we have had a fine sermon today," the preacher finally pronounces. "It wrenched my heart and made me pray for those of you that have not accepted Christ as your savior. I know some Sundays you like to get home quick, you've got Sunday dinner waiting, but today our ladies have prepared a fine dinner for us right here in the church basement, and we'll have our afternoon Revival Worship at one-thirty.

"Today there's no reason to hurry, so I'm going to say this:

If you can't take the time to speak to Brother Kingsley and say you enjoyed the sermon, it's just like a slap in the face. I hope each and every member of Gethsemane Baptist Church will take that to heart. Now, Brother Rufus Drennan, will you lead us in prayer?"

In the silence that grows overlong, heads begin to turn.

A thin whiny voice raises itself to be heard all the way to the front. One of the women sitting in the last pew.

"He done left, Brother Percy."

The wages of laughter is remembering that the feedlines in the chickenhouse tend to get plugged by midday.

"Brother Rollins, would you lead us in prayer?" the preacher amends, this time with his eye on his man.

Momma takes Laura by the hand to meet Brother Percy and Brother Kingsley. I go out the side door by the basement stairs into the noonday brilliance. We will not stay for the dinner, Momma has promised. Besides, Revival dinners aren't a thing like they used to be, she told me, knowing that I am remembering pimento-cheese sandwiches and homemade rolls out under the trees of the old churchyard across the road. The church basement, Percy said, and I do not doubt it.

Still, I gaze across the road looking for the two-by-fours, saw horses and long planks that used to bear fried chicken and peas and okra and barbecue and spice cakes with white mountain icing on top of the ladies' best cloths—and of course they are not there. What is there, and it runs a small shiver down my spine, is my father's grave.

I am standing and deciding to walk over there when the door opens behind me and Carrie Dean comes squinting into the sunlight.

"I thought I'd catch you out here," she grins, and we slip our arms about one another. "I'm just curious: What did you think of the message this morning?"

"Which message was that?"

"I'm talking about Reverend Kingsley, and you know it."

"He got me real interested in drinking cocktails and flipping my flapper, how about you?"

"You are a mess!" she exclaims, pushing me away. "Are you staying for the rest of the afternoon?"

"Not unless he takes back that stuff about the ERA."

"Well, why don't you come talk to him about it?"

"Right."

"Seriously! You might learn something."

"*He* might learn something. He might find out I'm tar-and-feather material."

"Awwww, Jeannine, it isn't that bad."

"Tell that to Delores Holloway."

"Now, Jeannine!" Carrie Dean has a long warning note in her voice, and she looks around to see who might overhear. She drops her voice. "She was running around on her husband! Garth's second cousin Everett!"

"And Everett was lily pure."

"Well no, but he promised to straighten up. Delores wouldn't even give the deacons her word."

"And did Everett straighten up?"

"He did for a while."

I look at her and shrug.

"What does that mean?" Carrie Dean demands.

"In my book that makes Everett a liar and a church member."

"You're bound and determined, aren't you?" she grins.

"Is Garth a deacon?"

"Yes. Why?"

"It's not important," I say, but my heart races. I want to say something about glass houses. I know it's at least biblical.

Carrie Dean suddenly clasps me. "I love you anyway," she says. "And the Lord loves you."

"I've had better," I tell her.

She pushes back again. Her tongue clicks behind the separate front teeth. "I think you're right to stay clear of the preacher! You might get tarred and feathered at that!"

We laugh then. She says, "I got a look at that little girl of yours when she changed places in the service. For a minute I believed I was five years old and should be settin' with her! She is just like you, Jeannine!"

Laura isn't just like me. All too often I see Larry looking up at me from those shining pale amber eyes she got from him.

"She must be just like me," I say. "She's full of the dickens."

The door to the church basement swings open, and there stands Garth, the very picture of domesticity, a Corning Ware lidded casserole taped shut in his hands.

"They'll be wanting this downstairs before long, hon," he says to her. "Nice to see you, Jeannine."

I manage a nod, and most of a smile.

"I expect they will," Carrie Dean affirms, and takes the dish he hands her.

He turns back into the doorway and holds the door wide for her. She flashes me a grin and says, "You sure you won't come on with us?"

I shake my head. I watch as the door closes behind them, closes on the sound of Carrie Dean's high heels on the basement stairs.

I cross the road to the graveyard while Momma shows off Laura to Eola and Old Mrs. Jefcoats, Mrs. Flowers and Uncle Spanner. I glance back to their little circle on the front sidewalk of the brick church, see Uncle Spanner squatting to Laura's height, his knees spread wide over his Sunday shoes. Momma's face is as radiant as Laura's, even when Laura turns shy and lifts Momma's skirts for a better hold.

I find the grave with no trouble, though after two years the earth is still too soft for the monument Momma plans. For the present there is white gravel inside a white wire fence, the kind used for flower borders. A glass jar of withered daffodil stems sits in front of the marker. Two azalea bushes have been planted on either side, though one of them has withered and died. No headstone.

I stand and stare at the brown rain stains on the white gravel, and the only thing that comes to me is the dining room, the day of the funeral, the food that came to the house with the visitors and covered the table and the buffet. Sweet potato pie with marshmallows, yes, but also brown-and-serve rolls in the package, buckets of fast-food chicken and layered desserts of Cool Whip and instant pudding. To me such offerings seemed crass— the mourners could fast or starve, as far as I was concerned, in the absence of something genuine. But this contrariness is mine, has nothing to do with him. But does anything? Does everything?

Soon I hear light running steps on the stones, and Laura comes speeding up the path. When she sees my face, she stretches to be picked up. In my arms she nestles her sweaty face next to mine and pats my shoulder professionally.

"Are you crying 'cause you miss your daddy?"

"Yep."

"I miss my daddy, too."

"Do you?"

"But I'm not crying. I get to see him in five more days on top of this day, Grandma said. You don't get to see your daddy, because he's down there, right?" She points. "But Grandma says he's in heaven," she observes, screwing up her face to show that such contradictions are to be expected. "Do you wish he was still alive?"

The question is shocking. I set her down on her feet.

"Yes."

"Why?"

"I don't know, Laura. I don't guess it would change anything."

Momma hurries up to us from the path, and bends to reach for the jar of stems. She shakes it empty behind the marker.

"I wish Verlie would come empty her own jars," she sighs. She notices the azalea bush.

"Poor feller," she declares, pulling the plant up from the earth by its roots. "He'll be dead for two years come September. Sometimes I can't make myself believe it. I talk to him, you know, me there in the barn right by myself, just like he was really there. I think he can't believe it sometimes, himself." She uses a hand to wipe her eyes, and allows a rueful smile for me.

"When I get him the headstone I want, that'll remind us both, I guess." She stretches out a hand for Laura. "Come on here, gal, you want to see that old telephone over there?"

There are three headstones of note in the Gethsemane cemetery: one with a white marble angel, one with two pink granite lambs and one with a telephone, its receiver off the hook. The one with the telephone has this inscription: "Buford Holloway, 1911/1953. Jesus Called Him."

19

The Malibu climbs the back road home to the Blue Rise. Pinpoints of full sunlight glare out from between the leaves of the trees. Walnut, pine, sycamore, pecan, chestnut, chinquapin. There are no more flowers on the honeysuckle vines, which languish on barbed wire in the heat, dull and heavy. Laura's hand clasped around my neck ceases to seem anything but another discomfort.

"That Brother Kingsley, he is a wonderful speaker," Momma is saying. She is also actually telling me why.

I slow the car at the end in anticipation of the two deep washouts, only to realize that the road has been resurfaced. The roadbed lies out flat, color bright as a new wound, and small ridges of loose clay mark the edges of the blade's path. Two sets of distinct tire tracks mar the new surface—not ours, for we took Laura to Sunday School by the highway this morning. The fresh clay smell hangs in the air like new plowing.

I interrupt my mother. "When did they redo the road?"

"Why, yesterday, I imagine."

"Road crews work on Saturday?"

"Saturday mornings, sometimes. Why? You act like something's the matter."

"Nothing." Woman, age thirty-five, desires to wave to the man in the county road grader. "Forget it."

When I stop the car in front of the porch and open my door, Laura scoots out from between the door and the back of my seat. The dogs run to greet her and she hugs their grateful heads, lets them lick her.

"Can you beat that?" Momma exclaims. "Remember when

that little squirt was scared to death of anything? She must have some Groves in her, after all."

"That must mean I have some. Logically speaking."

"Well, honey, it's hard to tell. You aren't fat and you aren't dumb."

I laugh with her, my eyes filling. I flick the keys dangling from the ignition.

"Momma, I called the airline this morning before church. I have a flight out tomorrow morning at six—"

"*Why?*" she cries out, her face twisted in disbelief.

"Laura can still stay till Saturday. I haven't told her I'm going yet. I have that to do, and the packing I didn't get done last night. I'd like to spend some time with her and you this afternoon. Maybe we could take a walk together in the woods?"

The tears already course down her face. "Where are you going, Jeannine? Are you going back to your husband?"

It is the first direct mention of Larry between us for days. I pick up the gathers of my silk dress one by one, and let them fall. Laura is over beside the front steps looking for a kitten that ran behind the lantana bushes.

"I am going back to Des Moines. Larry and I have some things to talk over before Laura comes back. I don't know about the rest."

She gathers her face in her hands and begins to shake. The mewing sound that she makes with her crying wrings my heart, wrings a tenderness I don't seem able to express. I do not dare so much as a touch, for fear her tears will turn to fury. I cannot risk her ferocity now. Only when I'm away from her can I remember the part I need to remember: that only a very frightened person needs to be that ferocious. When I am this close, I seem to be the only frightened person for miles.

"What can I do?" she sobs. "What can I do to help you?"

I let out a breath. "Mother, you can't help me. And I can't help you. I have to live my life and you have to live yours. That's all you can do: Live your own life."

"Live my life? Do you think·this is a life, an empty old

house and nobody to love and take care of and to love and take care of me? I suppose you think I could just up and leave here, live on air and thistledown?"

Laura comes stamping up to the car, her face a righteous scowl.

"Isn't anybody going to let me in the house? I can't open the door *myself.*" She yanks on my arm, throwing the full weight of her sturdy little body into the demand.

I shake my arm free and Laura sits down hard on the grass. She begins to cry angrily.

My mother glares at me. "You don't even appreciate what you've got!" She gets out of her door, slams it and goes to Laura. She picks her up and Laura clings tight, eyeing me over Momma's shoulder. The sight of that smug little face is all I need. I laugh.

As it happens, I appreciate exactly what I have got. I've got a daughter who knows how to get her needs met. If there is a touch of the tyrant about her, she will certainly be in good company with my mother for a few days.

The airplane is rolling away, nosing toward the sun that is just beginning to send a gold haze over the tops of the pine trees bordering the runway. I can still see Laura waving, waving inside the glass partition, can see Momma kneeling beside her, pointing at my window. Tears stream down my face. Tears of love for my daughter, tears of love and despair for my mother. For all the familiar strangers from my childhood. Something jagged and lodged in my heart argues that I won't be able to come back here. Or if I do, that I won't be coming back as the same person. Yes. I think next time I would have to come back as a grown-up.

Last night after I put Laura to bed, I called Carrie Dean to say good-bye. She said again that she would pray for me. She said she believed I would be happy if I had a marriage blessed in the Lord. I said I believed so, too.

"I'm going to have to ask your momma if I can't get Laura over here to play with Victoria one day this week." Carrie Dean enthused. "I wouldn't miss seeing that for nothing! I hope I don't just sit back and bawl."

"I think I would," I told her. I know that I would, and in truth I am glad to be spared that sight. My tears are spread thin enough as it is.

Then, later, when Momma went out to check things over for the night, I called Drew.

"You taking off tomorrow morning? Lord, lord. Your momma get all the way under your skin, or is it something else?"

"I'm just ready to go, is all."

"Well, listen, I want to talk to you before you leave here. Can I get in my car and come see you?"

"Don't do that, Drew. It's late, and we couldn't get anything said sitting around here anyway."

"Well, you're going to have to stand here and talk to me over the telephone, then. Did you have a good time the other night or not?"

"You remember that stick you were telling me about? The one we would need to beat off the other women? I could have used it on Raymond."

Drew laughed. "With Raymond all you need is a rolled-up newspaper. He acts like some kind of hot puppy sometimes. From what I've seen, though, men can't be expected to know the difference between family and fun. They get flustered any time something begins with f."

Drew broke through the sniggering to add, "I told you, didn't I, that the first man to call me after Rusty left was my momma's uncle, the preacher? I thought he was just goin' to come talk about Corinthians Thirteen, but you learn fast. Now tell me. Are you goin' to make me ask you?"

"Ask me what?"

"That was you and Raymond in my driveway the other night, wasn't it."

Not a question. A statement.

"I'm afraid it was."

Drew's laugh rang out. "Well, honey, what can I say? It's

just like in the western movies, you caught me with my britches down."

"Yeah, I figured."

"It's not funny to you, I know. You feel like you have to do the decent thing and let your old friend in on her secret?"

"Drew, I mostly feel like a ghost when I'm down here anyway. I can't think of anybody that much cares to know what I see. Let alone believe that I saw it."

"You're sore about it." Again, not a question.

"I *am* sore. I feel like I've been kicked all over. But it doesn't have anything to do with you. You're the only honest person I know—or at least you're dishonest in ways I can understand."

Drew cackles and relieves me of my high seriousness.

"Anyway," I finish, "I don't feel like I have to fight for my breath around you. And I thank you for that. From my heart."

"Lord, Jeannine, is there anything you don't take to heart?"

"Doesn't look like it. I'm working on it, though."

"All right, now listen, Jeannine. *He* don't know that it was you that came, and I won't tell him. Now, is it going to bother you about your friend? You answer me."

I deliver a deep sigh. Is this how people make moral decisions, over the telephone, a disaffected wife to a gay divorcee concerning a philanderer?

"Drew, what really bothers me, if you want to know, is that Garth Parrish is such a worm. Apart from that, it doesn't bother me which hole he's trying to crawl into."

Drew whistles into the receiver while I blanch over what it is that I have said.

"Ouch, Cousin!" she yelps. "I think it *is* time you flew on out of here. You're beginning to talk like *folks!*"

"Drew, I'm sorry, I didn't mean it to come out like that. I—"

"Sugar, you're just beginning to make sense. Don't get scared and quit your first time out. You keep on making sense, and pretty soon the rest will straighten out by itself."

"Drew? I really love you a lot."

"Yeah? Well, don't ever'body? Listen, I can't stand around makin' sweet talk all night, I got to get on with my bitchin'. Otherwise I don't feel right when I say my prayers."

"Good-bye, Drew."

"Come see me next time. If there is one. Bye."

We hung up and I finished my packing. Momma and I had a last cup of tea and talked about how sweet Laura is. We cleared the tea things together and I went to bed.

But getting to sleep was another matter. All that leave-taking, for one thing, and I have noticed that the full moon affects me this way: If I sleep, I wake up recalling dreams of being washed on the tides all night. If I stay awake, it feels like borrowing future time.

Last night what was on my mind, of course, was Larry. What I would say to him when I called from the airport. What we should decide to do. Ever since I talked to Drew that night at the Holiday, I had been stuck on the words that came out: I want a room of my own and a lock on the door. I had tried to put them aside, because they didn't have the sound of reconciliation.

Last night I didn't put them aside. I decided I had better pay attention. If what I was hoping for after all was reconciliation, there were steps to consider. You can't reconcile something that hasn't been separated. Larry and I had been struggling toe-to-toe, and desperately. We had not been separated. This time I spent with my mother didn't count, did it?

"Not hardly." It was Drew's voice I heard in my head—a welcome change of venue for my problem-solvers.

The first step, then, would be to separate.

Beginning with the expectations, with all the dependencies. I had depended on Larry to save me. He had depended on me to remain saved with what he chose to offer. Both of us needed re-training.

What really happens, of course, is that the ones who get close enough to do you in got that close in the first place because you let them. It was you who drew them in, awarded the trust, gave them a contract. It is reasonable for them to be pissed when they are doing their job and you decide not to do yours.

Larry and I need to find a way to separate, and to continue—if not for the best of reasons, then for the one that counts: We have not come far enough to stop. There is a feeling about that. I know it now when it comes, the feeling that a thing is finished.

I am finished with the bitterness over Daddy. I am finished trying to earn my mother's approval or her permission to live my life. I am finished with the kind of dependency that I have carried through my life like a touchstone.

I am finished believing that there is salvation by relationship.

And if I now open my hand to grasp something new, I must let something go. I am finished regretting the things that will slip away.

Larry and I are engaged in a struggle that is painful and critical, but we are engaged. Not finished.

When Laura and my mother are gone from sight, when the jet has climbed upward to put a layer of haze between us, I open my hand on the black jellybean that Laura has given me. It is a parting token of her affection. It is so representative of her five-year-old heart: a gift, but not something too dear. Not a red jellybean, or a white one. The picture of her deliberating over her bag of candy makes my throat throb with laughter. It is her intensity, her sanity, that is so moving. All the same I am glad not to have a seatmate to witness my pendulum swings of emotion.

There was one moment on the ground, just at the boarding gate. Laura, who lives in the present and who began to·see that presently I would be gone, suddenly announced that she was going, too.

"Five days," I said to her, holding up as many fingers. "Then your dad and I will meet you at the airport. I'll call you on the telephone tomorrow, and you can tell me about the chickens and the kitties and the dogs."

Laura was considering all this, but she hadn't brightened. The small chin was dimpling. "But if you go away for five mornings, I want—I want—"

Momma stepped in. She knelt to Laura's height, primped

her face and whined, "If you go off and leave Grandma, Grandma won't have anybody to help her, and she'll cry and cry and cry!"

I panicked. All the possibilities flashed across my mind: my child, browbeaten and her spirit broken. My mother, Bible in hand trailing ribbons, doing her emotional blackmail. Myself, convicted once and for all of child neglect. I hovered between delivering another of my foredoomed position statements and simply taking Laura on the flight with me.

But it was Laura who spoke, and with some heat. "Grandma! You in-wupted me!"

Thus disposing of my mother's whining, the child resumed. "If you go away for five mornings, Mommy, when you pick me up at the airport with Daddy, I want to eat at McDonald's."

"Okay, you're on," I agreed, laughing in relief. The Christians have traditionally been thrown to the lions, but here's a lion thrown to the Christians. For five days, I believe it may be a fair match.

The seat belt sign goes off, and the cigarette smoke begins to make its way forward in the cabin to the no-smoking section where I sit.

This much time spent courting the past, and I believe I can see the future. I know that after Laura is back and Larry and I have done whatever it is that we will do in order to go on, whether we finally separate or not, Momma will call me up one Saturday and say, "I just wanted to say that if you lived anywhere nearby, I'd just love to have lunch with you today."

Icicle juice will run down the walls of my heart, and then, after I hang up, I will understand. I will understand that I have been gone long enough for her to return to her fantasies, where she finds me still perched on the princess throne, still the daughter she ought to have had, still the pliant teenager. For she is thinking of the years in Houghton Park, a place where people have lunch together. Not Gethsemane. People don't have lunch in Gethsemane, they eat dinner or fix supper. My mother would like to meet me for lunch at Stouffer's in Detroit, and I will be wearing a ponytail.

On another Saturday she will call and say, "Jeannine, I want you to tell me something. Are you a part of America's health or a part of America's sickness?"

On alternate Saturdays we will continue to haggle over my life—for if it is mine, to do with as I choose, then I take something from her that she considers hers. I take the daughter that she has perfectly raised and turn her into someone alien. Of course she will fight for what is hers.

Separations can only be made by two people. If one lets go while the other holds fast, there can be no peace. Nothing goes forward. A pitiful and violent flapping, a sheet nailed to a staff at one corner.

Last night I lay awake in my four-poster bed in my mother's house and watched the light curtain billow and drift into the room in the moonlight. I got up and checked Laura, who breathed deeply in her crib, sound asleep in her new pink nightgown. Then I went out on the front porch. The full moon was beautiful, of course, sitting up over the Rise and washing the valley with silver, making inky pools out of the shadows.

I leaned against one of the columns and watched the moon ride the sky like some kind of radiant loophole, a glimpse of the promised land after all. Three small straight clouds presented themselves in formation just behind the glowing peephole, cartoonist's lines indicating speed and motion.

And I found the words for Larry that have been escaping me. They welled in my throat like seeds sprouting, and I knew that by the time I see him I will know each of them the way my mother knows each moon-laced flower in her yard. These words of mine will be formal, too, arranged and bordered neatly, no stragglers. It is possible to have order in some places, if not in others.

There are things that can be said. There are things worth being clear about, even when the big nouns are not called for. The marriage we made ten years ago is ended; we can begin with that. We can forgive each other, and ourselves, for the expectations we now let go. We can also let go of the ignorance we wore in the name of innocence. We can say that we end, as we began, in good faith. And if ending is not beginning, it can at least clear a path for hope.

Mississippi is disappearing below, the pattern of trees flowing and eddying like a deep green river around red patches of clay. These patches break wide into plowed fields and muddy ponds. I want to hold this in my mind, have it be a place apart, a place I know. But it all looks like that from up here. This could be Tennessee by now, for all I know.